Discover the series you can't put d...

'A high level of realism . . . the action scenes come thick and fast. Like the father of the modern thriller, Frederick Forsyth, Mariani has a knack for embedding his plots in the fears and preoccupations of their time'

Shots Magazine

'The plot was thrilling . . . but what is all the more thrilling is the fantastic way Mariani moulds historical events into his story'

Guardian

'Scott Mariani is an ebook powerhouse'

The Bookseller

'Hums with energy and pace . . . If you like your conspiracies twisty, your action bone-jarring, and your heroes impossibly dashing, then look no further. The Ben Hope series is exactly what you need'

Mark Dawson

'Slick, serpentine, sharp, and very, very entertaining. If you've got a pulse, you'll love Scott Mariani; if you haven't, then maybe you crossed Ben Hope'

Simon Toyne

'Hits thrilling, suspenseful notes . . . a rollickingly good way to spend some time in an easy chair'

USA Today

'Mariani constructs the thriller with skill and intelligence, staging some good action scenes, and Hope is an appealing protagonist'

Kirkus Reviews

'If you haven't read any Mariani before but love fast-paced action with a historical reference, maybe this one won't be your last'

LibraryThing

'A breathtaking ride through England and Europe'

Suspense Magazine

'This is my first Scott Mariani book . . . and I totally loved it. It goes on at a good pace, and for me Ben Hope was brilliant, the ultimate decent good guy that you are rooting for'

AlwaysReading.net

'Scott Mariani writes fantastic thrillers. His series of Ben Hope books shows no sign of slowing down'

Ben Peyton, actor (*Bridget Jones's Diary, Band of Brothers, Nine Lives*)

'A really excellent series of books, and would make a wonderful television series as well!'

Breakaway Reviews

'Scott Mariani seamlessly weaves the history and action together. His descriptive passages are highly visual, and no word is superfluous. The storyline flows from beginning to end; I couldn't put it down'

Off the Shelf Books

THE WHITE KNIGHT

Scott Mariani is the author of the worldwide-acclaimed action-adventure thriller series featuring ex-SAS hero Ben Hope, which has sold millions of copies in Scott's native UK alone. His books have been described as 'James Bond meets Jason Bourne, with a historical twist'. The first Ben Hope book, *The Alchemist's Secret*, spent six straight weeks at #1 on Amazon's Kindle chart, and all the others have been *Sunday Times* bestsellers. Scott was born in Scotland, studied in Oxford and now lives and writes in a remote setting in rural west Wales. You can find out more about Scott and his work on his official website: www.scottmariani.com

By the same author:

Ben Hope series
The Alchemist's Secret
The Mozart Conspiracy
The Doomsday Prophecy
The Heretic's Treasure
The Shadow Project
The Lost Relic
The Sacred Sword
The Armada Legacy
The Nemesis Program
The Forgotten Holocaust
The Martyr's Curse
The Cassandra Sanction
Star of Africa
The Devil's Kingdom
The Babylon Idol
The Bach Manuscript
The Moscow Cipher
The Rebel's Revenge
Valley of Death
House of War
The Pretender's Gold
The Demon Club
The Pandemic Plot
The Crusader's Cross
The Silver Serpent
Graveyard of Empires

To find out more visit **www.scottmariani.com**

SCOTT
MARIANI
THE
WHITE
KNIGHT

Harper
North

HarperNorth
Windmill Green
Mount Street
Manchester M2 3NX

A division of
HarperCollins*Publishers*
1 London Bridge Street
London SE1 9GF

www.harpercollins.co.uk

HarperCollins*Publishers*
Macken House, 39/40 Mayor Street Upper
Dublin1, D01 C9W8, Ireland

First published by HarperNorth in 2023

1 3 5 7 9 10 8 6 4 2

A catalogue record for this book
is available from the British Library

ISBN: 978-0-00-850574-5

Printed and bound in the UK using 100% renewable
electricity at CPI Group (UK) Ltd

This novel is entirely a work of fiction.
The names, characters and incidents portrayed in it are the work
of the author's imagination. Any resemblance to actual persons,
living or dead, events or localities is entirely coincidental.

MIX
Paper | Supporting
responsible forestry
FSC
www.fsc.org
FSC™ C007454

This book is produced from independently certified FSC™ paper
to ensure responsible forest management.

For more information visit: www.harpercollins.co.uk/green

In memory of my late brother Francis, my best friend (and a great chess player).

ACKNOWLEDGEMENTS

I didn't have the expertise to write this book alone, and without the invaluable contribution of certain highly skilled and knowledgeable individuals some parts of it couldn't have been written at all. My eternal gratitude, therefore, goes to International Chess Grand Master Malcolm Pein for his input in designing the epic (or at least, I think it is!) chess match played between Ben Hope and Silvano Scarpa in the novel. Among his many noteworthy credentials Malcolm is a former child prodigy and British Junior champion. He is Manager of the England chess team as well as the chess correspondent of the *Daily Telegraph*, and the founder of the charity Chess in Schools and Communities (chessinschools.co.uk) and the London Chess Centre (chess.co.uk).

Many heartfelt thanks also to Danny Rosenbaum, Mike Truran and Carl Portman of the English Chess Federation for their generous technical advice. And needless to say, I couldn't leave out my brilliant editor Genevieve Pegg and all the team at HarperNorth.

'A single person who stops lying can bring down a tyranny.'
Aleksandr Solzhenitsyn

'Imagine what would happen if all billionaires contributed to building a just world.'
Donna Maltz

'Mercy to the guilty is cruelty to the innocent.'
Adam Smith

PROLOGUE

The only sounds to be heard in the fine, sunlit room were the distant whisper of the surf and the occasional soft *clunk* as one of the two silent, deeply concentrated players shifted one of his chessmen over the board. For the last hour, neither had paid the slightest attention to the magnificent sweep of white sandy shore visible from the windows of the beachfront villa, the gently waving palm trees, the pure azure blue of the ocean under a cloudless, pristine sky.

It wasn't a large villa. Small, but perfectly appointed, with all the requisite luxuries provided for their guests. This island haven, privately owned and totally inaccessible to ordinary people, comprised another fourteen of them, for the use of the top-level delegates who had been helicoptered or yachted in from all over the world, for a very special and important reason.

The room in which the two chess players sat was cool and airy and brilliant white: white marble floor, white marble columns, white marble fireplace, the only splashes of colour provided by the oriental rugs and the artwork on the walls. Its furnishings were tastefully minimal, an artful blend of classical and modern. Such understated opulence was nothing unusual for these men, who had lived for nearly all of their lives in wealth and privilege.

Both were a long way from their European homelands. The younger of the pair was in his early sixties, slightly built with an intense expression and thick silvering hair swept back from a domed brow. He was Austrian by birth but no longer lived there, spending most of his time at his secluded retreat on Lake Balaton in Hungary. His German-born opponent was more than two decades his senior, but every bit as mentally keen in his elder years as he'd been so long ago, when he'd made his first billion as a young entrepreneur. The deep intelligence, cunning and strategic brilliance that had propelled him to become one of the world's richest tycoons were reflected not only in the boardroom but also in this game of tactics and war that had been his lifelong passion, and one at which he excelled to the point of being almost unbeatable. He honed his formidable chess skills almost every day, and the board and pieces with which he and his younger opponent were playing now accompanied him on his business travels all over the world, despite their unique historical provenance and extreme value: so priceless, in fact, that two of his security retinue were employed specifically to ensure their safety. It was a foible, perhaps a risk, but he loved the chess set so much that he would not play on any other.

The Louis XVI sideboard nearby (nicely positioned under a gilt-framed Thomas Gainsborough oil) contained an extensive selection of fine Cognacs, Armagnacs and Calvados – and while neither man was averse to a tipple even so early in the day, the cut-crystal glasses and decanter on the table at which they played contained nothing stronger than iced water with a twist of lemon. It was important that they kept their wits sharp, not just for the game but for the two-day conference that was due to begin shortly, their whole reason for being here. It wouldn't be long now before they were summoned to the meeting venue on the far side of the island.

All the more reason, then, to get this game finished before they were interrupted. The younger man was an excellent player by any standard. His winning strategy had been steadily unfolding for the last while, his black troops were strongly positioned and he fancied that he could see clearly four or five moves ahead of his opponent, with victory in sight. But what had started as a deceptively mild-mannered game plan on the part of the older man now suddenly began to reveal itself in its almost Machiavellian fiendishness. With the audacious sacrifice of his queen by which he'd lured the enemy straight into his trap, the white army was suddenly poised to unleash its unstoppable onslaught. The older man's face remained completely calm and impassive, but he played with a kind of contained cold fury that if anything had become more intense in the aftermath of his recent sadness. Those who knew him well – and very few did, as he tended to keep people at arm's length – knew that the last twelve months had been a painfully unhappy time for him.

The final slaughter was quick and bloody. One by one the black pieces were swept ruthlessly off the board until the black king was laid bare of his protecting rooks and knights, and became a fugitive running for his life while the white pawn that had been innocently creeping deeper and deeper into enemy territory now reached the finish line and the all-powerful white queen was restored to the board to devastating effect. Black's position was now utterly hopeless.

In three more moves the hunted king was helplessly trapped, cornered, pinned down, and the checkmate was complete.

'I lose count of the number of games I've lost to you,' the younger man said, shaking his head. 'Once again, Auguste, you have decimated and humiliated your poor old friend.'

'Not at all,' the older man protested, smiling modestly as he set the pieces back to their original positions. 'In fact it was a much closer contest than it appeared to be. You had the advantage several times.'

'Nonsense. You annihilated me as you always do.' The younger man laughed. 'I should be thankful that we don't play for money, or else you'd have stripped me of my fortune as well as my self-confidence.' A fortune that, at the last count, was high up in Europe's top fifty. 'Perhaps one day you will allow me to get my revenge,' he added, with a look in his eye that betrayed the truth that he did in fact take these losses quite personally.

'Next time, I'm sure,' said the older man.

Their conversation was interrupted at that point by the arrival of a delegation manager come to remind them with a polite smile, 'Gentlemen, the meeting is due to get underway. If you be so kind as to follow me . . .'

As they were about to leave, the older man went to get his dark suit jacket from the back of the chair where he'd been sitting. In so doing he accidentally nudged the chess table with his hip, causing some of the pieces to topple over and one of them, a white knight, to fall off the board and drop to the floor. 'Oh, no!' he exclaimed in horror.

Luckily, the table stood on a fine oriental rug – or else the precious old chess piece, carved centuries ago from a piece of Persian white opal into the most elegantly stylised horse's head, three inches in height, might have shattered into a hundred tiny pieces on the hard floor.

'Thank God, it's all right,' he said, inspecting it. 'I must be getting clumsy in my old age.'

'I'm glad it wasn't broken,' said the younger man. 'I must say, Auguste, that if I owned such a magnificent work of art as that chess set, I'd leave it safely at home. One of these days . . . it really doesn't bear thinking about.'

'I know, I know,' replied the older man, still turning the recovered chess piece over in his fingers and carefully scrutinising it for any cracks or chips he might have missed on first inspection. 'Perhaps I ought to take your advice.'

The younger man chuckled. 'That would be the first time you ever did that, my old friend.'

'Gentlemen?' prompted the delegation manager, looking at his watch. 'The car is waiting.'

'My apologies,' the older man said. 'Let's waste no more time.'

'And needless to remind you also,' the manager added obsequiously, 'that the usual rules apply, with regard to personal phones or electronics of any kind. I trust you have taken the necessary precautions?'

'Of course, of course.' The two delegates had been through this ritual many times before. Such devices were strictly forbidden at their ultra-secret conferences. The rules of their close-knit and highly covert organisation were nothing short of sacred, and to break them, according to the oath that each member was required to swear on admittance, was punishable by the severest penalties.

They left the villa and climbed into the long, luxurious car that had been sent to whisk them across the island to the meeting. The doors slammed, the engine purred into life and they took off.

And what his colleagues hadn't noticed was that the older man had discreetly slipped the chess piece into his jacket pocket.

Chapter 1

Twelve weeks later

At 11.49 on the morning it happened, Valentina Petrova was sitting in a classics lesson at her exclusive international boarding school in Switzerland, listening to her teacher Madame Chiffon talk about the chapter of Homer's *Iliad* that the students were going to translate from Greek. Valentina was a star pupil and usually highly attentive, but right now, as Madame Chiffon droned on, she was somewhat distracted by the view from the classroom window – the glitter of the midday sunshine twinkling across the waters of Lake Geneva far below, stretching away to the mountains in the distance – and thoughts of lunch. In just a few minutes she and her classmates would join the rest of their friends in the school refectory, where a grilled Swiss cheese sandwich awaited. A delicious blend of Sbrinz and Emmental, with a touch of Dijon mayonnaise and a slice of tomato. Her mouth watered at the prospect.

What the seventeen-year-old girl didn't yet know was that for her, the lesson would come to an end a little sooner. Interrupted by an unexpected knock at the classroom door that snatched Valentina from her dreamy thoughts, Madame Chiffon stopped mid-flow and said, 'Come in.'

The door swung open and in walked Frau Meier, the headmistress's tall, blocky secretary, whom some of the girls secretly nicknamed Frankenstein. Looking uncharacteristically nervous, Frau Meier apologised for breaking into the lesson, lumbered quickly over to Madame Chiffon and whispered something in her ear that made the classics teacher turn pale.

Madame Chiffon looked stunned for a moment, exchanged an anxious glance with the secretary and then turned to address the class. She was looking straight at Valentina.

'My dear, you're needed at the headmistress's office, right away,' Madame Chiffon said. 'You'd better hurry.'

Valentina felt herself flushing. The pang of guilt and the paranoia that she'd somehow been caught daydreaming quickly evaporated as she realised this could only be bad news. She rose uncertainly from her desk and followed Frankenstein out of the classroom, feeling the eyes of her friends on her as she stepped out into the corridor and the door closed behind her.

Her heart began to thump. 'What am I needed for, Frau Meier?' she asked as the secretary led her through the grand building, more like a magical fairytale castle than a school. Valentina had been a pupil here for the last five years, since she was twelve, and she loved it. Here she was treated like a normal person and not the sole heiress to the Kaprisky billions. It was a warm, welcoming and happy environment, even though academic standards were tough and much was expected of her. But the taut, grim expression on the secretary's face was anything but joyful, and she gave no reply to Valentina's question.

It was a terrible moment of déjà vu for Valentina, because she had been summoned away from the classroom like this once before. That had happened last year, when her grand-uncle Auguste had called her in floods of tears to break the awful news that her Russian father Yuri Petrov and her mother Eloise, Tonton's niece, had been killed in an avalanche while on holiday skiing in the Austrian Alps. Valentina's parents had been estranged from one another for much of their daughter's childhood, but in the last few years they'd got back together. Valentina had so many cherished memories of that time, before it had all been shattered.

The months since the accident had been the worst of her young life. She'd survived the crushing grief and heartbreak thanks mainly to the loving support of so many people around her, her classmates, her teachers, and of course Tonton himself, to whom she'd always been very close but who in the wake of their family tragedy had become even more like a surrogate father to her.

Now, just when she'd thought she had come through it all, Valentina was reliving the same horrible feeling all over again.

Frau Brunner, the headmistress, looked even more sombre as she stood behind her desk, talking in a low voice on the phone. As Frankenstein ushered Valentina into the large, airy office, Frau Brunner broke off from whatever she'd been discussing with her unknown caller and said, 'Here she is.' Before Valentina could say anything, the phone was being pressed into her trembling hand.

'Yes?' she said uncertainly, in a voice that sounded tiny and quavering. She could barely stand the way the headmistress and the secretary were frowning at her, so she kept her eyes averted downwards.

'Valentina, it's Gabriel.'

Gabriel Archambeau was the veteran lawyer and adviser who had looked after the affairs of the considerable Kaprisky estate since before Valentina was born, and was a close friend of the family. Based in Chartres in France, he often visited their residence near Le Mans. He was normally jovial and fun to be around, except of course for when her parents died, when she and Tonton had needed all the consoling friendship they could get. The tension and sadness Valentina could hear in his voice brought those awful memories closer again, confirming her fears that something else bad must have happened. There was a hard lump in her throat. Why wasn't Tonton calling her? Why Gabriel?

Gabriel had never talked down to her or treated her like a kid, even when she was much younger, and he broke the news with typical directness. 'Valentina, there's been an . . . incident. It happened just after ten o'clock this morning. I'm here at the estate, with the police.'

Valentina took in the deliberate use of the word *incident* and understood immediately that in Gabriel's precise, lawyerish way of speaking, it must mean something very different from the *accident* that had taken her parents away from her. Feeling numb with shock, she mumbled, 'What is it? What's happened?'

'It's . . . it's your granduncle Auguste. It's Tonton.' Gabriel's voice sounded close to breaking point.

Valentina's throat felt so tight it was like she was being strangled, and she could barely speak. She managed to say, 'Is . . . is Tonton dead?'

'No, he's not dead. He came out of surgery about ten minutes ago but . . .' Gabriel let out a deep sigh that sounded more like a wheeze, as though he'd been holding his breath for the last hour.

'But *what*?' she demanded, a jet of impatient anger piercing through her anxiety.

'I . . . I can't talk about this over the phone, Valentina. There are a lot of things I have to explain to you and it should be done in person. You'd better come home right away. I'm sending the plane.'

Three hours later, after a rushed and frantic trip aboard the Kaprisky jet, Valentina was whisked through the tall gates of the estate to find her home swarming with police. The ambulances and coroner's vehicles had long since disappeared. Gabriel met her, wearing a crumpled grey suit and looking a hundred years older as they hugged one another tightly.

'There's an Inspector Boche who wants to speak to you,' Gabriel said.

'I don't care about him. I want to see Tonton,' Valentina replied firmly, and Gabriel nodded.

The Kapriskys' private clinic adjoining the estate was just a short drive away in Gabriel's Jaguar. They called it 'their' clinic but in fact it was one of the best-equipped small hospitals in Europe. At this moment, Tonton was the sole patient in the state-of-the-art intensive care unit. The emergency surgery had succeeded in saving his life and all his vital signs were good – exceptionally good for a man of his age, and one who had just been the victim of a sustained and brutal attack. But though he'd managed to come through, he hadn't regained consciousness since the incident and was in a deep coma.

Valentina was shaking with dread as a tall, thin doctor called Theroux led her and Gabriel through a labyrinth of gleaming white corridors to a viewing window, the closest she'd be allowed to get to her Tonton for the moment. She had to force herself to peer through the glass. Her grand-uncle was a small, frail shape swathed in white sheets on a hospital bed surrounded by bleeping machines and attentive nursing staff. He looked peaceful, and if it hadn't been for all the tubes and wires and the oxygen mask over his face, he might have been sleeping normally instead of languishing in a state of profound unconsciousness, closer to being dead than alive.

Valentina turned to Dr Theroux. Her slender hands were balled into fists by her sides. She took a deep breath, jutted out her chin and mustered up all her courage to ask him, 'Is my Tonton going to die?'

'He's as strong as a horse,' the doctor replied after a moment's reflection. 'Few men half his age could have with-stood the initial trauma, let alone survived the anoxic brain injury he's suffered. His entire system shut down for several minutes after the attack, starving his organs of oxygen. That can be the only reason the attackers apparently left him for dead the way they did. Considering all that, he's doing extremely well. But it's still far too early to form a prognosis, with this level of damage and the number of complications that could still arise.'

He waffled on like that for a while longer, using all kinds of technical medical expressions that Valentina didn't understand and found increasingly confusing. She cut him off with a raised hand and another question.

'Will my granduncle ever wake up from this coma? The simple version, please. I'm not a doctor.'

Dr Theroux shrugged. 'The simple version? Basically, we don't know. In some cases patients can make a full recovery, given time. In others, the vegetative state can be persistent, or permanent.'

Permanent. Valentina couldn't, wouldn't, even contemplate that horror. She willed herself to cling onto hope. But still the terrifying doubts wouldn't go away. She asked Theroux, 'And if he does wake up, will he be . . . normal? I mean, will he still be my Tonton? Will he even recognise me?' Tears flooded her eyes and spilled down her cheeks as she said it.

Gabriel put an affectionate arm around her shoulders. 'We don't know that either, sweetheart. We just have to trust that Dr Theroux and his team are doing all they can, all right?'

Valentina sniffed, wiped her eyes and collected herself. Tonton wasn't the only one in the family who was tough. She refused to allow herself to cry openly in front of strangers.

'All right,' she said to Gabriel. 'Now take me to talk to the policemen.'

The detectives were waiting for them in front of the main house, which was still milling with uniformed officers and the forensic teams who came and went like ants, collecting clues and evidence. As Valentina and Gabriel stepped out of the Jaguar, Inspector Boche came forward to introduce himself to her and offer his deepest sympathies. He was a bullish man who looked as if he needed to shave twice a day and had one of those wispy tufts of hair in the middle of a bald scalp that Valentina found mystifying. Why didn't they just cut it off?

Boche launched into a well-practised spiel, offering his deepest sympathies at this difficult time, blah blah blah. 'Never mind that,' Valentina said. 'Monsieur Archambeau has already explained to me what happened. Now please fill me in on the rest of it. Every detail.'

She listened intently, her head slightly bowed and her young face taut and grim, as Boche ran back through the whole grisly account, or as much as they knew at this point. The enormity of what had happened was dizzying. It wasn't just her uncle. Twelve people she'd known for most, or all, of her life were now dead, brutally, ruthlessly murdered inside her home, while her beloved Tonton's life hung in the balance. But why? Who could have done this terrible thing?

Boche said, 'I know you have many questions, Mademoiselle. So do we. We're still in the very earliest stages of this investigation and it may take time to get to the bottom of what happened here. In the meantime we would be extremely keen to speak with Georges Roblochon, the kitchen assistant.'

Valentina frowned. 'Georges?'

'You know him?'

'Of course I know him. I've known him for as long as I can remember. But why do you need to speak to him?'

'Because he's the only staff member unaccounted for,' Boche explained. 'We know he was here on the estate shortly before the attack happened, from gate security footage showing him in the van with the cook as they returned from buying kitchen supplies in Le Mans.'

'Yes, Annick and Georges always go to the fish market on a Wednesday morning. But—'

'Annick Marceau's body was among the others recovered at the crime scene,' Boche said. 'But that of Monsieur Roblochon is conspicuously absent. So where is he?'

'Are you saying Georges is a suspect?' she gasped. 'That's not possible. Georges is the sweetest, gentlest man. It's absurd to think he could have had anything to do with this.'

'Then I look forward to speaking with him, so we can verify his innocence. But in my experience innocent men don't mysteriously vanish with such convenient timing. He hasn't returned home since the incident and his elderly parents in Le Mans haven't heard from him either. All of which makes him a person of interest to us.'

'I don't believe it,' Valentina said. 'You're getting this wrong.' The frustration overwhelming her, she was unable to stop the tears that rolled down her face. Gabriel was looking anxiously at her, and stepped in protectively to bring the torture to an end.

'I think that's enough information for Valentina to process at the moment,' he said to Boche.

The inspector nodded gravely. 'Yes, of course. I'm sorry. Just let me say, Miss Petrova, that you can rest absolutely assured that we will not rest until we find the perpetrators of this terrible crime and bring them to justice. I have my very top men working on this, and they will be working around the clock. There's nobody better.'

Valentina remained silent for a long moment, gazing into the middle distance as her mind worked furiously and she decided what she was going to do.

'No,' she said at last. 'There is someone better.'

Chapter 2

Ben Hope rested back in the plush cream leather seat and watched the green patchwork countryside skim past ten thousand feet below. The luxurious Airbus helicopter in whose rear passenger cabin he was travelling could accommodate thirteen, which gave its sole occupant plenty of elbow room. And plenty of privacy to sit there wondering what the hell this was all about.

Yesterday's urgent and unexpected phone call from a certain Gabriel Archambeau had interrupted a busy afternoon's work at Le Val, the tactical training centre that Ben operated along with his fellow ex-military colleagues Jeff Dekker and Tuesday Fletcher in their sleepy corner of rural Normandy. Sleepy, that was, except for the sounds of rattling automatic gunfire, roaring engines and popping flashbangs that could often be heard wafting across the fields when the Le Val team got into action instructing groups of trainees from all over the world. And except for those all too frequent occasions when a distress call came in on behalf of a friend in serious trouble.

A man with Ben Hope's background and experience could certainly never have been considered a stranger to trouble. The whole course of his past life was littered with crises, emergencies and often deadly conflict. But this time it sounded bad. Really bad.

Archambeau hadn't said much over the phone, but it had been enough for Ben to instantly drop everything and agree to do whatever he could to help. He'd spent the rest of yesterday fretting over what the hell could have happened. Then early this morning, the familiar gleaming bright red helicopter with the KAPRISKY CORP corporate logo emblazoned on its sides had touched down in the cropped grassy meadow that was Le Val's long-distance rifle range. Ben was already there waiting for it.

With its maximum cruise speed of over 300 kilometres an hour, the Airbus could make the trip southwards across France from Le Val to the Kaprisky estate in under sixty minutes. The magnificent residence and its thousand-acre grounds were situated within the commune of Champagné, fourteen and a half kilometres from the city of Le Mans. It was a place Ben knew well from his previous visits there. He had a long personal and professional acquaintance with its owner, the octogenarian billionaire Auguste Kaprisky.

Auguste had always been a bit of an odd bod – and Ben's friend and business partner Jeff Dekker wasn't a million miles off the mark when he likened the old guy to the famously crazy billionaire Howard Hughes. He was eccentric in his ways, notoriously stingy with his money (one of the enduring Kaprisky legends was that he used to place artificial flowers on his late wife's grave, because fresh ones were so expensive and short-lived), and was often dressed in the same old threadbare suit he'd owned for forty years, deliberately staying thin so as not to have to buy another. He was stiff and formal in his manner, famously reclusive and paranoid about security, and perhaps even more famously lacking in humour, having earned himself the nickname 'the man who never smiles'. Ben knew that wasn't entirely true. He'd seen the old man crack a dry smirk, maybe as many as twice or three times over the years.

And yet for all his peculiarities, and the extreme, almost reptilian coldness he could display when displeased, he was equally capable of great warmth and generosity of spirit. He absolutely doted on his grandniece, Valentina, and he was deeply loyal to his friends. When some years earlier a ruined former business rival had gone berserk and somehow managed to penetrate the residence's security cordon to pepper the house with an Uzi submachine gun, Auguste was convinced that only the expertise of his personal security guards, who'd quickly neutralised the crazed shooter before he could do more damage, had saved his life. And he'd freely acknowledged that he owed that live-saving expertise in large part to Ben Hope, the man who had trained them to handle exactly those kinds of contingencies.

That had been the incident that began the unlikely friendship between the ex-SAS soldier and the billionaire. The bond had grown even stronger when Ben had been called on to travel to Russia to pry little Valentina and her father, Yuri, from the hands of some very dangerous and ruthless people.

Over the years since, Auguste's gratitude had remained undiminished and he'd come to Ben's aid several times in whatever way his vast resources allowed, such as lending the use of his Gulfstream jet and crew when Ben needed to fly in a hurry to Africa on a mission to rescue his son Jude from Somali ship hijackers. On another occasion, the old man had offered his home as safe haven for a friend of Ben's who had found herself in danger. As if all that weren't enough, a crate of eyewateringly expensive champagne was delivered to Le Val each Christmas, much enjoyed by the team.

Ben had been off again on his travels – he couldn't even remember where to on that occasion – when Yuri Petrov and his wife Eloise had been tragically killed. He'd been unable to attend the funeral in person but sent his condolences. Since then, he and Auguste hadn't been in touch as frequently as in the past, and he sensed that the grief had hit his friend very hard indeed. He'd often meant to give him a call.

And then this had to happen.

Ben had always regarded the incident with the business rival and the Uzi as a freak occurrence, never to be repeated. Now it seemed not only that he'd been dead wrong, but that, this time around, the attack on the Kaprisky residence might have succeeded, and quite spectacularly, where the first had been doomed to failure. The difference? The first had been a bungled amateur hit. The second, seemingly, was anything but.

For the moment, until he learned more, Ben had been provided with only a handful of core facts: that a team of armed men had managed to penetrate and storm the residence in broad daylight, wipe out the house staff including all eight of the personal bodyguards, put two bullets in Auguste Kaprisky and make their escape, leaving him for dead. At this point the old man was in a critical condition and there was no saying whether he'd make it or not.

As for who might be responsible for the attack, the police apparently had no idea, other than that it must be someone highly organised and very smart, with an intimate knowledge of the estate's security systems. Many people worked on the estate – groundskeepers, gardeners, stable grooms, pool maintenance staff and an estate manager who oversaw them all – but the whole operation had been executed without alerting any of them, to say nothing of the armed personnel who manned the main gate and security barrier.

After a search of the grounds Gendarmerie officers had discovered an open access gate in a remote section of the perimeter fence, more than quarter of a mile from the house. Skid marks on the road outside the fence showed where a fast getaway vehicle had made its escape. It was being assumed that the intruders had used that route as a means of both entry and exit. How they'd managed to slip across the estate unseen on foot, let alone get inside the house itself, remained a mystery. The extensive network of CCTV cameras that surveilled the perimeter had been disabled somehow shortly before the incident.

Meanwhile, the perpetrators' motives for wanting Kaprisky dead were still unknown. The police's only lead was a kitchen assistant believed to have been at the house that day, but whose body hadn't been found, alerting their suspicion that he might in some way have acted as an accomplice to the attackers. A search was underway for the potential suspect. But until they knew more, much more, there was nothing but questions, more questions, and no answers.

In short, figuring out what the hell had happened here was a job for someone with a little more skill and experience than the local police could bring to the table. Ben was that person. Or he hoped he was, for the sake of his old friend.

They were getting close to their destination. Like a miniature model far below he saw the little private road that led to the estate's main gates with their security hut and barrier, where the guards checked everyone who entered and left. The cops had set up a cordon at the entrance and a couple of patrol cars were hanging around, but there was no sign yet of the TV news crews and paparazzi who'd soon be thronging around the gates like flies on fresh manure and circling the house in their helicopters. Less than twenty-four hours since the incident, Gabriel Archambeau was obviously working hard and pulling all the strings he could to keep the sensational breaking story out of the media for as long as possible, but even he couldn't work miracles.

Even from the air, the estate seemed to go on for ever. The helicopter overflew the lush greenery of acres of woodland giving way to emerald paddocks in which magnificent Arab horses galloped away at the sound of the approaching aircraft. Now the pilot was banking over the seventeenth-century château itself, giving Ben a bird's-eye view of the Kaprisky residence as little starbursts of sunlight sparkled off its towers and turrets. The fabulous home had once belonged to the Rothschild banking dynasty, before the German-born Kaprisky fell in love with France, changed his name from August to Auguste to make himself sound more Gallic, and badgered the Rothschilds into selling him the estate for cash. The joys of almost limitless wealth.

Ben had known a lot of very rich people in his time. He'd always been happy he wasn't one of them.

Moments later, the chopper came down to land on a circular helipad at the rear of the property, and Ben climbed out into the wind of the rotors' downdraught carrying his old green canvas bag, the only luggage he'd brought with him.

He'd half expected Gabriel Archambeau or some other employee to emerge from the house to meet him, but nobody did. He walked alone around the side of the château and across the courtyard, pausing to light a Gauloise and gaze around him, trying to visualise the scene as it had been during the attack. Outwardly, there was no visible sign of disturbance. The police presence and forensic vehicles had all gone, leaving the place itself physically unchanged in their wake.

It was just as Ben remembered it from his last visit. The breathtaking splendour of the great house and buildings, the perfection of the grounds. Water burbling and splashing from the baroque-style fountain, with its classical statue of Diana the huntress, at the centre of the circular courtyard in front. The scent of roses and freshly mown grass. The soft cooing of doves and the distant whinny of horses. The only thing that hadn't been here before was the haunting sense of something terrible having happened. Ben could feel it hanging in the air like a pall.

He flicked away his half-finished Gauloise and walked up the balustraded stairway to the grand entrance. The château's double front doorway was ten feet tall and carved out of solid oak. Ben tugged the sash of the ancient manual pull-cord doorbell, and from somewhere within came the faint chime, like the ringing of a gong. He waited patiently for a few moments, knowing it took an age for anyone to get to the door of the huge house. At last he heard the clunk of the lock, and one of the doors swung partly open.

Auguste Kaprisky's long-serving butler had been Jean-Claude Vautour, a dour little man who always wore the same black waistcoat and white gloves, with oiled-back thinning hair and sunken cheeks like Peter Cushing. But no more, he'd been one of the victims of the attack. In his absence, Ben was greeted by the dark-suited, square-shouldered hulk of a private security operative he'd never seen before. Moving fast, no expense spared, Archambeau had scrambled in a whole new team to replace the old one that had been wiped out.

The new guy was maybe eight years younger than Ben, and a good eight inches taller at about six-seven. Built like a silverback gorilla, with enormously long musclebound arms that threatened to pop the seams of his suit sleeves. Ginger hair buzzed short enough to stand straight up like bristles. He wasn't making any effort to hide the butt of the holstered auto pistol that protruded from his jacket. He was wearing a military-style radio and earpiece. The big fleshy face under the buzz cut was stony and expressionless.

'I'm expected,' Ben said. Wondering how fast the gorilla would be able to get that pistol drawn and into action if he made a move. Not fast enough, probably. It was getting harder to find the staff these days.

The gorilla glanced Ben up and down, gave a curt nod, then without a word to him spoke into his radio in a voice two octaves deeper than a normal human being. 'He's here.' Then he opened the door wider and stepped back to let Ben through. 'This way.'

'I know the way,' Ben said.

The hulk led him through the huge marble-floored entrance hall, their footsteps echoing up to the high domed ceiling adorned with fresco artwork and gilt. The walls were hung with a few examples from Auguste Kaprisky's extensive art collection, an eclectic mix comprising the old and the modern, from Dürer and El Greco to Picasso and Kandinsky. Ben recognised the names but he wasn't much into art. They made their way down a long, broad corridor that smelled of furniture wax and floor polish, and was lined with Greek statues on marble plinths. All more or less the way Ben remembered it from his previous visits here, though in all truth he'd never really paid any of it a great deal of attention.

The end wall of the corridor was adorned with an enormous oil painting of Napoleon Bonaparte, a particular hero of the old man's. More than two metres high, it depicted a younger, slimmer future emperor than most of his portraits, sitting astride a magnificent white horse rearing dramatically up on its hind legs with a craggy mountain scene in the background, a reference to Napoleon's crossing of the Alps with his army in 1800.

Ben couldn't recall if the painting had been there when he'd last come to the house, and he barely gave it a second glance now. On the adjacent wall to its right hung a vast early eighteenth-century gilt-framed mirror; now that item he *did* remember, because when Auguste had bought it at auction a few years earlier, he'd proudly told Ben that it had once belonged to Marie Antoinette. To Ben's eye the flamboyant rococo monstrosity represented one of the billionaire's occasional lapses of taste, but then what the hell did he know?

Opposite the mirror stood a tall, impressive doorway. The hulk stopped beside it, surreptitiously turned to admire his reflection in the glass, then rapped his heavy knuckles on the door and grunted in his sub-bass tone for Ben to go in. Attitude.

Through the door was a yellow silk-panelled room that was an accurate replica of one of the more opulent salons at Fontainebleau Palace. Ben had been inside the room many times but it had never felt so sad and empty. An elegant curve of windows at its far end looked out into the grounds, where a couple of the horses disturbed by the arrival of the helicopter had returned to their tranquil grazing.

Standing watching them through the window was a young girl Ben knew well but hadn't seen since their safe return from Russia. She'd been just a child then, although she'd handled herself bravely through more danger than most adults would ever see in a dozen lifetimes. Their last communication had been a handwritten note from her in a little pink envelope, given to Ben by her father, Yuri, because she was too bashful to do it herself.

Dear Ben,
Thank you for what you did for me, and my Papa. I will never forget you. I hope that you'll come and visit us very very often.
Love from your best friend in all the world.

She'd signed it with four kisses under her name. Yuri had laughed about the note, saying he reckoned his daughter had a schoolgirl crush on Ben and dreamed of marrying him one day when she was older.

She was still a schoolgirl, but those romantic dreams were a long way behind her now, and she'd grown up into a fine young woman. She turned away from the window as he walked into the room, and he saw that she'd been crying. At the sight of him, her tear-streaked face broke into a smile of joy, like sunlight bursting through the clouds.

'Hello, Valentina,' Ben said.

Chapter 3

'It's so good to see you,' she said as she hugged him, burying her face into the hollow of his shoulder and clasping him around the middle. 'Oh God, I can't tell you how happy I am that you're here.'

Ben could feel the tension and pain in her body. They stood like that for a long moment in the silence of the room, then she pulled away from him and gazed up into his face with the saddest eyes, filled with tears that glistened in the light from the windows. 'Let me look at you,' she said, as though she couldn't quite believe it was really him. 'It's been so long since I saw you last. But you haven't changed a bit.'

She herself very much had, though. Up close, the depth of maturity in her expression was startling. The last eighteen months of heartbreak and tragedy had entirely done away with the youthful Valentina he'd known and left her thinner, harder-edged, more serious, an adult before her time. Ben knew all too well what it felt like to lose someone. There'd been far too much of that in Valentina's young life. He wished he could tell her things would get better.

'How is he?' he asked.

She shook her head. 'The same. There's been no change since last night. I don't know if he's ever going to wake up.'

'I'm so sorry.'

'Would you like to see him?' she asked. 'They won't let us into the room with him, but you can see him through the window.'

'I'd rather not see him like that, Valentina.'

'Nor me,' she murmured, wiping a tear. After a silence she said, 'Who could have done this, Ben?'

'That's what we'll try to find out,' he replied. 'I'm here now. I'm not going home until we get to the bottom of what happened to your Tonton. That's a promise, Pumpkin.'

She managed a smile through the tears. 'That's what Papa used to call me.'

'I know.'

'I miss him too. I miss them all so much. I feel so alone and lost without them. At least I did, until you appeared.'

'Your granduncle's a fighter,' Ben said, laying his hands on her shoulders and looking earnestly into those heart-rendingly sad eyes. 'He always was. You haven't lost him yet, so let's not give up hope, okay?'

She sighed, nodded sagely. 'Thanks, Ben. You always make me feel better.'

'I'll always try,' he said.

'Are they here yet?' she asked, glancing nervously towards the window. 'The press?'

'Not yet.'

'They will be,' she sighed. 'It'll be hell. Why can't they leave us alone? Those horrible ghouls, prying into people's lives, feeding off their unhappiness.'

'Because of who you are,' Ben said.

'I hate it,' she said bitterly. 'I hate being rich. I wish we were just ordinary people, like everyone else. Then nobody would have wanted to hurt us like this, would they?'

You could always just give it all away, Ben might have said. But he didn't say that. 'We don't know why anyone wanted to do this. We can't assume anything right now. In any case, it's not only wealthy people who get attacked. There can be all kinds of reasons.' 'Maybe you're right,' she replied. 'I don't know about these things. I wish they didn't happen to anybody at all.'

'Me too,' Ben said. 'But that's the world we live in.'

'I suppose I must sound terribly naive saying that, don't I? But I'm not, at least not completely. One thing I do know is, don't attacks like this normally happen at night, under cover of darkness, when everybody's asleep? I mean, isn't it unusual that it happened during the day, in the middle of the morning?'

'It is unusual,' Ben agreed. 'Whether it means anything, we'll have to try to figure out. One step at a time, okay? Now why don't we sit down and you tell me exactly what happened, right from the beginning.'

Valentina nodded. 'Would you like a drink? Tonton told me you're fond of whisky. There's a bottle in the cabinet.' Pointing.

'No thanks, Valentina.'

'Well you won't mind if I do,' she said. 'I need it.' Seventeen years old and hitting the bottle.

'You should go easy on that.'

'I'm not a child any more, Ben,' she said with a note of firmness. Who was he anyway, to be lecturing anyone on the perils of drink? She crossed the room to an antique globe on a stand and opened up the hollow planet Earth to reveal a selection of drinks and glasses. He watched as she poured herself a small measure of Crème de Cassis into a crystal brandy glass. He might have guessed that if a teenage girl was going to take up boozing, her first choice would be some sticky, sickly liqueur. He was relieved that at least it wasn't the hard stuff. At her age, he'd already discovered a taste for single malt scotch that later became a little too much of a habit.

Valentina carried her glass over to an alcove window seat and settled on it, facing the window and making a little nest for herself among the velvet cushions. Ben sat with her and waited for her to speak first. She took several small sips of the liqueur, then set the glass down on the sill and folded her hands in her lap, staring helplessly at them. 'What can I tell you that Gabriel won't have told you already? Nobody has a clue about anything. You know about Georges?'

'The missing staff member? Only that he's a possible suspect. I take it he hasn't turned up yet.'

She shook her head. 'No sign of him. But I refuse to believe he had anything to do with it. If the police think otherwise, they're nothing but a bunch of idiots.'

Ben was generally inclined to feel the same way about police officers, a handful of rare exceptions notwithstanding, but he made no comment. He asked, 'Where is Gabriel? I'd expected to see him here.'

'I sent him away,' Valentina replied. 'The poor man is so upset by what's happened. There's nothing more he can do here for the moment, and I can handle things myself. Besides, I wanted to see you alone.'

'You've grown up into a very brave young lady,' Ben said, smiling at her with a real feeling of pride and affection.

'Oh, no. I'm really not.' She sighed, took another sip of her Crème de Cassis and gazed out of the window at the calmly grazing horses, getting her thoughts together. 'I was at school when it happened. Tonton was alone here in the house, or as alone as he ever can be. The bodyguards are' – she corrected herself – '*were* never too far away, hovering around him the whole time, as closely as he would allow. He's a very private person, as you know.'

'Gabriel told me that it was one of the estate maintenance staff who raised the alarm, some minutes after the attackers had left.'

'That's right. It was Marcel, the head gardener, who lives in a cottage on the estate. He happened to be driving past the house on his little tractor thing, when he noticed a back door open and saw what he realised was a foot sticking out of it. He ran over to investigate, and nearly died of fright when he saw the body.'

'Whose was it?'

'Gaston's,' she replied. Gaston Bonnet had been one of Kaprisky's personal close protection team. Ben remembered him well. 'And then poor Marcel saw there was another body close by. That was Vincent, Vincent Moreau. He was—'

'You don't need to explain to me who Vincent was,' Ben said.

'Of course, you trained some of them, didn't you? Anyway, Marcel was too terrified to go any further into the house, so he hurried off to tell the gate staff, and the police were called. If it hadn't been for Marcel, they certainly wouldn't have found Tonton in time to save his life.'

'So this back door was what, a tradesmen's entrance?'

'It's a little basement back kitchen and storeroom with steps up to the ground floor,' Valentina explained. 'Next to it is a utility room where I happen to know some of the bodyguards go to sneak a cigarette now and then. Tonton doesn't approve of anyone smoking in the house.'

'Which could explain why Gaston and Vincent were down there,' Ben said.

She nodded sadly. 'And the housekeepers, too, because the utility room is used for keeping cleaning equipment, mops and buckets and such. The police think that the intruders got in through the back kitchen, encountered Vincent and Gaston, then pushed further into the house and soon afterwards met Marie-Anne, the housekeeper, and her two assistants, Sophie and Clementine.'

'Who were all killed as well,' Ben said.

Valentina's mournful expression darkened to one of anger and revulsion. 'They shot Marie-Anne . . .' she hesitated, balking at saying it '. . . they shot her in the *eye*. The police said she was killed instantly, and I suppose she must have been. Clementine wasn't so lucky. She managed to crawl some way before she died. Clementine was only a year older than me. She was my friend.'

'I'm sorry,' Ben said again. It sounded so lame, but what else could he say? He moved quickly back to the practical facts. 'This back kitchen door, would it normally be left open?'

'It used to be, but not any more. There was a problem with some of the junior grounds workers going in there to help themselves to pastries and sandwiches, so Tonton said it should be kept locked.'

'And had the door been broken into from the outside?'

'No, that's the funny thing. The police didn't find any sign of forced entry.'

Gabriel hadn't given any of these little details over the phone. Ben made a mental note of them and said, 'Okay, and then?'

Valentina went on, 'It seems as if the next person they shot was Jean-Claude,' referring to Vautour, the butler. 'He was much more than just a butler to Tonton. They'd known each other since long, long before I was born. He was on his break, drinking coffee in the main kitchen, when he must have heard a noise and went to investigate. The police found his half-empty cup on the kitchen table. His body was on the stairs.'

'So the attackers were making their way to the upper floors when they shot him,' Ben said. 'What about the other bodyguards, apart from Gaston and Vincent? Where were they?'

'Pierre, Pierre Nord, he was found with Tonton, in Tonton's study on the second floor. Tonton was shot twice, you see.' She wiped a tear, seemed about to break down, then swallowed and went on in a tight voice, 'It seems that it was the first shot that hit him in the shoulder. They said it missed its mark because of Pierre, who got in between Tonton and the killers, trying to shield him. There were three bullets gone from Pierre's gun, but we don't know if he hit any of them. Then they shot him dead. After he fell to the floor, they fired the second shot at Tonton. That's the bullet that went into his chest. It stopped his heart. But he didn't die.' Another tear welled up, quivering on her eyelash, then rolled down the smooth curve of her cheek.

Ben remembered Pierre Nord well from their training sessions. A big, strong guy, tough and determined. He'd given his life to do his job. Ben said, 'I know it's hard for you to have to go through all this again. But I need a full account of the details to help me understand how it all happened.'

'It's okay. Like you said, I have to be brave. Or at least act as though I am.'

'You're doing great,' Ben said. 'All right, so far that accounts for three of the bodyguards. What about the others?'

'Two more of them, Jacques and Noël, were right behind Tonton. The police suspect they came rushing into the room just as those shots were being fired, too late to save him. Jacques's gun fired two shots. One of his bullets went through a clock on the mantelpiece and into the plaster of the wall behind it. The broken clock was how the police knew exactly what time it happened, six minutes past ten. Where the other bullet went, we don't know yet. As for Noël, his gun was still full, so that must mean he was killed before he fired a shot.'

'Yes, that's what it means. So that makes five, leaving Max, Denis and Lucas.'

'Lucas didn't work for Tonton any more,' Valentina said. 'He left two months ago, and was replaced by a new man.'

Ben was surprised to hear that. 'Who's the new man?'

'André something. I don't remember, you'd have to ask Gabriel. Anyhow, Max, Denis and André were found dead

34

in different parts of the house. The police said that Denis had eleven bullets in his body. *Eleven*, Ben. What kind of person does that to another person?'

One with a high-capacity weapon, most likely with fully automatic capability, Ben reflected inwardly. And one with the ability to place a string of rapid-fire shots on target in a high-pressure combat situation. In the hands of your average gunned-up criminal, the lively, squirming recoil of something like a small, compact submachine pistol could easily get out of control and produce a vertical spatter of bullet holes that mostly missed their target and stitched a line up the wall behind. That had been the case with the demented Uzi shooter who'd made the last attempt on the Kaprisky residence. This had been something totally different.

Trying to form the details into a coherent picture he said, 'So it all seems to have happened so fast, it took them completely by surprise and they weren't able to get into position in time, except for Pierre, who might just have been with your granduncle by chance at that moment, and Jacques and Noël who happened to be nearby.'

'Nobody even heard the shots. How could that be?'

'It's a big house,' Ben said. 'And if everybody was using sound suppressors, the reports wouldn't travel very far.' He could have talked about the attackers' possible use of special-ised subsonic rounds to reduce the noise even further, sacrificing a little velocity at the muzzle without compromising their effectiveness for a close-quarter massacre like this. It was how his SAS unit would have done it, back in the day. And often had.

'Okay, I understand that,' Valentina said, frowning. 'But I don't get how come these intruders were able to overpower Tonton's security men so easily. Why? You're the one who trained them. Can you understand it?'

There was no sense of blame or accusation in the tone of her question, just confusion and bewilderment. Ben couldn't realistically blame himself for the apparent failure of the bodyguards, either. He'd taught these men well. They were some of the more talented close protection operatives he'd worked with, and up until this incident he'd have been perfectly confident in their ability to shield their VIP principal from all but the most extreme scenario. There was no question of Auguste Kaprisky having been fobbed off with second-rate personnel.

And yet, this had happened nonetheless.

'Yes, I did train them,' he replied. 'All except the new guy, André. And they were pretty good. But the men who did this were better. That's all I can say. No matter how high you think you've climbed up the tree, there's always someone higher than you.'

'Except you, Ben. Nobody's better than *you*, surely.'

He shrugged. 'I can't say that.'

'So who are they? Where did they come from? Who were they working for?'

'The police will be asking the same questions,' Ben said. 'Someone out there knows something. And until they can find a better lead, the cops are going to keep coming back to Georges, the kitchen assistant. He's the missing link. The nearest thing they have to a real suspect.'

'I told you, Georges is innocent,' she said firmly. 'If you knew him, you'd understand how crazy it is to suspect him of any involvement. A simple soul like him wouldn't harm a fly. He was completely devoted to Annick, our cook. And to Tonton. He's about forty, I think, but he's got the mental age of a child and an IQ to match.'

'You're sure of that. Then where is he?'

'I don't know. But there's bound to be some explanation. Maybe he ran away when it all started happening. He must have been completely traumatised. The poor thing could be hiding somewhere, too afraid to come out. Or perhaps he's hurt, lying in a ditch somewhere, suffering. Oh God, what must he be going through?'

Ben was keeping an open mind on poor dear Georges, but he could see it was a dead end pressing her on that point. 'All right. Let's step back and look at the bigger picture. What's the motive here? The easy answer being money, of course. This house has more treasures in it than the Louvre Museum. Your Tonton's art collection, to begin with, all those Rembrandts and Van Goghs. And Napoleon on his horse and that gaudy gold mirror in the corridor outside. Not to mention all the rest of the stuff he's been cramming this house with for decades.'

'You don't like the mirror?' Valentina asked, managing another weak smile.

'Personally? I think it looks like something that came out of an oversized Christmas cracker. But not everybody would feel the way I do, and I'm sure it's also pretty damn valuable. As are all the rest of the little trinkets and baubles lying around that would be more portable and manageable for a thief looking to make a fast getaway on foot, which I'm assuming is what they did.'

'I don't think Tonton would approve too much of your calling them trinkets and baubles.'

'Then again, I'm not a fine art connoisseur,' Ben said. 'But I do happen to know that's a genuine Ming vase there on that mantelpiece, and that those are a couple of original Fabergé eggs either side of it, the one on the left a gift to your granduncle from Prince Rainier of Monaco. Basically everywhere you look in this house there are knick-knacks worth millions of euros. You'd only have to stick one of them in your pocket to come away a pretty rich man. And that's what's strange. These people could have had their pick of all this prime loot, and yet, from what Gabriel told me on the phone this morning, nothing at all was taken. Which means we have to rule out the most obvious motive.'

Valentina cocked her head a little to one side and looked at Ben thoughtfully. 'Yes, I expect Gabriel would have told you that. But it's not actually the case.'

Chapter 4

Ben looked at her. 'You mean, something *was* taken?'

Valentina nodded. 'Just one particular item. Or more correctly, thirty-two of them. The pieces from Tonton's chess set. His favourite chess set that he plays on the most. He has lots of them.'

'His favourite one being the Napoleon set.'

She seemed surprised. 'You know it?'

'I do know it.' Ben had actually had quite a number of games on it with Auguste over the years. He could play reasonably well, though nowhere near the level of the old man, who could give the world's top grandmasters a run for their money. As a wily strategist with a genius intellect and the apparent ability to think in five or six dimensions at once, chess was so much Auguste's game that it could almost have been invented for him. He'd been passionate about it all his life, and amassed a collection of sets dating back to various periods of history, some of them many centuries old. But just as Valentina had said, the Napoleon set was the one he'd lovingly bring out time and again.

He loved to talk about it, too. Ben had been told its history, oh, maybe ten or twelve thousand times, certainly enough to remember. It got its nickname from its famous erstwhile owner, who, when he wasn't going around

39

conquering much of the world at the head of his vast armies and crowning himself Emperor of France, had been a keen player of the grand old game – if not, according to Auguste, particularly skilled at it despite his undisputed talent for real-life military tactics.

Like Auguste, the Emperor had owned several chess sets. One, probably the most famous, was on display in the museum of Biltmore House, the palatial 8000-acre North Carolina estate and one-time residence of George Washington Vanderbilt. Kept under glass and never touched let alone played, it was Chinese in origin, the pieces carved from ivory, natural-coloured for white and stained red for black.

But the authoritative and completely trustworthy source from whom Kaprisky had obtained his own, much-prized 'Napoleon set' had assured him that this one, much more than the example at Biltmore, had been the Emperor's personal favourite and the one he loved to play the most. By contrast it originated from sixteenth-century Persia, the pieces exquisitely sculpted from white opal and lapis lazuli with a matching board. Even Ben, a self-professed ignoramus when it came to some of the finer *objets d'art*, had had to appreciate its beauty. He'd been quite shocked to hear that Auguste habitually took the chess set with him on his travels, albeit packed inside a protective case and with extra men to guard it whenever it was out of his sight.

'Then you know how important it is to Tonton,' Valentina said. 'Not for its financial value, of course. He doesn't really care about money.'

Because he has so damn much of it, Ben thought to himself. 'So the pieces were taken, but what about the board?'

'It's still there in its usual place,' she replied.

'On that little table near the fireplace?' Ben asked.

'You remember.'

'Hold on a minute,' he said. 'I don't understand. If the chess pieces are missing, why did Gabriel tell me nothing had been stolen?'

'Because that was true, as far as he knew then. I only just discovered this morning that they were missing. It was after I'd sent Gabriel away and the last of the police had gone, while you were on your way in the helicopter. That's when I decided to have a look around Tonton's study. I don't know why I did. I think some part of me believed that I'd find him sitting there reading, and that he'd be all right and this was all just some horrible dream. But he wasn't there, of course. No trace of him, except for the bloodstain on the rug where they found him. I stood there staring at it for ages. Then I just happened to look around the room. I wasn't expecting to find anything the police hadn't already found But I know every inch of the room so well, and I saw right away that something was different.'

'Did you tell Gabriel what you'd found?'

She replied, 'He would have been driving back towards Chartres at the time, and wasn't answering his phone. I've left him a voicemail and a text but I haven't heard back from him yet.'

'What about the police? Do they know?'

Valentina nodded. 'Yes, the officer in charge of the investigation, Inspector Boche, he gave me a direct line number, and I called it to tell him about the chess set. He didn't seem very interested. I think the police have just made the assumption that this wasn't a robbery, because of all the other valuable things that weren't touched. Then he asked me how I knew anyway, because Tonton's study was sealed off with crime scene tape. He wasn't very happy when I told him I'd cut the tape. I'm just a silly interfering little girl, it seems.' She shrugged. 'Well, that's fine. I don't care. You know, and that's all that matters.'

Ben said, 'Let's go upstairs to the study and take a look.'

Valentina led him from the yellow silk-draped salon and back along the passage to a sweeping double staircase. The gorilla in the suit was nowhere to be seen, but Ben guessed he and his colleagues would be lurking somewhere not too far away.

He followed Valentina up the stairs to the second floor, and along another long, wide art-filled corridor until they arrived at the door of Kaprisky's study. The crime scene tape that Valentina had irreverently snipped with scissors was hanging limp either side. She pushed the door open and Ben stepped in after her.

The large, dark-panelled room was very familiar to him, a much more masculine space than the airy bright salon downstairs. Oil paintings of historic naval battles from the age of sail hung on the walls, and a display of old flintlock pistols and muskets adorned the space between the two gothic-arched windows behind Kaprisky's enormous antique desk. Heavy satin drapes shut out much of the light. The room's silence was made more solemn by the slow tick-tocking of the tall long-case clock. A smaller but far more ornate clock, the sound of whose delicate mechanism had once complemented that of its larger sibling, now stood silent on the mantelpiece, its innards shattered by the bullet that had buried itself deep into the wall behind it, its frozen hands forever witness to the moment its owner had come face to face with his would-be assassins. The forensic team had done a lot of damage digging the bullet out of the plaster.

Near the grandiose fireplace was the small table, instantly recognisable to Ben, where he and the old man had spent all those hours playing chess – or, more correctly, where Ben had spent a lot of hours losing at chess. Many of their games had taken place after his return that time from Russia. It had been a rough mission that left him with a few minor injuries, and he'd stayed on the estate to be treated at the private clinic and recuperate before heading back home to Le Val. It was during that time that he'd got to know Auguste well. Seeing the room again filled him with a renewed surge of anger and sadness.

'Here, you see?' Valentina said, pointing at the empty chessboard that rested on the table. Like the pieces from the Napoleon set, it was fashioned out of moonlike opal for the white squares and rich blue lapis lazuli for the 'black' squares, the superbly crafted whole inset into a square piece of marble. But the pieces themselves were conspicuously missing, leaving the board looking naked and desolate.

'Are you sure about this?' Ben asked. 'He hasn't just put them somewhere else?'

'Now you sound like Inspector Boche,' she replied a little hotly. 'I'm not imagining it, if that's what you think. I'm often in this room and that's where the pieces always are, unless Tonton's away somewhere and taken them with him. He never takes the board, because it's so awkward to transport. But the pieces fit into their own little case. And look, there's the empty case sitting on the bookshelf, see? If Tonton had tidied them away anywhere, that's where he'd have put them. But he didn't. It can only mean one thing. So I'm right.'

'I stand corrected,' Ben said. 'Then if the attackers stole the chess pieces, that raises three questions. Is that the sole reason they came here, for a targeted robbery of that one specific item? And if so, what could be so important about a chess set that whoever's behind it would launch a raid like this and happily slaughter half the household? Especially with so many other valuables lying around.'

'And then the third question,' Valentina said, anticipating his thoughts, 'is why did they only take the pieces and not the board? I mean, someone does all these terrible things to steal a priceless antique chess set that once belonged to Napoleon Bonaparte, but then they only steal *half* of it? It's crazy. As though harming innocent people wasn't insane enough.'

'Unless they meant to take the board as well, but weren't able to for some reason,' Ben said. He slid three fingers under the corner of the board and lifted it an inch off the table. The dense material weighed about the same as a heavy paving slab, the smooth edges cool against his fingertips. 'Too heavy to carry, maybe.'

'But if they came here intentionally looking for the chess set, wouldn't they have known all about it?' Valentina asked.

'I'd imagine whoever commissioned the robbery would have given them the details,' Ben replied.

'In which case, they'd know the board was a solid, heavy object. They'd have been prepared to deal with it. And packed the pieces in their case to protect them, surely.'

'Makes sense,' Ben said, nodding. 'Even if nothing else does.'

Yet more unanswered questions, crowding his mind along with the rest. Why had the CCTV cameras watching the perimeter been put out of action, and by whom? Why had the back kitchen door been left unlocked, allowing the attackers to get inside the house? From whichever angle Ben tried to get a handle on the whole mystery, he couldn't make sense of any of it.

Valentina was frowning as though the same perplexing thoughts were churning through her own mind. 'But one thing's for sure, Ben.'

'What's that?'

'What I want,' she said. She stepped behind her grand-uncle's desk and sat in his heavy leather chair, framed by the gothic windows. She looked strangely as though she belonged there, as she laid her hands flat on the desktop and looked at Ben with a face that had become suddenly much harder. Her whole demeanour and tone were no longer those of the seventeen-year-old schoolgirl Ben knew. He was looking at the sharp-witted, steely-eyed hard-driving mature business executive of the future.

'There are a couple of things I haven't told you yet,' she said. 'To begin with, let me tell you something about Tonton's will. Something that until now, only he, the family, and Gabriel have known about. Now you will too.'

Chapter 5

'I'm honoured,' Ben said. 'And curious.'

Valentina explained. 'You see, Tonton has always lived in fear that one day he might lose his . . . I don't quite know what the best expression would be.'

'Lose his marbles?'

'That's one way of saying it. Not that there's ever been any sign of that happening; quite the opposite. But both his father and his grandfather before him suffered from mild senility by the time they reached the age of ninety. The thought of the same thing happening to him terrifies Tonton. For him, it would be worse than being dead. So he made a provision in his will that if at any time he was no longer fully in possession of his mental faculties, or his marbles, as you put it, then the control of the estate, the Kaprisky Corporation and the entire family fortune would revert to the next relative in line. Now I'm the only one left alive, that means me.' She gave a small wave of her hand. 'Oh, Gabriel will still be there to oversee the day-to-day running of the business and take care of administrative stuff, all those little things. But the big decisions will all be down to me, until Tonton recovers. So here I am, suddenly placed in charge of an empire. Which I suppose makes me the empress.'

Ben smiled. 'I suppose it does.'

'And so I've decided what to do next.'

Ben said nothing. The ponderous ticking of the long-case clock filled the silence. Valentina knitted her fingers on the desk. She said, 'Ben, I'm going to instruct Gabriel to put a bounty on the heads of the people who did this to Tonton. Not only to him, but to all the others they've hurt. People who were loyal to us. People I've known as long as I can remember. People I'm never going to see again, thanks to these murderers.'

Ben could see in her eyes that she was completely, calmly serious. There were no more tears on the horizon, no perceptible anger, no visible emotion at all. 'How much of a bounty?' he asked.

'One billion euros,' she replied evenly.

'That's a lot of money, Valentina.'

'It's only a fraction of what we're worth. If I need to raise it to three billion, five billion, then I will,' she said, nonchalantly tossing the colossal numbers about as though it were Monopoly money. 'I don't care. Whatever it takes to get justice done. I want these people alive, so that they can be made answerable for what they did. I want to be able to meet them face to face before I bury them for ever. And I want Tonton's chess set returned, because if he ever recovers I want to be able to sit at that table again and play with him the way we used to.'

Ben said nothing for a moment as he pondered what she was telling him. 'And you're asking me to act on your behalf to make all this happen.'

'That's why I asked you here, Ben. You were the only person in the world who could have saved me and my father that time. There's nobody else I trust to help me again now.'

'What about the authorities? You have this Inspector Boche and his detectives heading up the investigation. I can't imagine them taking too kindly to you stirring the pot like this.'

'To hell with them,' she replied flatly. 'I didn't call them in. Gabriel did. We don't need them and I don't want them. I told you, I want justice for Tonton. Boche can't deliver that. Not the way I want it. But you can.'

'A billion euros,' Ben said.

'Yes. That's the price I'm putting on the heads of these men. It's what I'm offering you to hunt them down.'

'And kill them.'

'Did they show anyone any mercy when they attacked our home? They deserve whatever's coming to them.'

'And if I said no?'

'Then I'd try and find someone else,' she replied simply. 'But I don't know who.'

'Do you have any idea what you'd be getting into?' Ben asked her. 'With that kind of money on the table, you'd have every desperado, contract killer, soldier of fortune and cannibal headhunter from here to Shanghai swarming at your door to offer their services. Those aren't the kind of sharks you want to go swimming with, believe me.'

'That's why I'm asking you. You're not just my first choice. You're my only choice. Help us. And the billion euros is yours.'

He said nothing.

'I've seen what you can do, Ben,' she said. 'Do it for me.'

'What I did then, the things you've seen me do, that's not the life I ever wanted, you know? I've been trying for a long time to leave it all behind me. To find peace. Or what-ever kind of peace can be found, for a guy like me.' It was rare for Ben to speak so much from the heart, unless to a very close friend.

'With so much money, you could have nothing but peace for the rest of time,' she said. 'You'd never need to worry about anything again. Please. I'm begging you. For Tonton. For me.'

Ben reflected for a few moments, then shook his head. 'I don't want your money, Valentina. Not for myself. But,' he added after another pause, 'I'll use whatever I need of it as expenses to find the men who did this.'

Her glum expression lit up. 'Then you'll help us?'

'You know I will. You knew that before I even got here.'

She jumped up from the big leather chair, ran around the desk and hugged him, suddenly the little girl once again. 'It's wonderful. I don't know how to thank you.'

'You don't have to thank me at all,' Ben said. 'You and your granduncle are my friends, and friends help each other.'

Valentina let go of him and started pacing up and down, burning with excitement. 'I suppose this is a job for a team, really. Top professionals, like you. But I don't want you hiring outsiders. Promise me that you'll only use the people you trust the most in the whole world to help you.'

'I promise,' he said. 'But I usually prefer to work alone.'

'However you want it to be, that's how it will be. You have carte blanche, Ben. I mean that. Total freedom to run this operation your way. Just remember what I said, though. You'll have all the resources you could possibly need at your disposal. Anything at all, just call me on this number' – scribbling it

49

on a Post-it note from Auguste's desk and pressing it into Ben's hand – 'and it will be taken care of immediately, without question. 'Cars, aeroplanes, helicopters, cash, accommodation, any kind of equipment you might require, it's yours.'

'And Gabriel agrees to all of this?'

'Gabriel works for me now,' she said matter-of-factly. 'He'll agree to whatever I tell him.'

Ben was amazed by how tough and determined a young woman the little girl he'd known had grown up into. Then again, he thought, she had Kaprisky blood – and Auguste, for all his eccentricities, was one of the toughest people Ben had ever met. But as he was reflecting on that, he remembered something else.

'You said there were two things you hadn't told me yet. What's the other?'

Chapter 6

Valentina looked coy. 'Well, I was really hoping like crazy you'd say yes. And deep down in my heart I was sure you would. That's why I didn't tell Inspector Boche and his men everything I know. I'd already decided I wanted you, and not them.'

'You need to be careful about things like withholding evidence from the police,' Ben said. 'That could get you into trouble, if they found out.'

She made a dismissive gesture, like swatting at an imaginary bluebottle. 'Oh, who cares? They'd only interfere.'

'Fine. What didn't you tell them?'

'The combination to the safe where Tonton keeps his private appointments diary,' she replied with a twinkle. 'I knew that if I let that Boche have it, he'd probably take the diary away. And I thought there might be some useful information in it for you.'

'How come you know the combination to Auguste's safe?'

'Because I'm his little sugar dumpling and he trusts me with everything,' she said brightly. 'Well, almost everything.'

'Have you already looked inside?'

'Of course. The diary's there, along with a few other things. Here, let me show you.'

She trotted nimbly across the study, dropped to her knees beside a large, solid antique dresser, and opened a cupboard to reveal the shiny black steel safe door concealed inside. The safe had a digital combination panel on its front. 'The combination number is the notation of the final moves of The Immortal Game,' she explained, tapping it into the panel.

'Anderssen versus Kieseritzky, 1851,' Ben said. 'I might have known it would be something to do with chess.'

'You know your stuff. I'm impressed.'

'Anyone who's hung around your granduncle long enough will pick up all kinds of valuable information like that.'

There was a soft click, the safe lock popped open and she swung the heavy door back, showing a deep felt-lined recess inside that was lit by small LED spotlamps.

'There,' she said. 'Take a look.'

Ben crouched beside Valentina and examined the safe's contents. There was a Smith & Wesson .357 Magnum revolver in a leather holster, a matching leather twin speed-loader pouch holding twelve hollowpoint rounds for the weapon, a thick sheaf of papers in a card folder marked AUGUSTE KAPRISKY: LAST WILL AND TESTAMENT, a chunky leather diary with gold-edged leaves, a black velvet jewel box containing a collection of cut diamonds that glittered in the light from the window, and a plain steel key with no label or markings on it.

'Why did he have the gun?' Ben asked.

'I didn't know he had one until I looked inside the safe earlier. Self-protection, I suppose.' She looked saddened by the thought of how little good it had done him.

Ben unclipped the revolver from its holster, unlatched the swing-out cylinder and saw that it was fully loaded with six more of the same .357 hollowpoints. Heavy blued steel and solid, hand-filling walnut grips to soak up the recoil. An old-school weapon, utterly reliable, powerful and built to last. A useful accessory for a man with dangerous enemies, as long as it wasn't stored uselessly out of reach inside a locked safe at the very moment you needed it most. The first rule of gunfighting: have a gun. He reholstered the revolver and laid it to one side.

'What about this key?' he asked.

'I can't tell you what it's for. There's nothing on it to say, and it doesn't seem to fit any of the locks I tried.'

'Okay,' Ben said, and opened the diary.

For an international businessman, Auguste Kaprisky made few appointments, for the simple reason that he didn't leave home a lot. As Ben leafed through the gold-edged pages he saw many of them were empty, here and there a scribbled note in blue fountain pen ink as reminders of things like Valentina's school term dates – an eye test, a doctor's appointment. As far as Ben knew, Auguste was in excellent health. There were a couple of other entries that were meaningless to him, one from several months ago and the other more recent, labelled simply with the letter 'F'.

'F, what does that stand for?' he asked Valentina, and she just shook her head.

But some other entries in the diary were marginally more comprehensible, as far as they went. One, from just a couple of weeks earlier, was a UK landline phone number with an Inner London area code prefix and a note in Kaprisky's handwriting to call someone called Lennox. That contact appeared only once in the diary, but two others cropped up more regularly. During the last four months Kaprisky had had three meetings with someone whose initials were SS, each one with a time specified but no clue about where the meetings might have taken place. That was, not until Ben found a number for this 'SS' scribbled beneath the earliest entry. It was another landline number – Kaprisky was well known for his scorn and loathing for mobile phones and refused to call one unless he had to. This one had the international dialling code for Italy and the 06 area prefix indicating that 'SS', whoever he or she might be, was based in Rome.

Ben asked Valentina, 'Do you know anything about this person he went to see in Italy?'

'Nothing. He never mentioned it to me. Going by the dates, I was at school each time he went there. Do you think it could be something important?'

'Right now, anything could be important.'

The last of the appointment entries in the diary was potentially more interesting. It was by far the most recent, having taken place just two days ago, the eve of the attack. Once again, frustratingly, the contact's name was only given as an initial, this time 'FK'.

But the details of the appointment were much more specific. It appeared that Auguste had travelled to Berlin for an 11.30 a.m. meeting with this 'FK' at the Ritz-Carlton Tea Lounge. Ben wondered what it could have been about. This time there were two phone numbers, one the usual landline, with the international German and Berlin area codes, and the other a mobile. It must have been a big deal for Kaprisky to stoop to calling one of those.

'Did your Tonton say anything to you about seeing this person in Berlin?' Ben asked.

'No, but we don't talk every day.'

Ben thought that if he needed to verify that Kaprisky had actually gone to Berlin, he could always check with the pilots.

It was all impossibly vague. 'Could "FK" be the same person as "F"?' he wondered. 'If "F" is a person at all?'

'How the FK should I know?' she replied, unable to resist. 'Sorry, I shouldn't joke. I truly have no idea.'

The rest of the diary was predictably blank, and there were no further entries in the notes section at the end. 'So we've got Lennox in London, "F" on its own which could be anything at all, "SS" in Rome and "FK" in Berlin, neither of which we have a clue about either,' Ben said, scribbling them all down on another Post-it note from Kaprisky's desk. 'Very instructive.'

'It's got to be useful information, though,' Valentina said hopefully. 'Doesn't it?'

'If only we knew what it meant. We've got some numbers here. Let's give them a call and see who answers.'

Taking out his phone he started with the London number. After two rings a cheery-sounding young female voice replied, 'Lennox Advisory. How can I help you today?'

So Lennox wasn't the name of a person, but a company. 'I'm sorry, I must have the wrong number,' Ben said, and hung up the call to check the place out online. Keying 'lennox advisory' straight into his phone's search engine, he quickly found that it was a high-end specialist fine art investment firm offering consultancy services to potential investors. Their website showcased a collection of extremely expensive works by a famous contemporary artist whose postmodern offerings were currently returning a 300 per cent profit for their eager buyers, for reasons Ben found hard to grasp. The paintings looked to him like the results of a pack of stray dogs barfing their guts out on a canvas after having gorged themselves on a mountain of decomposing pizzas. Scarcely Auguste Kaprisky's cup of tea either, but Lennox Advisory's expertise probably catered for the more conservative end of the market as well.

'So much for that,' he said to Valentina. 'He must have been looking to buy some new piece to add to his collection.'

'Then it means nothing for us,' she said, looking disappointed. 'What about the other numbers?'

Ben tried the Italian one first and drew a blank. No reply, no answering message. Then he tried both numbers for 'FK', with the same result each time.

'Damn,' Valentina muttered.

'I'll keep trying.'

'So what now, Ben?' she said, looking expectantly at him.

'Now, let's poke around the estate a little and see if we can't figure some of this out.'

Chapter 7

Ben spent the rest of the morning reviewing the house security and exploring every inch of the place to try to understand how the killers had got inside. His first port of call was to investigate the spot on the perimeter where the police believed the intruders had entered, and then made their escape afterwards. The south gate, as it was called, had been installed many years earlier as an access point for grounds staff. The only entrance other than the main gate, it had fallen out of use decades ago and its wrought-iron bars had become choked with weeds and brambles.

The south gate was a long way from the house, separated by large equestrian paddocks and areas of wildflower meadow. First Valentina led Ben to the utility room near where the bodies of Gaston and Vincent had been found, and took the old iron key from a row of hooks. Then they borrowed an all-terrain estate buggy from the groundskeeper's shed, and followed a little gravel track that eventually disappeared into long grass closer to the edge of the property where few people ever went.

Ben was an expert tracker, and he soon spotted a trail clearly made by a group of men on foot, who would have been moving in single file. The trail led all the way to the disused south entrance, where the weeds and brambles had been trampled around the foot of the gate. On further exam-ination he found recent scrape marks and traces of fresh oil on the old iron lock. The police had discovered the gate hanging open and relocked it again, on Gabriel's insistence, after the forensic tests had revealed nothing useful. The sole key had apparently been on its hook in the utility room the whole time.

'So either the intruders had a copy of this key, or the gate had been left open for them in advance,' Ben said. Opening the gate, he stepped out into the narrow, empty road running alongside the perimeter fence and squatted down to take a look at the traces of tyre marks left by the getaway vehicle accelerating off in a hurry. The tracks were those of some-thing large and powerful, with wide wheels. Maybe a big SUV with enough space for six or seven men, or a perfor-mance van like a Mercedes Vito Sport or a zippy VW Transporter. He walked back to the gate, relocked it and returned the key to Valentina, then stood looking thought-fully around him for a few moments.

'You don't look happy, Ben,' she said. 'What are you thinking?'

'I'm thinking there's no question that they used this gate to make their escape, after the fact,' he said. 'But they were taking a hell of a risk getting in this way. It's a long hike to the house, and in the middle of the morning there was a good chance of being spotted by one of the estate workers.'

'I suppose they were wearing masks, like those black ski masks terrorists wear,' Valentina suggested.

He nodded, thinking she was probably right about that. 'Of course, if they'd been seen running away *after* the event, it wouldn't have been a disaster for them. By the time the main gate guards were alerted and made it all the way around the perimeter to the south gate, they'd have been long gone and nobody could identify them. But it's the idea of them entering the property this way that bothers me. Even if the camera system was disabled, all it took was for a gardener or maintenance person to spot a bunch of armed men in ski masks sneaking across the grounds, and their whole plan could've been scuppered before they even reached the house. Yet they chose to launch their strike in the middle of the day when night time would have been a much safer option. Why?'

'It doesn't seem to make sense, does it?'

'Unless we're missing something here. Never mind. Let's go.'

On their return to the house he had Valentina lead him around the outside to the back kitchen, where he examined the door and quickly verified that the police had been right about its not having been forced open. Even if the lock could have been expertly picked without leaving a trace, the door was routinely secured from inside with a heavy iron bolt top and bottom. There was no possible way it could have been levered or smashed open without causing serious damage.

'Now take me to where all the rest of the bodies were found,' he said. He felt bad that he had to ask her to subject herself to such an unpleasant job, after all she'd already been through. But Valentina didn't utter a word of complaint as she stoically led him on the grisly tour of the whole house, pointing out the places where the forensic examiners had already done their work. Some of the bloodstains were still clearly visible on carpets and rugs, and plaster was missing from walls where bullets had embedded themselves. It was a sickening experience, even for someone as hardened as Ben. The sanctity of Auguste Kaprisky's haven had been so utterly violated that it was going to be a long time before this place felt like a home again. Valentina had wanted to bring in a cleaning agency and repairmen, but Inspector Boche wouldn't allow it until the forensics people had completely finished their work.

'That's all of them,' she said grimly when they'd spent a long while going from room to room. 'Except for Annick. She was the only person killed outside.'

'Show me.'

They walked back into the sunshine and along the side of the house, through an archway covered in climbing roses and to a small courtyard next to a walled kitchen garden with greenhouses and polytunnels.

'This garden was Annick's favourite place,' Valentina said sadly. 'It's where she cultivated all the organic vegetables for the kitchen. I helped her to plant that apple tree over there, when I was just six years old. See how it's grown. And here's where she was found,' she added in a different tone, pointing. 'They didn't shoot her. She was strangled with something like a metal cord. Those disgusting filthy—' It wasn't like Valentina to swear. She let her words trail off, and stared at the spot where the cook had died.

'And whose van is that?' Ben asked, looking at a Citroen Berlingo that was parked in the shade of the kitchen garden wall. It was the XL model with the extended wheelbase and extra cargo space. He knew it well, because his friend and associate Tuesday Fletcher at Le Val used the same type of van as a handy runaround for fetching supplies. Except Tuesday's was bright orange, in keeping with his cheery, outgoing character, and this one was a flat, dull shade of beige. It stood out from the rest of the Kaprisky estate fleet, which were mostly Audis, including the heavily armoured Q7 Premier Edition limousine Auguste was normally ferried about in, and all gleaming black.

'Annick's,' Valentina replied. 'She'd been out in it during the morning. It was just her bad luck that she wasn't still out when it happened. She wouldn't normally have been back so early, on a Wednesday.'

'Remind me why that is,' Ben said.

'Because every Wednesday morning, regular as clockwork, Annick goes – or went – to a fish market in Le Mans, near the cathedral. Georges always liked to go with her.'

'Every single Wednesday?'

'Oh, yes. Tonton's very set in his ways. He always has to have fish for his dinner on a Wednesday, and of course it has to be super fresh, bought that day. Annick would go and pick it up for him, even if there were no other groceries she needed. She's been making the journey every week for years.'

Ben had to say it. 'The guy's a multi-billionaire. He can't have everything he needs delivered to the house?'

She shrugged glumly. 'Oh, you know Tonton, the way his mind works. He's full of contradictions, as miserly as he's generous, as illogical as he's brilliant. The fishmonger wanted an extra fifteen euros to deliver the fish every week, but as he saw it, if he was paying Annick her salary anyway, by getting her to fetch it he was getting it brought to him for free.'

Ben inwardly rolled his eyes. 'Okay. Go on.'

'So anyhow, the way it looks is that they'd only just got back from town when they were attacked. Annick was just a couple of steps away from the van, with the driver's door open, when the police found her.' A tear appeared in the corner of Valentina's eye and she wiped it quickly away, trying to look brave.

Ben was thinking about the missing kitchen assistant. 'So what happened to Georges, if he was with her at the time?'

'I suppose he must have got away from them, and run off somewhere.'

Which Ben thought was pretty damned unlikely. He asked, 'How do we know that he was in the van with her?'

'From the main gate video footage,' she replied.

'I'd like to see that.'

Chapter 8

From the kitchen garden courtyard she led him back through a side door and then a maze of passageways to the room that housed all the monitors for the security system. One entire wall was covered in screens, and the mass of electronic equipment feeding the images through from the estate's many CCTV cameras, along with the alarm system, took up two large rack cabinets. It reminded Ben a little of the setup Jeff Dekker had installed at Le Val, only on a rather grander scale.

The monitor room had always been the domain of Kaprisky's close protection team, who in their role as house guards would take rotating shifts watching the screens for any suspicious activity. Because of the extreme infrequency with which anything exciting or dangerous actually took place on the estate, that part of their job tended to involve a lot of sitting around in comfortable desk chairs and drinking coffee.

And as Ben noticed when he and Valentina walked into the room, the new guys hired as replacements had been pretty quick to take to the same lazy routine. Three of them, including the ginger-haired gorilla Ben had encountered earlier, were lounging around slurping from mugs, apparently unperturbed by the total blankness of the security monitors and more interested in a Formula One race showing on the TV in the corner. The remains of their lunch littered the desk next to them. They were so intent on gawking at the race that they didn't notice they had company.

'Nice to see men hard at work,' Ben said, and all three heads jerked round to face him with startled expressions that quickly turned to glowers.

'Nothing's going to happen,' the gorilla mumbled. 'And we don't work for you anyway.'

'No, you work for me,' Valentina told him. 'And I'd like you to get out, please. Ben and I want to use the room.'

'What for?' the gorilla asked.

'You heard the boss lady,' Ben said, jabbing his thumb back over his shoulder in the direction of the door. 'Sling your hooks, boys.'

The three got up from their seats, set their half-empty mugs down on the desk and started skulking towards the exit. The gorilla turned to stare heavily at Ben and seemed about to say something.

'You have a problem?' Ben asked him, returning the stare.

'No.'

'Good. Then piss off.'

The three ambled out of the monitor room and the door closed behind them.

'I hope those goons aren't permanent replacements,' Ben said to Valentina when they were gone.

'They were all Gabriel could find at such short notice,' she replied, turning off the TV with a remote. 'I'll get someone better.'

'I know people,' Ben said. 'Good, reliable guys I've worked with in the past. Let me make some calls, okay?'

'Thanks, Ben. I know I can count on you.'

They cleared away the mugs and food debris. 'We've been so busy all morning, I hadn't realised it was lunchtime,' Valentina said. 'Are you hungry?'

'I might grab a bite later,' he said. 'You should have something.'

'I'll eat when you eat.'

Pulling two of the chairs up to the desk, they set about reviewing the security camera footage on the main computer screen. All the data from the CCTV system was transmitted to a central receiving unit in the rack and stored on a hard drive for forty-eight hours before it was automatically scrubbed. The police had already watched all the footage up until the moment where the images had abruptly stopped recording, minutes before the attack. Nothing had been stored on the hard drive since then, and its black box within the rack seemed to have lost all power.

'When did the system go down exactly?' Ben asked her.

'Three minutes past ten is when it stopped recording. That's what Inspector Boche told me, but they couldn't figure out what made the system malfunction. They said things break down.'

'That's it? It didn't bother them that the timing was a bit coincidental?'

She held up her hands. 'They said they would look into it.'

'Let's check it out,' Ben said, swivelling his seat away from the desk and rolling over to the rack. It took two minutes of poking around among the mass of wires at the back to discover the reason. 'I think I've found your problem,' he said, holding up a loose wire that he'd found unplugged and dangling free of its jack socket.

The wire feeding power to the hard drive. Seemingly he was the first to have noticed that it had come unplugged. In fairness to the detectives, you did have to look right into the back of the rack unit to see it. These things were so easy to miss. Perhaps they'd been too busy hunting down the perpetrators, fighting crime and righting wrongs.

'That's all it was?' Valentina said, raising her eyebrows.

He plugged the wire back into place. The system had been built with good, positive, old-fashioned connectors that took a little effort to push in and would require a deliberate yank to pull out. A small green power light reappeared on the hard drive as it began recording again.

'Voilà,' she said.

'Looks like there was no malfunction after all,' he said. 'Then again, these things don't unplug themselves.'

'Then someone must have unplugged it. But who?'

Another mystery to add to the growing list. 'We'll worry about that later,' Ben said. 'Let's check out the video.'

Using the arrow keys on the computer keyboard, Ben wound through yesterday morning's CCTV footage from the main gate camera. It had been business as usual from early in the day, when the night shift had handed over to their replacements just after dawn. Ben fast forwarded through the morning, letting the playback roll at ten times normal speed. The camera angle showed the security gate-house, the closed barrier, the gates and a stretch of the road beyond. A counter in the bottom corner of the screen showed the exact time, down to the second. Now and then the small dark figures of the security men moved about with comically accelerated motion, but nothing much was happening.

At 8.57 a.m. a post van arrived. Ben adjusted the playback to normal speed. The postman got out and passed a small parcel and a bunch of letters to the guard in the gatehouse, hung around chatting for a couple of moments and then drove off again.

Ben asked, 'What was in the parcel?'

'A CD of Josquin's medieval choral music that I ordered online, as a present for Tonton,' she said sadly. 'Now I don't know if he'll ever hear it. The rest of the letters were just bills and stuff.'

The images rolled on at high speed. No more vehicles arrived. The guards appeared to be having a pretty quiet morning. Then at 9.16 a.m. Annick's beige Citroen Berlingo came into view, rolling down the driveway from the house. Again, Ben slowed the playback to normal speed. The rear-ward camera angle, pointing towards the gates, meant that only the windowless rear of the van could be seen.

'There she goes, off to buy the fish,' Valentina said. The van paused by the gatehouse as the barrier came up and Annick exchanged a few words with one of the guards through her open driver's window. All that was visible of her was her left arm, and the sleeve of the bright green jacket she was wearing. When the barrier was fully raised, the van moved on, passed through the gate and turned right up the road towards Le Mans. The barrier slowly came back down again. Nothing more happened for a while.

Ben worked out the timing in his head. The town was fourteen and a half kilometres away, and the roads were mostly rural with a lot of sharp bends to slow you down, so he figured it would take maybe twenty to twenty-five minutes to drive there; plus time to park, then to visit the fish market, collect the shopping along with anything else Annick needed while on her travels; then return to the van and make the drive home: in all, he estimated that they should have been gone well over an hour. But at just 10.02, only forty-six minutes after setting off, the van was back at the main gate and being waved in through the barrier. The guards barely paid it any attention as it re-entered the estate. Then the van headed back down the driveway towards the house, and disappeared off the bottom edge of the screen.

'Oh, God, here they come,' Valentina breathed, eyes fixed on the screen. Her expression was tense and full of dread, because she knew what was soon to happen next as her friend Annick reached the house. 'Don't go in, Annick. Turn around and drive away again.' As though she could will something different to happen this time around. Ben put his hand on her shoulder and gave it a tender squeeze.

The van's return from Annick's shopping trip was the last thing the hard drive had recorded. Moments later, just as the time counter was hitting 10.03, the feed stopped and the image disappeared. The screen going blank was like a symbol of Annick's life being brutally snuffed out. Valentina looked down.

Ben was frowning. 'Let me see that again.' He rewound the playback to where the van arrived at the gate.

'You're going to make me watch it all over?'

'You don't have to look. Can I zoom in?' he asked, and Valentina leaned across him and showed him how to enlarge the image. Once more the van, now filling much more of the screen, was flagged through the security barrier and began to roll off down the drive. There was some sunshine glare on the windscreen, but the video definition was excellent and the two figures in the front seats were quite clearly visible through the glass. Annick, behind the wheel, was a heavyset woman in her fifties, with a large round face, Yoko Ono sunglasses and red hair that looked too vivid to be natural. She was wearing the same bright green jacket as before. The man sitting in the passenger seat was wearing a scruffy blue denim jacket with the collar turned up and a tattered grey cap sporting what looked like a New York Yankees logo. His face was lowered so that it was obscured by the cap's peak.

Ben said, 'That's Georges with her?'

'Yes, who else would it be?'

'You can't see his face.'

'But that's his jacket, and the same grubby old grey cap that he always wears. He bought it on a trip to New York years ago and can't be parted from it. Won't even wash it.'

Ben peered more closely at the screen. He asked, 'Does Georges have a neck tattoo?'

She shook her head and looked baffled. 'No way. That wouldn't be his style at all.'

'This guy does,' Ben said, pointing. It was a difficult angle, shot from in front and above, and the sun's glare on the windscreen made it hard to see. But there was definitely the top edge of a blueish ink design protruding from the collar of the denim jacket. 'He turned the collar up to try to hide it, but you can still make it out. Looks like a spiderweb tattoo. See for yourself.'

Valentina stuck her nose right up to the screen and gasped, 'You're right!' She turned wide, startled eyes on Ben. 'Then the man in the passenger seat wasn't Georges!'

'This is crucial, Valentina. You have to be sure. There's no way he could have had a tattoo done since you last saw him?'

'Not a chance. He'd be terrified of having it done, even if he wanted to. It's not Georges. It's someone else pretending to be him!'

Ben said nothing. He was already moving on, thinking fast, looking at the times. There was a four-minute interval between the van's return from Le Mans and the moment the clock in Auguste's study had been smashed by a bullet, at 10.06. A lot had apparently happened in those four minutes. Too much, for the chronology of events to fit the narrative. There was an anomaly here. One the police obviously hadn't picked up on.

'What are you doing now?' she asked. He made no reply as he minimised the screen window with the main gate footage and switched to another camera view, this one from the perimeter cameras watching the south gate and the road running past the fence. Like before, he reeled the time clock back to earlier that morning and let it play at ten times normal speed.

He already knew what he was going to see.

Nothing moved at the south gate. No vehicles arrived. Nobody entered the grounds. The road remained empty the entire time. Then, like before, as the time clock hit 10.03, the video recording went blank.

Ben turned away from the computer to face Valentina. 'Okay, so let's walk back through this whole thing. At two minutes past ten, Annick's van returns strangely early from the fish market, with a passenger who we now know wasn't Georges. They drive back in through the main gate and head towards the house. It's a long driveway, so say it takes two more minutes to get there, drive around the rear and park up in the courtyard by the kitchen garden. Then it would be four minutes past ten. Annick gets out of the van and is strangled almost immediately afterwards. Let's say it takes them a minute or so to do the deed and then get inside the house. So now it's 10.05. One minute later, assuming the clock in your granduncle's study was accurate, they'd worked their way up to the second floor and shot him.'

She nodded, uncertain where Ben was going with this. 'I do know the clock was accurate. The butler wound it up every day.'

'Yet the CCTV system was still working fine just three minutes earlier, because it didn't stop recording until exactly 10.03. And as we've just seen, until that moment there was no movement on the south gate. So for the police's theory to be right, everything has to have happened in that short time window. How realistic is it that the getaway vehicle rolled up outside the perimeter, the attack team got out, entered the grounds and covered quarter of a mile on foot to the house, took out their first victims and then stormed upstairs to shoot your Tonton, all in the space of three minutes?'

'It's impossible,' she replied, realising. 'Then it must mean—'

'That the intruders didn't get in through the south gate at all,' Ben said. 'Or else the cameras would have logged their arrival before the system went down.'

'My God. How could the police have got it so wrong?'

'Because their theory isn't a theory at all,' Ben said. 'It's no more than a hypothesis based on an assumption, based on the fact that nobody seemed to have come through the main gate and they'd found the south gate open. But you know what they say about assumptions, don't you?'

'No. What do they say?'

'"Assume" makes an *ass* out of *u* and *me*,' he replied. 'Big mistake to assume anything.'

'So then the attackers must have got inside some other way. But how?'

Ben said, 'Show me Annick's van again.'

Chapter 9

They hurried back out of the monitor room and to the kitchen garden courtyard where the Citroen was parked. 'I don't believe it,' she said as they walked. 'The police spoke to all the gate security men. There was never any suspicion about Annick's van. I suppose nobody thought twice about how she and Georges had come back early.'

Ben asked, 'And that also means none of the cops have examined the van?'

Valentina shook her head. 'No, I don't think so. They didn't think they had any reason to.'

'Then Annick's shopping must theoretically still be in the back.'

As they reached the van, Ben glanced in the driver's side window and saw nothing except empty seats. The rear cargo bay was screened off from the front cab by a vertical plywood partition and there were no rear windows. He walked around to the back doors and tried the handle. The van wasn't locked. He swung open both doors. A load of fresh fish would have been fairly rank by now, after sitting inside a hot vehicle under the sunshine all this time. If he'd expected to find it there, he'd have been bracing himself for the stench.

No smell. No fish. Nothing at all. The back of the van was empty. Just as he'd thought it would be.

'That's odd,' Valentina said. 'So what happened to the shopping?'

'Maybe there wasn't any,' Ben said. 'But why? Because the market had run out of fish? So early in the morning?'

'No,' he replied. 'Because Annick never got to the fish market.'

As he stood there with the back doors open, he was noticing something about the van floor. The vehicle was familiar to him because of Tuesday's van, different only in colour. But maybe there was another difference too, one not visible from the outside. The interior of the rear cargo bay looked a little strange, and he realised why: it was because the floor was too high. Another piece of plywood covered the bottom of the bodyshell from the rear doors to the vertical partition. Whoever had installed it had set it raised up at least ten inches above the actual floor, resting on runners the length of the cargo bay.

Ben leaned into the van and groped around under the edge of the plywood. His fingers found something there, like a small lever, a hidden catch. When he moved it, there was a click and a section of the floor popped up under spring pressure to reveal a hidden compartment underneath, ten inches deep. But used for what?

'I don't understand,' Valentina said, baffled.

'Was this Annick's own van or does it belong to the estate?' he asked her.

'To the estate. But she was the only one who used it.'

'I'm supposing you have an office for all the routine admin stuff around here?'

'Yes. I mean, I've never had anything to do with that side of things. But I know where it is.'

'May I see?'

Ben followed as she led him back inside the house, through another side entrance and through more passages. 'This is it,' she said, stopping at a door. 'We don't lock it.'

It was the usual kind of office with all the usual kinds of fixtures, not dissimilar to the one at Le Val where Ben hated spending time on admin chores. Desks, computers, filing cabinets. It was the last he was interested in. One large sliding drawer was labelled VÉHICULES and contained all the paperwork for the various vehicles of the estate fleet. It was all pretty well organised. Each vehicle had its own separate folder with all the relevant registration, warranty and insurance documents, test certificates, garage receipts and the like. Sifting through, he found the folder marked CITROEN BERLINGO. Inside were the usual documents, some receipts for various things done, like an exhaust change and a new set of brake pads three months ago. Nothing about modifications to the floor.

Ben took note of a few more details, then asked if he could see the van again. Valentina was baffled, but she bottled up her questions and walked back there with him in silence.

Ben opened the driver's door, reached in and popped the bonnet release catch. Then walked around to the front of the van and opened up the bonnet. He rested it on its support strut and ducked his head under the open lid to peer inside the engine compartment. It smelled faintly of petrol and oil. 'Aha,' he said. 'There you go. Just what I thought.'

'I wish you'd tell me what you're up to,' she said, with a note of irritation.

Ben had seen all he needed to see. He stepped back from the van. 'Everything about this van is right,' he explained to Valentina. 'The registration number, the colour, the whole works. Everything on the outside, that is.'

He could see she was completely bewildered, so he went on patiently, 'You see, all vehicles have their own unique individual ID numbers. One for the chassis, on that little VIN plate there. See it? And one for the engine, stamped into the casing. You have to look closely to read it. But the chassis and engine numbers on this vehicle don't match the ones in the paperwork on file in the office.'

'What does that mean?' she asked. The things that lay hidden in the grease and grime under the bonnet of a motor vehicle didn't enter into the world of a teenage schoolgirl.

'It means it's not the same van, Valentina.'

'But it looks the same.'

'Yes, it does. Because it was intended to look the same. And that's because the van is how the attack team got inside the estate.'

The glazed look of confusion on Valentina's face slowly turned to a stare of horror. 'Are you saying that Annick had something to do with what happened?'

He shook his head. 'No, I'm saying I think that Annick and Georges never got as far as the market that day, because somewhere between here and there they were intercepted by some men, maybe three of them. They would have chosen a quiet, empty stretch of country road to do it. There are plenty of those around here, before you hit the main roads towards Le Mans. So the ambush point would be not far from the estate, probably no more than a few minutes' drive. I think that these men hijacked the van at gunpoint, stuffed Annick and Georges in the back, then one of them went off in a separate vehicle while the other two drove this van to some remote location in the area, a woodland, maybe. Again, there are lots to choose from within just a few kilometres of the estate. The rest of their team were waiting for them. That's where they switched Annick's van for this replica, which they'd already had prepared with a hidden compartment ready-filled with certain equipment they'd need for what was coming next. Then I think they threatened to kill Annick if she didn't do exactly what they told her. Which was to use the modified van to smuggle the attack team back inside the estate, right under the noses of the security guards. The men were hiding in the back. There's plenty of room in there for five or six people, if they crammed up a bit. No windows, so they couldn't be seen.'

It was a struggle for Valentina to take all this in. In a low, shaky voice she asked, 'And Georges?'

'I think they used him as an example to demonstrate to Annick that they meant business,' Ben said. 'That's why his body wasn't found here at the house.'

She swallowed and turned a shade paler. 'You mean . . . they killed him?'

The girl was old enough, and had seen enough, not to have to be protected from the stark reality of these matters. 'They were always going to kill them both anyway,' he replied. 'It's just a matter of tactics as to how they played it. They could have brought his body to the house in the back of the van, so it would have been found with the others. You might say that not doing that was a mistake on their part. Maybe the rest of the team didn't fancy travelling with a corpse, though I doubt that would bother them. Or maybe it was very, very clever. Because by having Georges disappear and therefore setting him up as a potential suspect, they succeeded in diverting everyone's attention. Nice moves. Whoever set this up would make a pretty good chess player.'

'I can hardly believe what I'm hearing,' Valentina murmured.

'Then once they had poor Annick frightened out of her wits, they made her drive back to the estate with one of the men sitting up front, wearing Georges' cap and jacket. He'd have been holding a pistol under the jacket, ready to shoot her if she deviated in any way from their instructions. He kept his head down and the cap pulled low to hide his face as they came through the gate barrier.'

'That was taking a chance,' Valentina said.

'Not really. You saw the way the guards just waved the van through with barely a second glance. The weekly fish market run was a regular routine for them, every Wednesday morning since time immemorial. Then once the hijackers got inside the grounds, they made her park here in the usual spot in the courtyard. They didn't need her any more at that point. So they dragged her out of the van and one of them killed her, quick and quiet. At least she didn't suffer too much. Meanwhile the others were unloading their equipment from the hidden compartment.'

'What equipment?' Valentina asked, wild-eyed.

'They brought a lot of weapons to play with, because they knew they'd have to tangle with a bunch of highly trained, armed close protection guys. Probably also some kind of mobile signal jammer device, to prevent anyone within the house from raising the alarm on the outside or communicating with each other on the inside.'

'I didn't even know such things existed.'

'They do, and they work.' Ben could testify to that personally. There was actually one in the armoury at Le Val, left over from a past job. He went on, 'All that gear would have been pre-loaded aboard the replica van, well hidden just in case of any problems. These people were obviously meticulous. The fact that they went to the trouble and expense of creating an almost perfect replica of Annick's van tells us that they're also highly resourced. We're dealing with professional operatives at the highest level.'

'You can tell all this from a van?' Valentina said, looking at him in wonder.

'Not just the van,' he replied. 'It's a question of fitting the pieces together. Like the back kitchen door. They could have used Annick to get them into the house, but they already had a better entry point thanks to their person on the inside, who made sure it was left unbolted for them.'

'Their person on the inside?'

'The same person who'd been watching the place for a while, getting a feel for the routines, looking for the weak points. The person who located the south gate for them to use as an escape route, and probably had a copy of the key made on the sly to give to them in advance. The same person who told them about Annick and Georges' weekly trips to the fish market. *That's* why they chose that time of day for their attack, instead of hitting the place at night. It was so they could use Annick's van as their Trojan horse to slip through the gates unnoticed. The moment they were clear of the security barrier, they probably radioed their inside man, who then unplugged the video system ready for their exit. They knew they'd have to get out on foot and they didn't want to be recorded doing it.'

'That inside man could only have been one person,' Valentina said, thinking hard. 'The new man on the body-guard team. André. If he was one of their gang, he must have expected they would take him with them when they escaped. But instead they killed him, too. It's like you said about the chess moves. They were covering their tracks.'

'That's what I'm thinking,' Ben replied. 'But I have to probe deeper to be sure.'

'And then?'

'And then we're going to follow the trail until we find these people,' he said.

Chapter 10

Ben had travelled to the Kaprisky estate in the knowledge that he'd probably be staying here for a while. It wasn't unusual for him to be called away from Le Val for periods of time to respond to some crisis or emergency in some or other part of the world. He might often vanish out of contact with them for weeks on end, and his long-suffering team-mates were more than used to having to cover for his frequent absences.

This looked as though it might be about to turn into one of those times.

'I'm going to need something to drive around in,' he said to Valentina.

'That's not a problem,' she replied. 'We have lots of cars to choose from. Come and I'll show you.'

Some way to the rear of the house, between a tennis court and an indoor pool building, was a long, low garage complex fronted with a row of closed steel shutter doors. Valentina pressed a button on a wall panel, and the shutters began to roll up with a whirr. One half of the garage housed the all-black fleet vehicles, including the heavy armoured limousine Auguste sometimes travelled in, though in fact he more often drove around in his ancient Citroen Dyane because it was far cheaper to run than the massive fuel-guzzling behemoth. The other half of the garage was home to the old man's classic car collection.

Over the course of a lifetime of great wealth, Auguste had amassed a thoroughbred stable of some of the most iconic and expensive motor vehicles ever made. He collected them the way some people collected artworks, not to be put on display but purely for the private satisfaction of their owner. He never drove any of his collection, but made a point of keeping them in perfect condition, lovingly valeted, fuelled and ready for use if the fancy should take him to roll one of them out for a spin on his private track circuit. The oldest was a venerable Model T Ford dating back to 1908, and the most flamboyantly luxurious was a 1953 Rolls Royce Silver Dawn convertible. In between those two extremes Auguste had filled up his stable with, among others, a 1967 Lamborghini Miura, a 1975 Ferrari 308, a Jaguar E-type, a Shelby Cobra racing car and a 1957 Mercedes Gullwing roadster.

'Take whatever you want,' Valentina said offhandedly. 'I wouldn't know one from another. Cars don't mean anything to me.'

Ben passed on the Italian supercars, because his idea of automotive perfection wasn't having your arse dragged along an inch from the road. The E-type and the Gullwing were both too ostentatious and showy, the Cobra too raw. But as his eye ran along the line of gleaming cars it landed on a bright yellow late-1970s Lancia Stratos, a dart-shaped weapon of a car that was all wraparound curves and flared arches, capable of insane high speeds. To his mind, the only really practical sports car in Kaprisky's collection. It wasn't especially pretty or elegant, built not for flash but for brute real-world performance. In its day it had been the nearest thing on the road to a real rally car, with a string of championships to show for it. You didn't have to lie flat on your back to drive it, it wasn't as twitchy or highly strung as other road missiles, but it could still get you where you needed to go in a blisteringly short time. True, the rear-engined design, placing most of the car's weight over the back wheels, gave it a tendency to swing out under hard cornering – but then you'd already be going so fast there were a multitude of other things that could take you out.

'That one,' he said, pointing at the Stratos.

'It's yours.'

'I'll try to return it in one piece.'

'Whatever,' she said with a nonchalant gesture. 'The ignition keys are all on a rack inside that cabinet over there.' As he opened the cabinet and selected the key for the Stratos, she added, 'You'll have to have somewhere to use as a base, too. You can have the Swiss cottage for as long as you need it. It's just a simple little cabin, but it'll serve you as a pied-à-terre while you're around the estate. Here, take me for a spin in your new chariot, and I'll show you. It's too far to walk.'

Ben had seen inside some traditional bothies when he lived in Ireland, and he'd spent a night in a rural Alpine farmhouse in Switzerland while on a kidnap and ransom job years earlier. Built on a green hillside surrounded by huge oak trees, at the end of its own track far out of sight of the main residence, the 'simple little cabin' wasn't remotely like any actual cottage he'd ever come across – more like a picture-book fantasy chalet, with an overhanging roof, upper-floor balcony, highly ornate wooden facade and enough space to accommodate a whole minibus-load of skiers in high comfort. It beat hunkering down in a rock trench in full kit with a machine gun for three sleepless nights on the trot or going to earth in a jungle foxhole surrounded by hostile combatants intent on stringing you up and dismembering you, that was for sure.

'It's pretty basic,' he told Valentina. 'But it'll do.'

She didn't get the joke, because in her innocence she had no idea of the kinds of places Ben had had to rough it in his time. 'There's lots of other accommodation to choose from on the estate. I just thought you'd like this best. Or maybe you'd prefer to stay somewhere else. The Château du Grand Lucé is quite nice. Or we could rent you a villa nearby? Whatever you want, the choice is yours.'

'No, this is fine,' he said, smiling.

'I'm glad it's okay. Help yourself to the food and wine, and the wi-fi is pretty good.' She looked at her watch. 'I'd like to pay a visit to Tonton now.'

'I'll come with you.'

Ben disliked hospitals at the best of times, and the visit to the private clinic was a far cry from being one of those. Auguste looked so frail there in his bed, hardly even visible for all the respirator tubes and equipment that surrounded him, that he seemed barely alive. The doctor with whom Ben and Valentina spent a few moments talking said that there had been a slight flicker of a response that morning. No more than the briefest flutter of an eyelid, though it could have been an involuntary muscle twitch and it was too early to get one's hopes up. They were doing all they could, but he admitted that amounted to very little.

Five minutes was all Ben could stand before he had to leave, thoroughly depressed and wishing he hadn't gone in. He waited outside for Valentina, then dropped her back at the house. She was upset and wanted to rest a while. By the time the Lancia rumbled to a halt back outside the Swiss cottage, Ben's sadness had morphed into a cold, simmering rage.

As he walked inside his temporary residence and dumped his bag in a chair by the door he realised it was after two and he still hadn't eaten a bite all day. He grabbed a bag of peanuts and a banana from the chalet's well-stocked kitchen, munched them quickly and washed down his lunch with a glass of red wine – a very fine vintage Châteauneuf that was far too good to be swilled down on the hoof, but what did it matter? Stepping out onto the chalet's balcony with the sweeping views of the estate spread out below, he lit a Gauloise and got on the phone to Jeff Dekker to give him the latest.

'Call me anytime you need me,' Jeff said. 'I'll be there like a shot.'

'Thanks, Jeff. Appreciate it.'

Next Ben called Gabriel Archambeau at his law offices in Chartres. Gabriel's English was as fluent as Ben's French, and they could have talked in either language but settled for the former. 'I received Valentina's messages,' Gabriel said. 'I've been trying to call her back, but there's no reply. We seem to keep missing each other.'

'She was with me. It's been a busy morning. I wouldn't disturb her now.'

'I assume there's been no change in Auguste's condition.' It wasn't a question.

'If there were, you'd be the first to know.'

'*Merde*,' Gabriel muttered under his breath, reverting back to his native language for an instant. 'What a nightmare this is. My heart bleeds for that poor girl, after all she's been through.'

'We'll resolve this,' Ben said. 'One way or another.'

'And I'm extremely grateful for your involvement, Monsieur Hope. Or should I call you Major? I understand that was your military rank.'

'Just Ben,' Ben said.

'Extremely grateful, as I say, *Ben*, for Valentina's sake as well as Auguste's. Though I must admit, I'm a little unclear what exactly she had in mind bringing you on board. I gather you'll be working in the capacity of a kind of private investigator?'

'Just doing all I can to help, that's all,' Ben said.

'In which case I imagine you'll be liaising closely with Inspector Boche and his team? I'll let them know you'll be in touch, but I'm not sure how they'll take to working with a private investigator. In my experience the police are generally uncomfortable with such arrangements.'

'I'll be pursuing my own line of enquiry,' Ben said. 'No need to contact them.'

'But anything you learn from your own investigation, you'll naturally pass on to the authorities.' The lawyer's mindset.

'Naturally,' Ben assured him.

'Good, good. I admit I was a little uneasy when Valentina mentioned involving you.'

'She only wants what's best for Auguste.'

'As do we all. Please tell me what I can do to help.'

'I was calling about André. The new guy, Lucas Dennim's replacement.'

'André? You mean André Becker?'

'I'm curious about him.'

'Curious in what way? The poor man's dead.'

'I'm aware of that,' Ben replied. 'I gather he hadn't been on the team for long. It was the first I'd heard of a new addition. Since the rest of the team had trained with us at Le Val, and given how important it was to Auguste, it seemed to me a little odd that he didn't come through me for a recommendation, or at least mention it.'

'He wasn't that new,' Gabriel replied, sounding perplexed. 'He joined us about three months ago. I'd have to check the employment records. But what you tell me is a little confusing. I was under the impression that André *had* trained with your organisation, like the others. That was the main reason Auguste hired him right away, irrespective of how highly recommended he was by the agency, or how impressive his CV was.'

Ben frowned. 'No, I definitely don't recall anyone of that name having trained with us.'

'Are you sure? He had all kinds of paperwork to show for it. Signed by you personally, as I recall.'

Ben thought that was weird. He normally had an excellent memory. Surely he couldn't have forgotten?

'I have all the records on file,' Gabriel said. 'I'm away from my desk right now. Give me a few minutes, I'll check and get back to you.'

'Talk then.' They hung up the call and Ben immediately called Jeff again.

'That was quick,' Jeff said. His voice sounded echoey and the phone reception wasn't good. Ben guessed he must be down in the underground armoury, where all of Le Val's extensive weapons and ammunition arsenal was kept under lock and key.

Ben asked him, 'Does the name André Becker ring any bells? He's supposed to have done a close protection course with us, but I don't remember him.'

Jeff paused, thinking. 'Me neither, off the top of my head. But maybe we're getting doddery in our old age, mate. I was just going through the armoury inventory with Tuesday. Hold onto your knickers a mo while I scoot over to the office and check the trainee records.'

Ben waited. Then a couple of minutes later, Jeff came back on the line saying, 'Not getting that doddery, Ben. We were both right. The files don't show any record of an André Becker having ever trained with us. There's André Chastain, remember him? Right character, *he* was. And of course there was that complete tosser André Hoofnagel, who you booted out for being pissed as a fart on the shooting range that time. But nobody called Becker. You sure you've got the right surname?'

'Quite sure.'

Ben thanked him, got off the phone and then redialled Gabriel Archambeau's number.

'I was just about to call you,' Gabriel said. 'As I thought, the estate employment records show that André Becker was hired almost exactly three months ago. I'm looking at his Le Val Tactical Training Centre course completion certificate right here on my screen, with your signature on it. Am I missing something?'

'You said Becker was recommended by an agency. Which one?'

'Uh, let me bring that up for you as well . . .' Some tapping of keys, and Gabriel's breathing on the phone. 'Yes, here it is. The Carlson Agency based in Brussels. They sent me copies of André Becker's professional credentials. As I said, it all looked impressive enough to me. Auguste thought so, too.'

'Can you email them over to me right away?' Ben asked, and Gabriel said he could do that while they were still on the line.

Ben already knew what he was going to see. Because there was no Carlson Agency in Brussels, or anywhere else for that matter. He'd been in this business long enough to know it through and through, and there was no doubt in his mind that they didn't exist. That was confirmed when he opened up the emailed documents from Gabriel and saw their letter of recommendation for Becker, along with the faked Le Val training certificate and his own forged signature. It was pretty well done. No surprise that both Auguste and his lawyer had been taken in by the deception. Under different circumstances, even Ben might have believed that he'd signed his name to the document, and simply forgotten.

'Do you mind telling me what's going on?' Gabriel asked, sounding unnerved by Ben's silence on the phone.

Ben ignored the question and asked, 'Why did Lucas Dennim quit the team?'

'Where are we going with all this? He just came to us one day, what is it now, four months ago, and said he wanted to quit.'

'Just like that?'

'Yes, it was very sudden and unexpected. He said he didn't want to work any longer, had come into some money – quite a substantial inheritance, from what I gather – and was taking early retirement. But he gave virtually no notice, wanting to leave right away, and I was under pressure to replace him because Auguste absolutely insisted on not being a man short. Luckily the agency came through just at the right moment. It was real serendipity.'

'Sounds like it,' Ben said. 'Thanks, Gabriel, I'll be in touch.'

'Wait – you still haven't told me why you w—' Gabriel started to say, but Ben hung up the call.

Chapter 11

Surrey, England

It was a warm afternoon, a vivid blue sky almost unbroken by just the occasional puffy white cloud that drifted above on the soft breeze. The bumblebees in the flowerbeds hummed in the background and the sprinklers made rainbows in the sunshine as the two associates walked slowly down the ornamental gravel path that ran alongside the long, immaculate lawn. The gardeners working on trimming the maze hedge and clipping roses at the south end, near the great Tudor-period house, were far enough away for the pair's conversation to remain completely confidential. So were the armed men in dark suits and sunglasses who loitered discreetly around the sides of the garden. It was an extremely secure environment, as befitted the nature of the two men's discussion.

They weren't young men, and the elder of the two walked slowly with a cane as the other ambled by his side, respectfully careful not to outpace him. The elder man was wearing a Panama hat and a crisp white blazer over a striped shirt open at the neck, and smoked a cigar. The only people he tended to frequent were as extremely wealthy, or almost, as he was; and like most very rich people he owned several homes in different corners of the world, but this secluded country manor in the south of England was where he chose to spend much of his time nowadays. His visitor was more formally dressed, though he'd slackened his tie a little in the warmth. His suit was uncrumpled from the two flights, the first by private jet and the second by helicopter, that had brought him here for this very private talk.

From somewhere in the distance, beyond the house, could be heard the excited piping voices of great-grand-children and the barking of the hounds as they played together on the front lawn. The women were busily preparing a garden party for later in the day – Pimms, cucumber sandwiches and canapés in the marquee, musical entertainment and dancing – all silly nonsense that the older man couldn't be bothered with. By the time the guests started arriving in their chauffeur-driven Rollses and Bentleys he'd be back in the sanctity of his study and library, relaxing alone with a decanter of sherry and his treasured *Iliad*. He disliked social events and preferred to avoid the trivial conversation that they inevitably entailed. The only subjects he considered worthy of his attention were those that could, by their very nature, never be shared outside of the close-knit and highly exclusive circle to which he and his visitor belonged.

The older man had been silent for the last minute or two as they walked, puffing ruminatively on the cigar and frowning with discontent.

'You were soft,' he said at last. 'Which I find disap-pointing. I had expected better of you, my friend.'

'I wouldn't call ordering a man's death being soft,' his visitor replied.

'Ordering, but not achieving. You had the opportunity. You failed. Frankly, I'm surprised at your handling of this, given your track record.'

'I've known him for a long time,' the visitor said. 'If it had to be done, then so be it. He knew our rules. He brought it on himself. But it was the least I could do to ensure the job was carried out quickly and cleanly.'

'A machine gun is a rather effective tool for that purpose,' the older man said.

'I have some idea of what such weapons can do to a man. I didn't want my old friend to be cut to pieces by automatic gunfire, so as to be unrecognisable in his casket. Two shots maximum, one to the chest and one to the head. Those were my instructions. Two large-calibre pistol bullets, well placed by an expert, should be enough to kill anyone. Especially a person of his advancing years.'

The older man didn't need to be told about advancing years. He grunted. 'Except it didn't work out as planned, did it? It would seem that your friend was tougher than you gave him credit for. Thanks to your sentimentality, this operation has been irreparably bungled. Getting to him now will be nigh on impossible.'

The visitor shook his head. 'I see no need for that, in any case. The man is deep in a coma. He no longer represents any threat to us.'

'What if he wakes up?'

'From what my sources have given me to understand, that's unlikely to be the case.' The visitor's inside information came from a junior police officer in Le Mans who had been approached by two mysterious men bearing a bag of cash and instructions to report on all developments. He couldn't have refused, given what they knew about his side interest in child pornography. 'Even if he does wake up,' the visitor added, 'his doctors agree that the chances of a full recovery are slim.'

'Meaning what, that he'll remain a vegetable for the rest of his life?' The older man didn't mince his words.

The visitor shrugged. 'Time will tell. I, for one, am not losing any sleep over it. And with all due respect, I don't see this as a failed operation.'

'His survival isn't the only issue here,' the older man said. 'There's the matter of the *item*.'

'The item is safely hidden,' replied the visitor. 'I wouldn't worry about that either.'

'Who said I was worried?' the older man rasped. 'Other than the fact that it didn't exactly yield the result we hoped for, did it? After all our meticulous planning, months of preparation, no expense spared, no detail overlooked. It was perfect. Or should have been. Now it turns out that this much-vaunted "item" was a blind alley. More of a white elephant than a wh—' That was enough. His devotion to absolute discretion didn't allow him to finish his sentence, even in such a private setting. No names or specifics were to be mentioned anywhere except within the ultra-secure confines of their boardroom meetings.

The visitor pursed his lips. They walked a few more steps in silence. Carefully measuring his words he replied, 'I admit, I too was disappointed by that outcome. It may be that we mistook the situation.'

'Alternatively, it may be that we were simply fooled. And that the information he stole may still be out there, in some other form.'

'With all the precautions we take? I doubt it. No, the only other way he could have stored it was in his memory,' the visitor said, tapping the side of his own head with a finger. 'Which is now effectively erased.'

'Let's hope so, at any rate. And the journalist?'

'He didn't learn anything of importance, above a few unsubstantiated generalities.'

'You can be sure of that?' the older man asked doubtfully.

'The individual employed for that task is a specialist. If he was unable to extract anything, it means there was nothing there to begin with. The bulk of the information had yet to be passed on.'

The older man puffed his cigar. They walked on. 'I still don't like it,' he grunted. 'Too much rides on this for even the slightest element to be left to chance. And as for the *item*, am I to assume it will now be destroyed, along with the rest of what we retrieved?'

The visitor hesitated a moment, then replied, 'There'll be no trace of it for anyone to find. I guarantee it. The incident is now behind us.'

'You'd better be damn well certain of that too,' said the older man. 'We can afford no more mistakes.'

Chapter 12

Ben had been fairly well acquainted with Lucas Dennim, as with all the trainees who came to hone their expertise with his team. Le Val's 'classroom' included not only its actual sit-down lecture theatre but also its killing house, a replica of the SAS's own live-fire training facility where realistic targets were engaged with real bullets; its short and long shooting ranges; its defensive driving track and skid-pan; its new unarmed combat dojo and the surrounding countryside where they practised capture evasion and fugitive recovery skills. Each aspect of the training experience was designed to mercilessly expose the trainee's weaknesses – and no person alive didn't have them – with a view to raising the bar as high as humanly possible.

When you pushed a man to his limits like that, both physically and mentally, you learned a lot about him. Outside the classroom too, during the evenings spent relaxing around the big farmhouse table when conversation flowed as freely as the food and wine and they got to know one another at a different level. It all served to form a strong bond between pupil and teacher, not one that might necessarily be called friendship as such, but something akin to the camaraderie that was forged between military comrades.

And so even if Ben wouldn't have described Lucas Dennim as a friend, he knew a lot about the guy. Thirty-nine years old, born in New Brunswick to a French-Canadian mother and an American father. The family had moved to Europe when Lucas was thirteen, a smart kid who excelled in sports and was fully bilingual in English and French, which he spoke with a slight Canadian accent. After a short but exemplary military career he'd done a spell with the GIGN French anti-terror police before getting into the private security world and moving to Clermont-Ferrand, where he still kept a home base as far as Ben knew. He'd already been outstanding at his job by the time he was hired to join Auguste Kaprisky's bodyguard team. His training at Le Val, soon after getting that job, had made him even better.

You didn't get to know a person that well without gaining an understanding of how their mind worked. Which was what was troubling Ben, because this sudden decision to quit his job and run off without warning or notice didn't sound at all to Ben like the behaviour of the man he'd known.

Dennim had his faults, of course. He was given to procrastination, which meant he was less well suited to leadership roles. He loved his material comforts and he had more of a roving eye for the ladies than perhaps was quite good for him. But as part of a well-disciplined team, where his foibles could be kept under control, he shone. Dennim scored highly in armed and unarmed defensive skills, had sharp reflexes and quick wits, and would give his life to protect his principal. Ben would have recommended him to anyone.

And someone that good just didn't act this way, letting the side down, abandoning his mates, compromising the team's ability to carry out its shared duty. Not unless there was a very good reason for it, and now Ben was interested in finding out what that reason was.

'Me again,' he said to Jeff.

'I'm popular today. Makes me feel all fuzzy and warm inside to be so needed.'

'Do we have a phone contact for Lucas Dennim? Should be on his file, if so.'

It was just like Jeff not to hesitate or ask questions. He put Ben on hold while he dug up the file and came back a moment later. 'Got a landline and a mobile, which do you want?'

'Give me both,' Ben said, and copied them down.

'So what's up? Onto something?'

'I don't know. Maybe.'

'Let me know if you need anything else, okay?' Jeff said.

'There is one more thing, Jeff.'

'Name it, mate.'

'I'm not happy with the new security team that Kaprisky's lawyer dredged up to replace our guys. Your typical bunch of juiced-up wannabe warriors who think they're Chuck Norris.'

'Never trust a lawyer,' Jeff said acerbically. 'Want me to make some calls?'

'We'd be looking at six or eight men. Military background, ideally, with additional close protection training that they've either had from us or from someone we'd vouch for. I want the best of the best. Money won't be an issue.'

'Most of the blokes that come to mind would do it for free, after what's happened. Leave it with me and I'll get onto it right away.'

Ben gave Jeff Valentina's number so that he could liaise directly with her. Once Jeff came up with the goods, as he could be utterly relied upon to do, Valentina would be more than happy to give Gabriel's replacement team their marching orders.

With that taken care of, Ben got back to thinking about how he was going to handle Lucas Dennim. If there was something fishy going on, a direct approach might scare him off, drive him underground. But then, that kind of response would also tell Ben a lot. And then he'd have a real lead to go after instead of just sniffing at clues. If Dennim did a runner, Ben would hunt him and find him.

He tried the mobile number first, but it had gone out of service. If Dennim was basking in early retirement thanks to this big cash windfall, then he might be at home in Clermont, which the landline number's regional code fitted with. Ben dialled it, still standing on the sunshine-dappled balcony of the Swiss cottage. After several rings, just as the answering message was about to kick in, the voice of a woman came on the line, speaking French. Dennim's personal life was one area Ben knew little about. He assumed this must be a wife or a girlfriend.

'Good afternoon, Madame,' he said in French. 'Wonder if I could speak to your husband, please?'

'My what? I don't have one,' came the slightly fazed reply. Her voice was sluggish, as though she'd just woken up.

'Well, is Lucas at home, please?'

99

'Nah, he doesn't live here any more,' she said vaguely. 'I'm his sister Rosalie. Moved into his place now that he's gone off on his travels, living the dream. Looking after some rich guy's pad, he said. Who's this?'

She sounded pretty dreamy herself. Or high on something, it now occurred to Ben. He should have guessed from the touch of Canadian French in her accent that this was the dippy hippie younger sister he remembered Lucas having once mentioned.

'Hi there, Rosalie. My name's Bernard Thibaud and I work for the Kaprisky Corporation, where Lucas was formerly employed.'

'Right,' Rosalie said uninterestedly. 'Didn't I see something on the TV about that? Like a robbery or something?' She seemed hazy on the details.

'You might well have,' Ben said. 'But hey, you wouldn't happen to have a mobile number for your brother, would you? Only I need to speak to him quite urgently.'

'I don't use them,' she said. 'Microwave radiation rots your brain and turns you into a zombie.'

So does whatever you're smoking, he thought. 'I'm sure you're right, Rosalie. But passing on his number won't hurt you. Do you have it?'

'No. What would I want it for?' Like even calling a mobile number could turn you into a zombie, too.

Ben sighed. 'Well that's a shame. The thing is, you see, it appears from our records that Lucas is owed some back pay from us. I've got records of two different bank accounts for him and I was calling to enquire which one he'd like the money paid into.'

'Oh yeah?'

'Though I don't suppose he needs it,' he added jokingly, 'now that he's come into a fortune.' Sometimes when you joked around with them a little, you could bring them out of their shell. Rosalie might still actually be useful for something.

'He has, has he?' she said, suddenly coming much more to life. Money talk often had that effect on people. 'First I heard of it. And I can't imagine who left him anything, in this family. What a load of bullshit.'

'Oh. Must be my mistake, sorry. In that case, he'll be happy to hear from me. It's rather a substantial amount we owe him.'

Rosalie let out a loud snort. 'Lucky for some. I have an email address for him, if that's what you're after. Snail mail, too. He left me a note of them when he went off. We're not in touch much. He's a prick. I only agreed to look after his place 'coz it's rent-free, you know? Hold on, I have to find where I put the note.'

'That would be great,' Ben said, and when Rosalie finally came shuffling back to the phone after spending a long time searching, he noted down the addresses as she read them out. He wasn't as interested in the email as he was the postal address, which made him raise an eyebrow. Miami, Florida. Not too shabby a place for a fellow to retire to, recently cashed up thanks to a mystery windfall.

'You've been a big help, Rosalie,' he said.

'Anything in it for me?'

'Just my undying gratitude.'

'Yeah, well, when you talk to my prick of a brother you can tell him to stick it up his *trou du cul*.'

So much for undying gratitude. Ben said, 'You take care now, Rosalie. Look out for those zombies, won't you?'

'Huuh??'

Ben ended the call and ran down to his car.

Chapter 13

Back at the house, Ben quickly outlined to Valentina what he'd found out and why his first step should be to travel to Florida. She didn't bat an eyelid. A three-minute phone call to Gabriel Archambeau put the wheels in motion, and within a short time Ben was back at the wheel of the Lancia Stratos speeding towards Le Mans Arnage airport.

The Kaprisky Gulfstream G650 was housed in its own hangar, ready to fly twenty-four-seven with a flight crew on constant standby. The seven thousand or so kilometres across the Atlantic from Le Mans to Miami was just half the range the jet was capable of at a stretch, travelling at a steady Mach .85 with anything up to nineteen passengers on board. This wouldn't be the first time Ben would be able to zip halfway across the world at a moment's notice courtesy of his friend's mighty resources and the power of the Kaprisky name to pull a lot of bureaucratic strings, though he'd never dreamed he would ever be doing it under such circumstances.

Just seven hours after takeoff, the jet was approaching Miami International. Ben could have spent his journey feasting on five-star gourmet delicacies and drinking champagne, but he'd contented himself with a plain ham sandwich and some bottled water. He watched from his wing seat as they left behind the azure blue of the ocean and dropped altitude over the coastline. Funny how a 500-foot megayacht could look like a child's bathtub toy from so high up. And funny how the super-rich and their privileged friends could waltz through international borders with only the most cursory checks. On landing at the private terminal he was through customs in about thirty seconds flat, treated like a foreign dignitary – albeit a very peculiar breed of foreign dignitary who travelled oddly light with just a discreditable old canvas bag for luggage, wore a scuffed brown leather jacket and boots and hadn't shaved in three days – and shown to the high-performance Cadillac Blackwing that had been provided for his use, charged to the Kaprisky corporate account like everything else. Which was good news for him, having been banished for life by pretty much every car rental company on earth – thanks to all the vehicles of theirs that had ended up riddled by bullets, burnt to a cinder, crushed flat or sunk to the bottoms of rivers whilst in his care.

Miami was six hours behind Le Mans, and so in effect Ben had got there just an hour or so after departing France. That kind of time efficiency suited him just fine. He used the Cadillac's GPS to locate the address that Dennim's hippie sister Rosalie had given him, and headed through the big wide open streets and boulevards lined with palm trees, dazzling sunlight reflecting off towering white apartment buildings and glittering high-rises against the cloudless blue sky, here and there a glimpse of the ocean.

Ben had travelled around the United States of America before, frequenting its rural and wilderness areas more than its cities. Miami was giving him the same impression he'd had elsewhere: everything seemed larger and more spread out than in Europe, the buildings spaced far apart, lots of leg and elbow room just as there was in this big American car. It was hot, but only about twice as hot as France this time of year, and the Caddy's air-conditioning kept the cabin ice cool. The GPS insisted on talking to him in a smooth, silky female voice that he turned off. He whirred down the windows and lit a Gauloise.

Lucas Dennim's address was in an area of Downtown Miami called Coconut Grove. Ben worked his way south through Little Havana, past colourful streetside cafés and restaurants shaded under lush palm trees, then hit South Bayshore Drive and threaded through the heavy traffic along the broad boulevard flanked by fine high-walled homes and parks. His destination was a tall luxury waterfront condo tower off Bayshore in the heart of Coconut Grove, separated from the street by an expanse of emerald-green lawn and overhanging trees. He drove slowly by, checking the address, then pulled into a shaded parking area by the foot of the imposing building.

The sun hit him like a hammer as he walked from the car. He ducked inside the coolness of the apartment block and rode the lift up to the sixth floor, emerging onto a broad, fragrant marble-floored landing with a giant picture window overlooking the calm green lagoon waters and jetties of Dinner Key Marina, where countless sailing boats, a forest of masts, gently bobbed and glittered under the sunshine. It was a far cry from the classical magnificence of the Kaprisky estate, but not at all an unpleasant environment for an ex-security guy to spend his retirement in.

Dennim's condo was at the end of the hallway. Ben paused outside the door, listening carefully and hearing only the sound of silence from within. Nobody was around. He knocked, rang the doorbell, and after a while was satisfied that Dennim wasn't at home.

Ben was pleased about that, because it gave him a chance to poke around the condo and see what was what, rather than dive straight into a confrontation with the guy. It was hard to predict exactly what Dennim's reaction would be at seeing his old acquaintance turn up so out of the blue, but there was little doubt he'd be fairly freaked out. Especially if, as Ben strongly suspected, there was something more than a little dubious about the sudden turnaround in his fortunes.

Ben had a long history of breaking into places. It took him less than three minutes to pick the lock and defeat the alarm system before it started raising hell. Once safely inside, he looked around him at the palatial interior and gave a low whistle. Dennim's living room was all glass at one end, with the same impressive east-facing view of the marina and the deep blue ocean beyond. Modern furnishings, acres of gleaming hardwood, lots of white leather. Ben toured the rooms for signs of recent habitation, and found enough to convince him that Dennim had been here until not long ago. There were clothes in the bedroom wardrobe and cabinet drawers, toiletries in the bathroom, and food and drink – lots of drink – in the fridge, the only non-alcoholic of which was an opened carton of semi-skimmed milk that was still fresh. There were an impressive number of empty booze bottles in the recycling box under the kitchen counter. Beer, whiskey, tequila, vodka and wine. Dennim had been enjoying himself, that was for sure. On a smoky glass-topped coffee table by one of the leather armchairs in the living room lay a copy of the *Miami Herald* dated three days ago, and next to it a couple of leisure boating magazines and a brochure from a local yacht brokerage company.

The brochure was the most interesting. Tucked inside it Ben found paperwork showing that a certain Mr L. Dennim had recently become the proud new owner of *Spirit Dancer*, a sixty-foot sailing yacht prominently featured in the brochure. The images were of a stunningly beautiful, sleek white vessel with a distinctive blue stripe down her hull. She was a Gulfstar 60, built in 1982, fully reconditioned and modernised with all the state-of-the-art features, a tasteful teak and rosewood interior, four cabins, three heads, walk-through galley, powerful Perkins diesels, and an asking price of just a shade under three hundred grand. The sales receipt was for the same amount, paid all in one lump sum by wire transfer. A separate sheet of paper folded inside the brochure was a boat slip hire agreement, whereby *Spirit Dancer*'s new owner had signed up to shell out an additional thirteen hundred bucks per month for a year's moorage rental contract at the Dinner Key Marina conveniently located within a stone's throw of his condo.

Curiouser and curiouser. Apart from anything else it meant that Lucas Dennim had no current intention of returning to France. But where was he now? Ben walked over to the big window and gazed out at the tethered boats on the water down below. A pair of binoculars lay on the sill, through which Dennim could presumably admire his prize possession from the comfort of his home. Ben used the binocs to slowly scan the rows and rows of gently bobbing white vessels, searching for a sixty-footer with that distinctive blue stripe. He couldn't see one, but there were so many boats tightly packed together at the jetties that it was hard to be sure.

Ben helped himself to an ice-cold beer from Dennim's fridge and sat in the armchair to drink it, while pondering what to do next. Then he left the apartment, leaving the alarm disabled in case he might want to return, and took a walk down to the marina.

Chapter 14

He soon found the pier he was looking for. The softly rippling tide lapped at the jetty as he walked out along it under the hot sun, past the moored boats of various shapes and sizes, ranging from fast motor cruisers to full-scale sailing yachts capable of long ocean crossings. He reached *Spirit Dancer*'s allocated slip and, not especially to his surprise, found a gap of empty water where she should have been. So that was where Dennim had gone, apparently off for a trip in his new toy. Ben wondered where to, and for how long he'd be gone. A four-cabin yacht could carry a lot of stores, and for a single person it would be a fully self-contained floating home that could stay out at sea for weeks on end.

Most of the other boats on the pier seemed to have nobody aboard, but not all. A few slips further down the jetty from *Spirit Dancer*'s empty space was a smaller and scruffier ocean cruiser whose owner, a lean and deeply-tanned sea salt in his late fifties wearing a flowery shirt and a straw hat, was stumping about the deck carrying out some maintenance work and swearing to himself. Ben stopped and gazed at his boat, pretending to admire it. The guy noticed him standing there looking, and they exchanged greetings.

'Fine day,' Ben said.

'Sure is that,' the guy replied, squinting up at him from the deck with one eye closed against the glare of the sun. 'You on vacation, mister? Ain't from around here, are ya?'

'Just visiting. I was supposed to meet a pal of mine here, to go fishing together. But it looks like he's gone off without me.' Ben pointed back towards the empty slip a few spaces down the row.

'Oh, that guy. Met'm. He's new here. Canadian, right?'

'That's right. Dennim, Lucas Dennim.'

'That's him. Friendly dude. Likes to shoot the breeze. And show off that neat boat of his. Yeah, he headed out yesterday.'

Ben turned to gaze out at the flat blue ocean horizon, empty apart from a few smaller leisure craft and a couple of giant multi-storey superyachts the size of tankers, and shook his head. 'Couldn't wait, damn it.'

'Weren't alone, though. Had a lady friend with him. Pretty hot little number, too.' The guy grinned. 'Guess three's a crowd, if you know what I mean.'

Ben grinned back. 'Yeah, I guess you're right about that. You wouldn't happen to know where he was headed?'

'Matter of fact I do. Your buddy told me he was fixin' to check out Treasure Cay, Great Abaco Island, hang around there for a few days, maybe a week or so. Thinking of renting a beachside villa there, he said. Must be pretty damn seriously loaded, if he can afford a place there.'

'He's done all right for himself,' Ben said.

'Lucky for some,' the guy replied ruefully. 'What is he, some tech wizard who came up with the next big thing and then cashed out?'

'He cashed out, all right,' Ben said. 'But I don't think there was a lot of wizardry involved.'

Treasure Cay was in the Bahamas, some two hundred miles east of Miami. If Dennim was planning on hanging around there for a week or so, there was no desperate hurry to catch up with him. Ben let himself back into the condo, locked the door, reset the alarm, and went to the luxurious bathroom where he took a quick, cool shower. When he was dried and dressed he headed for the kitchen and cobbled together a meal from tinned beef and Mexican-style refried beans. Lathered with hot chilli pepper sauce it tasted not too terrible. He washed down the volcanic concoction with more of Dennim's beer as he sat poring through the back ads in the boating magazines.

Once he'd found what he was looking for and decided on his plan of action, he returned to the car, set the sat nav and headed northeast up the coast along South Bayshore Drive and then hooked up with South Miami Avenue. After Alice Wainwright Park he hung a right turn for the Rickenbacker Causeway. The long road bridge across Biscayne Bay's glittering blue waters connected Miami with the barrier islands of Virginia Key and Key Biscayne. Traffic was light and Ben sped quickly away from the city.

From out to sea, the high-rises of Downtown looked as though they were rising up out of the water. Crossing the first stretch of causeway he reached Hobie Island Park, flanked on both sides by white sands and palm trees. Nearby was another marina crowded with even more boats and yachts. A little further from the marina lay the place he'd found in the back ads of Dennim's magazine, called Vinnie's Seaplane Charter.

Ben followed the track down to the beach and parked the Cadillac under the shade of the palms. Vinnie's operation consisted of a couple of tin sheds and a long white wooden pier at which a dozen or so amphibious aircraft sat bobbing on their ski-like floats. They all looked shiny and well-maintained. Seeing them made Ben think about Abbie Logan, the pilot and charter business owner he'd met in Australia's Northern Territory and become romantically involved with for a brief time. He wondered what Abbie was doing at this moment.

At a separate jetty a few yards further down the shore was moored a solitary plane that gave a rather different impression from the rest, visibly older and somewhat scuffed, discoloured and battered from a lifetime of hard use. One of its floats appeared to have snagged a reef or some other sharp object and been patched up with gaffer tape. It reminded Ben of Jeff Dekker's ancient Cessna Skyhawk, which Tuesday referred to as a flying coffin.

Over by one of the tin sheds, a couple of men in greasy mechanic's overalls and baseball caps were working on another seaplane that had been wheeled up onto the beach and stood partially dismantled as they worked under the engine canopy. Ben walked over to them and offered a friendly smile as they turned to greet their prospective customer. The older of the two guys, heavyset and bearded, introduced himself as Vinnie and his younger associate as Danny. 'So, bud,' Vinnie said with a toothy grin, wiping sweat from his face with the back of his hand and leaving an oily black smear. 'You lookin' to charter a seaplane? Then you came to the right place. We got the best selection in Florida.'

'I was thinking I'd like to take a tour of the islands,' Ben said. 'Check out Treasure Cay.'

'That'd be no problem at all,' Vinnie replied, turning with a grand wave at his small squadron. 'Any of our aircraft would suit you just fine. When were you thinking of flying?'

'Right now,' Ben said, looking at his watch. 'I'd like to get underway as soon as possible.'

Vinnie and Danny exchanged glances. 'Right *now*?' Vinnie shook his head at Ben, his grin wavering a little. 'No can do, bud. Soonest I can book you in would be a couple hours. I gotta finish this engine and I don't have another pilot available until later this afternoon.'

'That's okay,' Ben said. 'I don't need a pilot. I'll fly the plane myself.'

Vinnie's grin wavered a little more. 'I can't let you fly one of my planes. Forget that, mister.'

'What about that one over there?' Ben asked, pointing at the battered older aircraft moored alone at the other jetty. 'Does it go?'

'She goes just fine, mister,' Vinnie said. 'She'll do anything you want her to, take you anywhere you want, even if she don't look like much. But she ain't for charter.'

'No, I was wondering if she was for sale,' Ben said. 'That way I don't need to hire a pilot to take me out, do I?'

'Why don't you want to hire a pilot, dude?' Danny asked, squinting at him curiously.

'I just like my privacy,' Ben told him.

'You ever flown a seaplane before?'

'I'll fly pretty much anything,' Ben said. Which was true enough. In his time he'd flown a motley variety of aircraft including military helicopters and even his own sister's flashy prototype turboprop, which he'd admittedly dumped in Lake Toba in Indonesia while being threatened with destruction by air force F-16s. His one experience of flying a seaplane had been in a veteran Supermarine Sea Otter in the Cayman Islands, years ago. That plane had suffered a fiery end when he'd crash-landed it onto the deck of a ship like a flying bomb, laden with high explosives. On that occasion, at least, the crash had been deliberate. He'd been wilder then, back in his reckless youth. God forbid he should ever attempt anything like that now.

'Are you blowing smoke, mister?' Vinnie asked, deeply unsure about all this.

'Perfectly on the level,' Ben said. 'I'm buying, if it's available.'

'You'd have to talk to Pepe. It's his plane.'

'I'll do that. Where can I find him?'

He was directed over to the second tin shed, where Pepe and another of the staff were filling jerrycans from a large fuel drum. Ben introduced himself. 'I hear you're the owner of that seaplane over there?'

'Heard right,' Pepe said, wiping his hands on a rag. He was a guy of around thirty-five, with a long face made longer by a goatee. A ponytail down his back and a T-shirt under his overall that said LET'S GO BRANDON.

'Wouldn't brag about it, though,' said the other guy. 'It's a piece of shit.'

'Zip it, Tee Jay,' Pepe grumbled at him.

'How'd you like to sell it to me?' Ben asked. 'I'll give you seventy-five thousand dollars. Shake on the deal now and you can have the cash wired to your account within thirty minutes. Then when I'm done with the plane, you can have it back. You keep the money, of course.'

Pepe stared at him in bewilderment. He scratched his goatee. 'Hold on a minute there, mister. Let me get this right. You're saying you wanna buy my plane from me and then let me have it back, gratis?'

'That's what I'm saying.'

'Are you nuts? That's the most dumbass thing I've ever heard.'

'Take the deal, man,' Tee Jay urged him, poking an elbow in his ribs. 'This guy's a coupla cards short of a fuckin' deck.'

Pepe gave Ben a suspicious frown. 'This for real, mister? You yankin' my chain?'

'Why don't you try me and see?' Ben said. 'You have nothing to lose.'

'Gotta be a catch, right?'

'Take the money, for Chrissakes,' Tee Jay hissed. 'Before he changes his mind.'

'Shut up, Tee Jay. I don't know, mister.'

'Better decide fast, Pepe,' Ben said. 'I'm in a hurry.'

They wrangled over it for a couple more minutes before Pepe relented, stuck out his hand and said, 'You gotta be out of your mind, man. But hell yes, I'll take the deal. Though I won't believe a word you're tellin' me until I see the colour of your money.'

Ben couldn't blame the guy for that. He'd have balked at the idea, too. As did Gabriel Archambeau two minutes later, though for different reasons, when Ben, leaning against the wing of the Cadillac smoking a Gauloise, told him the sum of money he wanted wired to the account at the Bank of Central Florida.

'You can't be serious. I understand Valentina gave you carte blanche, but all the same. I don't have the authority to sanction such a payment.'

'She does,' Ben said. 'Call her if you need to. But make it quick, Gabriel. I've got things to do.'

Five minutes after that, the lawyer called back to say that the money had been wired. It appeared that Valentina had given Gabriel a severe roasting for hesitating even for a second to give Ben whatever he wanted. He sounded suitably contrite, with repeated apologies and the assurance that it wouldn't happen again.

'Don't sweat it, Gabriel,' Ben told him, ended the call and walked back to the shed where Pepe and Tee Jay, joined now by Vinnie and Danny, were huddled in a group, darting looks his way. Shortly afterwards, an astonished Pepe, unable to unglue his eyes from the internet banking app on his iPhone, confirmed that the transfer had indeed come through as promised, every penny of it. 'Holy shit, man, I thought you were shining me on.'

'Are we fuelled up and ready to go?' Ben asked.

'This guy don't fuck around, does he?' Danny said with a chuckle.

Pepe accompanied Ben down the white sandy beach to the jetty where the old plane heaved gently on the glass-clear water. Ben cast off the rope from its mooring point, jumped down from the jetty onto one of the floats and clambered into the small two-seater cockpit. The inside of the aircraft was just as scuffed and worn as the outside, but everything seemed to be in reasonable order. He quickly ran through the controls, refamiliarising himself with all the switches and dials. Flaps, water rudder, one plunger control for fuel mixture, another for throttle. Pretty simple and straightforward. Like riding a bicycle.

As Pepe stood watching from the jetty, still quite stunned, a new thought came to him and he called anxiously over, 'Hey, you got all the paperwork to fly this thing, right? We're all legal and all?'

'Don't worry about a thing, Pepe,' Ben called back with a reassuring smile, buckling himself in and donning his headset. 'I'll see you later.'

All clear. Contact. Then the plane's single engine spluttered into life with a puff of blue smoke and the spinning propeller whipped up a fine spray from the water. Ben taxied away from the jetty, brought up the revs and the aircraft began to accelerate through the gentle surf. Faster, faster, the engine note clattering louder, vibrations filling the cockpit. Then he was soaring upwards, the vibrations smoothed out and the shore, the tin sheds and the upturned face of a worried-looking Pepe were quickly falling away beneath him.

The seaplane gathered altitude, buzzing happily through the warm air. Ben set his course and levelled off at fifteen hundred feet, high enough to give him a pretty good bird's eye view of the ocean, settled back and relaxed into the ride.

The small leisure boats and great tri-deck superyachts passed by far below. Somewhere over the flat blue horizon was Great Abaco Island and Treasure Cay, where with any luck he'd find *Spirit Dancer* waiting for him.

And when that happened, Lucas Dennim was about to get the second biggest surprise of his life.

Chapter 15

It wasn't long before Ben had sunk the last glimpses of the Miami skyline behind him and there was nothing but open blue water for as far as the eye could see: a seemingly infinite circular horizon that surrounded him on all sides and made it easy for the mind to start persuading itself that this was the sum total of all reality and nothing else existed. That might not have been such a bad thing, he reflected, gazing around him at the beauty of it. The ocean was almost perfectly flat with barely a speck of white, the most vivid blue-green, so pure you could almost see the bottom, its surface shimmering and sparkling with a zillion diamonds. On and on, the steady drone of the engine becoming hypnotic.

The many islands that collectively made up the Commonwealth of the Bahamas were widely spread out over a vast tract of ocean. The largest, Andros Island, and the smaller New Providence Island that was home to the capital city of Nassau, lay far off to the south, on his starboard wing, while the northernmost land mass of Grand Bahama was to his other side. Directly ahead on his present course was the long, thin island of Great Abaco, which curved from Fox Town at its northern tip to Sandy Point at its southern end. His destination, Treasure Cay, was situated on the far side, though he would need to keep a sharp eye out for Dennim's yacht from the moment he sighted land.

At last, Ben spotted the island far off in the distance, a green and white slash against the vivid blue. He dropped some altitude on his approach and scanned from one end of the horizon to the other for any sign of his target. The western shores of Great Abaco were clustered with many smaller islands, some of them apparently uninhabited and thick with mangrove. There were a few boats dotted about on the ocean, none of them the one he was looking for. Now he was buzzing inshore, the aircraft's shadow skimming in the shape of a cross over the treetops as he gazed down at the splendid villas and mansions that nestled among the verdage. Much of the development was clustered along the far side of the island. A single highway ran its length, and beyond it the white sands of Buckingham Beach and Treasure Cay itself, with its luxury beach hotel and golf resort, the ubiquitous marina teeming with boats, boats and more boats. The coast was dotted with the waterfront homes of extremely rich people. Dennim's neighbour at Dinner Key Marina hadn't been kidding: this place was the ultimate paradise hideaway of sun-seeking millionaires and billionaires. If you were lucky enough to find a nice little pad for rent and had to ask the price, then you probably couldn't afford it. And if Lucas Dennim really was in the market, he must have come into even greater sudden wealth than Ben had thought. Where the money had come from – that was another story.

The seaplane buzzed over the far shore and out across the bay. Miniature figures down below of people sunbathing, walking along the shore, splashing in the water. A coastguard helicopter was scudding over Buckingham Beach. A fast motorboat was towing a water skier through its long white wake. A little further out across the bay, stately yachts glided swanlike over the blue. Ben swooped down a little lower to get a better look at them. His heart jumped momentarily at the sight of a gleaming white hull with a blue stripe – but as he banked overhead his excitement sank again as he saw the vessel was a catamaran. Close, but no cigar.

He was still pretty confident of finding *Spirit Dancer* as he ranged further out to sea. Beyond Treasure Cay were the smaller islands of Green Turtle Cay to the north and Great Guana Cay to the south. In the middle of them lay the tiny island of Whale Cay. The seaplane roared over a sprawling great billionaire mansion that sat in splendid isolation among the trees. Tennis courts and a helipad, and the virgin beach and the stunning blue ocean all around. All perfectly lovely, if only Ben had been here for the scenic view.

His optimism was beginning to sour, thoughts encroaching on his mind that maybe this hadn't been such a good idea after all; that maybe Dennim had had a change of plan; that maybe he'd been feeding his neighbour at Dinner Key Marina a load of bullshit. The reality was that, footloose and fancy-free, Dennim and his lady friend could sail off wherever the hell they wanted.

Just as the doubts were beginning to crowd in on Ben's mind and he was thinking about Auguste's seventy-five grand gone up in smoke, and how he might explain this to the lawyer without appearing totally stupid, he spotted the tiny lone white speck far away to the east, miles beyond the other side of Whale Cay.

Ben altered his course a few degrees and the plane banked in its direction. He kept his eyes fixed on the white speck as it grew slowly bigger and cleared. A boat – but what kind of boat? One with a single mast and a sail, he could make out now. And then he could see the distinctive stripe, and his spirits soared again. There she was.

Coming down closer to the sea he curved around in a wide circle and was able to discern the figures of two people on deck. Hard to get much detail at this distance, but enough to tell that one was a woman with long blond hair, the other a dark-haired man in cargo shorts and an open white shirt. He couldn't make out their faces, but it was clear enough that the woman was wearing very little. Three's a crowd, all right, he thought.

Spirit Dancer's occupants were standing at the deck railing looking up as the plane looped overhead. Ben came round once more, levelled out for landing and touched down on the smooth water about sixty yards from the yacht's starboard side. He lowered his throttle speed, engaged his taxi rudder and started making his way towards the vessel. Looking through the binoculars he'd taken from the condo he was pretty certain the man on deck was Lucas Dennim, though he hadn't seen him in a while. Ben wondered again how Dennim was going to react to his former trainer's surprise appearance.

The answer soon became apparent when, as the plane came within some thirty yards of the yacht, the guy who looked like Lucas Dennim suddenly tore away from the starboard railing, disappeared into the wheelhouse and re-emerged an instant later clutching an object whose identity Ben was in no doubt over at all. It was a pump-action shotgun. The kind of utility weapon you could walk in and buy from any K Mart store in America. Ideal for home owners defending their property. Or for paranoid yachtsmen anxious to stave off the attentions of mysterious and unexpected visitors in the middle of the ocean.

Ben was very interested to know who, exactly, Dennim was so worried about. But now wasn't the time to be puzzling over mysteries. The plane was close enough to the yacht for Ben to be certain he'd found who he was looking for. It was also close enough to be within effective range of that shotgun.

The unmistakable pump-action *clack-clack* sounded across the water, followed an instant later by Dennim's angry yell, 'Hey! Whoever the fuck you are, you'd better get away from my boat!' Dennim pointed the barrel of the weapon in the air and let off a booming shot. He shouted, 'I'm warning you!' Then as the plane kept floating closer he levelled the weapon and fired again. His second shot kicked up an eruption of white water a foot away from Ben's port float. Then the third shot punched a colander of buckshot pellet holes into the float itself. The fourth shattered a window, showering Ben with broken glass.

Ben didn't think Dennim had recognised him yet, but he wasn't inclined to sit around waiting to find out if the guy would act any differently when he did. That was an eight-shot tube magazine on that shotgun and it was certain to be loaded up full. Ben scrambled out of the cabin, jumped down onto the float and dived into the milk-warm water, cleaving the surface like a seal as a fifth shot sent up a burst of spray very close by.

Ben was a strong swimmer, even fully dressed and wearing stout shoes. In a few strokes he'd gone deep under the water. Glancing up he could see the yacht's gleaming bottom, the dapples of sunlight playing on the white fibreglass. Then the mirror-smooth surface overhead was shattered as another shot blew up the water like a depth charge. The buckshot sank harmlessly around him, trailing little threads of bubbles. Ben swam on, deeper, the water roaring in his ears, until he'd passed beneath *Spirit Dancer*'s keel. In a couple more strokes he was right under and propelling himself powerfully up the other side. His head broke the surface, and there was the smooth curve of the yacht's hull above him, its port rail just about within reach. He grasped it and hauled himself up towards the deck, streaming water.

Across to the starboard side of the deck, Lucas Dennim was bending over the rail scanning left and right, waiting for his unknown and unwanted visitor to show himself so he could blast him again. Dennim's blond-haired lady friend had run away aft towards the wheelhouse, hurriedly putting on her bikini top. Neither noticed as Ben silently climbed over the rail behind them.

'I think I must've got the sonofabitch,' Dennim was muttering to himself. 'Eat lead, asshole.'

In four fast strides Ben crossed the deck and was on him. He wrapped a pincer-like arm around Dennim's neck, jerked him backwards off his feet and at the same time locked onto the shotgun, twisting it violently out of the man's hand and letting it fall with a splash into the sea.

Lucas Dennim was a big, strong guy and he'd spent many years learning how to handle himself in a fight. He struggled hard, but Ben had him tight and quickly forced him down on the deck, pinned and helpless. The blonde was watching from the wheelhouse, now decent again, and apparently frozen in panic. Ben was glad about that, because the last thing he needed right now was to have to deal with her, too. He blocked a backward elbow strike determinedly aimed at his face, grabbed a fistful of Dennim's hair and whacked his head against the deck boards a couple of times to subdue him a little. Dennim's muscles went limp, but only for an instant before he started struggling again, as desperate as a trapped wild animal. He managed to break Ben's grasp on his hair, leaving a few tufts behind, and with a concerted jerk of his body was able to flip over onto his back. Ben hit him again, pinning his arms as they came up to grab his throat.

Then Dennim's eyes opened wide with horror and recognition as he realised who he was fighting.

He gasped, 'Holy crap, it's Ben Hope!'

Chapter 16

Ben let go of Dennim's arms. 'Are we done? Then stop messing around and let's talk, okay?'

Dennim was staring in total confusion as Ben let him get to his feet. 'Honey, what's going on?' the blonde called out in a high-pitched, sugary voice tinged with fear. 'Speak to me, honey! I'm scared!'

'It's all right, Candi,' Dennim said hoarsely, finding his voice. 'I know this guy.'

'Who is he?' the blonde bleated. But Dennim was too stupefied to reply to her. He leaned against the rail, wiped a smear of blood from his lip and muttered, 'I can't believe it's you, man. What the hell are you doing here, turning up out of the blue like this?'

'Just thought I'd drop in and say hello,' Ben said. 'Not much of a welcome, though. Do you normally pop off twelve-gauge buckshot rounds at your old friends come to visit?'

Dennim spluttered, 'I'm sorry, man. But how was I supposed to know it was you?'

'Who did you think it was?' Ben asked him.

'I . . . I thought . . . hey, I mean, you never know. Some guy comes out of nowhere and next thing he looks as if he might be trying to board your boat.'

'The famous seaplane pirates,' Ben said, raising an eyebrow. 'I heard about that. They're a big problem in these waters.'

Dennim sighed heavily, hung his head and rubbed his eyes. 'Fuck, I need a drink.' Looking over to where his lady friend was still standing there looking nervous he called, 'Candi, get me a beer, would you? Get one for my buddy Ben here, too.'

Candi nodded dumbly, biting her lip, then turned like a gazelle and disappeared below. She reappeared a moment later with a couple of bottles of chilled beer. Dennim took them from her without thanks, handed one to Ben, twisted the cap off his own and drank half of it down in one swallow. Ben set his bottle down on the deck without opening it.

'Look, I'm sorry,' Dennim repeated miserably. 'I just got jumpy. I carry some cash on board, a little bit of walking-around money. I thought you'd come to rob me.' It was an obvious lie and he made a bad job of it.

Ben nodded. 'I understand, Lucas. A man of your means can't be too careful, after all.'

'My *means*?' Dennim blustered, putting on a look of astonished surprise that would have hands-down failed any amateur dramatics audition. 'You saying I'm rich or something? What gives you that idea? The boat, right? Well, it's not mine. Belongs to a friend.' He took another long swig of his beer.

'And so does the condo in Miami, I suppose.'

Dennim's beer went down the wrong way and he sprayed it all out. He stared at Ben so hard that his eyes bulged. 'The what?'

'The cosy little bachelor pad in Coconut Grove,' Ben said. 'Next to the marina. You know the one. Does that belong to your rich friend too?'

Dennim's mouth opened and closed a few times, but no sound came out. He managed to say, 'Th-that's right. It's his place.'

'And that nice coffee table must be his, too,' Ben said. 'The one with the yacht broker's brochure lying on it, with the sales receipt for this tub. A receipt with your name on it.'

Dennim had turned pale, and now his face flushed red. 'You broke into my place?'

'So it is your place,' Ben said. 'Like this is your yacht. Have you found that nice villa to rent in Treasure Cay yet?'

'Okay, okay, enough of this shit. What are you really doing here?' Dennim demanded, pointing the beer bottle at Ben.

'I came to give you the latest update about your former employer. I'm sure you've been worried about him.'

'Kaprisky?' Dennim blinked, uncomprehending. 'What about him?'

'Oh, you hadn't heard. Been too busy enjoying the good life and sailing around the Bahamas to be watching the news.'

'What news?' Dennim blurted. He really didn't know.

And so Ben told him.

Dennim's head sank into his hands as Ben talked. The empty bottle fell from his fingers and rolled across the deck. 'Oh God,' he kept repeating in a shocked murmur. 'Oh Christ. All of them?' Talking about his ex-colleagues in the close protection team.

'Every last one,' Ben said. 'Including your replacement. A guy called André Becker.'

'Do . . . do they know who did it?'

'Not yet,' Ben replied. 'Neither do I. But I'm working on it. And I've a pretty good idea that the people behind the attack are the same ones who paid you all that money. How much did they offer you, Lucas?'

Dennim's eyes were glazed with agony and he couldn't meet Ben's gaze. 'Five million,' he muttered.

'Euros, pounds or dollars?'

'What does it matter? Euros.'

'I won't ask who paid you off,' Ben said. 'Because I'm sure you have no idea. All you knew was what you were told, that the money was yours, cash in the hand, if you just agreed to walk away from your job. Correct?'

Dennim nodded. 'They just called me one day. I thought it was a hoax at first.'

'But you didn't tell anyone.'

'No. Then ten grand appeared in my account, ping, there it was. To show me they were serious.'

'No questions,' Ben said. 'That was the condition, wasn't it? You didn't know what they were planning. You didn't know they were going to fill your place with an inside man with a phony résumé, whose job it would be to help the attack team to get into the estate. You knew nothing. Right?'

'Right,' Dennim whispered, and Ben believed him. If he hadn't, Dennim would have been in the water for the sharks to eat.

'But you must have wondered,' Ben said. 'It must have crossed your mind once or twice, to question why some anonymous person would offer you five million euros for no other reason than you give up your job. You didn't find it strange?'

129

'Of course it was strange,' Dennim snapped, suddenly looking up. 'I thought I was having some kind of weird dream at first. But who's going to turn down five million euros? It was there for the taking. What choice did I have? I'm pushing forty years old, Ben. I've been in the private security game for a long time and frankly I was getting burned out. Reaching the end of my shelf life. Now I'll never have to work again. I mean, what would *you* have done?'

'I might have thought it was a little bit suspicious,' Ben said. 'I might have asked myself why this mysterious bene-factor was willing to invest so much in having me gone. Nobody throws cash around like that without a very particular reason. I might have wondered if maybe, just *maybe*, they had some ulterior motive, perhaps planning to do something unpleasant, and that by taking the money I was facilitating that, and more than a little bit complicit. I might even have mentioned it to my boss instead of feeding him a pile of lies about an inheritance.'

Dennim said nothing.

'And if it meant getting blood on my hands,' Ben said, 'I wouldn't have taken the five million. I wouldn't have taken a hundred trillion, not if I was starving in the street. But you jumped at it. What does that say about you?'

'I didn't think it was going to be a hit!' Dennim protested.

'No. You didn't think at all.'

'I'm sorry. I'm so sorry.' Dennim began to sob.

'You look it, too,' Ben said. 'But what you are most of all is a damn fool. I hope you're enjoying your blood money. Except I don't think you can even do that, can you? Because now you're so paranoid about losing it that you see robbers and pirates everywhere and go around with a shotgun, ready to open fire on any stranger who gets too close. Or maybe you knew deep down that these crooks would come after you one day. Five million and no strings attached? Maybe you've been expecting a little visit from them. And maybe you should expect it, Lucas. Because how do these people know you can be trusted to keep your mouth shut for ever? You're a loose end just waiting to be tied up.'

Dennim slumped on the deck. The sobbing racked his body and made his shoulders quake. Then the floodgates opened, and he wept like a child. Ben picked up the unopened beer and held it out to him. Dennim pushed the bottle away. 'I don't deserve it.'

'Probably not,' Ben said. He lobbed the bottle over the side. The blonde was still hovering in the background, hugging herself and watching and listening uncertainly with huge Bambi eyes. Ben said to her, 'Miss, why don't you go and work on your tan or something?'

She hesitated, watching Ben warily, then disappeared back down the companionway to the lower deck.

Dennim went on weeping for a minute or two, saying over and over, 'It's all my fault. It's all my fault.' Then he looked up at Ben, his face covered in tears. 'So that's the reason you came looking for me, right? To punish me. Beat the shit out of me. Or blow my head off and leave me out here. Right?'

'Until I got here, I wasn't sure what to do with you,' Ben said. 'Now I see you, Lucas, frankly, I think killing you would be a waste of effort. I think you should be allowed to live a very long life, for years and years after all the money's burned up, the beach bunnies and bimbos have moved on and you're all alone in misery and squalor. And you can spend that time thinking about how you sold out the men you worked with, and the man who trusted you with his life, just out of pure greed and stupidity.'

'What am I going to do now?' Dennim mumbled, close to desperation.

'Keep your head down and pray the bad guys don't catch up with you again,' Ben said. 'Good luck, Lucas.'

The wind had come up while they'd been talking, and the sea was rising, making *Spirit Dancer* roll and pitch on the swell. The seaplane was beginning to drift further away. It was time for Ben to leave. Without another word he swung his legs over the rail and dived into the water and started swimming for the plane.

Chapter 17

As he headed back towards Miami he was asking himself what he'd learned for Kaprisky's seventy-five thousand dollars. Dennim's revelations had been vague and cloudy, as vague and cloudy as the man's understanding of the way he'd been used. Despite that, a few things had now become clearer in Ben's mind. It was more obvious than ever that the payoff had been arranged so that André Becker, if that was even his real name, would become the operation's inside man.

It was also increasingly clear that Becker had been deceived and eliminated in order to leave no trail, avert too many questions being asked. These were powerful, wealthy and ruthless people, as capable of fabricating highly convincing false credentials as they were of dispensing millions in bribe money or rubbing out their own people for the sake of operational security. The scale of their operation kept getting bigger and more elaborate.

But the biggest piece of the puzzle remained missing, because Ben still knew nothing about who they were.

By the time he got back to Vinnie's Seaplane Charter, he'd been gone over six hours and used up most of his fuel. Vinnie and Pepe happened to still be there, working late. As Ben tied up the plane to its mooring point he saw the two men walking down the beach towards him.

'Didn't figure on seeing you again,' Pepe said.

'I said I'd return your plane,' Ben replied. 'I've no further use for it.'

'You're lucky the cops weren't here waiting for you,' Vinnie grumbled.

'Now why would you want to go and do a thing like that?' Ben said.

'Hey, what the hell?' Pepe had noticed the smashed window and shotgun blast holes in the float. 'Oh man, look what you did to my fuckin' plane!'

'So get it fixed,' Ben told him. 'You can afford to now.'

Some people were just never happy.

He left them at the jetty and headed back to his car, squelching in his wet boots. Traffic was lighter at this time of the early evening as he sped back across the Rickenbacker Causeway into Miami. At a late-opening clothes store in Mary Brickell Village in the heart of Downtown he bought some new black jeans, a cotton shirt and a pair of tennis shoes. The boots and jacket would dry off. The rest of his old stuff, he dumped in a garbage bin at the side of the store. Then he bought some spicy Venezuelan takeout food from a shiny red street stall called Alpha Dog, advertising THE BEST HOT DOGS EVER!, and ate it in the car before he drove back down south along the coast to Coconut Grove. He was thinking that since Lucas Dennim probably wouldn't come skulking home with his tail between his legs for a while yet, he might as well make use of the guy's condo while he was in town.

Ben helped himself to some more of Dennim's diminishing beer supply, lounged in one of the white leather armchairs and checked in on Jeff Dekker, who said he'd already been in touch with six of their contacts in the VIP

134

close protection business, five of whom had said they were interested. Jeff had several more candidates on his list and had already been in touch with Valentina.

Ben thanked Jeff, and then tried again to call the two remaining phone contacts from Kaprisky's diary: the as yet unidentified 'SS' in Rome and 'FK' in Berlin. It would be after midnight there by now, but he called them anyway. Still no reply from the Italian number, and none either from 'FK's' mobile number. But the last one he tried, the German landline number, scored a hit.

After five rings his call was answered by a teary-sounding woman, who'd clearly been in the middle of a late-night crying session when the phone rang. '*Ja?*' she sniffed.

Ben hesitated, taken aback. Before he could say anything she'd managed to compose herself a little and asked, '*Suchen sie Fritz?*' *Are you looking for Fritz?* From which Ben deduced that Fritz must be the F in the initials FK.

His spoken German wasn't as fluent as his French, not enough to pass for a native, but good enough. He replied, '*Entschuldigung, dass ich so spät anrufe. Darf ich mit ihm sprechen, bitte?*' *Sorry for calling so late. May I speak to him?*

'He's dead,' she replied, and immediately burst into tears again. Through the gasps and sobs she added, 'He was killed yesterday.'

'I'm so sorry to hear it,' Ben said after a beat. 'My condolences.'

She blew her nose. 'Thank you. Are you a colleague of his, another reporter?'

More key information. A suddenly deceased reporter was always interesting, because some reporters had a habit of sticking their noses in where they weren't welcome. Playing along to learn more, Ben replied, 'That's right. My name's Peters, Justin Peters.' He talked in a soft, reassuring tone that he knew from experience was effective at gaining people's trust and getting them to open up to him.

'You're British. I thought so, from your accent. So you're not based in Berlin, like Fritz?'

She seemed to want to talk to someone. He felt sorry for lying to her. 'No, in London. But we've known each other for a long time.'

'Justin Peters,' she said thoughtfully. 'Yes, I think he might have mentioned you. I don't really remember. Everything seems like a dream.'

'This is terrible,' Ben said. 'I'm in shock.'

'We were getting engaged. My poor Fritzi.' Her voice broke up into more bitter weeping. Ben waited for her to compose herself again. 'What happened?' he asked gently.

'They say it was an accident,' she replied, anger piercing through her tone. 'I don't believe it. Now *this* has happened too. Look at this place. Can it be coincidence? What's going on?' Her emotions were so fraught that she was letting it all pour out to a complete stranger, just to get it off her chest.

He asked, 'What else has happened?'

She didn't reply but went on, her words gushing out faster and faster in such a stream of quick-fire German that he had to listen hard to keep up. 'That's why I can't believe what the police say, that it's just a coincidence. First this so-called accident. Next his apartment has been burgled. The whole place is completely wrecked. How am I supposed to deal with this? He had no family and I'm the only one who can do it and I've only got until the end of the week

136

before the lease on this place is up and there's no way I can afford to keep two places and I've no idea where to even start going through all his things. I've been here for hours and you'd hardly know it. I don't like being on my own here at night. This building gives me the creeps. Especially now, when you just don't know who could be hanging around. I'll have to come back here during my lunch break tomorrow, but the office is right on the other side of town and I only get an hour and . . .'

'Shh, take it easy,' Ben said calmly.

'That's what they said at Hoffmann Design, too. Where I work. They said, "Mia, you need to look after yourself, take some leave, all the time you need." But I can't. I'm better when I work. It's the only thing that keeps my mind off all of this. I have to keep moving or I'll just . . .'

As she was still gabbling away he put her on speaker and looked up Hoffmann Design. It was an interior design consultancy in Berlin. The company website had a tab marked 'Unser Team', listing all their design consultants, each with a little bio and a thumbnail image. Mia Brockhaus had been employed there for seven years and had a nice little portfolio of interior design projects. Her picture showed an attractive, smiling woman in her thirties, with lustrous green eyes and dark hair bobbed above shoulder length.

Mia wasn't smiling now, that was for sure. 'I should go home and try to get some rest,' she sniffled. 'There's nothing more I can do here tonight. Thank you for calling, Herr Peters. Fritz would have appreciated it.'

'I'm very sorry for your loss,' Ben said. 'Please take care. *Auf wiedersehen.*'

'*Auf wiedersehen*.'

And it would be *wieder sehen*, quite literally, because Ben had already decided where he'd be heading from here and he'd be seeing her again soon, though she didn't know it. The moment the call was over, he was straight back on the phone to Gabriel Archambeau.

Gabriel must have been tucked up asleep in bed. He didn't sound overjoyed at being disturbed. 'It's you. Do you know what time it is?'

'How's Auguste?'

'I was on the phone to Valentina two hours ago. Still more or less the same, I'm sorry to say. Now and then a tiny flicker of eyelid movement, but the doctors say it could be just a nerve twitch.'

'Say hello to her for me,' Ben said. 'Meantime, something's come up this end. Is the jet still here in Miami?'

'On standby and ever at your disposal, just as Valentina ordered,' Gabriel said, with just the tiniest tinge of resentment discernible in his voice. 'Are you willing to share this latest development?'

'No. I'm leaving for the airport now. Call the crew and tell them to get ready to fly to Berlin, now, right away.'

'Berlin? What for? Auguste was there only a few days ago, for some unexplained reason. Nobody ever tells me anything.'

Which confirmed the entry in Kaprisky's diary, about his meeting with Fritz at the Ritz-Carlton Tea Lounge. Ben wasn't about to start explaining his movements to the lawyer. He hung up.

Less than ninety seconds later, he was stepping out of the lift and leaving Dennim's condo building for ever.

Chapter 18

Gabriel's instructions had come through and the jet was getting prepped for takeoff by the time Ben got to the airport, while all arrangements were being made for a hastily scheduled flight to Berlin. Once again the might of the Kaprisky empire was flexing its muscles, just so that one man could be whisked back across the Atlantic like a magic carpet ride. This was what it must feel like to be a billionaire.

As he handed back the keys to the Cadillac it occurred to him that this was probably the first time he'd ever returned a car in one piece. Maybe he was getting tame. Who knew – if this kept up, perhaps the rental companies who'd blacklisted him might even reconsider and start trusting in him again. As long as they didn't go and talk to the guys at Vinnie's Seaplane Charter.

While he was waiting for the Gulfstream's crew to make their final pre-flight checks he sat in a corner of the empty VIP lounge at the private terminal, making do with a double measure of Glenfiddich single malt in lieu of his favourite Laphroaig and checking out what he could find online concerning the recent accidental death of a Berlin reporter. Fritz Kohler, 35, a journalist for a well-known, left-leaning newspaper (weren't they all these days), had been found dead by a railway line on the edge of the city. The alleged 'accident' had happened on the evening of the same day as the attack on Kaprisky's home. Ben tended to think Mia was right about her fiancé's death having been no coincidence.

He was about to widen his search for more information about Kohler when one of the Gulfstream crew came to say that they were ready to leave. As he was boarding the plane, Ben was able to catch a moment to speak to the co-pilot, a guy called Michel whom he'd got to know quite well from his previous flights. As casually as possible, Ben asked Michel about their recent trip to Berlin, two days before the attack. Michel looked downcast at the mention of what had happened. They were all deeply upset over it.

'Did the boss happen to say anything about why he was going there, who he was meeting with?' Ben asked. It was a long shot, but Auguste might have mentioned something in passing to these guys who'd flown him around for years.

'No, he never talks to us about business. His being there, is that the reason we're going back?'

'I think it might be,' Ben said. He made his way into the cabin and settled in his seat, deep in thought.

The jet left Miami at 19.18, local time. Eight hours and forty minutes later they touched down at Berlin Brandenburg Airport, just another transglobal hop and a skip for the Gulfstream and its single passenger. Berlin being six time zones ahead of Florida, it was now almost ten in the morning there. Ben had had plenty of opportunity for a decent night's rest in the ultra-luxurious cabin, but he'd been too troubled by nagging thoughts to sleep much. Partially restored by a breakfast consisting of three strong black coffees gulped down in quick succession, he emerged into the German drizzle. After another cursory customs wave-through, a pretty airport staffer called Liesl escorted him to a parking area where another car was waiting for him, again courtesy of the Kaprisky business expenses account.

When in Germany, you drive a Mercedes: in this case a sleek S-class sports saloon. Ben signed for the keys, jumped in and was about to get moving when his phone began to vibrate in his pocket.

The caller ID was Valentina's. As he answered it, his immediate instinct told him that something bad had happened. That Auguste was dead. Or that there'd been another attack. His imagination mushroomed.

'Ben, he moved his finger!' she almost yelled with excitement the instant he answered the call. 'They let me sit with him for a little while this morning and I was holding his hand, and he actually moved his finger! He was able to lift it right up and sort of waggle it. He did it twice. His eyes were closed, but I'm certain he knew I was there. It was as if he was trying to communicate with me. I'm sure of it! Oh, Ben!'

His heart lit up inside him. 'That's fantastic, Valentina.'

'Isn't it just? Maybe there's a chance . . . oh God, I can hardly dare to think it . . . I'm so terrified I can hardly breathe . . . but maybe he's going to recover!'

'You want me back there?' he offered.

'No, you have things to do. Gabriel says you're going to Germany.'

Ben thought she was going to ask him why, but then a sudden and dramatic change in her tone of voice made him realise that she had something else on her mind. 'But listen, that's not all I was calling about,' she said sombrely. 'Inspector Boche called me a few minutes ago. They've found something.'

The tension that had drained out of him on hearing the good news came flooding back just as quickly, and he clutched the phone tight against his ear. 'What?'

'It was exactly as you said, Ben. It happened early this morning. A man was walking his dogs in the woods just a few kilometres from the estate when they came across an abandoned van. It had been set on fire. Completely gutted. He called the police.'

'Annick's van?'

'Yes. That thing you said about the engine and chassis numbers? They've checked and it turns out it's the real van. Everything just the way you predicted. And .. .' – she took a deep breath before saying it – 'they found a body inside. '

Ben didn't have to make any kind of a wild guess as to whose it was. 'Georges?'

'They're almost sure it's him. Though it's hard to tell. He's . . . he's all burnt up, Ben.' She sounded as if she wanted to throw up. 'And half his head is missing from where they shot him before they torched the van. The police are going to have to use dental records to check it's really him. Someone has to go down to the morgue in Le Mans to identify him as well. His parents are old and sick and the poor things must be in a state of shock, so I've offered to do it in their place. One of the security men will drive me there.'

'I'm sorry you have to go through that, Valentina.'

'I'll be all right,' she said stoically. 'I've done it before, you know. When Maman and Papa died. So now this whole

142

place is full of police again. They've taken away the fake van that was dressed up to look like Annick's, and they're going to take it apart and go through everything for more clues. Though I don't believe they'll find anything you didn't already work out.' She paused. 'I haven't told the police about you, Ben. Gabriel's been going on at me that the authorities need to be kept informed, but I've ordered him to keep your name strictly out of it. I hope that was the right thing to do. I see this as a family matter. And as far as I'm concerned, you're part of the family.'

Ben was touched by her words. 'You did the right thing, Valentina. The less I have them breathing down my back, the better.'

'I don't know why you had to go to America and Germany,' she said. 'And I'm not going to ask. All that's important to me is that you catch these men.'

'I found out some things. I'm going to find out more.'

'I'm trying too,' she said. 'That strange key we found in Tonton's safe? I've been testing it on every lock I could find, everywhere in the house. Of course it might be a key to something that's not in the house. But I'll keep on.'

'You do that. Take care, Valentina.'

The Mercedes started up with a blast from its quad exhausts and Ben roared away from the airport. Valentina's update had left him with mixed feelings as he spurred the fast saloon on its twenty-kilometre northward journey towards the heart of the city. He was just as excited as she was to hear that Auguste might be working his way back to some kind of recovery. But now that the layers of this whole intrigue were slowly peeling apart in his mind as he learned

143

more, his thoughts were haunted by a looming new sense of danger, as yet undefined, gathering in the distance like dark storm clouds.

That was what had been keeping him awake through the night. Around two in the morning, too unsettled to sleep, he'd delved deeper into Fritz Kohler's internet presence and found his journalism blog, with links to a number of articles he'd written in the past. The guy was more than just some lefty newspaper hack. He was a full-blown investigative journalist of the old school, specialising in exposing corporate corruption, dirty dealings and high-level fraud. He hadn't been afraid to take aim at some pretty mighty targets in his time, including a major German banking conglomerate exposed in a scandal over risky mortgage-backed securities – stuff that was over Ben's head but had resulted in a class-action lawsuit worth a few billion, thanks partly to the revelations from Kohler's research – and a leading motor manufacturer suspected, and later charged, for falsifying emissions data. Some important players had got their fingers burned in that one, and again Fritz had been right in the middle of it.

A professional dirt-digger like Fritz Kohler was bound to have made a few powerful enemies over the years. The kind who might show their gratitude by having you 'accidentally' squashed by a speeding train. Guys like him were magnets for trouble. You didn't go to them unless you had a particular reason for doing so. Specifically, unless you had certain information to pass on.

Which could only make Ben wonder what on earth Auguste Kaprisky was doing, flying off to Berlin to meet with someone like Fritz Kohler? Within days of that mysterious meeting one man had come close to being killed, and the other was now thoroughly dead.

Something was unfolding here. Something that Ben didn't like at all. What dangerous secrets were locked away inside the old man's comatose brain? Whose interests did it serve if they remained hidden in there for ever? More disturbingly, what might be the consequences if he recovered from his coma with his memory intact?

Ben couldn't mention these misgivings to Valentina. He was just going to have to find out more.

His destination was Mia Brockhaus's workplace, the offices of Hoffmann Design, which were located in a central business district near Potsdamer Platz. He cut through the heavy Berlin traffic with Courtney Pine playing live in concert on a radio jazz station, his wipers beating away the light rain and Gauloise smoke trickling out of his open window. It was sultry and humid, the sky a mass of scudding grey cloud. Welcome home to Europe. A long way from the waving palm trees, white sands and superyachts of Miami Beach and the Bahamas, but such was the life of the hard-pressed sleuth in search of clues and, so far, finding little of any real value.

The Hoffmann Design building was a slick modern steel and glass affair on Leipziger Strasse, a stone's throw from the Berlin Spy Museum. It was nearly eleven in the morning. Ben found a parking spot where he could observe the building's entrance. From what Mia Brockhaus had told him over the phone he expected her to be at the office today, preferring to bury herself in her work rather than sit pointlessly grieving at home. And she'd said she would be using her lunch break to return to Fritz's apartment, to go on trying to tidy the place out. All the same, it was worth checking, so he pulled the company phone number from their website and called reception to ask politely whether Fräulein Brockhaus was available. 'Hold on, please,' said the receptionist. Then, 'Shall I put you through?'

Ben said, 'Sorry, I have a call on the other line. I'll phone again later. Thank you,' and hung up.

So now all he had to do was sit and wait. He'd eaten nothing since his fast food in Miami, and even though he wasn't hungry he was concerned about getting low on calories. He left the car briefly to hurry up the street and grab a coffee and a doughnut from a food stand. The doughnut was one of those with no hole in the middle, filled with jelly and called a Berliner. When John F. Kennedy had proclaimed to a bemused West German public in 1963 that '*Ich bin ein Berliner*', he'd been describing himself as one of these very same jelly doughnuts. Ben ate his presidential snack and drank his coffee at the wheel of the Mercedes, and went on waiting. He'd done a lot of that in his career, whether it was urban surveillance like this or sitting in a hole in the ground with a rifle, waiting for the enemy to show themselves. He was good at it.

Time passed. The sugary doughnut had done its job but he was still tired from his sleepless night, and risked another run up the street for more caffeine. German coffee might just be about the worst in Europe, almost as bad as what they dished out to you in Britain. He soldiered through a second cup of the bitter brew and went on watching the Hoffmann Design office entrance. A few people came and went, but none of them was Mia Brockhaus. At 11.39 a.m. an electrician's van arrived and the guy disappeared inside the building, returning back and forth a few times to fetch tools and equipment from his van. He had a big belly and a bushy moustache. and definitely wasn't Mia Brockhaus either.

Then just after 12.20 p.m. Ben saw a slim, petite dark-haired woman matching the photo on the company website emerge from the glass doors, wearing a light blue jacket and carrying a small handbag, and hurry over to a little white Opel Corsa hatchback in the staff car park.

He said, '*Guten Tag*, Mia.'

Ben started up the Mercedes, tossed his crumpled coffee cups and doughnut wrapper in the back like a real police detective, waited for the Opel to filter out into the traffic and then followed her at a discreet distance, leaving two or three cars between them but careful not to let her slip away from him at a traffic light.

It was a long drive across much of Berlin, heading north and east into what had once been the communist-controlled sector the other side of the wall. Several times he nearly lost her, when a bus or lorry would block her from his view and he was worried she might have taken some unexpected turning or disappeared down a side street. The Opel led him into an area of old East Berlin called Friedrichshain and down a long avenue called Karl-Marx-Allee where many of the lugubrious apartment blocks dated back to the brutalist architectural style of the Stalinist era. Some parts of Friedrichshain appeared more gentrified, slowly evolving away from their Cold War days to become hip and trendy, but the street where Fritz Kohler had lived wasn't one of

147

them. Mia pulled up at the kerb outside a slab-sided, dirt-streaked older apartment building.

As Ben drove slowly past he watched her get out of her car, looking uptight and tense and clutching her handbag, and scamper nervously towards the mouth of a narrow alley to the side of the building. He ducked into a parking space across the street, walked quickly in the direction she'd gone and reached the alley just in time to see her disappear into a doorway.

He followed. The alley was dingy and uninviting, and would be very dark at night. He could see why she didn't like coming here alone. But it was easy to imagine why a guy like Fritz Kohler would have chosen to live here, as a kind of political statement. The abode of the rebellious investigative reporter, Man of the People, dedicated to taking down the corrupt structures of capitalism everywhere. If the relationship had lasted long enough for them to get married, Ben suspected that Fritz's lifestyle choices might have become a bone of contention for the couple.

The interior was as stark and bleak as the outside. The entrance lobby had cracked plaster on the walls, no lift and a square spiral stairway. Peering upwards Ben could see Mia climbing the steps towards the second floor. He followed quickly and silently, padding up the staircase two stairs at a time after her. There were four apartments on each landing. As he reached the second he saw one door partly ajar and could hear sounds of someone moving about inside.

He slipped into the apartment. Mia Brockhaus was in a living room at the end of a long, narrow passage. She'd left her handbag on a small table in the hall where the landline telephone was, hung up her blue jacket and put on the kettle in the tiny, bachelor-esque kitchenette to brew some tea while she got on with her work.

The living room was a bomb site, even worse than she'd described it on the phone. Whoever had burgled the place had pretty much torn it apart. Books and papers littered the floor, furniture had been upended, drawers tipped out, all the usual hallmarks of the classic ransacking job Ben had seen many times before. Mia stood in the middle of the chaos with her hands on her hips and shaking her head in helplessness as though wondering how she could get through it all. There were already four large black garbage sacks full of stuff, and enough mess everywhere to fill another dozen. It was clear she had an almost impossible task on her hands.

Ben stepped into the living room behind her. She whirled around with a sharp gasp as she saw him, and backed away in alarm. He held up his palms to show he was no threat. 'Easy, Fräulein Brockhaus,' he said in German. 'I'm sorry I frightened you.'

'Who are you? How do you know my name?'

'I'm the man you talked to on the phone last night,' he replied. 'Now I'm here in Berlin, because I wanted to speak to you in person.'

'Herr Peters? Justin Peters from London? What are you doing here? How did you find this place? What's going on?' The terror was imprinted on her face.

'I'm not going to hurt you, Mia. Trust me, that's the last thing I'd want to do. But I lied to you last night. My name's not Justin Peters, it's Ben Hope. Call me Ben. I understand

149

you have a lot of questions. So do I, but I'll try to explain all I can.'

'You said you were a friend of Fritz!'

'I lied about that too, Mia. I never met your fiancé. I'm working on behalf of the man I believe Fritz had a meeting with the day before he was murdered.'

At the sound of that word, she flinched as though she'd been slapped across the face. Ben saw her shocked expression and nodded. 'That's right. Like you, I don't think that what happened to Fritz was a coincidence and I'd like to talk to you about it.'

'W-why me?' she stammered.

'Because people are dying,' Ben said. 'And we need to figure out why.'

Chapter 19

Twelve hours earlier

Nearly five thousand miles away, Lucas Dennim lay sprawled out half drunk in his recliner on *Spirit Dancer*'s deck. His state of mind was not good. After the departure of his unexpected visitor that afternoon, he'd got Candi to fetch him a six-pack of beer from the galley fridge. When he'd finished gulping that one down he'd got her to bring him another, in the hope that getting filthy drunk would alleviate his crippling feelings of shame and guilt over the things Ben Hope had told him.

It hadn't worked too well, so far. Now the deck was littered with empties, rolling from side to side across the varnished planking from rail to rail with the gentle rocking of the yacht. Dennim sat watching their back and forth motion as though hypnotised, his head swimming from the booze. Nothing mattered to him: not the radiant warmth of the sun soaking into his bones, not the blue sky and ocean all around him, not even the allure of the half-naked Candi hovering around the deck and attending to his every need, her long blond hair golden against the caramel tan of her skin, her bare feet padding over the boards, the dazzling charm of her smile. He was oblivious of the whole lot of it, because all he could think about was what an idiot he'd been. Thanks to him, thanks to his weakness and stupidity and pathetic greed, all his former colleagues were dead and gone. He'd betrayed them, abandoned them, and now their wives were widows and their kids were fatherless, and all for the sake of five lousy million euros. He would give it all back in a heartbeat to be able to undo what he'd done. The feelings of regret and self-blame were killing him, making his head throb and his stomach muscles knot up and his neck as tight and hard as a palm trunk. The tension was unbearable. When he tried to roll his head around, he could feel something crackling and popping in there.

'Candi?' His voice sounded thick and slurry from all the drink.

'Yes, babe?' Instantly attentive, ready to obey his every command. 'You want some more beer?'

He shook his head no, and winced at the pain it caused. 'Need a massage,' he slurred.

'Sure thing, honey,' she replied, beaming at him with those amazingly perfect white teeth. 'Whatever you want.'

Whatever I want, eh, he thought bitterly as she vanished below. She reappeared a few moments later carrying her lightweight folding massage bed, a towel, some oils and a little zippered pouch that presumably contained more of her muscle-relaxing gizmos. She might be as dumb as a box of rocks but when it came to massage, she was a world-class expert.

'Come and make yourself comfortable, honey,' she cooed, setting the bed on the deck. Clumsy and discoordinated from the beer, he heaved himself out of his recliner and she helped him off with his shirt. 'Jeez, look at you, you're all bruised,' she commented, eyeing the fresh marks that the fight had left on his arms and chest. 'That Ben Hope guy really beat the crap outta you.'

'Leave him out of it,' Dennim muttered incoherently. 'He's a good man. The best. He's the only friend I have left.'

'Sure, honey. Lie down, now.'

He did as she said, flat on his belly with his arms hanging down limp to the deck. 'You just relax, my poor sweet baby,' said her soothing voice in his ear. 'Close your eyes and lie still, and I'll soon make you feel better.'

This was just what he needed, he thought as he closed his eyes and let himself begin to drift. Thank goodness for Candi and her magic healing touch. As she got to work he felt her splash a little oil on one shoulder, then the other; then her strong, lithe hands began to caress and knead his tense, tight muscles. 'Hmmm,' he mumbled dreamily, 'that feels better already. Up a bit. Left a bit. There. Oh, yes. That's it. Don't stop.'

'Hold on, honey,' said her soft, comforting voice. 'I've got something here that will help you even more.' She paused what she was doing, and from far away in his reverie he heard the sound of her unzipping the little pouch she'd brought up from below deck. 'This is something really special,' she purred. 'Just for you.'

'Hmmm.' His lips curled into a little smile of anticipation. As the tension drained out of his body, the pressure inside his head was already easing and those tormenting guilty feelings were melting away. 'You're such a treasure, Candi,' he murmured. 'An angel sent from heaven. I'm so glad I found you.'

Where he'd actually found her was in a bar in Coconut Grove, within easy staggering distance of his condo. He'd been hanging around the place for three afternoons in a row, throwing dollars around, buying rounds, his cash-stuffed wallet lying on the bar next to him for all to see and his expensive new gold watch on open display. On the fourth afternoon he'd been sitting on a bar stool nursing his fifth or sixth beer and idly watching some baseball game on the TV in the corner when she'd appeared as if out of nowhere, this goddess in painted-on jeans and a skimpy top that exposed her tanned, toned midriff, and perched her perfect form on the empty stool next to his. He'd been fully aware of all the other guys in the bar craning their necks to ogle her, while to his amazement he'd been the one she'd seemed to exclusively want to latch onto.

Dennim wasn't an idiot – not in his opinion, anyway. He'd been around and knew how the game worked. And yet this beautiful girl truly didn't appear interested in him for his money. There was a real connection there as she sat very close, drank all the drinks he bought her, laughed at his lame jokes and smiled that beguiling smile, her long-lashed blue eyes, deep as lagoons, never leaving his. Having this sensational young lady pay him all that attention made him feel like a teenager again. She said she was a masseuse – and we all know what *that* means, Dennim had thought to himself.

Naturally, he'd done all he could to impress her with his newfound wealth. At the mention of his latest acquisition, his pride and joy moored in the marina just down the street, she'd been blown away with excitement and readily accepted his invitation to come sailing around the islands with him the next day. They'd barely been a hundred metres from shore when off had come the bikini top and he'd thought his eyes were going to pop out.

That yacht trip had been followed by another, then another. She seemed to enjoy hanging around him. So far, none of the hot action he'd droolingly anticipated had come about. But it was surely only a matter of time before his charms won her over all the way.

At least, that's what had been predominantly on his mind, until the sudden and very unexpected arrival of Ben Hope and the deeply unnerving news he'd brought with him had wiped away all Dennim's enthusiasm. Now Dennim couldn't have risen to the occasion even if the bikini bottom had come off too.

Back in his present reality, he murmured, 'Come on, baby, that felt so good. Keep going.'

'Don't you worry about a thing, honey,' cooed her sugary voice, so close and yet so far away. 'You just lie still and let me take care of you. It'll all be over in a minute, you'll see.'

From somewhere in the back of his brain came the thought, '*What* will all be over in a minute?' But as soon as it formed it drifted away again, like a cloud on the ocean breeze.

And then the cold steel of the ice pick pierced deep into the base of his neck. A howling scream wanted to erupt from his lips and he tried desperately to struggle, but Candi was an expert at more things than massage. The long, slim, needle-pointed spike had penetrated with surgical precision right through to his spinal cord, causing instant catastrophic damage and already shutting down much of his central nervous system so that he could do no more than open and close his mouth soundlessly, like a landed fish skewered on a hook.

With the last bit of strength left in his body he managed to twist his head upwards, and caught a glimpse of her face looking down at him. He saw a hard, fierce expression in those lovely blue eyes that he'd never seen before. Saw her slim fingers wrapped around the handle of the ice pick buried in his neck, the red of his own blood. The gold of her hair and the blue of the sky above her. And then the darkness rose up like a black mist and he saw nothing more at all.

When Lucas Dennim was dead, Candi withdrew the steel spike, wiped it clean and zipped it back inside its pouch. Then she left him lying there on the massage bed and calmly paced down the companionway to the below-deck cabin where she kept her things. Taking a two-way radio handset from her bag she turned it to the preset frequency channel.

'It's done. Come and get me.' She spoke using her real voice, which was lower in pitch than the squeaky tones 'Candi' had talked in, and had a completely different accent that wasn't easily pinned to any particular nationality but certainly wasn't American. She didn't need to tell her radio contact where she was. The GPS tracking device had been planted aboard *Spirit Dancer* days earlier, so the handlers onshore knew exactly where to send the helicopter.

It wasn't the first time she'd been in contact with them that day. While Dennim had been lounging in his recliner knocking back his six-packs earlier, she had slipped quietly away to inform her handlers of the surprise visitor who'd turned up in a seaplane that afternoon. She'd given them his name, an accurate physical description and a concise report of the conversation he'd had with the asset. The handlers' response had been as she'd expected, issuing her with the order to terminate Dennim without delay. 'Candi' would then cease to exist, and return to her base where she would await the instructions directing her to her next job.

She anticipated that the helicopter would take about thirty minutes to get here. She used that time to wash the blood off herself in the water, then climb back aboard and dispose of the bikini and the blond wig and change into jeans and a T-shirt and a pair of sandals. There was still a large amount of blood pooling on the deck and seeping through the cracks in the planking, but that was of no importance: the evidence would be erased soon enough. Dennim's death would not officially have been caused by a stab wound. The deep puncture wound made by the ice pick's long, thin blade would show as no more than a tiny red hole on the back of his neck, barely noticeable from the outside and all but completely erased once she'd finished with him. The pathologist would write it up as death by misadventure. That had already been taken care of.

The chopper arrived shortly afterwards, right on cue. It hovered low over the boat, whipping up the water with the blast of its rotors. Her Miami contact appeared in the open side hatch, signalling down at her and dropping down a rope ladder to the deck. The last two tasks she performed while still on board *Spirit Dancer* were to douse the body with gasoline and arm the detonator of the compact but powerful explosive device in her bag. Then she clambered nimbly up the rope ladder, her short, spiked black hair ruffling from the downdraught of the rotors.

As the chopper regained altitude and sped away from the drifting yacht, she took out the bomb remote. 'Nice knowing you, moron,' she said as she thumbed the trigger.

Spirit Dancer was instantly engulfed in a violent explosion that shattered her hull like an eggshell and swept a wave of ultra-hot fire over her deck, consuming everything in its path. The mast toppled sideways, making the blazing vessel list to starboard. Nothing of Dennim's remains could be seen through the raging flames. In moments the onboard gas cylinders ruptured in the heat and a secondary blast ripped the bottom out of the yacht.

The chopper banked around for a few sweeping passes, until the fiery wreck finally slipped beneath the waves taking the charred body of its owner down to the ocean floor with it. Just a scattering of smoking debris floated on the surface. Soon that would disperse on the waves, leaving little trace of *Spirit Dancer*'s existence for the coastguard divers to find – and none whatsoever of that of the mysterious Candi.

The watchers on the helicopter had seen all they needed to see. The pilot levelled out and started heading back towards the Florida coast.

Chapter 20

'You want to talk?' said Mia Brockhaus. 'Okay, then let's talk. But you first. Then I'll decide if I can trust you or not. You could be anybody.'

'You're right to be careful, Mia.' Ben showed her his Le Val trainer's card. 'I used to be a soldier. I became quite good at it. Later I started using the skills I'd learned to help find people who'd become the victims of kidnappers.'

She carefully examined the card, then handed it back to him. 'That's an unusual kind of occupation. I didn't realise anyone did that. Other than the police, I mean.'

'It's a bad world out there,' Ben said. 'Someone has to try to make things right.'

'May I ask what made you become involved in it?'

He sensed that she was sounding him out, still trying to decide whether to trust him. Plain open sincerity and human empathy were the best ways to gain that trust. 'My little sister,' Ben said. 'She was taken captive by human traffickers in Morocco when she was a child. I was just a few years older when it happened, and it changed my life.'

She was looking at him differently now. '*Mein Gott*, that's terrible. Did you ever find her?'

'Let's just say Ruth is alive and well and living in Switzerland now. Not every story has such a happy ending.'

'Is that what you're doing now? Looking for someone in trouble?'

He shook his head. 'I wish I was. Because then there'd be a chance of rescuing these people's victim before any harm had been done. It's too late for that. A friend of mine was shot. I'm looking for the people who did it.'

'I'm sorry.'

'So am I. And I'm sorrier now, since I heard what you had to say. I believe the same people who broke into my friend's home, killed a lot of innocent people there and left him in a coma are responsible for what happened to Fritz.'

Mia was listening hard and connecting ideas together in her mind. 'You said Fritz had a meeting with this person the day before.'

'At eleven the previous morning, at the tea room at the Ritz Carlton hotel here in Berlin. My friend travelled from France to Germany to talk to him. I discovered it from his diary, which only gave the time and date of the appointment and Fritz's initials and phone numbers. That's why I had to pretend to be someone else, when I called you. I had no idea who I was even calling.'

'I understand,' she said. 'So how much do you know about this meeting?'

He replied, 'Only that it must have been very important for each of them. And it seems it was also very important to the people who wanted to eliminate them both. My friend is, or was, a wealthy and influential man with a lot of high-level connections in the world of business and politics. Your fiancé specialised in exposing wrongdoing in that same world. Putting it together, I'd take a wild guess that the purpose of their meeting was to pass on some information that my friend felt Fritz should know about. But perhaps you can tell me more.'

He sensed she could. That she was holding back from revealing everything until she'd finished fishing for everything he knew. She was a perceptive, quick-witted woman. There was a lot of intelligence shining through the pain in her eyes.

Mia sighed. 'You have to understand, Fritz had his own views about the world. His ideas could be somewhat radical. That's why he left the first big newspaper he worked for, because they were too mainstream. He and they didn't see eye to eye on the issues he felt really mattered most. Then when we started going out together two years ago, he used to tell me some things. I found it hard to accept them at first, because I'd never met anyone like him before. In fact to be honest I thought some of the things he told me were plain crazy. I was ready to dismiss them as conspiracy theories, paranoid fantasies. We used to argue about it.'

'It's not a theory any more,' Ben said. 'Not when someone's really out to get you.'

'Fritz was convinced, and became more convinced as time went by, that the world is run by just a handful of people, very powerful people. That these few people control virtually everything: the media, business, science, technology, politics, government policy, even our health and education. Going by that worldview this control is global, and getting tighter and more orchestrated every day. He believed these controllers, these elites as he called them, had for years been systematically burrowing deeper and deeper into every aspect of our lives, furthering their influence over everything we do or even think, so that eventually they would own us completely and take away any kind of freedoms we ever had, turning our whole civilisation into a dystopian nightmare. And that most people are completely blind to the fact that we're already nine tenths of the way there.'

'Fritz wouldn't be the only person to hold those ideas,' Ben said.

Mia shrugged. 'Of course I was never brought up with such notions. I came from a very safe, happy background. A loving and supportive family, a stable home. I thought the world was a wonderful place and people who thought this way must be very unhappy at best, maybe even crazy. But Fritz was the least crazy person I've ever met, and so that confused me even more, because surely this stuff he was so passionate about couldn't be true? Could it? I didn't know. I'm an interior designer. I'm not interested in politics or economics, but Fritz was really into that whole world and spent hours reading and researching. He wrote a blog and posted videos on alternative media platforms that attracted hundreds of thousands of views. Then he was employed by another newspaper, one much more in line with his ideas. His opinions were gaining traction. Meanwhile he was pursuing an independent career, hounding dishonest politicians, businesspeople, state officials, revealing their lies and hypocrisy to the public. He's never looked back.'

'I've seen some of his work,' Ben said kindly. 'He was very clever and dedicated. People like him make the world a better place.'

'If you had known him, you'd know there was much more he was working on besides what he made public. Things even he was afraid to write about or even talk about to the wrong person. Even to me.' She fell silent for a moment. 'Then quite recently he was approached by someone very important. He didn't tell me who, but he was terribly excited about it. This person apparently had some explosive information to share, and wanted to meet him.'

'Do you know why?'

She shook her head and looked sad. 'I wish I could say yes. Or perhaps it's better not to know. As I said, he didn't tell me everything. For my own protection, he used to say. And so all I can tell you is that what this man, your friend, was offering to reveal to Fritz was something huge, massive. A bombshell, Fritz kept saying. He couldn't wait for the meeting. Afterwards he called me to say that the things he'd learned were even more amazing than he'd imagined. And that was just a taste of it, apparently. There was more to come, much more.'

'They were planning on talking again?'

'Yes, it was only a preliminary meeting. But even so Fritz sounded quite blown away by what the man had revealed to him. Shaken up, even. Fritz always said that nothing could surprise him any more. He wasn't easily shocked. But this was different.'

'He didn't say what it was that had shocked him so much?' Ben asked, wondering what the hell Auguste Kaprisky could possibly have passed onto him that was this explosive. 'Not even a clue?'

'I think he was going to. He sounded as though he was bursting to share it with someone. We arranged to get together for dinner that night, at a restaurant near my office that we often visit. When I got there, there was no sign of him. It wasn't like him to be late. I tried calling and texting him, left several messages, but there was no reply. After an hour I was starting to get really worried, but what could I do but just go home and keep trying to phone him?

'Next morning, still no reply. Then my phone rang and I thought it was him. I was so relieved. I expected he'd be full of apologies, saying something had come up, wanting to meet for lunch and tell me all his news.' She shook her head. 'How naive I must be. Instead it was the police, calling to inform me that my fiancé had been hit by a train and killed. I was so stunned I couldn't speak, couldn't breathe. Next thing I knew, I was having to go to the morgue to identify him. It was awful. Every time I shut my eyes I can see him lying there. There was hardly anything left of him.'

Mia's voice had been growing more strained as she talked, and now she broke down into floods of tears. But under all that bitter sorrow was a hard core of red-hot rage, and it was the rage that was keeping her going. It made Ben think of Valentina, and what she was going through. It made him think of himself, too, when the worst things had happened in his own life.

When her crying had subsided she went on, 'The accident happened on a quiet stretch of the Stadtbahn network near the Charlottenburg district, right out to the west of the city. It makes no sense. The police found his old Volvo parked among the bushes a short distance from the railway line. His phone was inside. That's how they got my number. I'd been calling and calling him all through the night.'

'Do they know what he was doing there?'

'They don't know anything,' she replied, dabbing her eyes with a tissue from her pocket. 'Just that his bloodstream was full of alcohol. That's apparently all the evidence they need to concoct their theory. The official story is that Fritz got blind drunk, drove aimlessly around the city until he was completely lost and confused, then abandoned the car and wandered off on foot. Then he somehow managed to stumble onto the railway line, where he must have fallen unconscious. The train driver never even saw him.'

Ben's next question was a necessary but difficult one to ask. 'Mia, can we know for sure that's not what actually happened to him?'

'Yes, we can be totally sure of that,' she snapped back, flashing an angry look at him. 'Because my Fritzi didn't get drunk, not ever. Everyone who knows him knows this. Many times I've heard him tell the story of how he once drank a whole bottle of spirits when he was a student and made himself ill, and vowed never to intoxicate himself like that again. A glass of wine at Christmas, the occasional light beer at a barbecue party, but that was his absolute limit. If there was a large amount of alcohol inside his body when he died, it's because somebody put it there. You can believe me or not, I don't care. I know the truth.'

'I do believe you,' Ben said. 'It's the oldest trick in the book. But I had to ask. Did you mention this to the police?'

'Of course I did, and all I got was the brush-off. Oh, but don't you know, your boyfriend just fell off the wagon. A secret drinker who managed to get himself found out the hard way. All that *scheisse*. And it's just a coincidence that his apartment gets turned over at the same time. Hey, burglaries happen.'

'You think the burglars were looking for material that Fritz might have been passed at the meeting?'

'What else? This meeting is the reason he's dead, pure and simple. That's what I think. And you think it too.'

Ben said nothing.

She looked at him. 'We've only just met and I don't know you very well. But from what you've told me I understand that you're a man of justice. And you were a soldier. What will you do?'

'What the police won't,' Ben said.

She nodded. A silence fell between them for a few moments. They could hear a siren passing by in the street outside. It wailed off into the distance. Then Mia said, 'There's something I haven't told you. But I think I trust you now. I'm going to tell you.'

'I appreciate your trust, Mia. I know how difficult this is for you.'

'You asked me just now if the people who did this' – she motioned around her at the mess of overturned furniture and Fritz's possessions scattered all over the floor – 'were hunting for something Fritz might have brought away from the meeting. Information, evidence, whatever that "something" might be. Well, if that's what they were after, they wouldn't have found it here at his apartment. He was far too clever for that. And far too careful. You can imagine that some of the investigations he was involved in were often risky, even potentially deadly. Over the years he and his associates have exposed corruption at the highest levels of the corporate establishment. We're talking about powerful people. It's not unknown for investigative journalists who probed a little too deep into secret affairs to disappear in the middle of the night, never to be seen again. Or to be found dead from suicide. The kind of suicide where the person somehow managed to blow out their brains with their hands tied behind their back, and dispose of the gun afterwards.'

'That kind,' Ben said with a grim smile.

'And so, Fritz was sometimes in possession of certain documents, photographs, recorded evidence and other material that he couldn't afford to be caught with. For his own protection, and the protection of his sources.'

'You're saying he had a secret hiding place for that material.'

She nodded anxiously. 'Somewhere nobody would know about or be able to find. If Fritz *was* given anything at the meeting, then that's where he'd have put it. He had several hours free between when the meeting ended and our dinner date. Plenty of time to drive there and stash whatever it was away safely. It's not very far away. A little over an hour's drive from Berlin.'

Ben realised this new revelation could blow the lid off the whole mystery. 'And do you—?' he began.

'Know where it is?' She gave another furtive nod. 'I do know. Fritz once told me that if anything should happen to him, someone else ought to be informed of where the information was kept secure, so that it wouldn't be lost. Someone unconnected with his work, someone he trusted never to tell a soul. Now here I am, revealing his secrets to a stranger. It's a rundown old house in the countryside, rented for cash under a fake name. Beneath the house is a disused cellar where they used to store cheese. He called it his hidden grotto. It's where he stashed all his materials.' She added bitterly, 'He even used to joke sometimes about how he could use the place as a safehouse to hide out in, if his work ever got him into trouble with the bad guys. He thought that was funny. Ha.'

Ben asked, 'Have you been to this place since he was killed?'

She shook her head emphatically and replied, 'Frankly, after what's happened, I've been terrified to know too much about what Fritz had got himself into. I haven't been near the place and I don't want to. This is all too hot for me to handle on my own.'

'Except you're not on your own any more,' Ben said. 'I'm here now.'

'I . . . I don't have time for this,' she stammered. 'I have to get back to work.'

He shook his head. 'Under the circumstances, I don't think your boss will hold it against you if you take the afternoon off. Why don't we get in my car, and then you can take me to the old cellar?'

She reluctantly agreed, then retrieved her handbag from the stand in the hallway, locked up Fritz's apartment, and they headed back down the stairs to the alleyway. Ben led her across the street to where the Mercedes was parked. As they drove off, she directed him northwards away from Friedrichshain and took out her phone to call the office and say she wouldn't be back in that afternoon.

Ben drove. They'd done so much talking already that they lapsed mostly into silence, each preoccupied with their own thoughts, Mia now and again pointing out the way ahead. He felt he was getting close to the truth now. But what lay in store, he still had no idea.

And if he hadn't been so focused on those troubling concerns, then perhaps he'd have noticed the metallic brown Volkswagen Tiguan SUV that had been parked up the street from Fritz's place and was now on their tail, threading discreetly through the traffic a few cars behind them.

Chapter 21

Fritz Kohler's secret safehouse was tucked away in wooded countryside near the town of Lübbenau, some eighty kilometres to the southeast of the city. It might have taken Fritz an hour to get there in his old Volvo, but Ben planned on getting there much more quickly. As he blasted down the highway he checked in again on Jeff to find out how things were moving along with the recruitment of the Kaprisky estate's new security team. Jeff now had seven strong possibles, six of whom were firmly committed and waiting for their green light.

'We need to revise that number,' Ben said. 'I want a couple of extra guys on Auguste at all times. And on Valentina too. She could be a target. Call it a ten, no, a twelve-man team, if you can get them.'

Jeff instantly understood that Ben's concerns had grown much more serious since last time they'd spoken. 'Jesus Christ, sounds like we're raising a bloody army here. What's going on, mate?'

'Let's just say the old man might have got himself in deeper than we reckoned on,' Ben said.

'Silly old bugger. Copy that. I'll be in touch.'

'Who are Auguste and Valentina?' Mia asked when Ben got off the phone.

'A couple of people who mean a lot to me,' he replied. 'And I'm damned if I'll let any harm come to them. Or to you, Mia,' he added. 'That's a promise.'

'I feel as if I'm locked in some kind of nightmare. When does this end?'

'When Fritz and all the other victims get what's coming to them.'

'It's not enough. It will never be enough.'

From the highway they turned off the main roads into a countryside region called the Spreewald, a river delta filled with waterways and forest. Mia explained that it was a protected nature reserve and largely a tourist attraction, famous for its flora and fauna, its pretty villages and hundreds of canals – but some parts were less developed and remained pretty much the way they'd been during the more austere days when the then DDR had been under Communist rule.

It was in one of those areas that Fritz had found his safehouse, an old-time dairy built on a scrap of farmland surrounded by forest and marshland. He'd always expected that one day the place would be snapped up by some property developer, but until that day came, the cheap rent and the remote location made it the perfect hiding place for his sensitive data.

The winding country roads forced him to slow down a little as they cut deeper into the Spreewald. They passed through picture-postcard villages, over old stone bridges and along the banks of canals. Locals still navigated the waterways in traditional flat-bottomed boats and punts, some of them sturdy enough to transport heavy cargo, farm machinery and livestock feed. It seemed like another world after the cut and thrust of the modern city. The further they ventured, the more the villages thinned out and the forest thickened. By now the road had narrowed to a single track with a ridge of tall grass growing down its middle.

'That's the place there,' Mia said, pointing through the trees. Around the next bend was a dilapidated gateway, where the track narrowed even more with overgrown foliage encroaching on both sides that scraped the car's windows as they went bumping and jolting up to the old farmhouse.

It was immediately clear why the place was so cheap to rent. The tumbledown outbuildings were only in slightly worse repair than the farmhouse itself, whose woodwork was badly rotted, its roofline slumped in the middle like a prolapsed spine between its two chimneys, and several of its windows broken or fallen out. An old grain silo and milk pumping machinery stood slowly disintegrating with rust. The adjoining fields where the dairy farmer had once grazed his cattle were a jungle of reclaimed forest. Ben rolled the car to a halt on the weed-strewn yard, and they got out. Recent heavy rain had left a smell like decay and fungus in the air. The only sounds were the cawing of some crows that had been disturbed by their arrival and were returning to their roosts among the treetops.

Mia said, 'Come, this way.' She led him along a muddy path skirting the house and around the back, where some mossy concrete steps led down to the badly weathered door of what had once been the dairy's cheese cellar. Mia seemed hesitant, so Ben trotted down the steps and pushed against the door, which was unlocked and swung open with a creak.

172

'There's a metal inner door ahead,' she told him, tentatively following him into the darkness beyond. 'Fritz kept it locked, but he gave me a copy of the padlock key. Hold on, I have it here.' She groped blindly in her handbag for it. 'I can't see a thing. There's no electricity here, unless you get the generator going.'

'No need for that,' Ben said, and reached into his own bag for the compact but very powerful torch he always carried on his travels. He shone its bright beam on her until she'd found the key, then turned it towards the inner door.

That was when they saw someone had already been here before them. The lock hasp had been smashed away from the door frame with a heavy hammer or crowbar and the door itself was hanging open an inch.

'Scheisse!' Mia gasped.

'Get back from the door,' Ben warned her. He pushed it carefully open and shone the torch through into the darkness of the cellar, tensed and ready for trouble – but the only living thing inside was the rat that scuttled away into the shadows. Whoever had forced the door had been and gone. But they'd left plenty of traces of their presence. Fritz's secret storeroom had been as badly trashed as his apartment. Ben's torch beam swept over the mess of emptied files, the photos and computer printouts that covered the dusty concrete floor.

'No good,' he said to Mia. 'If there was anything of value to us here, it's been taken.'

'It can't be. Nobody knew about this place!'

'They do now,' Ben replied.

'But how?'

'We can worry about that later,' he said tersely. 'Right now, I'd suggest we need to get out of here.' His sixth sense was buzzing and he was getting a bad feeling about this place.

'Wait,' Mia protested, bending down to sift through the mess. 'There might still be something—'

'Forget it, Mia. Let's go.' He took her arm, gently but firmly, and led her back out of the cellar and up the steps. She was wriggling to get free of his grip as they emerged into the pale daylight and started towards the car.

'Where are we going?'

'Back to Berlin. We'll have to figure this out some other way.'

'But that was our only chance! Ouch, you're hurting my arm!'

Up above, the crows started cawing more loudly, and flapped away from their roosts as though something had startled them. Ben thought he heard another sound through the trees. He tensed. Froze still and put a finger to his lips. 'Shh. Be quiet.'

She was about to retort angrily when she caught the hardening look on his face and her eyes widened in alarm. 'What is it?'

'Too late,' he said, pulling her back behind the corner of the house. 'They're already here.'

Chapter 22

What Ben and the crows had heard was the soft, silent approach of a car coming down the track. Peering cautiously from behind the corner of the wall he saw it now: a metallic brown Volkswagen SUV, rolling towards the house. The play of the tree-dappled sunlight on tinted glass made it hard to see inside. But whoever it was, he didn't think they were property surveyors come to check the old place out for potential redevelopment.

The VW came pattering the rest of the way down the track and pulled up near Ben's Mercedes. The doors swung open and two men got out. Property surveyors might have been wearing high-visibility jackets and hard hats and carrying clipboards. These two were dressed in black nylon jackets and beanies and carrying compact black Steyr AUG assault weapons, one fitted with a grenade launcher. Military-grade hardware that Ben had trained with, back in the day. The way these men handled them, it was clear they'd been pretty well trained as well. Professional operators, without a doubt.

That was when Ben knew for sure that he'd inadvertently let himself be followed here from Berlin. Or that someone had planted a tracking device on his car, or both. Whatever the case, it was a fair guess that these two men belonged to the same gang who'd trashed Fritz's apartment and this place as well. Almost certainly also to the same organisation who had killed him. And they were intent on taking out anyone else who messed with their plans.

He swore under his breath. Through his career, both in and out of the military, he'd seldom been out of reach of at least some kind of effective weapon. For years he'd maintained a network of bank safe deposit boxes in all the main European cities, each containing a handgun, so that wherever he travelled in search of kidnappers and their victims he could be assured of being properly armed for the job. Now he was empty-handed. Being caught napping and unarmed in the presence of professional killers with automatic weapons was about as comforting an experience as finding yourself naked in a pit full of rabid baboons. But there was little use crying about it. He'd walked himself and Mia into a trap. Now he was going to have to get them both out.

She was pressed against the wall next to him, staring at him like a rabbit in the headlights. He put his finger to his lips again. With what he hoped was a reassuring smile he took her hand and whispered into her ear, 'Stay close to me. Don't let go of my hand. We'll be fine.' She swallowed hard.

The two men were nearing the house now. For a moment they were out of sight, but Ben anticipated that they would split up to patrol both sides of the building in a pincer movement to flush out their prey. That was what he'd have done, in their shoes. How to get out of it?

Glancing around him, he thought he saw a way he and Mia could outflank them both and make their escape. One of the tumbledown tin shed outbuildings was just a few steps away from the back corner of the house, separated by a narrow gap that they might with luck be able to cross unnoticed. Then they could work their way down the side of the outbuilding, through the straggly overgrowth of bushes that had grown up thickly all over the place; from there past another nearby semi-derelict stone barn and the junkyard of ancient farm equipment, and if they got that far they'd only be a short run from the car.

It was the only plan that might offer them any chance of getting out of here in one piece, but they'd have to move fast. Any moment now, one of the gunmen would reappear around the front corner of the house.

Ben turned to Mia and signalled what they were going to do. She looked terrified at the idea, but nodded. He squeezed her hand, slung his bag over his shoulder and they took off at a sprint. For two chilling seconds that felt like a minute they were exposed right out in the open. It was a gamble, but it paid off: they crossed the gap and ducked behind the rear of the outbuilding a heartbeat before one of the gunmen emerged on their side of the house, as Ben had expected.

Made it. Now all they had to do was reach the car. Very cautiously, very quietly, keeping their heads low, they moved along the side wall of the building, forcing their way through the tangle of bushes. Mia was clutching Ben's hand in a death grip. At any instant a storm of gunfire could come ripping through the flimsy rusted metal sheeting as though it were made of paper. Silence. Just the soft pad of their running feet and Mia's rapid, shallow breathing right behind him.

They cleared the end of the first building, crossed another narrow gap and kept running, heads low, until they'd reached the end corner of the stone barn next to it. So far, so good. Ben peeked out from behind his cover. They'd managed to flank the whole length of the house unseen and gained more than half the distance to their car, now less than twenty yards away. Meanwhile, the two gunmen had finished circling the house and met at the back. He could see them well from here, through a couple of the barn's dusty windowpanes. Some men would have been annoyed and angry at being eluded by their targets, but not these. They appeared totally calm and impassive as they exchanged signals. One of them jabbed a finger towards the open cellar door, as if to say, 'Bet they're hiding in there.' The other one nodded.

In those few moments, Ben was able to observe the two men carefully. They looked strikingly similar in height and build, with a Nordic kind of look about them. The one doing the pointing at the cellar door had what appeared to be a purplish port-wine stain birthmark on his right cheek, though it was hard to tell at this distance.

An expert in his trade watching another at work can learn a great deal at just a glance, and Ben could see the high level of training in the slick, smooth way these guys operated as they slipped inside the cellar door, first one and then his comrade. They wouldn't be in there long before they realised it was empty. Just a few seconds was all the time Ben and Mia would have to make the dash across the remaining open ground to their car. But they could do it. They had little choice but to try.

He gripped her hand again, and they broke from cover and made a dash for it. Two fast running strides. Three. Four. The car closer and closer now. Every second counted.

And then, as they were just a few metres short of the car, Mia's phone went off inside her handbag like a sonic hand grenade. The damn thing was set to one of those jaunty musical ringtones that Ben had always hated. And he hated them more now than ever as the cacophony rang out loud and clear across the yard. It seemed to reverberate even more shockingly in the space between the house and the shed. Which could have been Ben's imagination. But it was certainly noisy enough to be heard by the gunmen inside the old cheese cellar, who now came bursting back outside a whole precious couple of seconds sooner than Ben might have wished, while he and Mia were still stuck out in the open ground and in full sight.

The gunmen were taking no prisoners. The rattle of automatic gunfire filled the air, drowning out Mia's phone and her scream as Ben yanked her violently out of the path of the bullets that tore up the ground where they'd been standing and hammered into the parked Mercedes. The car's windscreen and headlights blew apart and holes punched the driver's door and bonnet. Ben felt a fluttering jerk as a round passed through the bag on his shoulder, missing his body by a hair's breadth. Mia stumbled and fell, and for a heart-stopping instant he thought she'd been hit too. Still clutching her hand, he wrenched her back up to her feet and they scrambled away.

The shooters came on, shoulder to shoulder, spraying bullets. There was nowhere for Ben and Mia to run – nowhere except the cover of the old milking machinery a few steps to their right. The sleeve ripped half off her jacket as Ben propelled her across the yard and spun her bodily behind the rusting hulk of some kind of disused storage tank. Whatever its purpose might have been back in the day, he neither knew nor cared – but it saved them now as he hurled himself behind it and the furious stream of bullets chasing close behind impacted against the heavy-gauge steel like a hundred tiny peen hammers.

'Move, move!' he yelled at her over the din. Sparks were flying, ricochets pinging off bits of pipework and angle iron and howling past their ears. She was so filled with terror that she was as limp as a bag of rags as he pushed her deeper behind cover. Suddenly there was a lull in the firing as the shooters dumped their emptied magazines and slammed in fresh ones from the pouches on their belts, running as they reloaded. In that short breathing space Ben was able to shove Mia back towards the stone barn and yank the door shut behind them. Its thick walls would at least shield them from gunfire and buy them a few more moments while he tried to figure out a new way out of this.

The barn was cluttered with all the usual farm junk, empty fuel drums and old fertiliser sacks. The floor was spongy underfoot and smelled of rats and mouldy straw. The only light was what little filtered through the filthy windows and down through the cracks between the roof slates. But darkness could only be a good thing when you were being hunted to the death by men with automatic weapons. Ben knew he had only a few moments to figure out some kind of alternative plan. He found it, in the shape of a three-foot length of rusty iron pipe. One good swing, and a man's brains would be pulp. That would shorten the odds, at least. Ben decided to make his stand here, in the hope that the killers would pass on trying to shoot through the windows and doorway and instead try to come in after them. First one in the door would find himself on the receiving end of the metal pipe before he knew what was happening. Then Ben would snatch up his weapon and use it on the other guy. It would be close, ugly combat from which there could only be one survivor. With any luck they wouldn't both die right away, allowing him to find out who the hell they were.

That was Ben's plan, at any rate. But he soon saw it wasn't going to work out that way. To come blindly storming in after their targets would have been too obvious a move for these two men, who seemed to have anticipated the danger of a trap as though they knew exactly who they were dealing with.

He heard voices outside the barn. Then he heard another sound. One that was unpleasantly familiar to his ears. The hollow metallic clunk of a 40mm grenade being loaded inside the stubby tube of its launcher and the action being snapped shut ready to fire.

Not good.

Chapter 23

Ben just had time to grab Mia and haul her towards the rear window of the barn before the grenade blasted a fist-sized hole in the barn door. What kind of grenade it might be, there was no way of knowing until it went off: could be tear gas, incendiary, fragmentation or the even nastier flechettes, those little two-inch steel darts that would be hurled outwards in all directions by the force of the explosion and perforate anything in the vicinity.

He had no intention of hanging around to find out. He used his body to smash through the filthy windowpane, rolling out backwards through the jagged hole and dragging her with him just as the whole interior of the barn erupted into a huge fireball. A tongue of flame rolled out of the shattered window and seared them as they tumbled to safety. Then the rotted timbers, blown apart by the shockwave, collapsed and the whole roof came crashing down.

For a moment everything was obliterated by dust and smoke. Ben was lying on his back at the foot of the stone wall with Mia on top of him. He felt her stir, heard her groan. No time to ask if she was hurt. He didn't think he was. His bag and leather jacket had saved him from being badly lacerated by the broken glass. He rolled out from under her, sprang to his feet and yanked her up after him and started running blindly through the smoke. He had little idea where he was going, except away from the shooters – who any moment now, as the smoke dissipated, would spot them and open fire again.

Ben tore through bushes, came to a flimsy wooden fence and smashed it down with a kick, and saw that they were heading towards the thicket of forest that had been encroaching for years on the abandoned farmland. 'The car!' Mia gasped. 'What about the car?'

'Forget the bloody car. Keep moving.'

Into the trees now, running as fast as they could through the dense undergrowth. Low branches whipping at their faces and tearing at their hair and clothing. One slip, one fall, would be fatal – because the crackling of twigs behind them told Ben that the shooters were in pursuit again. A moment later, another rattle of gunfire clipped leaves and bark from a tree a foot to his right. He urged Mia on faster, taking a zig-zagging motion through the foliage that slowed down their rate of progress but made them just a little less easy to hit. A pause in the firing caused him to snatch a backward glance over his shoulder and he saw, with fleeting satisfaction, that one of their pursuers had blundered into a thicket of brambles and the other was having to help him out. That would buy Ben and Mia a few precious moments to widen the distance between them and the guns.

Deeper and deeper into the forest, pressing their advantage for all it was worth. The gap had widened by maybe forty metres, but Ben knew that if he didn't come up with some way to delay their pursuers further, neither he nor Mia would leave these woods alive.

'What's happening?' she asked breathlessly as he slowed his pace.

'Keep running, Mia. Straight ahead that way.'

'But what about you?'

'Please. Just go. I'll catch up with you. Go!'

She hesitated, staring at him, chest heaving, then turned and hurried on alone.

Ben crouched in the bushes at the foot of a large tree, hidden by the foliage of its low-hanging branches, and peered back through the woods. The shooters had lost sight of them and split up, following a parallel course fifteen metres apart to widen their search, weapons shoulder high and poised to open fire at anything that moved. The one on the left was well off course to stumble upon Ben's concealed position but the other, the man with the port-wine birthmark on his face, was heading right for him. Ben had about half a minute to work out the best plan of attack.

Looking up from his hiding place at the tree next to him, he saw there was a thick, heavy branch jutting out horizontally around chest height to a tallish man. Carefully rising to his feet he grasped the branch and pulled it back a little to test its flexibility. With a bit more effort he had it bent right back like the limb of a crossbow. He eased it back into position, then quickly doubled back a few steps the way he'd come. He'd been trained to stalk through the thickest jungle without leaving a trail that even the most astute predator, human or otherwise, could follow. But now he deliberately trampled down the ferns and bushes, so that it looked as though a blind rhino had come barging through here.

The guy with the wine stain was coming closer. Ten seconds to enemy contact. Ben quickly, silently returned to his hiding place by the tree. He grasped the horizontal branch with both fists and bent it right back again, as far as he dared flex it before it snapped.

Five seconds to contact. Peering past the edge of the tree trunk Ben could see the guy's gait and body language stiffen as he noticed the rhino path beaten into the ground. For an instant Ben thought he was about to summon his friend over, but instead he tightened his grip on his weapon and moved stealthily along the path. Closer, closer. Ben could see his eyes under the hem of the beanie hat scanning warily from side to side for any sign of his prey.

Three seconds to contact. Ben had the branch under full tension. His muscles were beginning to ache from the strain. So close now that he could almost smell the guy's breath. And he could also see that what he'd initially taken to be a birthmark on the guy's face was actually an old burn scar. It must have happened a long time ago, and it had been a nasty burn that disfigured the corner of his right eye and left a mottled, reddish-brown patch of raised scar tissue down his cheek. Must have been pretty damned painful at the time.

This was going to hurt like hell, too.

As the guy stalked into the trap Ben placed the last few pounds of strain on the branch, praying it wouldn't snap at this critical point. Then at exactly the right moment he released it, and it sprang powerfully away from him with a lashing *whoosh* of foliage. The mid-section of the branch, as thick as Ben's arm, caught the guy across the chest like a sideways swipe of a baseball bat in the hands of a very strong ball striker. The Steyr AUG was knocked from the guy's grip and the heavy blow sent him sprawling backwards off his feet with a winded OOF! and the distinct snap of a rib breaking. As he crashed down to the ground Ben burst out from the bushes. If there'd been time, he would have delivered a lethal trachea-crushing kick to the man's throat. Instead he made a dive for the fallen weapon. Shoot the other guy first, then turn it on this one. He was already injured, but if he needed disabling a bit more then Ben was happy to oblige him with a bullet to the shoulder or leg. Then the interrogation would begin.

Except once again, Ben's plan was thwarted. His lunging hand was just two inches from the weapon when the second guy reacted with the kind of speed he'd have more expected from a Special Forces soldier than a regular combatant. Super-fast and almost as accurate. The blast of gunfire blew fountains of dirt up from the forest floor and forced Ben to give up on the fallen weapon and roll away behind the cover of the tree. He was on his feet in one spring and running again, chased by bullets that smacked off trunks to his left and right and whizzed past his ear. He was cursing under his breath as he ran. Whoever these guys were, they were good. Too damn good.

Ben had failed, but he could console himself that he'd also succeeded in part, because now the uninjured shooter had to help his comrade, who certainly had at least one broken rib and would be in a great deal of pain. That should slow them down a good bit while Ben raced through the forest to catch up with Mia.

Moments later, he wasn't so sure it had slowed them down all that much. Bullets raked the trees as he went, dangerously close. The two men were relentlessly determined to eliminate their targets and the only way to stop them would have been to kill them.

Sprinting hard, Ben spotted the running figure of Mia up ahead. They'd crossed the whole patch of forest, and she was emerging from the trees into an area of open meadow that led down to the bank of a canal. She glanced back, saw him following her and turned towards him with a look of relief. 'Thank God!'

'Thank him later,' Ben said. 'When we're out of here.'

He took her hand again and they rushed down the bank towards the water's edge. There was a flat-bottomed river boat with an outboard motor chugging its slow way up the canal towards them. An elderly man in a flat cap sat at the tiller, puffing a pipe. Strapped down under a tarp on the river boat's deck further forward was his cargo, a big heap of firewood cut ready for seasoning ahead of winter. He might have been transporting it up the canal to sell, or maybe he lived nearby and was heading home to stack the logs in his wood store. A gentle, pleasant, close-to-nature kind of way to spend an afternoon. He probably hadn't planned on having a couple of extra passengers on board, least of all two fugitives from an armed manhunt. But right now a boat was the only way Ben and Mia had any chance of making their escape.

And they'd better do it fast, because now the gunmen were emerging from the trees after them.

Chapter 24

'Oh, no. There they are!' Mia looked back in horror. From the treeline they now came running over the meadow separating the forest from the canal. The one with the burn scar was hobbling and bent over from the pain in his chest, but he'd recovered his weapon and was still in the game.

Meanwhile the river boat with its cargo of firewood continued burbling peacefully down the canal towards the point of the bank where Ben and Mia would reach the water's edge. Its elderly pilot, contentedly puffing his pipe with one hand on the tiller bar, didn't appear to have spotted the two armed crazies rushing down the slope. Ben rushed to the bankside with his arms raised to get the old guy's attention, both to warn him of the danger and to tell him they needed to get on board. He'd have been happy to offer the guy money, anything, if there'd been time to negotiate.

But before Ben could speak to him, the shooters suddenly opened fire and the tranquillity of this peaceful setting was shattered. Ben grabbed Mia and the two of them rolled down the bank, off the edge of the ancient wooden sleepers that lined the canal and into the water with a splash. Bullets raked at the canal's surface, sending up little explosions of white spray, and splinters flew from the firewood pile on the boat's deck. The shooters keep coming, firing on the move. The old guy at the tiller staggered to his feet in a panic. Then he let out a cry and clutched at his heart as bullets punched into his chest. He fell against the tiller handle, his weight shoving it sideways, and the boat instantly veered towards the bank.

'I can't swim!' Mia gasped, thrashing in the water and fighting to keep her head above the surface. Ben told her to take a deep breath, wrapped his arm around her body and dived deep under pulling her down with him. The water was cold and tasted brackish. Bubbles streamed from her mouth and she was on the edge of panic, struggling against his grip, but he held her tight. The flat bottom of the boat slid over them. Bullets were popping all over the surface and hitting the aluminium hull. Reaching the other side of the boat Ben threw his free arm up out of the water, grasped the edge of the bow and hauled himself up, dragging her after him. In the few moments they'd been underwater, the shooters had almost reached the bank. Gunfire was slamming into the boat, but as they crawled aboard Ben and Mia were shielded by the stack of firewood.

Struck again and again by the relentless stream of bullets, the old man's body slipped off the tiller and jerked the handle the other way as he slid off the boat's stern and into the water with a splash. The boat started veering away from the bank, heading back out towards the middle of the canal. But it was still moving much too slowly, the outboard motor chugging away at little more than idle speed.

Risking everything, Ben scrambled out from behind the wood pile and cracked the throttle wide open. The burble of the engine soared to a roar, white water churned from the propeller and the boat thrust harder through the water, leaving a curve of foaming wake as it left the bank behind.

For a moment Ben thought that the shooters were going to dive into the canal after them, but instead they just kept firing from the bank. Bullets were drilling the side of the boat, shredding the hull, water beginning to pour through the holes. If a bullet strike killed the outboard motor, they'd be sitting ducks. And if the shooters had brought any more grenades to play with, forget it.

But no, suddenly the distance between them and bank was widening fast as the boat kept on accelerating away. Up ahead, an old wooden bridge spanned the water. The shooters ran along the side towards it, the firing pausing again as they reloaded fresh magazines, then starting up once more. One of the straps holding the tarp down over the firewood cargo snapped, and some logs fell from the pile and splashed into the water. Ben yelled at Mia to keep her head down.

The boat was moving faster and faster, sending up a foamy bow wave as they passed under the bridge. The shooters were trying to follow them, but the support wall of the bridge was blocking them from getting any further along the bank. If they'd had any hopes of reaching the bridge in time to climb up onto it, allowing them to fire directly down at their targets, those were dashed too. They fell into a crouch, rested their weapons on the wall for a more stable aim, and went on loosing short bursts and single shots at the escaping boat, but their accuracy was beginning to lessen as they were left behind, and fewer strikes were hitting the boat.

Ben sat up behind the tiller and steered away from the bridge, heading for a bend in the canal. The firing slackened, then stopped. Ben looked back and saw the figures of the shooters, receding smaller and smaller into the distance, turn away from the bank and start running back up the slope towards the trees. He wondered if they thought they could get back to Fritz's farm, jump in their car and head the boat off somewhere downstream. He wasn't planning on staying on board long enough for that to happen.

Then the boat reached the bend and the disappearing shooters and the forest were blocked from sight. They burbled on past pretty little waterside houses, under another bridge. Ben checked Mia for any damage and found nothing worse than a few scratches from their dash through the woods. They'd been lucky. Ben didn't like depending on luck for his continued existence.

'Are we all right now?' Mia kept asking. Her face was pallid and her voice was shaky.

'I'll be happier when we get back on land,' he said. Among other reasons, so many bullet holes had been punched through their hull that the boat wouldn't float for much longer. He felt bad about the old man and wished that he could go back and attend to him properly – but the police would soon be descending on the whole area, and they wouldn't just be searching for the lunatic gunmen who'd shot the place up.

A kilometre or so further downriver, they entered a village that straddled both sides of the water. Barges and open tourist boats were moored along the banks, and people were milling around on a pontoon. But they were no crowd of happy tourists. Some were talking agitatedly on phones; others were acting scared, jabbering among themselves, gasping, hurrying away to safety. From the palpable sense of anxiety in the air it was clear that news of what had happened was spreading fast among the local population.

'This is where we get off,' Ben said. As he pulled the slowly sinking boat up to the side and helped Mia clamber out, he was very conscious of the looks they were getting: two slightly scorched-looking individuals, dripping wet, filthy and ragged, were bound to attract attention and suspicion.

From the pontoon a wooden walkway led inland towards the rest of the village. They emerged into a little cobbled street flanked by picture-postcard traditional houses and shops. Off a nearby square was a small café, and a couple of stands selling food and gifts for the tourists. Ben was looking around him for a bus stop, a taxi rank, some means of transport out of here. Mia had other, more immediate priorities. 'Do you have any money?' she asked. 'My purse was in my handbag.'

He felt for his wallet, sodden in the inside pocket of his leather jacket. 'Why do you need money?'

She pointed at the cafe. 'I need to clean myself up. We can order something and I'll use the bathroom.'

Ben shook his head. 'We don't have time for that now, Mia.' And sure enough, even as he spoke he could hear the wail of police sirens in the distance, growing steadily louder. 'We need to go. Right this minute.'

She looked at him. 'You're worried about the *polizei*? Not me. I'm looking forward to seeing them, because now we can report these crazy people trying to kill us.'

Could she be serious? 'Great idea,' he replied. 'Especially if you want to spend the next several days in custody explaining the whole story to them over and over again. Meanwhile these crazy people have a lot more power and influence than you understand. They'll soon find a way to get to you.'

'But we've done nothing wrong,' she blustered. 'This shouldn't be happening to me. I'm a citizen, with rights.'

This was no time or place to be having this conversation. 'Trust me, Mia. You go to the police now, you'll be dead within two days. You want to be found dead, like those other fake suicides you were telling me about?'

Ashen-faced, she asked, 'Then what am I meant to do?'

'Survive,' he said.

The sirens were getting closer. At that moment a motor-cyclist came down the street, pattering carefully over the cobbles at little more than walking pace. The bike was an old flat-twin BMW. The rider was a young guy in a full-face helmet and armoured leathers. Well protected from spills and bumps, so Ben didn't have to worry about hurting him when he stepped out into the road, grabbed him by his belt and hauled him out of the saddle and tumbling to the ground. The bike toppled over on its side with a crash.

But these old bikes were built to take the odd knock. Ben reached down for the handlebars and hauled the machine upright, ignoring Mia's horrified stare and those of the passersby. To the fallen rider, who was dazedly struggling back to his feet rubbing his elbow, he called out, '*Entschuldigung!*' Then to Mia as he swung his leg over the seat and restarted the stalled motor, 'Well, hop on, then.'

'What the hell are you doing?'

'Getting us out of here by the most expedient means possible.'

Looking dubiously at the motorcycle, she said, 'I don't know what to do. I've never been on one of these before.'

'Just hold on tight and try not to fall off,' he replied. With a worried frown she clambered onto the pillion seat and clasped her arms around his middle. He gunned the twist-grip, clicked into gear, dumped the clutch and Mia let out a yelp as they took off.

Behind them the first police car had come tearing into the village, siren whooping, lights flashing. In his mirror he saw the motorcyclist limping up to the cops, gesticulating wildly in the direction of his fast-disappearing machine. Moments later, the police car was giving chase, followed soon afterwards by a second, then a third.

Not long before, Ben and Mia had been running from murdering criminals. Now they were fleeing from the law. He could only guess what she was thinking about that, clinging onto him for dear life as they sped out of the village and onto a country road. For him, these sorts of things happened all too often.

This was the other reason why people wore helmets on motorcycles. Not just for impact protection, but because the full naked blast of a 135-kilometre-an-hour wind threatened to tear Ben's head off and made him narrow his eyes as though he were riding into a sandstorm. The road was long and twisty, and the three screeching cop cars were glued to their tail. What the thirty-year-old BMW gained in handling through the undulating bends, it lacked in top-speed perfor-mance on the straights, where the police cars began to inch closer and closer in Ben's mirror. He was screaming along on full throttle and the speedometer needle was trembling against its stop, and still they kept coming. Then the straight ended in another series of tight bends and he took full advantage of them, heeling the bike over hard from side to side and scraping the flat-twin cylinder head casings on the road left and right. Mia's grip on his middle was squeezing the breath out of him.

The police cars fell back a little, then started catching up again on the next straight. The road was a blurry green tunnel. How long he could keep this up before he wrapped himself and his pillion around a tree, he wasn't quite sure. Then a sign flashed past, almost too quickly to read, saying FAHRRADWEG, with a symbol prohibiting motor vehicles. He spied the entrance to the cross-country cycle route coming up rapidly on his right and hit the brakes hard. The bike's front forks plunged under sudden deceleration and his rear wheel locked up, tyre hissing, Mia's weight pressing against him. Then he was back on the gas and veering at a sharp angle of lean into the mouth of the cycle path, wobbled through a set of gates designed to admit two-wheelers only, and heard the screech of brakes and the crunching tail-end collision behind him as the police cars skidded to an emergency stop and piled into the back of one another.

Ben allowed himself a small smile of satisfaction, cracked open the twist-grip throttle and thundered away down the cycle track. Some mountain bikers, clad in their flimsy helmets and garishly coloured cycling gear, scattered out of the way like minnows parting for a shark as the motorcycle came blasting through at high speed. He knew that the cops would be scrambling to block as many exits to the maze of cycle routes as their available manpower would allow, if indeed they didn't manage to deploy a search helicopter. He doubted they'd be able to cover them all, but it was impossible to tell which.

So when he found the right spot, deep in the heart of the nature park through which the maze of cycle routes crisscrossed, he dumped the motorcycle in a clump of bushes. A few hundred metres further on, a courting couple had left their bicycles propped against a hedge while they disappeared into the long grass for a romantic interlude. When they finally re-emerged, they'd find their bikes had been commandeered by someone with a greater need.

Police sirens could still be heard not too far off in the distance when Ben and Mia, having reached a main road, abandoned their bicycles and continued on foot in the hopes of hitching a lift in the direction of Berlin. The last warmth of the afternoon sun helped to dry them out a little as they walked, but Mia was flagging and complaining, 'I can't take much more of this.'

Just a couple of kilometres later they were picked up by a friendly truck driver, who listened sympathetically to their sad tale about their car being stolen, and dropped them off at a nearby bus station. Mia hardly spoke all the way.

Two hours later, they were back in the city. After a stop-off at a cheap clothes boutique for Mia, they checked into a sleazy hotel under the names Herr and Frau Weber and spent an hour getting cleaned up. It was evening by the time they found a quiet wine bar a few minutes from the hotel, and sat wearily winding down with a couple of scotches for Ben, several glasses of Riesling for her. The TV in the corner was showing a news segment about the shocking incident that had taken place earlier that day in the countryside near Lübbenau. The victim was identified as Heinrich Vogel, 74, a retired schoolteacher. Police were still searching for the perpetrators, and also wanted to trace an unidentified man and woman reported by witnesses as fled the scene following a dramatic chase. In the wake of the shooting, the usual line-up of opportunistic politicians eager never to let a good tragedy go to waste were baying for tighter gun controls, blah, blah, blah. After a few minutes Ben and Mia turned away and stopped watching.

'Well, it's been an interesting day,' she said broodingly. 'I suppose I should thank you once again for saving me. But the truth is I have no idea what to do now. I woke up this morning as Fritz's grieving ex-fiancée, with no idea how simple my life was then. Now I'm a target for professional killers and also a fugitive from the police, apparently.'

'I'd be more worried about the other guys,' Ben said.

'I am, and what worries me most is that, if they knew where Fritz kept his secret materials, they must know everything else too. Who I am, where I work, where I live, all of it.' She looked at him. 'I can't go home again, can I?'

He shook his head. 'Not now. Maybe never. I'm sorry.'

Mia was silent for a minute. 'There's nothing for me here now, in any case. Fritz was my whole life.'

'We can get you a new life.'

'If only you could,' she said with a sad smile.

He asked, 'Do you trust me?'

She shrugged. 'Who else do I have?'

Ben said, 'Then come with me.'

'Where are we going?' she asked.

'On a plane ride.'

Chapter 25

The other end of the ultra-secure, encrypted video call showed the study of the large old country house in Surrey. Its owner sat at his desk, his gaunt, lined, white-haired face filling most of the big screen, bookcases and the fireplace in the background. This end of the call was at the private island location far away, where the older man's associate had his personal base.

The video call had been set up in a hurry. Their organisation had been thrown into a quandary by the report from their agent in Florida that a new player had unexpectedly and dramatically entered the picture. They were already familiar with this ex-military major, Benedict Hope, from his connection to Auguste Kaprisky's bodyguard team. But they hadn't anticipated his direct involvement in the affair. Now that the attempt to eliminate him in Germany had failed, their situation was growing more complicated.

'We cannot permit this man to go running around free,' the older man's deep, gravelly voice came rumbling through the speakers either side of the screen. 'He's a liability and risks finding out far too much. Do you hear me, Speer?'

The younger Austrian, called Klaus Speer, was irritated by this breach of protocol on his superior's part. Even on a secure call like this one, the personal identities of high-up members of the organisation weren't supposed to be uttered out loud. He would never have dreamed of addressing his superior by his actual name, Sir Simon Asquith, or even by his title of 'Chairman'. Masking his annoyance he replied calmly, 'I promise you that he will be dealt with very soon.'

'Promises, promises,' the Chairman grumbled. 'That's all I hear from you. You promised the Kaprisky situation would be taken care of cleanly, and look how that turned out. Now this man Hope is making a fool of you.'

'Our assets have never failed before,' Speer said. The particular men he was referring to were known to them, and to anyone else in that shadowy world, as Messer and Kugel. 'They won't fail again.'

It was just a glitch – or so Speer hoped. Their plans had been so long in the making, so painstakingly prepared, so much more ambitious than anything that had ever been attempted throughout the history of their organisation, that the stakes were dreadfully high. The whole Kaprisky business had been an unforeseen setback. How could any of them have predicted that their once trusted associate, a senior member of their organisation, would try to betray them like this? Well, in truth, Speer and some others had been increasingly aware of Kaprisky's discomfort as the long-discussed scheme had crept closer to becoming reality. Perhaps it was simply so vast in scale, so monstrous in concept, that for years he'd never believed they were really serious about carrying it out.

In any case, the swift and decisive response that the organisation had placed Speer in charge of had nipped that crisis in the bud. At least, that's what Speer believed. The Chairman remained far from convinced, and now this latest development had him riled yet further. His face on the screen was flushed an unhealthy, mottled red. 'It's one balls-up after another,' he seethed. 'First you fail to recover any evidence from Kohler—'

Another too-explicit reference that made Speer wince inwardly. He cut in, 'With respect, sir, we went over this the last time we spoke. I'm quite certain that the person in question knew nothing. If he had, it would have been revealed to us. He was quick enough to tell us about where he kept his research information. Nobody could have resisted that kind of pressure. He was telling the truth.'

Speer had been present at Fritz Kohler's brutal torture, a deeply unpleasant memory, though it wasn't the first time he'd witnessed such scenes. He was perfectly correct in saying that no man alive would have been strong enough to withhold information in the face of that kind of cruel punishment. By the end of it, the half-dead victim had been so mutilated that to throw him under a train was the only means of hiding the marks of his interrogation. Speer could still hear Kohler's bubbling screams of agony, the pleas for mercy, the repeated and evidently sincere denials that Kaprisky had passed anything tangible to him, his insistence that their initial encounter in Berlin had been only a preliminary meeting. If it had ever happened, the follow-up rendezvous at Kaprisky's home would have revealed far more detailed, solid evidence of the agenda they were aiming to expose. Needless to say, it hadn't.

'So you say,' the Chairman grumped. 'However, it would appear we now have a whole new problem on our hands.'

'Not for long,' Speer insisted.

'Good. Because I'm sure I needn't remind you of the consequences if we should ever be found out. Not just for you, but for all of us.'

Such a discovery would be more than devastating, Speer knew very well. It would be the biggest political scandal of all time. The total ruination of some of the most powerful and influential men in the world. Should the public wake up to the horrifying reality of what was being planned for them, there would be no place for even those extremely high-up players to hide. Their only way out would be to swallow the cyanide pill – both metaphorically and perhaps literally. Aware of the tacit threat in the Chairman's words he replied, 'No, sir, you don't need to remind me. We're all in this together.'

The Chairman went on angrily, 'And I'm also sure I don't need to repeat what I said last time we talked, Speer. There are to be no more mistakes. I have no intention of convening the committee to tell them that we're pulling the plug. Things must go ahead as planned. Which means this Ben Hope has to be caught, made to tell us what he knows and then silenced before he can do us more damage.'

Speer actually suspected that even if they did now decide to abort their scheme for fear of getting caught in the act of the biggest crime in history, the plans were so intricate and far advanced that it could be too late at this point to prevent things from running their natural course. Once the boulder began to roll down the mountainside, there might be no stopping it.

He said, 'You have my assurances, sir. Hope is a dead man.'

Chapter 26

'Where the hell are you?' asked Gabriel Archambeau when Ben called that evening to instruct him to get the plane ready again. From his tone, one might have construed that the lawyer was mildly put out.

'In a sleazy hotel room in Berlin,' Ben replied. 'With my new bride, Frau Weber.'

'I suppose that's an attempt at humour. At least I hope it is. But let me tell you that nobody here is laughing. Have you the slightest idea what trouble your antics are causing for me? The car we arranged for you – the *very expensive* car, I might add – was found riddled with bullets at an abandoned farm near Lübbenau.'

'Oh, that,' Ben said.

'Yes, that. Valentina had me concoct a whole cock and bull story about its having been stolen, and forced me to go to the most inordinate lengths to keep your name from being mentioned. What on earth is going on? And I hardly dare to ask how many other laws you must be violating while you're out there running around doing God knows what.'

'You'll get my full report when this is over,' Ben said. 'In the meantime, I'm returning to base. But I'm not coming in alone. And that's something else we need to discuss.'

'My God. You weren't joking. There really is a woman there with you? Who is she?'

'Her name is Mia Brockhaus,' Ben told him. 'It's too dangerous for her to stay here any longer, so I want her to be accommodated at the estate while you arrange a new identity and a new life for her somewhere else. A whole new start. She isn't asking for much. But she'll need some money to help her get on her feet. I'll leave that to you.'

'It sounds very costly,' Gabriel said, sounding extremely leery of the idea.

'Cheaper than having an innocent person's death on your conscience,' Ben said. 'Get the flight crew ready for takeoff, Gabriel. We're on our way.'

They were at the airport by midnight, and ninety minutes after leaving German soil the Kaprisky jet landed at Le Mans Arnage, where they were met by a chauffeur-driven limousine. For Mia, who'd seldom ever flown before let alone in a private jet, the whirlwind journey and the sudden massive changes in her life were overwhelming, and she was asleep by the time the limo had whisked them back to the estate.

'We'll take good care of her,' Valentina promised some time later, when she and Ben were sitting alone in the yellow salon deep in the night, neither of them able to sleep. She was sipping on a mug of cocoa, to which Ben was glad to see she'd added nothing alcoholic. Her hair was tied back in a ponytail, and in this light she looked much more mature than her seventeen years. It was easy to forget he was talking to a kid. 'She can live here for as long as she likes,' Valentina went on, 'and Gabriel will arrange anything she needs for the future. You can count on it, Ben.'

'I know I can.'

'You look tired, Ben. Why don't you take a break from this? Spend some time with us on the estate for a day or two, help your friend Mia to settle in, and see Tonton. I know he'd appreciate a visit from you, even if he doesn't show it much.'

'I'm just getting started,' he said. 'Auguste's diary gave me an important connection. But there's another lead to chase. And no time to waste.'

'I wish there was some adequate way I could express to you how grateful I am for all you're doing.'

'I know that too.'

'Just please don't get hurt. I couldn't bear it.'

'How is he?' Ben asked, changing the subject.

'Every day brings a little more improvement,' she said, brightening up visibly. 'Today he not only managed to twitch two more fingers, but while I was holding his hand and talking to him, like I do all the time, I felt him give mine a squeeze. I'm certain he's communicating with me. One squeeze for yes, two squeezes for no. We could have all kinds of conversations that way, even if he still can't talk or open his eyes.'

'What do the doctors say?'

'That it's still too early to be sure, and that it mightn't mean anything. But what do they know? I'm so excited, Ben. Imagine, if he made a full recovery!'

And imagine if he woke up still remembering all those same secrets that he nearly got himself killed for the first time around, Ben thought. He just nodded.

Still fired up, Valentina told him about the other developments happening at the estate. The security team Gabriel had hired were soon to be history, because Jeff Dekker had come through for them and the replacements were due to arrive in the morning. Nine men, with the last three scheduled to appear in a few days' time, once they'd freed themselves from other commitments.

For Ben, the arrival of the new protection team couldn't have come at a better time. He didn't want to alarm Valentina by saying too much, but he'd feel a lot better about leaving here knowing they were around.

Around three in the morning, after tiredness had finally caught up with Valentina and she crawled off to bed, Ben silently climbed the stairs, past the room where Mia was sleeping and along the passage to Auguste's study. Valentina's words were still echoing in his head. *Please don't get hurt.* He didn't much fancy getting hurt, either. He'd been lucky to survive this far without a weapon. That was something to be remedied now.

He crept into the study, silently closed the door behind him and flicked on the desk light. Valentina had replaced Auguste's diary in the safe inside the antique dresser, along with the strange key that didn't seem to fit any lock in the house, and the Smith & Wesson revolver in its leather holster. Ben had watched her enter the combination code, the chess notation for the final moves of the classic Immortal Game of 1851. He wouldn't have remembered it otherwise, but he had a sharp eye and an uncanny memory for small details. He dialled in the long, convoluted mixed-digit code and the safe door swung open. At this moment he had no interest in the key, the diary or any of the other things inside. He reached into the safe and took out the gun and the speedloader pouch containing the spare hollowpoint cartridges.

A useful accessory for a man with dangerous enemies, indeed. It hadn't done Auguste much good, but the .357 Magnum with eighteen rounds of ammunition should be enough to deal with most kinds of problems, if the two killers should catch up with Ben again on his travels.

Alone in the study, Ben looked wistfully around him and his mind flashed back to his convalescence after his escapade in Russia, when he and Auguste had spent a lot of time playing chess here in this same room, on the very same Napoleon set around which this whole mystery somehow revolved.

Ben could picture the scene vividly: the two of them sitting at this little chess table, bent silently over the board, deep in their contest. The old man's consuming passion for chess showed in every pore of his skin, but there were times when Ben felt anything but love for it. In a moment of irritability he'd asked, 'Just what *is* it about this damn game that you love so much?'

Auguste had smiled kindly, sensing his friend's frustration.

'Are you asking me what is chess, Benedict? Why, chess is many things. It is not an art, nor is it a science, and most certainly it is not a game. Instead it is something much more profound. At one level it is a fight, a war, a struggle for survival. At the same time it is a deeply creative activity through which we can experience the purest beauty and truth, almost like a divine revelation. To be fully awake and intensely aware, free from all the noise and ugliness that taints the world outside of these sixty-four sacred squares. Some have said chess is life. I would say yes, chess is life – only better.'

Then the memory faded like a dream, and Ben was alone again in the study. He closed up the safe, left the room as silently as he'd entered and carried the weapon back downstairs. Two of the soon-to-be-replaced bodyguards were hanging around outside the house. Ben exchanged a few brief words with them, then returned to the Swiss cottage.

He knew there was no way he was going to get any sleep that night. His head was too full of all that was happening, and right now he still had more questions than answers. He stood on the balcony with a whisky and a Gauloise, deep in thought. He was still standing there when the sunrise broke red and gold in the eastern sky. Then he pulled out his phone and dialled the number of someone he had in mind to ask for advice and information. Someone he trusted implicitly.

Jaden Wolf had once been a highly talented SAS soldier, before quitting the regiment to refocus his considerable skills on an alternative career as a professional killer. Some might have argued that wasn't as much of a transition as it might appear. Maybe they'd be right. But Wolf's successful and lucrative new line of work had brought him into close contact with a whole world of which Ben knew very little. The two men had fallen out of contact for several years, before a series of chance events had renewed their friendship. Having cut his ties with that former phase of his life, Wolf now led a quiet, solitary existence in the mountains of southern Spain. Ben was wondering if his old friend might be able to help him identify the two men who'd tried to kill him and Mia.

Why ask Wolf? Because these were no ordinary thugs for hire. Ben had come up against plenty of those in his time, and knew their ilk well enough to tell that the pair he'd encountered in Germany were different. They were pro assassins of the kind who would only work for the top-paying employers: that was to say, the world's most powerful and elite villains. Which included government agencies, in Ben's book; but it also included the more shadowy kinds of forces who would have orchestrated a hit on someone like Auguste Kaprisky. In short, these top-ranking killers were exactly the type of men with whom Jaden Wolf had once rubbed shoulders.

Wolf was an early riser. Ben tried his mobile number three times in the space of thirty minutes, but there was no reply. In the age of communication, nobody ever seemed to answer calls any more. He tried twice more. Still no answer. Wolf must be busy.

As the red sun climbed over the horizon Ben headed out for a three-mile run around the estate. The faster he ran, the more clearly it helped him to think and the more he forced the fatigue and tension out of his system. Returning to the cottage he pounded out a dozen sets of twenty press-ups and the same number of sit-ups, followed by a cool shower and a pot of hot coffee. Still no reply from Wolf. By now it was late enough in the morning to make another phone call. This time Ben dialled the Rome landline number he'd got no response from before, for the contact called 'SS' in Auguste's appointments diary. It was his last remaining lead.

This time, there was an answer. Looked like the age of communication was alive and well after all.

It was a man's voice on the line, an older man's voice, crackly and throaty. And instantly hostile. 'Who the hell is

208

this?' the voice demanded in Italian. It wasn't the most promising start to the conversation.

Ben's fluency in Italian was about midway between his French and his German. He said, 'You don't know me, but please don't hang up. My name is Ben Hope and I'm calling you about Auguste Kaprisky.'

There was a long silence on the line. It felt as though the man was debating whether or not to hang up. But then curiosity must have got the better of him, and he growled, 'You know Auguste Kaprisky?'

'I'm working for him.'

'Then you know what's happened to him,' the Italian said.

'Not all of it,' Ben replied. 'But I'm trying to find out. Specifically, who did it. How much do you know?'

'I've seen the news,' the Italian replied defensively. 'What are you, a cop?'

'No chance.'

'Private dick?'

'Not exactly that either.'

'Then how did you get this number?'

'It was in his diary,' Ben said. 'Which tells me you know him too. I was hoping perhaps you might be able to help me. Perhaps I could meet you in Rome.'

'How'd you know I was in Rome?'

'Because your number has a zero-six prefix,' Ben said. 'Let's not play games, all right? How about you start by telling me your name? I already know your initials, "SS".'

'How am I supposed to help you? I don't know anything,' the man said, not very convincingly.

'I'd still like to talk. If I come to Rome, will you agree to meet?'

'*Vaffanculo.* You take me for some kind of *idiota*? I've no idea who you are!' He sounded about half a heartbeat away from hanging up the phone.

'You can trust me,' Ben said. 'You want me to get his grandniece Valentina Petrova to vouch for who I am? I can do that with one call.'

That seemed to soften the Italian's attitude a little. 'Valentina,' he grated, sounding marginally more human. 'I met her once. She was just a tiny *bambina* then. No more than two or three years old.'

'So we have mutual friends in the family,' Ben said. 'And you have no reason not to meet me. If you give me an address, I'll come and see you there. I'll make it worth your while.'

'Money,' the voice spat. 'I don't want your money. I've known Auguste Kaprisky since before you were born.'

'Fine. Then you can do it for Auguste's sake. What happened to him needs to be put right. If you're his friend, then I'm sure you feel the same way.'

A pause. 'Okay. When?'

'As soon as you like. How about today? Just tell me the time and the place.'

'I'm not giving you my address.'

'Fine, then how about we meet somewhere public? Then if you decide you can trust me, maybe we can continue our conversation in private.'

Another pause. Getting blood from a stone was like juicing ripe oranges next to trying to extract anything out of this guy. Then the voice said, 'Antico Caffè Castellino. Via Cesare Battisti, next to Piazza Venezia. This afternoon, one-thirty.'

Ben looked at his watch. There was time. 'I'll be there.'

'You better not be wasting my time.'

Ben replied, 'I might say the same thing.'

'How will I know you?'

'I'll wear my red baseball cap,' Ben said. And at that, the mysterious and not-so-forthcoming 'SS' hung up the call.

Chapter 27

Ben didn't have a red baseball cap. Arriving in central Rome with an hour to kill before his rendezvous, he bought one with ROMA tackily emblazoned across its front in an over-priced sporting goods boutique, and carried it with him as he strolled the streets, like just another tourist doing the rounds of the dizzying number of sights in the ancient heart of the city.

The September sun was still very warm, the traffic was hectically doing what the traffic always did in Rome and the crowds were out en masse. Ben was being watchful of strangers, carefully but discreetly scanning the throngs of passersby for anyone who might happen to be a hired assassin on his tail. He saw nobody he might have to shoot, but the concealed bulk and weight of Kaprisky's .357 Magnum pressing against the back of his right hip was a comforting presence all the same.

He wandered the old forum for a while, gazing around the patchwork of ruined temples and basilicas, then made his circuitous way on foot into the Capitol, in the direction of Piazza Venezia and his rendezvous point. He climbed the steps up to the Piazza del Campidoglio, a haven away from the traffic fumes and the squealing of brakes and honking of horns, and sat there for a while quietly smoking, admiring

Michelangelo's facade of the Palazzo dei Conservatori and thinking of all the classical artworks inside its museum galleries that would have had someone like Auguste Kaprisky weeping in frustration that he could never own them. Then he wandered back down the street level and ambled along Via del Teatro di Marcello, past the monstrous great white marble Victor Emmanuel Monument, the 'wedding cake' as the locals had disparagingly dubbed it, which blotted out the view of the Capitol from Piazza Venezia. His destination, Antico Caffè Castellino, was situated just up the street across the other side of the square, with a sprawl of tables outside in the sun and busy waiters tending to the lunchtime clientele. The main historic attraction in sight of the café was the slab-sided, fortress-like Palazzo Venezia across the square, with its infamous balcony from which Mussolini had made many of his key speeches, including his 1940 declaration of war against France and Britain.

Ben still had a few minutes to spare before his 1.30 p.m. rendezvous, and he killed that time strolling westwards down the uneven pavements of nearby Via del Plebiscito while contemplating how he was going to handle his anonymous and totally unknown contact. 'SS', whoever he was, seemed a cagey sort of customer. Ben wanted their meeting to take place in private as much as possible, because if the guy wasn't amenable to talking to him, he might have to resort to certain methods to persuade him.

He was weighing the problem in his mind when he happened to come across the incongruous sight, for the historic centre of Rome, of an Irish pub called the Scholars Lounge. That was when the sound of a solitary fiddle reached his ear. The music wasn't coming from inside the Irish pub, though it ought to have been. A few metres further down Via del Plebiscito a skinny young busker had set up on a street corner and was sawing out a fast, energetic and note-perfect rendition of a traditional Irish reel that Ben hadn't heard since his days living in Galway.

Ben looked at his watch. He still had a little time before he'd need to turn back towards Piazza Venezia. He stopped and listened as the fiddler finished his tune. A few other pedestrians walked by without paying much attention. The cloth cap that the skinny young fiddler had placed on the pavement at his feet was almost completely empty, containing just a dismal smattering of coins. Ben took out his wallet, laid a twenty-euro note in the hat and weighed it down with a generous fistful of change from his pocket.

'*Grazie, signore,*' said the busker in a strong Irish accent, lowering his fiddle. He looked lean and hungry and badly down on his luck.

'That was the best "Jackson's Reel" I can remember hearing outside Dublin,' Ben said, in English. 'Or in it, for that matter.'

The fiddler's face lit up. 'Hey, where are you from?'

'Around,' Ben said. 'Name's Ben.'

The beaming young guy shoved his bow under his arm and stuck out his hand. 'Padraig.'

'You're a long way from home yourself, Padraig.'

'Aye, tell me about it,' Padraig replied, with a darker look back at the Irish pub. 'Thought I could set up with me fiddle in there, but they kicked me out, so they did, the bastards.

Not that they'd know proper Irish music if it crept up and bit them on the arse. They're all in there listening to reggae and Bruce Springsteen, if you can believe it.'

'Figures,' Ben said.

'So here's me, standing on this street all morning, playin' me heart out, and look what I had to show for it, until you came along. Hardly enough for a friggin' cup of coffee.'

'Maybe Rome isn't quite ready for your talents yet,' Ben said.

'You can say that again,' Padraig replied sourly. 'I don't know why I ever left Sligo to come to this fookin' place. Land of culture, they said it was. Now the auld cow at me boarding house is threatening to throw me out on the street if I don't pay her a hundred euros by tomorrow. I haven't eaten for two days.'

'Tough break,' Ben said. He glanced up the street. It was time to be moving on. Then a thought came to him and he said, 'Listen, why don't I pay your rent for you?' He reached into his wallet for more cash, and showed him.

Padraig narrowed his eyes and looked suspicious. 'What would you want to do that for?'

'I wouldn't do it for free,' Ben said. 'I'd ask a small favour in return.'

The suspicious look deepened. 'Oh aye? What's the favour?'

Ben smiled. He pointed up the street. 'There's a nice café on the square, three minutes' walk from here. I'd like you to sit at a table outside on the terrace and have yourself a slap-up lunch. Which I'll pay for too, whatever you like. Nice bottle of wine, all the food you can eat, on me.'

The suspicious look vanished and Padraig stared at him in amazement. 'You're not shitting me, are you? *That's* the favour you want from me?'

'Absolutely not shitting you,' Ben said. 'The one other thing I ask is that you put this on.' He held out the red baseball cap. 'Wear it the whole time you're having your lunch and don't take it off.'

'Seriously, like. What's the catch?'

'There is no catch,' Ben assured him. 'No hidden strings, no surprises, no questions. Nobody will give you a hard time, I promise. Just enjoy yourself, earn your cash and wear the hat. Come on, Padraig. It's easy money.' He looked at his watch. It was 1.26 p.m.

Padraig thought about it, but not for any longer than about ten seconds before he took the deal. He gathered up his busking earnings, stuffed the fiddle and bow into their case, and eagerly slapped the red cap on his head. Ben walked with him to the piazza. As they approached the cafe, a well-dressed older couple who'd been having their lunch at an outside table were getting up to go.

'Run and grab that table,' Ben said to Padraig, pointing.

In a sudden moment of self-doubt, Padraig hesitated and looked self-consciously down at his threadbare clothes. 'Christ, the state of me. I look like a dosser.'

'Anyone gives you any crap,' Ben said, handing him a wad of several hundred euros, 'just wave this money in their face and tell them you want their best bottle of champagne. They'll think you're an eccentric millionaire.'

'Nobody's that eccentric.'

'You have no idea,' Ben said. 'Now get a move on.'

He crossed over to the far side of the piazza and sat on a bench, watching from a distance. It was now 1.30 exactly. Moments after Padraig sat down at his table, a waiter appeared, and Padraig went through his motions as instructed. The waiter stared at him, looked at the money, shrugged resignedly, and spent a long while scribbling in his notepad while the youth apparently ordered half the menu. Then the waiter stalked back inside the café to fill the order.

1.40 p.m. came and went. Padraig's food arrived, a mountain that required two waiters to bring it to the table, and a third to carry the ice bucket with the champagne in it. The young guy seemed to be enjoying himself immensely, scarcely able to believe his luck as he got stuck in. True to his instructions he kept the red cap on the whole time.

Ben went on watching the street. 1.45 p.m., and no sign yet of his mysterious contact. Five more minutes went by.

Then, just as Ben was beginning to wonder if he'd been stood up, 'SS' suddenly made his appearance.

Chapter 28

Ben saw him emerge from a side street at the corner of Via del Mancino, a few steps from the café. A small, thin, stooped man of probably around seventy-five, wearing an elegant beige linen jacket and a Panama hat, with silvery curls protruding from under its rim.

It was his furtive, nervous body language that made him stand out from the crowd. As he approached the café terrace he was obviously looking for someone. When he spied the unsuspecting Padraig sitting there wolfing down his lunch with the red cap on his head, he hastily retreated to the street corner where he stood lingering and staring at him for a long moment. Nobody had ever instructed this man in the art of covert surveillance, though his amateur skills were good enough to conceal his presence from Padraig. Next he snatched out a phone and, while the young fiddler was still quite oblivious of being watched, snapped a photo of him before turning around and heading off back down Via del Mancino.

Which was pretty much the kind of sneaky behaviour Ben had anticipated, given the man's manner on the phone. He'd never intended to make contact – just wanted to get a good look at whoever was wanting to meet with him. It seemed that Ben's idea of using Padraig as bait had worked out well.

Ben quickly crossed the square and skirted past the café terrace in no danger of being noticed by the young guy, who was too deeply absorbed in his meal. Reaching the corner of Via del Mancino he looked down the narrow street, lined with dozens of parked scooters and motorcycles, and spotted his man hurrying off down the left-side pavement. 'SS' moved well for a guy his age and must keep fairly fit, despite the stoop.

Ben followed, in the hope that 'SS' would lead him straight back to his place, or perhaps to some other location where they could talk privately. Down the maze of narrow streets they went, Ben hanging thirty paces back. After a couple of hundred yards the guy paused outside a backstreet shop front, took out a ring of keys that he used to unlock the shop door and went inside, closing the door behind him with the tinkle of a bell.

Ben hurried his step and reached the shop a few moments later. The sign on the door said CHIUSO, closed. He peered through the streaky glass and saw no sign of 'SS' within. Inside the window stood, and hung, a dusty and somewhat neglected-looking display of antique lamps and light fixtures of all shapes and sizes, from ancient candle chandeliers to hundred-year-old kerosene lanterns of the Petromax type Ben had used on hiking trips in the mountains of Wales and Ireland. So was this who 'SS' was, a trader in outdated lighting appliances? If that was his line, he didn't seem to be doing great business, judging by the appearance of his shop front.

Inset into the grimy, grafitti'd stone wall to the side of the shop was a barred black iron gate. Through its bars Ben could see a narrow fenced aisle running up the side of the building. It might offer a more discreet way of getting inside than barging in through the front door.

A crowd of clamouring teenagers were ambling down the street towards him, capering about and shoving one another as they came. Why did Italian kids always seem to be the noisiest in Europe, even more obnoxious in public than the French or the Spanish? He turned away to light up a Gauloise and waited for them to pass. With the coast clear he nimbly scaled the seven-foot wall and dropped down on the other side. He moved quickly up the side of the shop building, which was many centuries old, long and narrow on three storeys with a bowed red-tile roof, and much bigger than it appeared from the street. He came to a little door around the back, glanced around to make sure nobody was watching. The lock was old and flimsy and took him under sixty seconds to open with the little set of wire lock picks he always carried in his wallet. There was no alarm on the door. Ben quietly slipped inside.

He found himself in the tiny, faintly dank-smelling hallway of what seemed to be a private apartment adjoining the back of the shop. Maybe 'SS' lived as well as worked here. Ben stood very still, listening hard, hearing nothing. From up a corridor wafted the scent of freshly roasted coffee. He moved towards it, which he might have done anyway, under different circumstances. As silently as a ghost, he stepped through a doorway into a small, fairly basic kitchen with a simple table and a plain wooden chair. The beige linen jacket was hanging over the back of the chair and the Panama hat lay flat on the table. On a gas stove stood a traditional Italian Bialetti espresso percolator, just beginning to bubble up and filling the kitchen with its deliciously rich aroma.

'SS' had been here just seconds earlier, but now the room was empty. Seconds later, the sound of a toilet flushing nearby, to a chorus of ancient dodgy plumbing, explained where he'd gone. Ben stepped over to the chair and felt for a wallet in the inside breast pocket of the linen jacket, slipped it out and checked inside. The bank and Italian citizen's ID cards gave the name Silvano Scarpa. Suddenly our man 'SS' had a real name.

The toilet had finished flushing. Ben replaced the wallet and retreated quickly behind the kitchen door as Scarpa came back into the room and went over to the stove to take the bubbling, steaming percolator off the gas. He was wearing a white silk shirt. With the hat off, the silvery curls formed a ring around the base of a tanned, wrinkled bald crown. His back was turned towards the door. He clearly had no idea he wasn't alone. As Ben watched, Scarpa opened an old-fashioned fridge with more chrome on it than a 1957 Chevy Impala, poured milk from a carton into a small saucepan, heated the milk on the gas flame, added a splurt of black coffee from the percolator and served it into a flowery cup. Carrying it towards the table he took a sip and muttered to himself, 'Hmm, *gustoso*,' in the same gravelly voice Ben had heard on the phone.

That was when Ben stepped out from behind the kitchen door and said, '*Buongiorno*, Signor Scarpa.'

Scarpa whirled round in shock and let go of his cup, splashing coffee down the front of his shirt. Staring at Ben with round eyes he wheezed, '*Chi diavolo sei*?'

'Who am I?' Ben replied in Italian, stepping towards him. 'I'm the guy you didn't want to meet with earlier. So I decided to pay you a visit at home. Nice lamps, by the way. Do a good trade with those, do you?'

A normal citizen, faced with an intruder, would generally start threatening to call the police around now. Scarpa didn't do that. Which Ben found mildly interesting in itself. He motioned to the chair. 'Please. Take a seat, Mr Scarpa.'

'You're not the man I saw at the café.'

'He was a decoy. I had the strangest idea you'd play silly games with me. And I wanted to meet you alone.'

'Are you going to kill me?' Scarpa asked in a tight voice.

'Why would I kill the man I need to help me catch a killer?' The very fact that Scarpa had that on his mind, Ben was thinking, implied he knew more about what was going on here. 'I told you, I'm not one of the bad guys.'

'These days, who can tell? The things you said on the phone, anyone could have known them.'

'Is that why you ran?'

'I trust nobody. A man in my position can't afford to.'

Ben wondered what he meant by that. 'Believe me, Signor Scarpa. If I meant you any harm, you'd have known it by now. I came here because I sincerely need your help. I've come a long way to see you, and time is of the essence here.'

'Time? Why time?'

'Because it was only by chance that Auguste survived that attack. I believe that if he wakes up from his coma with his memory intact, which he might do any day, these men will come back to finish the job. And they might succeed second time around. I need to know what this is all about, so I can find them and stop this thing before that happens.'

The Italian was scrutinising Ben very closely through slitted eyes. 'I hear what you're saying. But what exactly makes you think I can help you?'

'You might start by telling me why Auguste came to meet you three times in the last four months,' Ben said. 'The entries are in his diary, where I found your number.'

'That's none of your damn business,' Scarpa snapped back. 'And you shouldn't be reading his private diary.'

Ben had expected some resistance, naturally. There were many ways to press information out of a recalcitrant inter-viewee. Some of the harsher ones, Ben wouldn't use on anyone. Other gentler options, like dangling them out of a twenti-eth-floor window by the ankles or putting a gun to their head, he'd found effective in the past. But he could see that strong-arm measures weren't going to work on this guy, even if he'd had no qualms about leaning heavily on a much older, frailer man. Scarpa was a tough cookie. He had it written all over his face.

'You say you've known Auguste for years and years,' Ben said. 'If you've managed to stay close to him all that time, that makes you a rare individual. Someone he really trusts. Someone he confides in, maybe. Possibly, someone he's done business with. Except that I don't think he's in the market for a bunch of old brass oil lamps.'

'And you, what's your relationship to Auguste?'

'He and I have helped each other out in the past. I took care of some security issues for him. And there was a problem with his grandniece in Russia some time back, which I had to deal with.'

Understanding and recognition dawned on Scarpa's face. 'Ah. I know who you are. You're the British soldier.'

'Was,' Ben said. 'Not any more.'

'He's talked about you. He said you were a good friend. That's not a word he uses easily.'

'If he's told you all that, then you know more about me than I know about you,' Ben said. 'How about we fix the balance?'

Scarpa nodded. 'You want to know how long I've known Auguste? Then come with me. I'll show you.'

He led Ben from the kitchen and along a passage to a plain, basic living room with simple, cheap furniture. The place hardly seemed like the abode of a man who was close friends with a billionaire and received regular visits from him. Maybe all was about to be revealed.

Scarpa took a framed picture from a sideboard, gazed at it fondly and showed it to him. 'This was the first time we met.'

The photo was grainy black and white and showed a much younger Silvano Scarpa, no more than about twenty or twenty-two. With him was an equally younger Kaprisky, in his early thirties with dark hair. The two of them were sitting either side of a chessboard, intently absorbed in a game that appeared to have been going on for some time, judging by the state of the board.

'It was an international tournament in Kiev, 1969,' Scarpa explained. 'Back in the days when Auguste was much less reclusive than he later became. Neither of us made it past the first couple of rounds of the competition. We were no match for the grandmasters in those days. This was a friendly we played after we'd both been eliminated.'

'Which it looks like he won,' Ben said, looking at the board in the photo. The image was fuzzy, but it was possible to make out the positions of the pieces.

'You can tell?'

Ben shrugged. 'I'm no expert. But at a glance I'd say he was about three moves away from checkmating you. Am I right?'

'As a matter of fact it took him four moves from that point to deliver mate. It would appear you play, then.'

'A bit. Auguste and I have had quite a few games together over the years.'

'How did you do against him?'

'He usually won.'

Scarpa arched an eyebrow. 'Usually?'

'I've got lucky once or twice,' Ben said, wondering why he was being asked these questions when it was him who needed answers.

Scarpa said nothing for a moment, standing watching Ben with his head cocked slightly and a pensive twinkle in his eyes. He looked as though some kind of crazy idea was brewing. Ben didn't like it much.

'You want information, yes?' Scarpa said. 'The truth of the matter is a little, shall we say, *delicate* to reveal. But I'll give you what you want.' He held up a gnarly finger. 'That is, on one condition.'

'What condition?' Ben asked warily. He was getting the feeling it wouldn't be to wear a red baseball cap.

'You and I will play a game of chess,' Scarpa said, with a triumphant glitter as if he'd already won. 'You beat me, I'll tell you everything I know.'

'And if I lose?'

Scarpa shrugged. 'Losers get nothing. That's the nature of the game, my young friend. As I'm sure you know perfectly well. That's my deal. Take it or leave it.'

Ben made no reply. He was reconsidering those alternatives that had occurred to him earlier, like dangling Scarpa from the edge of the Tarpeian Rock or jamming Kaprisky's .357 in his mouth with a live round in the chamber and the hammer thumbed back until he spilled the goods. But either still seemed like an unlikely proposition. And no way to treat a lifelong pal of Auguste's, no matter if the guy was a kooky old oddball and probably half-mad into the bargain. There was something here to learn, and Ben had come too far to turn away now.

He thought, *Fuck it.*

Said, 'All right, Scarpa. I accept the challenge. Let's play.'

Chapter 29

'Excellent,' Scarpa said, glowing with satisfaction and suddenly looking about ten years younger.

'So where do we do this?' Ben asked, looking around him for any sign of a chessboard in the small, simple living room.

'You'll see,' Scarpa replied enigmatically. 'This way.' He beckoned for Ben to follow.

He led Ben back along the passage towards the kitchen, then turned through a doorway and up a flight of creaky stairs to the first floor. Another bare passage, with a bedroom to one side, ended in a blank wall covered by a tall built-in bookcase. Scarpa stopped there.

'You want to show me your book collection?' Ben said.

Scarpa didn't reply. With a mysterious little smile he ran his finger along the rows of book spines, then reached for one of them, an old antiquities auction catalogue from 1979. Instead of pulling the book out he pushed it in, and to Ben's surprise the *click* of an opening latch sounded from somewhere behind the rows of volumes. Next thing, the entire bookcase swung out like a door, revealing a whole other room behind it.

More than just one room, Ben realised as Scarpa led him through the concealed doorway. There was a whole suite of them back here, like another apartment in its own right. Not only that, but this secret domain was far more opulent and richly decorated than the humble living quarters downstairs.

Silvano Scarpa was a man with a lot of secrets, all right. Anyone who thought Auguste Kaprisky was a little bit of an odd fish hadn't met this guy. A very peculiar gentleman, indeed.

Ben followed him through a luxurious lounge full of beautiful antiques, into a smaller side room. What he saw there made him blink. The room was completely devoted to the game of chess. Dozens of sets were arranged on tables all around the walls, each table with a chair either side ready for the players to get straight down to business.

To Ben's fairly dispassionate eye, one chess set had always seemed pretty much like another. Now he could see that was anything but the case. Some were large and decorative and colourful, others smaller and plainer. But all old, and clearly valuable exhibits in Scarpa's personal chess museum. He wondered how many people the Italian ever trusted enough to invite into his secret domain to challenge to a match. Or did he just play himself all the time? No wonder he was crazy.

'Choose your weapon,' Scarpa said, grandly waving his arm around him.

Ben walked over to the nearest table and looked at the set laid out on it. The small, hunched-looking pieces appeared carved out of stone and had few features to tell them apart, making it hard to distinguish a king from a queen or even a rook.

'An ancient Islamic set,' Scarpa said, gazing at it like a beloved pet. 'Magnificent, though perhaps not a good choice for a beginner.'

Ben picked up on the mind game the old man was playing, trying to psych him out before the real contest had even begun. He said nothing, passed on the Islamic pieces and stepped over to the next table. This one was more recognisable to him as a chess set, not too decorative, exotic or ancient. Though still a little unusual.

'A beautiful Jaques of London set from the nineteenth century,' Scarpa said. 'The boxwood and ebony pieces designed by a compatriot of yours called Howard Staunton, a famous Shakespearean scholar who was widely acknowledged as the first world chess champion. This style of pieces is still the standard used in world championship matches today. Though you'll notice the unconventional colour scheme of this particular set. It was the fashion at the time to paint the black pieces red.'

After a moment's hesitation Ben passed on that one too, and moved to the third table. Now this one was much more the kind of thing he was used to. A classic, familiar and timeless design with proper black and white pieces, though the finials on top of the kings were of the opposite colour. He could live with that.

'This one,' he said, pointing.

'Ah,' said Scarpa with an approving nod. 'You have chosen the Soviet set. It has an interesting history. After the six-month-long and inconclusive match between Garry Kasparov and Anatoly Karpov in Moscow in 1984 to '85, the pieces they played with were returned to the chess museum on Gogolevski Boulevard in Moscow but then mysteriously disappeared.'

'This is them?'

'Oh, yes,' Scarpa said, and his eyes glittered. 'Thanks to dear Auguste, who employed the best private detective in the USSR to track them down. He gifted them to me as a birthday present. I value them extremely.'

It surprised Ben a little to hear that his old friend, this apparently harmless eccentric, was capable of such underhand and quasi-criminal dealings. But it was the idea of another stolen chess set that mostly caught his attention. 'Do chess pieces often go missing like that?' he asked.

'Anything at all can go missing,' Scarpa replied, 'or can be made to go missing, if there are collectors out there who prize it highly enough. Some people will stop at nothing to get what they want, no matter how odd it may appear to the outside world.'

Ben watched him closely for any sign in his eyes that he might know about the Napoleon pieces taken by Auguste's attackers. The Italian could have been hinting at something, but Ben was a very acute judge of such things and he didn't believe that was the case here. For a second he toyed with telling Scarpa about it, on the off chance that anything could be learned from doing so. Then he dismissed the idea. There were already far more than enough clues to suggest that it had been no ordinary robbery carried out on the whim of some lunatic collector.

'So it's agreed,' Scarpa said. 'We will play on the Soviet set. Now we must choose sides, black or white.' He took a pawn from each side of the board, one in each hand, and switched them around a few times behind his back before holding out his clenched fists for Ben to choose.

Ben had an old rule that had become almost like a super-stition with him. *If in doubt, always pick left.* He pointed at Scarpa's left fist. Scarpa opened his fingers to reveal the black pawn.

'Black it is,' Ben said.

'And may the best man win,' Scarpa said.

They pulled out chairs and sat down opposite one another across the board. Ben looked at the array of his black army in front of him. His pick of colour meant he would be under pressure from the start, since white had the first move. But then, he'd be under a lot already, going up against a far more experienced and expert player, who was obviously highly confident of victory. Ben was already beginning to regret that he'd agreed to the game. What a stupid way to extract information from someone, he thought to himself.

Scarpa's wrinkly face was lit up like a schoolboy's with contained excitement. He rubbed his hands in anticipation of the imminent slaughter and he couldn't sit still. Then his expression became granite hard and inscrutable, as stony as a poker player's. He briskly reached out a bony hand to make his first move.

And then the game was on.

Chapter 30

Scarpa's opening gambit, innocuous enough and yet oddly menacing at the same time, was to shunt his king's pawn forward two squares. Ben had learned enough to know that that move was described as e4 in the language of chess notation. He responded in kind by moving his own black pawn out two squares to meet Scarpa's white pawn head on: e5, in chess parlance. It was the only counter-move in his limited repertoire.

With the battle now formally underway, the stone-faced Scarpa wasted no time in starting to deploy more of his white forces: first a knight, then a bishop, emptying out his rear rank so that he was already prepared to castle early in the game freeing up the heavy artillery of his rook to go out and wreak havoc on the enemy. Ben's grasp of chess opening theory was sketchy at best, but his past experience learning from much more gifted and passionate enthusiasts, like Auguste Kaprisky and Père Antoine of the Carthusian monastery where he'd spent some time years earlier, enabled him to recognise white's strategy as the so-called 'Italian game'. It seemed appropriate enough, given the nationality of his opponent. He wondered if Scarpa was having some little private joke at his expense.

Ben mimicked Scarpa's opening moves by getting his own knight and bishop into action. Nothing to worry about so far, he thought. This was the same old familiar pattern that had been played millions of times before in the history of the game and felt like reasonably safe ground to him. But the speed and decisiveness with which Scarpa responded to his moves unnerved him, as the Italian unhesitatingly flashed out an unexpected pawn sacrifice, offering his foot soldier with a move to b4.

Ben couldn't understand it at first. Why would Scarpa expose one of his own men like this, as though sending him out to the slaughter? Sensing some fiendish trap laid out for him to blunder into, Ben stared at the board for a long time. But unable to see the downside in doing so, he went ahead and took the offered pawn.

Too late, he remembered Auguste successfully throwing this same trick at him in one of their games from long ago. It was a particularly cunning little deception that Auguste, chuckling at his opponent's misfortune in falling for it, had explained to him after winning the game: the so-called Evans Gambit, invented by Pembrokeshire ship captain William Davies Evans, who had used it to topple one of the great players of his day back in 1829, was an aggressive means of allowing white to take control of the centre of the board. And it seemed that the well-used old trick was as effective as ever, with Ben having now idiotically fallen victim to it twice in his otherwise totally unremarkable chess-playing career.

For the first time since the start of the game, Scarpa let his poker face slip and gave the sly smile of a man who knew the scales had just tipped strongly in his favour. 'Shades of Fischer versus Fine, New York, 1963,' he said. 'We hated him for taking our world championship, but we respected his ability.'

From what had seemed like a fairly easy-going start, Ben now found himself hemmed with stunning speed into a losing position with the key strategic ground completely dominated by the enemy, who was able to move in against his black forces from multiple angles. Scarpa was relentlessly lining up his queen and bishop on Ben's king, who quickly fell into check and was deprived of his right to castle into safety. Ben knew that castling was something you had to do in every game – but now his king was leading a nomadic existence, singled out and vulnerable and fighting for his life in the centre of the board. The king's best defender, a knight, was forced to the g4 square, out of the action and unable to defend his charge.

Whatever fledgling strategies Ben had been trying to develop now lay in disorganised tatters, playing defensively just to save his men in the face of a withering enemy advance. Scarpa developed his pieces at speed and then thrust his f-pawn forward in what looked to Ben like the beginning of a decisive assault.

Ben stared helplessly at the board. Was it really all going to end so badly for black, and so fast? It certainly looked that way. Scarpa wasn't even hiding his sense of inevitable triumph any longer, letting the sly smile grow into a grin that spread across his face. If Scarpa won the game, Ben would have to honour his end of their deal and simply walk away empty-handed without the important information he'd come all this way for, and which the Italian was dangling in front of him like a taunt. He'd been a fool to allow himself to get into this situation.

Yet just as all seemed lost, at that moment an inspiration came to him. Could that last move of Scarpa's have given him a chance at turning this thing around? Ben cast his mind back to another chess game from long ago, one of the many that he'd played with Père Antoine in the serene silence of his chambers within the medieval monastery, looking out at the snowy Alpine mountainscape in the distance. 'Queen and knight,' the old monk had said in his soft, wise way. 'They're all right.' Ben had learned from him how those two pieces could complement one another and combine in a tactical duo known as Philidor's Mate, named after François-André Danican Philidor, an eighteenth-century French master who had been one of Père Antoine's chess heroes.

And now, suddenly, the hidden patterns in the layout of the chessmen in front of him seemed to yield their secret and shine a light towards a possible escape from his seemingly hopeless predicament. If he could just get his queen into a position where it could give check to the white king, then to his amazement he could see a way that it would combine with the knight and give mate in five moves. It would be a surprise attack that Scarpa clearly had no idea was coming, given that Ben's knight in question had been sitting on the sidelines as a non-combatant spectator for pretty much the entire game.

The trick would be not to let Scarpa read his mind until the trap was ready to be sprung. With an air of resignation,

Ben flicked his c-pawn forward one square, apparently a defensive move to cover an attack from Scarpa's bishop on Ben's undeveloped rook in the corner. As Scarpa brought his last piece into play, the queen's rook, ready to launch the final offensive that would wipe the black army out once and for all, Ben saw from the Italian's overconfident move that his feint had worked.

Ben checked his analysis a second time, took an inward deep breath and shifted his queen from d8 to b6. He knew that experienced chess players didn't announce check, and that doing so was a sign of a beginner – but he couldn't stop himself on this occasion.

'Check.'

Scarpa leaned forward in his chair, stunned. He knew he'd been tricked and that the threat of being checkmated was suddenly very real. A deep frown knitted itself on his brow. But then the frown cleared and Ben saw something creep into the Italian's expression, maybe thinking that his opponent might not have the skill to execute the coup de grâce and bring off a victory. Surely a player of Silvano Scarpa's calibre could quickly reclaim the advantage against his enemy. He reached out and shuffled the white king into the corner, out of check.

Exactly as Ben had anticipated. Ben moved his knight forward.

'Check.'

Now the frown was back on Scarpa's face, only deeper and darker this time. He moved his king back to where it had come from. Maybe he could keep running the king out of trouble until the shadow of threat lifted.

But any lingering hopes Scarpa might have had of rescuing his situation were blown to pieces as Ben confidently moved his knight backwards, giving check both from the knight and from the queen simultaneously. It was the first time Ben had ever been able to spring a double check on a chess opponent. Scarpa again was obliged to move his king into the corner. Now Ben had to rack his brains to remember the crushing manoeuvre that Père Antoine had used against him, the spectacular queen sacrifice that would end the game in two moves.

Ben reached for his queen and slammed it down next to the white king.

'Check.'

Scarpa's only possible move to liberate his king was to use it to take Ben's threatening black queen. But then by doing so, the white king was walking eyes wide open into a so-called 'smothered mate' where Ben could execute the kill shot with his knight. A bullet to the head. No possible means of escape.

Scarpa's eyes were darting up and down, back and forth over the board, as though in search of a miracle. None was forthcoming, or would be. Only an earthquake that brought the building down about their ears could save him now. Tight-lipped, he raised his scrawny hand and let it hover there for a moment before his fingers came to rest on his king. But just as Ben thought the Italian was going to do the inevitable and take the queen, instead Scarpa laid his king down on its side in resignation.

Scarpa let out a long hiss of a sigh and leaned slowly back in his chair, looking at Ben with something like real hatred in his eyes. He truly hadn't expected this inexperienced foreigner to best him at the game of which he considered himself a master.

'You lose, Scarpa,' Ben said. 'Now you talk. That was the deal.'

Scarpa was silent for a long-drawn-out moment. Then, with his eyes still fixed on Ben with that same glowering resentment, he shook his head. '*Penso di no.*'

Ben looked back at him over the top of the chessboard and the recumbent white king. 'You don't think so. You mean you didn't think you'd have to.'

Scarpa shook his head again. 'It is not possible. To do so would be to compromise myself and my clients.'

Ben had had enough of this crap. He slipped his right hand down off the chess table, drew the revolver from his belt and pointed it in Scarpa's face with the hammer cocked.

Auguste would have hated him for doing this. But Auguste wasn't here.

Ben said, 'This will compromise the state of your brains, when they're all over that wall. I know you're deep into something. While you're messing me around, the people who tried to murder your friend are still out there and getting further away. So now you're going to let me in on your little secret, or you won't live to regret that you didn't.'

Chapter 31

All of a sudden, Scarpa was rather more willing to cooperate. And now Ben was about to discover the reason why the Italian had been so reluctant to reveal his 'delicate' information before now.

'Please put the gun away,' Scarpa said wearily. The hate in his eyes had all washed away now and he looked suddenly older and frailer. 'There's no need for violence.'

'Fine,' Ben said, and stuck the revolver back in his belt.

Scarpa invited him to sit in the lavishly furnished living room, and poured them a glass of arzente from a cut crystal decanter. Then his story began.

'I make things,' he admitted. 'Copies of valuable items that people wouldn't be able to have otherwise. So much like the originals that nobody can tell the difference.'

'You mean you're a forger,' Ben said.

'I prefer to think of myself as an artist,' Scarpa replied with a thin smile. 'But yes, you might describe me as a highly specialised counterfeiter.'

'One who offers his services to billionaires like Auguste Kaprisky. But why?'

'To explain that, we have to go back in time. You see, when Auguste and I first met, all those years ago in the late sixties, I was a struggling young artist barely able to feed or clothe myself. It's become something of a joke, the idea of the penniless painter or sculptor starving in his freezing garret, but believe me, it's not a happy existence. It wasn't that I didn't have talent. But my abilities were of the wrong kind. I had hopelessly little imagination for creating original works of my own. However, when it came to *recreating* beautiful things that someone else had already produced, whether it be a classical painting, a sculpture, even an old woodcut, I found that I had a rare ability to reproduce them in almost perfect detail, virtually indistinguishable except to the most expert eye.

'I couldn't understand it at first. It seemed as if God had put a curse on me, to give me this natural talent and yet render me incapable of using it to create anything original. But then one day in 1969, when I was just twenty-one, I happened to show my new friend Auguste some of my best sculptures, and he was impressed. I knew he was quite wealthy, but I had no idea how much, or that he would offer me a handsome commission there and then to produce something for him, a replica of the Medici Venus that stands in the Uffizi Gallery in Florence. The original statue was made in the first century BC, and it's been one of the most widely copied pieces of art in history. King Louis XIV of France possessed no fewer than five replicas of the same statue, and Auguste wanted one as well, to put in his hallway. I got straight to work. All of a sudden, my strange talent made sense to me. That was what set me on my new career path.'

And a lucrative enterprise it must have turned out to be, Ben thought, looking around him at the opulence of the room. The fact that Scarpa had built himself a secret luxury hideaway behind a concealed door suggested that not all of his activities were strictly legal. The basic apartment and lamp shop downstairs were certainly just a front for his real operations. No wonder he was cagey.

Scarpa went on, 'As the years went by, Auguste remained one of my best customers. By now I had perfected my skills as a painter to the degree that I could create flawless forgeries of any grand masterwork my clients cared to name. Even though a man of Auguste's immense wealth could easily afford to buy the Mona Lisa, should it ever come on the market, he was frustrated by the fact that neither museums nor private collectors would easily be persuaded to part with some of the magnificent works of art that he coveted.'

'You painted the Mona Lisa for him?' Ben asked.

Scarpa smiled. 'No, not that one. Although several of my clients, including an oil sheikh and a former United States President do have copies of that particular work hanging on their walls, for which I charged them a great deal of money. Auguste's tastes have always been on a somewhat grander, more heroic scale. One of the last paintings I did for him, some years ago, was a copy of one that he had tried to buy from its owners at the Château de Malmaison gallery near Paris, to no avail. You would be astonished by the amount of money he offered them for it, but they turned him down at any price. A very well-known piece of artwork indeed. I'm sure you would know it.'

Ben said, 'Art isn't my strong point.'

The forger looked pityingly at him. 'Obviously your passions lie elsewhere. There's no accounting for personal tastes, I suppose. But it's not only paintings he's commissioned

241

from me over the years. Old clocks, even jewellery and other ornaments. Those Fabergé eggs on the mantelpiece in his yellow salon? I was rather proud of how exactly those resemble the originals. Auguste amuses himself by telling visitors to the estate that they're the real thing. They're always fooled.'

Ben had been one of those fools. He felt irrationally stung, knowing that Auguste had lied to him.

Scarpa went on, 'It's a funny thing, how people change through the years. As younger men he and I used to meet up quite often, talk about art, discuss future projects, play many, many games of chess together. I was one of the few who could beat him. But then, as my dear old friend became more reclusive in his ways and was increasingly reluctant to leave his estate except for pressing matters of business, I tended to hear from him less and less often. As I said, the last painting I did for him was the one I mentioned earlier, which I won't bother to describe to you as you know nothing about art. A fascinating project, with one particularly curious feature . . .'

'Go on and cut to the chase,' Ben said irritably, tired of hearing about forged paintings. Maybe he should get the gun out again.

'Then one day in June of this year, he called me out of the blue to say he had a new job for me. Of course I would never refuse my old friend and patron, no matter how occupied I might be with other projects. But I thought it was very strange.'

'Strange how?' Ben asked.

'This time it wasn't a classic painting or a statue he wanted to have recreated for his collection. It was a chess piece. A single piece, a white knight. One of the pair from a set Auguste owns that once belonged to a rather famous historical figure.'

'Napoleon Bonaparte,' Ben said. His mind was suddenly shooting back to the chess pieces stolen from Auguste's study. This couldn't be a coincidence. 'I know. But—'

'Why? On the face of it, the reason was simple enough. Auguste told me that he had accidentally knocked the original piece onto a hard floor and caused it to smash to pieces, some of which he couldn't find. Naturally, he was devastated and guilt-stricken at having broken something of such historic importance, not to mention its financial value. But since nothing could apparently be done to mend it, there was no option but to make a replacement. He brought me the remaining white knight from the set and asked me if I would produce an exact copy to take the place of the broken one.'

Ben realised that must have been the first of the trips to Rome that Auguste had recorded in his diary. 'This was in June? Four months ago?'

Scarpa nodded. 'Needless to say, the replacement white knight had to be perfect in every way, made from the very same material, a rare kind of marble that is uniquely creamy-white in colour. Auguste had sourced a sample from the same part of Persia, now Iran, where the original had come from. I was honoured to be given the task, though quite intimidated by the responsibility of having the remaining original knight in my possession while the work was being done. And also, I was somewhat baffled by one particular aspect of Auguste's instructions.' Scarpa shook his head. 'I asked him why he would specify this, but he wouldn't say.'

'Specify what?' Ben asked.

'Well, you see, the original pieces were solidly carved from opal and blue lapis,' Scarpa replied. 'But unusually, Auguste wanted the replica knight to be made with a small cavity in its base, which would be covered by the disk of green felt attached to its bottom. He was very specific about the dimensions of the cavity, requesting it to be an eighth of an inch wide and one and a half inches deep. I warned him that drilling a hole into the middle of the piece was a delicate operation as the material was quite brittle and could easily split. Yet he was insistent. He had even calculated how many grams of weight would be lost from making the cavity. And in order to ensure that the finished piece still weighed exactly the same as the remaining original, the extra half inch of depth of the hole was intended to allow for a small plug of a rare metal called osmium, twice the density of lead, to seal off the cavity and compensate in weight for the removed material. This way, the replica white knight would feel no different from the original, when handled. That was extremely important to him, and as you can see, he was prepared to go to great lengths to ensure it.'

'What was the reason for the cavity?' Ben asked.

The forger shrugged his narrow shoulders. 'As to that, I must admit I have no idea. Auguste didn't volunteer the information.'

'You didn't ask?'

'I was curious, naturally, as it seemed such an elaborate extra complication in the creation of the piece. But in my experience Auguste Kaprisky isn't a man who will tolerate being badgered with questions. I had others, too.'

'Such as?'

'Such as the fact that Auguste didn't offer to supply me with the osmium plug to fit into the cavity. The reason for that is that he wanted to fit it himself, even though he's not a practical kind of man. He barely knows how to change the cartridge in his fountain pen. Yet he was adamant that he would personally attend to those finishing touches to the replica white knight, inserting the plug, gluing it into place and then affixing the felt disk to the bottom of the base. I found it odd that he would take it upon himself to do those things, when I could have done them myself in the space of two minutes. It certainly wasn't an attempt on his part to save money. Very baffling indeed. One can only hazard guesses as to what ulterior reasons he might have had, and for what purpose he needed the chess piece made that way. Auguste is a man of many secrets, you know.'

'I'm getting that impression,' Ben said. 'I only wish I knew what they were.'

'He's a good man,' Scarpa said. 'A very good, decent, generous and kind man, in his own way. The dearest friend to me, and his grandniece Valentina adores him like no other. But nobody is above sin, I'm afraid. Auguste Kaprisky is no angel.'

'In what sense?'

'As an example, on occasion he obtained pieces of art whose provenance wasn't, shall we say, entirely legitimate. They sometimes came from dubious sources. I tell you this in the strictest confidence, of course.'

'You mean they were stolen,' Ben said.

'That's a blunt way of putting it, but yes. The art world is a hive of illicit dealings and corruption, and for a man with all the money in the world, the temptation to lay one's hands on certain items might be too much to resist. In such cases he would employ me to produce replicas with deliberate slight imperfections, to exonerate himself in the event of an investigation. If challenged over his alleged ownership of something he shouldn't have had in his possession, he would simply laugh it off as a misunderstanding by showing them the copy and pointing out the telltale signs that it wasn't genuine. Once his accusers backed off, he would switch the original back into its place. It never happened, but he was ready just in case. A man of great cunning, always thinking of every eventuality. What else would you expect of a superb chess player?'

'Nice,' Ben said. It was a glimpse of a side of Auguste he hadn't known.

'But I've long known that my old friend harboured darker secrets too,' Scarpa said. 'He made no specific allusion to them in his conversations with me over the years. But the secretive phone calls that would draw him away from the chess table for long periods of time, the days when he seemed deeply, silently preoccupied by what I could only guess were thoughts and ruminations of the most troubling kind. The occasional oblique references that suggested to me he had certain insights into the world of politics and economics that were far above what is revealed to the general public. All these things made me wonder about the real nature of his business affairs, and the kinds of people and shadowy dealings he might have been involved with.'

'Then you've known him better than I ever have,' Ben said.

Scarpa shook his head and smiled sadly. 'It's painful to learn that someone we call a friend keeps secrets from us. But you're not alone. As close as I've often felt to him, closer than a brother, I don't think there's a living soul in this world who truly understands the real Auguste Kaprisky. Not even little Valentina, the most precious thing in his life, has ever been aware of the deeper, darker side of her beloved grand-uncle or the secret parts of his life. Now I'm concerned that he must have got himself mixed up in something extremely dangerous. What else could explain this attack on his home? It seems he must have got on the wrong side of some very bad people. That's why I have to be more cautious than ever, in case they should show an interest in coming after any of Auguste's other business associates. Alas, one never knows.'

'Can you tell me more about who these people might be?'

Again Scarpa shook his head. 'I wish that I could, my friend. But I've already gone past the limit of my knowledge and into the realms of speculation. If poor Auguste had died in that attack, or if he tragically never wakes up from this terrible coma, then his secrets would be destined to stay locked away out of our reach for ever. From what you've implied, though it hurts me to say it, that might even be for the best. I hate to think of anything else happening to him.'

He looked down at his feet and was silent for a moment, reflecting. Then he looked up again at Ben, the twinkle returning to his eye. 'But we've talked long enough. I propose that we play another game. You have to allow me the chance to redeem myself for having lost the first.'

'Don't beat yourself up,' Ben said, standing. 'I'm sure it was just a fluke.'

'You're leaving? Don't you want to come up to the top floor and let me show you my studio? You might see something you'd like to commission from me. A Rembrandt, or a Monet?'

'No, thanks. I don't have the wall space Auguste has.'

'What a pity. Let me show you out the front way, through the shop. Perhaps I could interest you in a nice lamp before you go.'

'I found your company illuminating enough,' Ben said. 'Goodbye, Signor Scarpa. And for your own sake, don't go talking to any more strangers. You never know who might come knocking at your door.'

As Ben walked back along the narrow street towards Piazza Venezia, he was thinking about the white knight. There was only one reason for wanting to create a hollow space within the chess piece, and that was to conceal something inside. Something that would be well hidden by the metal plug glued in to seal the hole, and the felt covering over the base.

But to conceal what? And why?

Ben had to leave that puzzle to one side for the moment, because just then his phone began to burr in his pocket.

It was Jaden Wolf, calling him back.

Chapter 32

'Sorry for not getting back to you right away,' Wolf said. 'I got a bit waylaid.'

With Jaden Wolf, that could only mean one thing. Ben asked, 'Trouble?'

'Nothing I couldn't handle,' Wolf replied off handedly. 'Hardly worth mentioning, really. You remember the little spot of bother I had with those local boys a while back?'

Ben did remember. Not long after Wolf had moved to his peaceful little corner of Aragón in Spain, he'd got into an altercation with a gang of ne'er-do-well thugs he'd caught trying to set fire to a stray dog. Wolf was very fond of animals, and he didn't take kindly to people who did cruel and evil things to them. Soon after that incident, some friends and relatives of the pieces of trash he'd put in the hospital had formed an armed posse and come hunting for him in the rugged hills outside Albarracín, looking for revenge. Several bodies had ended up being disposed of in a ravine as a result. Ben had just happened to be there at the time – not that Wolf had particularly needed a helping hand.

'Well, the silly sausages only went and got it into their heads to come back for another go,' Wolf said.

'Dear me. Some people never learn, do they?'

'I think the lesson ought to stick this time. But never mind me and my dull, boring life. To what do I owe the pleasure of your call?'

Ben had reached the café. He scanned the terrace tables looking for Padraig, but the young guy was long gone. Walking on, he said to Wolf, 'I had a run-in with a couple of members of your former profession, near Berlin. It occurred to me that with your past experience and connections, you might know someone who could help me identify them.'

Wolf chuckled. 'Up to your usual tricks, I see. Some things never change.'

'Look who's talking,' Ben said.

'Ha, ha. What are you doing running around ze Vaterland?'

'I'm not,' Ben said. 'Right now I'm in Rome. But in a couple of hours I'll be back in Le Mans. My old friend Kaprisky's in trouble. I'm helping him out.'

'As one does. So, these two blokes you had a run-in with. Tell me, are we talking about identifying a pair of stiffs?'

'Not yet,' Ben said.

'Shame. Then you don't have a pic you can zap over by email. That would have made things simpler.'

'I didn't really have time to get the gentlemen to pose for a photo. But I got a good look at them.'

Wolf listened as Ben described them. 'Pros, and not just anybody. They don't hesitate to take out anyone who gets in the way of the job. And your regular gun for hire doesn't generally come equipped with Steyr AUGs and forty-mil grenades, so there's some money and organisation behind them. Physically in excellent shape, between thirty and forty. Some kind of Nordic ethnicity, it looked to me. Maybe

Scandinavian. Both about the same build and height as me, five-eleven-ish. One of them has what I thought was a birthmark on his right cheek but it's actually a burn scar. Apart from that they're very similar facially. You could almost take them for brothers.'

'That's because they are brothers,' Wolf said.

'You know them.'

'Small world,' Wolf replied. 'As you might have guessed, I knew most of the players in it, back in the day. These two were already well established by the time I came into the game. They look like twins, but they were born a year apart. And they're not Scandi, either. Close, but no cigar. They're Balts, born and raised in some little backwater peasant village in Lithuania. Didn't stick around there long, though. Still in their teens when they left their homeland for the bright lights of Poland, then Germany. Made quite a reputation as hitters for the organised crime clans, Chechen mafia, Albanian mafia, Remmo family. The list goes on. Made quite a reputation.'

'Names?'

'Nobody knows their real names. In the German underworld they were called Kugel and Messer.'

'Bullet and knife,' Ben said. 'Subtle.'

'About as subtle as the way they make their living,' Wolf said. 'You remember the rule I had, back in the days when I was on the job?'

'No women, no kids. You wouldn't touch any assignment that would bring harm to either.'

'Right. And I damn well stuck to it. But not everyone in that line of work had those scruples. And Kugel and Messer

251

had none at all. They were more than happy to take on the kinds of contracts that I'd have refused. It was well known within the business. They'd do anything, no matter to whom, the nastier the better. The one with the scar is Kugel, the older brother. Story of that goes back to when they were teens in Lithuania and their violent drunk of a father chucked a pan of boiling milk at them. Messer got out of the way in time. Kugel didn't. A couple of years later, when they were big enough and hard enough to take the old man on, they shut dear daddy in a wooden shithouse, wrapped a chain around it so he couldn't escape, doused it with petrol and burned him alive inside.'

'Lovely,' Ben said.

'That's kid stuff, compared to the things they did later. Which made them quite sought after in certain circles. It also made them very expensive. These days the word is only the richest bad guys can afford to enlist their services, at ten million a hit. If Kugel and Messer are on to you, you've got enemies in very high places. Seems you've been pissing off the wrong people, Ben. Then again, that's the story of your life, isn't it?'

'Thanks for reminding me.'

'I'm not going to even ask,' Wolf said. 'But whatever you've got yourself into this time, you know where to come if you need help. God knows you've been there for me enough times.'

'You've been a big help already, Jaden.'

'They're good, Ben. Really good. I mean, so are we. But these guys didn't waste time training to yomp over hills and mountains in full kit or survive for weeks behind enemy lines living off the land. All they know is killing. Knives, guns, poisons, explosives, hand to hand, up close and personal or a thousand yards away through a rifle scope. They've made an art of death, and they're masters at it. So watch yourself out there, all right?'

Reassuring words.

The Kaprisky jet was waiting for Ben at Ciampino Airport, half an hour's taxi ride from the centre of Rome. He'd learned a lot during his short few hours in Italy, and now it was time to take that information back to base. Ben boarded the plane, returned to his now familiar regular seat and fell into such deep thought that he barely registered the whoosh of the engines and the sensation of takeoff.

The more he reflected, the more Ben was convinced that Silvano Scarpa's counterfeit white knight was right at the heart of this whole complex affair. It was becoming clearer in his mind that the attack on the estate had had a two-fold strategic purpose. Firstly and most obviously, to eliminate the billionaire himself and thereby prevent him from revealing whatever dangerous secrets he possessed to the likes of Fritz Kohler. Secondly, to acquire the Napoleon chess set. Ben had known that already, but what he hadn't understood until now was the reason why the raiders would have made off with the chessmen alone and left the board behind. The board was just as historically important as the pieces themselves, and to separate one from the other would be highly detrimental to the set's value to a collector. So you could rule out the financial motive. Problem was, until now, that had also seemed to rule out any kind of logic to the deal.

What Scarpa had told him changed everything. It wasn't even the whole of the thirty-two pieces they'd been after. It was just the one white knight that somehow had special significance for them, because they'd somehow got wind of what it was. Ben wondered why they'd grabbed the whole bunch: was it simply because they were in a hurry to make their escape? Had it been a deliberate ploy to cover up their real intentions, as a smokescreen? Or was it perhaps that whoever had masterminded the attack didn't *know* which of the chess pieces they were looking for?

Those were all unanswerable questions at this moment. But the one that burned the hottest in Ben's mind was the reason for the hollow knight's creation. More specifically, how could a chess piece, a simple piece of opal carved in the shape of a horse's head, possibly be such a threat to powerful interests that they'd kill to obtain it?

Ben thought about the cavity that Scarpa had been commissioned to drill out of the underside of the knight. One and a half inches deep, minus the amount of space needed for the osmium plug that would compensate for the small loss of weight. What could be fitted inside that small space?

Racking his brain, he could only think of one possible option. Some kind of recording device. A tiny miniature mic and digital hard drive that could be used to bug a room, capture sensitive information and be used as evidence – perhaps as a means of blackmail, or for some different purpose. Either way, someone must stand to lose a great deal if that information was passed on.

But why a chess piece? Ben wondered why Kaprisky had planned it that way. If his intention was, say, to secretly record a conversation or meeting, why not just use a mobile phone? The fact that he'd gone to such lengths was extremely significant. It could only mean that the secret conversation he'd recorded had taken place within a highly controlled environment. Perhaps only certain people could be physically present at that discussion. And perhaps strict security arrangements were in place to protect the confidentiality of whatever was being aired. In effect, no mobile phones or other electronic gadgets permitted inside the room. No allowable leakage of information, on pain of death.

It boiled down to this: a clandestine meeting, involving high-level individuals who absolutely did not want the content of their conversation being divulged to anyone on the outside, and would stop at nothing to keep it safe. Moreover, a clandestine meeting to which Kaprisky must have been not only privy but an invited participant. A member of a group of powerful people who had little notion that he was in fact betraying their trust and recording whatever sensitive, dangerous, perhaps ruinous, information was being shared among them.

Ben remembered Scarpa's words: *Auguste Kaprisky is no angel.* The forger had been talking about Auguste's crooked little sideline in stolen, or at any rate dubiously obtained, works of art. But what if the old man had been mixed up in something far, far more dangerous? Something that could result in a much worse fate than ending up in jail?

The kinds of secret meetings Ben was imagining were the kind that mafia bosses and drug cartel chiefs held behind closed doors, in luxury mansions guarded by men with machine guns and fierce dogs straining at their leashes. Any hint of betrayal would mean a bullet to the head, if you were lucky. More likely, those guys would carve you up with a chainsaw and dissolve the remains in quicklime. But the notion of Auguste Kaprisky as a master criminal or organised crime kingpin was so ludicrous that it forced a dark smile to Ben's lips. It just didn't fit. An absolute non-starter of an idea.

Then again, maybe there were other ways a man like him could get embroiled in risky games. Ben recalled something else Scarpa had said, when he'd been speculating about Auguste's *certain insights into the world of politics and economics that were far above what is revealed to the general public.*

'What did you get yourself mixed up in, Auguste?' he muttered out loud.

Somewhere there had to be another clue that would uncover the truth. Ben thought back to the contents of the safe in Auguste's study. Now that the diary had yielded all the secrets it had to give, there was only one item left whose meaning was still elusive, and that was the unmarked key they'd found among Auguste's things.

The key, the key. Everything depended on it. Valentina had said she'd been trying to match it to a lock somewhere inside the house. If she'd had any success since he'd last seen her, she would have called him to say so. But now that Ben had come this far, he was damned if he wasn't going to crack its secret too. He felt so close now, as if just one more push would swing the door wide open.

It was getting towards late afternoon by the time the jet touched down at Le Mans. Ben thanked the guys for the ride and hurried to the private hangar where he'd left the Lancia Stratos. He tossed his gun onto the passenger seat, screeched out of the airport terminal and started driving fast back towards the estate.

And that was when the ambush happened.

Chapter 33

The return journey from the airport was only the second time Ben had had the opportunity to put the Stratos through its paces on the open road. In his dark, brooding frame of mind and his hurry to get back to base with what he'd learned, he pushed the car much closer to the limit of its performance.

And it was fast. Almost too fast for a road vehicle – and he'd driven some rockets in his time. The steering was so sharp and the handling so responsive that it felt as though the car would do anything at all he asked of it. One touch on the gas and the sensation was like sitting on the head of an arrow propelled from a high-tensile crossbow, reeling in the horizon at such a velocity that his senses could hardly keep up and the sides of the road became a blur. Such a pure-bred driving machine required all Ben's focus and concentration not to let its intoxicating power get out of hand.

He'd got about halfway back to the estate, hurtling along empty country roads that snaked between fields of vines, maize, sunflowers and bright yellow rapeseed, when a black Range Rover Sport with dark tinted windows suddenly came bursting from the mouth of a leafy lane on his right and tried to block him off. Ben reacted lightning-fast and darted around it with a juddering squeal from the Stratos' fat tyres.

In his mirrors he saw the Rover weave, straighten up and then accelerate hard after him.

Ben didn't think it was some grown-up boy racer larking about. Trouble had found him again. But finding him was one thing, and catching him was another. He stamped down on the gas and the Stratos dug effortlessly into its power reserves, surging eagerly forward with the gauge needles and the engine note soaring. The Rover must be tuned for extra performance, but it couldn't hope to compete with the power of Kaprisky's road missile and the boxy black shape in his mirrors quickly started falling back. *Nice try*, he thought to himself.

How the hell had they found him? Nobody had tailed him from the airport, and the road had been empty for several kilometres. More to the point, who were they? His instinct told him his old friends Kugel and Messer were back, but there was only one way to find out.

The loaded .357 Magnum was lying within easy reach on the passenger seat next to him, and for a crazy moment he was seriously tempted to slam on the brakes and become better acquainted with the hidden figures behind that dark-tinted windscreen. But that might not be such a good idea, he reflected, because as they'd failed to get him in Germany with a two-man hitter team, this time around they might very well have hedged their bets and sent more. Kaprisky's revolver carried six rounds and the twin speedloaders in his pockets another dozen. Eighteen rounds wouldn't be enough to deal with four, five, or even six military-grade assault weapons and God knew what other ordnance they'd brought to play with.

So casting aside that temptation, Ben accelerated harder and the gap between him and the pursuing Rover widened.

He flew through a series of bends with the rapeseed fields to his left and right a yellow blur. When the road straightened out again the Rover had dropped even further behind, wallowing all over both lanes in its desperation to press on the chase.

But then, suddenly, it was no longer just him and the black Range Rover. Ben felt, more than heard, the heavy pulsing thump somewhere overhead. He'd no sooner realised what it was than a blaze of machine-gun fire from above tore up the road and punched bullets through his roof. The bullets poked through the thin sheet metal like a steel skewer through wet paper. One burst open the padding of his driver's seat, an inch from his right thigh. Another ripped a six-inch chunk out of the steering wheel right between his hands, turning an O into a U and going on to drill a hole through the floor pan. Then the fast-moving dark shadow of the helicopter was swooping down over the road, overtaking the Stratos and roaring by with its nose angled down and its tail up, skimming close to the road.

The stricken car went into a violent wobble in its wake as Ben fought to prevent himself from going into a skid, grappling the wheel like a rally driver. Revs and speed were dropping. In his mirrors, the Rover was catching up again. Up ahead, the chopper banked around in a tight turn over the edge of the field, so low it almost shaved the heads of the yellow rapeseed crops to come roaring and clattering back for another pass. A Bell Jet Ranger, sleek and powerful and capable of flying a hell of a lot faster than he could drive the Stratos unless he was on a racetrack. He could see the twin machine guns slung under its nose, probably activated by a trigger on the pilot's cyclic control. It was no helicopter gunship, but it was something uncomfortably like it – and now it was streaking straight back towards him, approaching at an angle so that its fire wouldn't rake its allies in the Rover that was now fast closing the gap from the rear.

All Ben could do was throw the Stratos into a hard weave from side to side, in the hope that the ruined steering wheel wouldn't break off in his hands, and that his crazy slalom would throw off the helicopter pilot's aim and allow him to dodge the worst of the gunfire. The lightweight bodyshell and flimsy door skins would offer him as much protection from high-velocity rounds as a paper cup.

Here it came. He braced himself for the worst and ducked down as low as he could and still see to keep the car on the road.

Muzzle flash twinkled from the mouths of the guns. The Stratos went into a spin as bullets slammed into its front and side. Windows shattered and Ben felt the lurch as one of his tyres blew out. He sawed at the smashed steering wheel and somehow just managed to save himself from veering right off the road and into a ditch, or through the post-and-rail fencing that separated the raised banks of the verges from the yellow fields either side. Now the Stratos was out of its spin and pointing the right way again. He stamped on the gas and the engine responded with a throaty howl and the acceleration pressed him back in his seat. No time to grab the gun and shoot back. No time for anything, except to try to make it out of here in one living, breathing piece.

The chopper wheeled around after him, its deafening turbine screech filling the air and a wide circle of crops flattened under the downward blast of its rotors. But it couldn't fire because the Rover was coming up fast on his tail, the two targets too close together. Now it was the turn of the Rover's occupants to inflict some damage. A figure leaned out of its passenger window, jacket fluttering in the wind, teeth clenched, a cut-down semiauto shotgun in his fists. To the sound of a muffled boom from behind, the Stratos' back window shattered into a million pieces. Ben kept accelerating. The car was veering badly from side to side because of its burst tyre and the broken steering wheel felt in real danger of coming apart in his hands. A second blast, and Ben felt the impact judder through the car. They were trying to blow out a rear tyre too. To immobilise him, then reduce the Stratos to a shredded heap of wreckage with their victim inside. If Wolf had been right about the killers' million-a-hit fee, then the paymasters would get their money's worth.

Not if Ben could help it. The Stratos was limping like a three-legged greyhound but there was still a chance he might get away from them.

Then that chance suddenly vanished. Because about eighty yards up ahead, and closing fast, was another side road. And out of that side road was lumbering an articulated lorry with a long chromed tanker trailer that said ECOFUELS. Instead of turning one way or the other it cut straight across both lanes and stopped, blocking the entire road and, with it, Ben's escape route.

It was a well orchestrated attempt to take him out.

And if he didn't come up with something pretty damn soon, it looked as though it might actually succeed.

Chapter 34

In moments like this, you had to settle for whatever choices were open to you, if any at all. As he hurtled towards the truck with the Rover close on his tail still pumping shotgun blasts at the rear of the Stratos and the helicopter preparing to reopen fire with its machine guns, Ben was rapidly running out of road. So he did the one thing he could.

Which was to get off it. To his right, the side of the road was screened with trees. To his left was the thirty-acre field of bright yellow rapeseed crops, with nothing between it and him but a narrow grass verge and a wired post-and-rail fence. He swerved hard to the left. The Stratos hit the verge and exploded through the fence, pieces of splintered wood bouncing off his windscreen and over the roof. A momentary sensation of weightlessness as the car left the ground; then it landed in the field with a bone-jarring impact that hammered the suspension against its stops and visibility ahead was instantly reduced to near zero as he went ploughing through the curtain of crops. Tattered bits of vegetation covered the windscreen. He hit the wiper switch and kept pushing on as fast as the bucking, bouncing vehicle would let him. The old Stratos rally cars might have dominated the dirt in their heyday but they weren't made for belting across loose earth and plough ruts.

The Range Rover was. It came storming through the gap in the shattered fence and right after him, following the furrow of flattened crops in Ben's wake. The guy with the shotgun was still leaning out of his passenger window, pounding buckshot into the Lancia's rear. If something penetrated through to the vulnerable engine compartment, Ben would suddenly find himself in even more trouble than he already was. But even as that thought flashed through his mind, he knew he was about to have a bigger problem. Now the chopper was hammering overhead and coming back around in a tight banking curve for a third pass at him.

This wasn't a situation he was going to be able to survive much longer.

Ben thought, *enough*.

Barely slackening off his speed he yanked on the handbrake and slewed the Stratos violently around in a storm of shredded crops. The car rocked to a halt, turned about in a one-eighty and facing his pursuers as they came streaking towards him from different angles. Time to turn the tables. The hunters hunted. Ben stamped down hard on the gas and charged them. His engine howled and the blown front wheel was scrabbling for grip but he kept it steady as he could, aiming for the space between the Rover and the helicopter. Shotgun blasts slammed into the front of the Stratos and his windscreen dissolved into a web of cracks. At the same instant the helicopter's machine guns opened fire, sending up explosions of dirt in parallel twin tracks that came snaking fast towards him. There would be no escaping the torrent of bullets once they ripped into their target.

Ben had no intention of being in the way when that happened. With his foot down to the floor he was hurtling towards the enemy like a Japanese Kaiten suicide torpedo pilot of World War II. Then at the very last instant before the helicopter's gunfire shredded him to pieces he veered straight towards the Rover, snatched the revolver from the passenger seat, kicked open his driver's door and threw himself out of the car.

When you jumped from a plane you had time to plan your landing to avoid broken bones and serious brain damage. With just a few inches to fall, Ben struck the ground and instantly started tumbling and rolling. Bailing out of a fast-moving car on the road he'd have left most of his skin and flesh smeared over forty metres of tarmac. As it was, the soft earth and the dense crops cushioned the impact.

He came to a stop barely in time to see the Stratos hit the Rover. The driver of the oncoming vehicle had tried to swerve out of the way before it was too late, but he hadn't reacted quickly enough. The two cars smashed into one another head-on at a combined speed of a hundred miles an hour. The little two-seater weighed only a fraction of the big luxury SUV but the impact was enough to lift them both off the ground in a violent cartwheel of destruction. Bits of wreckage flew in all directions. A torn-off wheel was flung high into the air. The helicopter had stopped firing and now roared overhead, its massive wind crushing the yellow crops flat in a wide circle.

Ben was a little bruised and cut up from his tumble, but he sensed no critical injury. He leaped to his feet with the revolver in his hand and looked around him. The helicopter had gained altitude and was hovering above as though the pilot was momentarily stunned by what had just happened, waiting for what might happen next and trying to decide what to do himself: finish the job or fly away? On the ground, the wrecked cars had come to a rest a few yards apart. The Stratos was totalled. The more solidly built Rover had upended on its roof. At least one man was dead inside, blood smeared on the broken glass of the windscreen on the driver's side. The guy who'd been firing the shotgun out of the passenger window had been wrenched forward so hard in the collision that his spine was snapped and his face a red pulp where it had smacked against the roof pillar. One rear door had been ripped clean off. The other swung open on buckled hinges and the passenger inside crawled out.

Dazed, but not that dazed. And clutching a small Scorpion EVO submachine pistol with a folding stock. He saw Ben and scrambled to his feet. But he didn't stay there very long, because Ben shot him twice in the chest from fifteen yards away, the high-pitched report of the .357 Magnum almost inaudible over the clattering roar of the chopper, the sharp recoil thumping his palm. The man went over backwards like a felled tree. Then before any more survivors could come crawling out of the wreck with automatic weapons, Ben moved quickly behind the cover of the smashed Stratos.

While that was happening, the helicopter's pilot had got back in the fight and was swooping the aircraft around in a circle and lowering his altitude for yet another pass. Ben soon would be caught out in the open with nowhere to run from its machine guns. There was nothing much he could do about that right now, since three more men were emerging from the overturned Rover and jumping to their feet. One of them Ben had never seen before – but as he watched from his position crouched behind the Stratos he recognised the other two as the Lithuanian hitman brothers Messer and Kugel. All three were armed with the same kind of EVO submachine gun as their comrade on the ground with Ben's revolver slugs in his chest.

It would take more than a devastating car crash to slow these professional assassins down. Quickly assessing the situation, they and their third associate started trying to work their way around both sides of the Stratos, intending to pin him down in a diagonal crossfire. Three fully automatic weapons, each with a thirty-round box magazine whose contents it could spit out nineteen to the second.

Before he found himself in the middle of a firestorm he brought the revolver up over the wing of the wrecked Stratos, levelled his sights at the nearest two opponents, Messer and his unknown associate, and loosed off the four remaining rounds in his cylinder as fast as he could work the trigger double-action. Messer ducked down as the .357 hollowpoints drilled the bodywork of the Rover behind him. The unknown associate cried out and slapped a hand to his shoulder, then disappeared behind the car.

Kugel kept coming. His burn-scarred face was spattered with someone else's blood and looked more striking than ever. The EVO submachine gun was raised and ready.

Ben quickly unlatched the cylinder and dumped out the spent cases from his empty revolver, grabbed a speedloader from his pocket and fed in another six rounds, slapped the cylinder shut and was ready for action again. But even the most proficient modern-day sixgun shooter took a couple of seconds to go through the motions of a reload, and in those two seconds Kugel had reached the wreck of the Stratos and was bearing down on Ben with his finger on the trigger.

Ben brought his own gun up to bear, but Kugel fired first and the shocking jolt of a bullet impact on his right forearm put Ben's aim off and his shot went slightly wide, hitting the side of Kugel's neck, blowing off the lower lobe of his left ear and making him spin around on his feet. Kugel let off another wild burst, missed, took another step towards Ben with his weapon coming back on target. His eyes were cold, impassive and as blank as a shark's. Killer's eyes.

Ben would have wanted to keep the brothers alive for questioning. But this man was far too dangerous to keep alive.

They're good, Ben. They've made an art of death and they're masters of it.

But some people could be even more dangerous. And Ben Hope was one of those.

Chapter 35

In a move that had been drilled into him so many times that he could execute it almost too fast for the eye to see, he switched the revolver from his compromised right side to his left, planted the square blade of the foresight against the oncoming target of Kugel's head and squeezed off a single shot.

Point-blank range, the hollowpoint launched from the revolver's barrel at something north of 1200 feet per second, struck Kugel dead centre an inch above the bridge of his nose and printed a red third eye there. Kugel came one more step forward, the same implacable expression on his face, like some kind of automaton that lacked the reasoning to understand that it was catastrophically damaged. For a surreal fleeting instant, Ben thought that a man whose name was 'bullet' might be magically impervious to them. That maybe it would take a silver dagger or a stake through the heart to finish him. But then the neurological impulses from the pulped cerebral cortex to the central nervous system shut down and Kugel stumbled and collapsed face first into the dirt and flattened crops, stone dead on his feet before he'd even started falling.

Ben's right arm was on fire and there was blood dripping from the sleeve of his jacket, but there was no time to check how bad the wound might be. Clutching the revolver left-handed he turned towards Messer and the third man, who were re-emerging from behind the Rover. Messer was screaming in Lithuanian. If someone had just shot Ben's brother in the head, he'd have been screaming too. Bits of the Stratos' bodywork and windows flew as Messer let rip with a sustained blast from his EVO. Ben ducked for cover and fired back, *BLAM BLAM BLAM,* the shots punching the air. Another half a cylinder gone. Ten rounds spent in total, more than half of what he'd started out with. Not good.

Thirty yards away across the field, the helicopter had made its turn and was now coming back for a renewed assault. Nose down, tail up, the front tips of its skids almost raking the ground and its hurricane downdraught laying waste to the bright yellow crop. Muzzle flashes twinkled from its underside. The machine-gun fire ripped up the ground in a parallel track heading straight for where Ben was hunkered down behind the wreck of the Lancia.

With nowhere to run, Ben cocked the hammer of his weapon, took aim at the oncoming chopper and held his fire until he could clearly see the pilot behind the windscreen. The FBI and US Highway Patrol men who'd been issued with the first .357 Magnums back in the 1930s used to call them truckstoppers, because no other handgun round before had had the power to penetrate the engine block of a car. It could punch through other materials just as easily, including toughened aircraft Perspex. The recoil kicked against Ben's hand. A neat round hole a third of an inch wide appeared in the helicopter's windscreen and somewhere behind it he thought he saw something spatter red.

In the next instant the helicopter began to spin wildly out of control, machine guns still hammering away. The parallel tracks of gunfire deviated off target and went snaking towards the Rover, ripping up everything in their path. Messer stopped firing and hurled himself flat as the machine-gun rounds chewed through the bodywork of the overturned SUV and sent up fountains of dirt and pulped rapeseed all around it. Messer's companion failed to take cover in time and the continuous stream of gunfire cut him in half, separating his legs at the hips before he could utter a sound.

Now the chopper had spun right around on its axis and its tail, just a couple of metres above the ground, swung towards Ben, who scrambled out of its path to avoid being sliced to pieces by the tail rotor blades. The screech of the turbine and roaring clatter of the main rotor were deafening, the dust blowing up so thick that it was impossible to see. Ben fired three more pounding rounds into the helicopter's fuselage, and at this range it was like shooting at a barn door. Smoke instantly began pouring from the back of the gyrating aircraft as his bullets hit something critical inside. It followed its wild, uncontrolled course for a few more instants and then came down right on top of the wreckage of the Rover.

Ben ran and took cover among the rapeseed. A second later, the crashed helicopter exploded with a dull, ripping CRUMP and a mushroom of orange flame and black smoke rolled upwards. It was followed by a secondary explosion as the reserve tank erupted, tearing the flimsy shell apart.

Then all was silence, apart from the crackle of the blazing fire. Ben still had one round left in his gun but ejected it, dropped the cartridge in his pocket and fed in the last six as a tactical reload. Better to have it and not need it, than to need it and not have it.

A whole area at the heart of the field was devastated and blackened, with burning debris scattered everywhere. Black smoke belched from the ruins of the aircraft and the Rover buried underneath it, and climbed in a tower to the sky. Ben emerged from the ocean of tall yellow stalks and moved cautiously towards the scene of destruction, swivelling the revolver left and right in search of anything that moved. His right arm felt quite numb now and he let it hang loose, blood dripping from his fingertips and making a trail of spots on the ground. A sharp pain in his side told him he might have sprung a rib when he jumped from the car. But what was pain?

Kugel's body lay in a dark pool near what was left of the Stratos. The first man Ben had shot was sprawled twisted on the ground a few steps away, staring upwards with his gun hand outflung. The man he'd wounded in the shoulder had still been sheltering behind the Rover when the helicopter had come down on top of it, and him. All that was visible of him was a charred arm sticking out from under the fiery wreckage. Nearby were the grisly remains of their colleague who'd been sawn in half by the machine guns. His severed legs were lying in a patch of flames and burning from the feet up.

Which all added up to one man still unaccounted for: Kugel's younger brother Messer. Where the hell had he gone? Ben paced warily around the blazing debris, ready to shoot at the slightest movement of anything living. But the

Lithuanian seemed to have simply vanished, as though he'd drifted away on the wind with the smoke.

Ben stuck the gun in his belt and crouched down to check the bodies he could get close to for ID. There was nothing at all in their pockets, as he'd expected. He wondered whether Kugel, Messer and their associates had been part of the team that had attacked the Kaprisky residence. His curiosity was answered when he examined the legless corpse of the half-severed guy and found the spiderweb tattoo on the side of his neck. The man who'd taken Georges' place in the passenger seat of Annick's van.

As Ben stood up, a movement caught his eye from across the field and he turned to see a distant running figure making his escape through the rapeseed. Messer. He was heading towards the articulated lorry that was still parked sideways across the road beyond.

'There you are,' Ben said. He wouldn't have figured the Lithuanian assassin for a coward who'd run away when things got tough. But it looked as though Messer must have lost his weapon in his haste to get away from the crashing helicopter.

Ben drew the revolver from his belt and took careful aim. It was a long shot to make left-handed. And in any case, shooting a fleeing unarmed man in the back wasn't really Ben's style, even if it had been the right thing to do tactically. He sighed and lowered the gun. The running figure had reached the truck now, and was clambering up inside the cab to join the driver. Sooty diesel smoke puffed from the truck's exhaust stacks as the driver restarted his engine. It was too late to do anything to stop them from getting away.

Or was it? Ben watched as the long vehicle shunted backwards and forwards a short distance, then again. He could hear the impatient revving and see dust and dirt spinning from the truck's wheels as the driver tried to get it moving. Ben realised that the driver had got himself jammed at an angle in the narrow road, unable to reverse the huge trailer far enough to get turned around. Now he'd spun his front wheels so hard into the grassy verge that he'd well and truly got himself dug in and stuck fast.

Which meant there was still a chance that Ben could catch Messer alive and make him talk. He started running towards the truck. He didn't know if the driver was armed or what spare weapons the team might have loaded aboard, and he wasn't going to take any chances that they might start shooting at him as he ran. He raised the gun and fired, saw the driver's window shatter and the two heads inside the cab duck down.

Nobody fired back. Ben ran faster, ignoring the ache that lanced through his ribs with each step. He'd have fired more rounds at the truck to keep the enemy pinned down, but with only five shots left in his gun he needed to conserve ammo. Then as he was just sixty or seventy yards from the truck he saw its cab doors fly open and Messer and the driver jump out and start making their escape on foot down the road, back the way they'd come.

Damn it. They were too far away, with too much of a head start, for Ben to catch them. He hesitated, then raised the gun again. Maybe shooting them was the only option after all.

But just then the sound of an approaching car made him stop and turn around. A red Peugeot 206 hatchback coming from the opposite direction had been forced to a halt by the truck blocking the road. Its two occupants, a tall thin guy and a woman with sandy hair, had noticed the column of smoke rising from the middle of the field and got out of their car, craning their necks to stare over at the blazing wrecks of the two vehicles and the helicopter. Ben knew the couple wouldn't waste any time in calling the police. Nothing he could do about that either, except get out of here before the entire local gendarmerie turned up in force.

And Ben's best means of doing that had now arrived. He tucked his gun out of sight and hurried towards the couple with the red car. Clambering over the fence and flashing his Le Val card too fast for them to make out what it was he said in an urgent tone, 'Police officer in pursuit of a suspect. I need to commandeer your vehicle.'

Before they could react, he'd jumped in behind the wheel of the little Peugeot and taken off, leaving them standing there on the roadside boggling at their departing car. He hated stealing from people, but his need was greater than theirs. That was how he justified it, anyhow, as he went tearing up the grass verge, battered down the fence ripping off both wing mirrors, sped along the edge of the field to get past the obstructing truck and then back onto the road through the ragged gap he'd made earlier.

The road on the other side of the truck was still clear of traffic. Nor was there any sign of Messer or the truck driver. Ben drove a fast quarter mile down the road and saw a hundred places where the fleeing men could have made their escape cross-country. He swore, gave up the search and started looking for an alternative route back to the Kaprisky estate.

As he drove, he knew there would be real trouble when the police investigated the scene of the battlefield, gathered up the dead bodies and started asking hard questions. And he also knew that he'd be right in the thick of it, because when they took away the wreck of the Stratos they'd soon trace it back to him through Auguste. Moreover the couple back there would be able to identify him as the man who'd taken their car claiming to be a police officer. Even some of the blood the forensics people might find at the scene was undeniably his own.

It wouldn't be the first time in his life he'd found himself on the wrong side of the law. He'd always managed to get out of it somehow in the past, and maybe he would again. But all the same this was a new twist he could have done without. He drove on, trying to disregard the concerns that crowded his mind like the dark, threatening clouds that were gathering in the late afternoon sky. At least the estate would offer some kind of sanctuary from trouble, for the moment.

Though little did he know that when he arrived back there, more unexpected developments lay in store for him.

Chapter 36

By the time Ben was rolling up to the gates of the Kaprisky estate, the clouds were gathering closer and darker and the atmosphere was slowly building ahead of the coming thunderstorm. He was in a sullen mood and his injured arm had begun to hurt badly now that the numbness was wearing off.

But as the gate guards ushered him through the checkpoint he was pleasantly surprised to see some newcomers among them: faces he instantly recognised as those of Clark Jenner, Cormac Wallace, Liam Walker, 'Baz' Baczko and several other men he'd trained with before. The new security detail had arrived. And to Ben's amazement, through the small crowd that gathered around his car to welcome him appeared the even more recognisable and unexpected figures of Jeff Dekker and Tuesday Fletcher.

'Hello, mate,' said Jeff, beaming in Ben's car window. 'Surprised to see us? A couple of the guys couldn't get here in time, so we decided to fill in for them until—' Then his smile and cheery expression fell away as Ben hauled himself awkwardly out of the car and Jeff saw the blood soaking his jacket sleeve and running down his hand from the bullet wound.

'Jesus Christ, what's happened?'

Ben told his friends about the ambush that had just taken place, and the attack in Germany before that, and their looks of confusion and consternation grew as dark as the rolling storm clouds overhead. 'I don't have a lot of time to explain, folks,' Ben said. 'Things are happening, and they're going to start happening faster. The police are going to turn up here before too long and they'll be looking for me. Meantime, we have a lot of work to do.'

First off, the little Peugeot was going to have to be taken away as far as possible from the estate and dumped. A quick conference among the men resulted in Baz Baczko and Liam Walker being elected for the task and minutes later they headed off, Baczko driving the hot car and Walker following in Jeff's beefed-up Ford Ranger pickup. While that was being taken care of, Ben tore himself away from his worried friends, went inside and used one of the Kaprisky residence's many bathrooms to get himself cleaned up and examine his wound.

He'd been lucky, because the bullet had only creased the flesh. But it had gouged a deep trough in the top of his forearm and wouldn't stop bleeding. He daubed it with antiseptic cream, wrapped a makeshift bandage around it, and was emerging from the bathroom when Valentina, having been with her Tonton when she'd learned of Ben's return, came running to find him.

'My God, I just found out what happened. Are you all right?'

'Two of them got away,' he explained. 'And we're not much closer to finding out who's behind this.'

'Never mind that for now. Look at you, you're hurt!' She pointed at his arm. Blood had already started soaking through the bandage.

'I'll survive.'

'You need medical attention.'

'There's no time for that, Valentina,' he tried to protest, but she couldn't be denied. 'Don't be ridiculous, Ben. What's the point of having your own private hospital on site if you don't take advantage of it? We're going to get that poor arm of yours seen to right away, before it drops off.' She pulled out a phone. Two minutes later, a staffer was waiting for them outside in an estate golf buggy, to whisk her and her reluctant, frustrated charge to the clinic. On the way, she filled Ben in on the latest news of Auguste's recovery and he realised why, despite all that was happening, she was full of irrepressible happiness.

'He's out of the coma, Ben!' she gushed. 'Opened his eyes and smiled at me! It's fantastic! Though he's still terribly weak and asleep most of the time, and it'll be days before he starts to get his strength back. The doctors are sure he'll soon be able to start talking again, and after that it's only a matter of time before he can get out of bed. He's going to be all right!'

Ben was pleased to hear that Auguste was now under close guard by two of the new security guys brought in by Jeff and Tuesday. Less pleased that Inspector Boche and his detectives were still sniffing around and had turned up at the estate only that morning; but he was relieved that Valentina was keeping them at arm's length. 'I had to tell them Tonton was out of the coma. And now they want to bombard him with a ton of questions – but there's no way I'll let those idiots stress him out until he's completely recovered.'

Valentina's other news was that, during Ben's absence, Mia Brockhaus had left the estate and was now checked into the nearby five-star luxury Château du Grand Lucé under the name Molly Steiner. The long-suffering Gabriel Archambeau had been charged with the task of fixing her up with new identification, passport, bank account, credit cards and a well-salaried job within the Kaprisky empire. The corporation had branched out into property development as a new sideline some years earlier, and an opportunity had recently come up for an architectural designer to work on some of their building projects in Europe and the USA. Mia's professional experience made her an ideal fit.

'I appreciate what you're doing for her,' Ben said.

'She's one of the family now. Gabriel's moaning about it, of course. But he moans about everything.'

He might have good reason to moan even more, Ben thought, when he found out about the latest turn of events. How soon the police might turn up with their questions and arrest warrants was anybody's guess, and as he and Valentina arrived at the clinic he was anxious to get out of there and press on as fast as possible before they did. He fought to contain his impatience while the same weary doctor who had been with Auguste day and night attended to his injured arm.

'It's a very curious kind of wound,' the doctor said, carefully examining the deep crease made by the bullet. 'How did you say it happened?'

'I fell out of a tree,' Ben said.

'This could require a graft.'

'Just patch it up as best you can, doc. I'll be fine.'

A couple of painful injections and a dozen stitches later, the golf buggy delivered Ben and Valentina back to the house. The electrical storm feeling in the air was stronger than ever as the dusk began to fall. When the heavens broke, they were in for a spectacular light display.

While Ben had been getting stitched up, Jeff and Tuesday along with a few of the other guys had gathered around the TV in the security monitor room. But not to watch Formula One races. 'You're all over the news, mate,' Jeff informed Ben as they met up again outside the house. 'Jesus, it looks like a bloody battlefield. Burnt-out choppers and cars and bodies and a zillion coppers running all over the place. You should come and see.'

Ben froze. 'What are they saying?'

'"Dramatic incident near Le Mans,"' Tuesday said. 'That's all, along with a ton of wild speculation about terrorists, drug gangs, alien invasions, whatever comes into their heads. They've no idea who did it.'

'Or if they do, they're not telling yet,' Jeff added helpfully.

Ben agreed. It was only a matter of time. And there wasn't a moment to waste. He left his friends to go back to watching the news and led Valentina quickly up the stairs and back along the passage to Auguste's study. As she watched, full of questions, he knelt down in front of the old man's safe, keyed in the chess game combination and swung open the door to retrieve the key. 'Here we go,' he said. 'Now let's see what we see.'

'That's what you wanted?' she asked him. 'What for? I told you, I've already tried it on every single lock in the house, and all the outbuildings and cottages and everywhere else I could think of, and it doesn't fit any of them.'

'Then we'll try again,' Ben said. 'If it was in the safe with the diary, it must be important.'

'You try them all again, then, if you don't trust me to do things properly,' she answered back irritably, with colour rising in her cheeks. 'It only took me hours and hours. There are rather a lot of locks on the estate, you know.'

'I do trust you. If you say it didn't fit, it didn't fit. But we must be missing something.'

'Like what?' she said, shaking her head.

'Could be something simple. So simple we can't see it, for thinking too hard. All I know is, this key matters. And it's our last lead, Valentina. If we can't figure out what it's for, why Auguste saw fit to keep it hidden in here, then we're fresh out of ideas.'

'I already am,' she protested. 'As far as the key is concerned. I really don't know where else we can look.'

Ben gripped her shoulders and looked hard into her eyes. 'He's your granduncle. Your blood. Nobody else in the world is closer to him or knows him as well as you do.' Even as he said it his mind flashed uncomfortably back to the things Silvano Scarpa had told him about those hidden aspects of Auguste's life that nobody could have guessed at, and about his covert dealings with Fritz Kohler, and he felt a twinge of doubt. Did she really know Auguste, the real Auguste, as well as she thought? Did anyone? But he buried that doubt and pressed on. 'Try to think about it from his point of view. Put yourself in his shoes. If you had a huge, huge secret that you wanted to keep safe, where nobody could ever find out about it, where would you hide it?'

'What secret?' she asked helplessly, shaking her head. 'I don't have any idea what you're talking about.'

It was a long shot, and he knew it. But maybe, just maybe, there was something buried in her memory that she just wasn't seeing. Something her Tonton might have told her in passing. Even just the smallest hint. 'The biggest secret in the world,' he said. 'It doesn't matter what it is. Close your eyes. Take the key and hold it tight. Let your instinct guide you.'

She took the key from him and clasped it between her palms, screwed her eyes shut and thought hard for a long moment. 'I'm sorry, Ben. Nothing's coming to me. Where would I hide it? I . . . I . . .' She was straining so hard to find an answer that tears began rolling down her face. 'It would have to be somewhere impossible to guess, or even to find by accident. Somewhere totally bombproof.'

Bombproof. That was the word that set off a white flash of illumination like a starburst inside Ben's head, took his breath away and made his heartbeat start to race faster.

Valentina saw the change in his expression. 'What?'

Chapter 37

'You're right,' Ben said. He grabbed the key from her hands, leaped towards the doorway and set off down the passage at a run. Valentina followed, bewildered, calling after him, 'Hold on! Where are you going?'

Ben didn't answer. He pounded down the stairs, sprinted through the vast entrance hall with Valentina chasing after him, and burst outside so fast that Jeff and Tuesday, on their way back from the security monitor room, had to jump out of the way to avoid being run down.

'Where the hell's he off to in such a hurry?' Jeff asked Valentina as she emerged from the house in Ben's wake.

'You'd have to ask him,' she replied breathlessly, not slowing down.

'He's onto something, that's what,' Tuesday said, and nudged Jeff's arm. 'Come on, let's find out.'

Evening was beginning to fall, and the heavy atmosphere of the impending storm had grown even more intense while Ben had been inside the house. It wouldn't be long before the weather broke. He heard the running footsteps behind him, but he was too set on his purpose to look back or slacken his pace until he'd sprinted all the way from the house, past the equestrian paddocks behind it, to the multi-car garage where the Kaprisky fleet and Auguste's own car collection were housed. He pressed the wall panel button, the steel shutter whirred up and the interior of the garage was automatically lit up by halogen spotlamps that gleamed on the polished curves of the classic sports cars. But it wasn't those Ben had raced here to look at.

Turning round, he saw that not just Valentina had followed him from the house, but Jeff and Tuesday as well. Valentina was the only one slightly out of breath from the sprint. Swiss finishing schools obviously didn't keep their pupils trained to a peak of combat-ready fitness.

'What's up, Ben?' Tuesday asked.

'Bombproof,' Ben replied. 'That's the word you used just now, Valentina. It got me thinking.'

'Great,' she said, bemused and frowning at him. 'But I have no idea what you're talking about.'

'You want bombproof, here it is.' He pointed along the gleaming row of garaged cars to where Auguste's hulking black limousine sat among the assembled Kaprisky fleet vehicles. 'This thing's got enough armour plate built into it to roll through a minefield without a scratch, or withstand a direct hit from a rocket-propelled grenade.'

'Sure, so the guy's a bigwig and bigwigs like to be protected. So what about it?' Jeff asked, no less confused than Valentina.

'It also happens to have another special addition,' Ben said. 'Auguste was never much of a shooting man. But I happen to know he once had a bespoke gun safe fitted into the back of the car. For those times when you just *have* to transport your fifty-thousand-euro Purdey doubles to an exclusive grouse shoot in Scotland. I know, because the same guy who built our security vault for the Le Val armoury did the work for him.'

'Dubreuil?' Jeff said, remembering. 'If he built it, it'll be as secure as a bank vault. He's an artist, and no mistake.'

'And a gunsafe needs a key,' Ben said. He held the key up.

'I looked *everywhere*,' Valentina gasped. 'I'd never have thought of this.'

'Of course you wouldn't,' Ben said. 'Nobody would have. Your granduncle's a very wily man.'

She stared at the key in his hand. 'You think it will fit?'

'Only one way to find out,' Ben said. He didn't like relying on guesswork but he trusted his instincts, and they were often right. He stepped over to the cabinet that contained the rack with all the vehicle ignition keys, picked out the one for the limousine and used the fob remote to bleep open its central locking system. The limo's indicators flashed and the doors and boot unlocked with a *clunk*. Opening the lid on the cavernous boot and lifting back a carpeted panel revealed the shiny walnut veneer of the steel safe inset into a cavity in the floor of the boot. It was a beautiful piece of work, the wood grain as exquisite as the finest crafts-man-made furniture.

Now for the moment of truth. Valentina, Jeff and Tuesday gathered close around him as he located the safe's keyhole under a small circular cover and offered the key up to it.

The key went into the hole an eighth of an inch and stopped. He put slightly more pressure on it. No result. It felt as if the keyhole was blocked solid.

It was a bitter truth to swallow. But he had to accept that he'd let his enthusiasm run away with him. The key from

Auguste's study was completely the wrong fit for the lock. It wouldn't insert, let alone turn.

Ben's heart sank. He replaced the carpet panel over the locked safe door and closed the boot lid and stepped back from the car.

'Shit,' Jeff said. 'Or maybe not, then.'

Tuesday shook his head, gazed down at his feet and looked glum.

'Now what?' Valentina said.

'We'll just have to keep looking,' Ben replied.

'But where else, apart from the million places I've already tried?'

'I don't know. But I'll find it.'

Valentina was silent for a second, thinking hard. She sighed. 'Maybe the key's not that important, Ben. Maybe we should just forget about it and come up with some other idea.'

'It is important.' Of that much, he was still rock-solid certain. 'Got to be.'

'If only Tonton could recover faster, he might be able to tell us,' she said sadly.

'He will, kiddo,' Jeff reassured her.

Ben didn't reply, because there was another possibility in his mind that he felt it better to keep to himself. Because Valentina was assuming that her granduncle would *want* them to know what the key was for. But what if, in fact, he didn't? A man of so many secrets might well not be willing for the truths he'd worked so hard to hide to be exposed. Whatever he'd been prepared to reveal to Fritz Kohler was one matter. Perhaps the key could reveal deeper, darker truths that Auguste wouldn't have shared with anyone. Truths that could even shed a sinister light on his own role in whatever he'd been into. And the last person in the world the old man would want to see him that way was his cherished grandniece, the apple of his eye.

The four of them stood there in gloomy silence. Ben was acutely aware of the mounting pressure as his time window grew smaller and smaller. Any minute now the police might turn up in droves at the main gate. Enough time had passed since the ambush for them to have sifted through the evidence, interviewed the witnesses and traced the wrecked remains of the Lancia to its registered owner.

If that happened, he'd have no choice but to face the music. Whatever tricks Gabriel Archambeau had been able to pull with the German police to cover up Ben's involvement in the incident near Berlin, there was little chance of his being able to repeat them this time around, so much closer to home. And equally little chance that Ben could convincingly deny the many charges the cops would surely throw at him.

Just then the first big raindrop fell – followed by another, and another, and within moments the oppressive storm clouds finally made good on their threat. The heavens opened and the rain lashed down in curtains. The downpour drummed noisily on the garage roof, cascaded from the guttering and ran in rivers over the ground.

'Should've brought our umbrellas, guys. Looks like we're in for a right soaking,' Tuesday muttered, peering up at the sky. As if in response, a lightning flash lit the clouds, followed an instant later by a long rumbling growl from above.

Feeling suddenly very weary and despondent and not giving a damn if he got drenched to the bone, Ben left the garage and started walking back towards the house. He heard light footsteps following behind him. A small hand laced its fingers between his own with a comforting squeeze, and Valentina's voice at his shoulder said, 'Don't feel bad, Ben. You've done your best.'

'It's not enough.'

Her hair was already plastered to her brow from the rain. 'You should get out of the wet,' he told her.

'I'm staying right here with you,' she insisted.

'And me,' Jeff said, catching up quickly. Tuesday was just a step behind him. Ben felt a pang of emotion at the loyalty of his friends. Right now, he wasn't sure that he deserved it.

They walked on through the pouring rain. Valentina was clutching Ben's hand. Passing by the equestrian paddocks on their way back towards the house, they saw a team of grooms in raincoats hurriedly catching the horses to lead them to the shelter of their stables. Some of the animals were acting skittish and agitated by the sudden storm. One in particular, a beautiful but highly-strung grey Arab stallion that was whinnying and prancing about, tossing his head and giving his handler a hard time. Just then, another dazzling white lightning fork split the darkening sky, followed almost instantly by a growling clap of thunder. The frightened horse shied violently, jerked the halter rope from his handler's grip and reared up on his hind legs with a high-pitched neighing, pawing the air with his front hooves. The grooms scattered out of the way of the powerful animal and then tried to close in around him to regain hold of his rope, but he surged by them and took off at a pounding gallop across the wet paddock, tail and mane flying.

'They'll have a hell of a job catching that one,' Jeff commented.

'That's Prince Ahmed,' Valentina said, following the horse with an anxious gaze. 'He's always terribly nervous of storms. I hope he's going to be all right.'

Ben said nothing. Even as Prince Ahmed went charging off into the dusk pursued by three grooms, he was staring dumbstruck at the empty spot where the stallion had been magnificently rearing up on his hind legs a second earlier. Because the moment of realisation that image had triggered in his mind couldn't have hit him harder if the fork lightning had struck him right between the eyes.

Everything seemed to come together in his head all at once. Jeff's strangely meaningful words a few moments earlier, 'He's an artist.' The vision of the rearing horse, imprinted like a photographic negative on his retina. A stunning flash of inspiration. Ben might have been staring at the now vacant patch of dusky ground where Prince Ahmed had broken free of his handler, but what he was seeing in his mind's eye was the artwork that hung on the wall of the Kaprisky residence, opposite the doorway of the yellow salon. The painting of Napoleon Bonaparte sitting astride his rearing white charger on his crossing of the Alps.

The painting that Kaprisky had tried and failed to buy from the art gallery in Paris, and had commissioned his favourite art forger, Silvano Scarpa, to reproduce for him.

The forged copy that Scarpa had described as having 'one particularly curious feature'.

Gripped by another rush of absolute conviction, Ben started running back to the house.

'Whoa, hold on, buddy!' Jeff yelled as he, Valentina and Tuesday all chased after him through the lashing rain.

'Where the hell's he off to now?' Tuesday asked.

'Beats me, mate,' replied Jeff, his voice half drowned out by the next growl of thunder.

'No time to explain!' Ben shouted back at them, and kept running.

'You know him better than I do,' Valentina said as they hurried after him. 'Is he always this crazy?'

'Frankly, love,' Jeff told her, 'I'm surprised it took him this long to start acting up.'

Reaching the house completely soaked through to the skin, Ben dashed through the hallway and all the way down the long passage to where the painting hung. And there he was, the young, skinny Napoleon Bonaparte, much more dashing and heroic than in the better-known artistic renditions of him as a short, chubby little man with his hand stuck in his waistcoat, fixing the viewer with a bold, devil-may-care warrior eye as he rode his feisty stallion across the mountains to glory. You could see why Auguste had wanted so badly to obtain the painting, one way or another. The big, impressive artwork was just the way Ben remembered seeing it before, over two metres high and almost as wide, surrounded by a heavy gilt frame – but now suddenly he was seeing it in a very different light. And not just because he now knew it was a forged copy painted by one Silvano Scarpa.

The others had caught up with him, dripping wet and making puddles on the marble floor. 'What the hell are you doing?' Valentina yelled as Ben, completely ignoring them, started grappling with the picture and trying to pull it off the wall.

'This is it, people,' Jeff said, staring at his friend and shaking his head in disbelief. 'He's well and truly lost it this time. Had to happen someday.'

The painting was too heavy and too well secured to the wall for Ben to be able to shift it. He stood back from the wall, scrutinising the picture from top to bottom, corner to corner, thinking hard. What could Scarpa have meant by a 'particularly curious feature'? If only Ben hadn't been so impatient for him to get to the main point of what he was telling him, then it would all be much clearer now. And if Ben's instinct was right this time, all this confusion and messing around could have been avoided.

Then he found something. In the foreground of the picture the artist – or in this case the forger in the guise of the original artist – had depicted the name of his subject carved on a rock, like a kind of martial graffiti. Next to it were the names of Hannibal and Charlemagne, who in earlier periods of history had led their armies on that same epic mountain crossing. What Ben had noticed was that the letter O in the name BONAPARTE, about chest height, looked unusual. Its shape stood slightly proud of the vertical surface of the canvas. On closer inspection, the black outline of the O appeared to have been cut around with surgical neatness using a razor or a scalpel, in a perfectly regular oval that was barely visible from any distance away. As though someone had deliberately removed the whole shape of the letter from the rest of the canvas and then carefully, almost seamlessly, stuck it back into place again. But why?

Ben reached out a tentative finger and touched it against the centre of the O.

To his amazement, it pressed in like a button.

And if that wasn't a 'particularly curious feature' for a copy of a classic old oil painting to have, then Ben didn't know what was.

Chapter 38

There was the muted click of some catch or mechanism being released, and in front of the astonished eyes of Ben, Valentina, Jeff and Tuesday, the whole painting began to swing slowly away from the wall, hinged on one side like a huge door.

For Ben, it was a stunning déjà-vu replay of another Scarpa creation, the fake bookcase doorway to his secret apartment.

'Well, fuck my old boots,' Jeff breathed.

'Watch your sodding language, arsehole,' Tuesday scolded him. 'You're in the presence of a lady.'

Jeff shot an embarrassed look at Valentina and muttered, 'Sorry.'

'Why, do you guys think girls don't learn to swear at Swiss finishing school?' Valentina asked sweetly. Then she saw what was behind the painting and came out with an expression that made Jeff blush. 'Unbelievable,' she added. 'I've lived in this house for most of my life and I had no idea this even existed.'

Just as Scarpa's fake bookcase hid a secret, so did his forged painting. Behind that huge painted doorway was another. A steel safe door like the entrance to a bank vault, flush to the wall with a recessed handle and hinges as unburstable as the ones on a submarine hatch. And instead of a dial or combination keypad, the way to unlock it was via a single old-fashioned keyhole.

'Go for it, Ben,' Tuesday said, grinning his trademark grin that could dazzle a sightless mole from fifty metres.

Ben took the key from his pocket, stepped up to the steel door and, for the second time in a few minutes, offered the key up to a keyhole with no idea what was about to happen, or what – if anything – he might find behind that locked door. This was his second chance. It was unlikely there'd be a third.

Ben held his breath as he inserted the key. An eighth of an inch; a quarter of an inch; no apparent resistance. In it went, all the way, as silky smooth as dipping a warm spoon into chocolate cream. Then he turned it anticlockwise and he felt the cuts on the key engage with the slick mechanism of levers and tumblers inside the lock. With just the lightest torque pressure the lock turned and he heard the faint scrape of deadbolts drawing back.

The lock was open. Ben breathed again. He gripped the recessed handle and gave the door a tug. It was heavy. For a man as old as Auguste Kaprisky, it must have taken all his strength to open. Once it began to move, its weight gave it the momentum to swing out more easily.

And he stared into the space that had opened up behind it.

As in the car garage, the opening of the door triggered automatic lighting that brightly illuminated the interior of the walk-in safe, while a folding metal step whirred smoothly out of a recess at the bottom to allow easy access. What could only broadly be described as a safe was really a room in its own right, at least twenty feet deep and just as wide, its walls and ceiling clad with the same kind of heavy-gauge steel as the door and its floor a thick slab of concrete that was no doubt steel-reinforced. Lining both sides and the end wall were various shelves and alcoves, all of them crammed with valuables.

Ben climbed up the metal step and walked into the safe, followed by a dumbstruck Valentina, Jeff and Tuesday, all gazing around them in utter bewilderment. One whole section was filled with neat bricks of cash, arranged into separate heaps of US dollars and euros, more paper money by far than Ben had ever seen in one place before. It would have taken several people hours to count it all, but at a glance its value had to be in the scores of millions. That was mere pocket change compared with the section on the opposite wall that was solid with glittering gold bars. Stacks of them, packed tight into a cuboid mass four feet high and eight feet long that must weigh several tons. Auguste seemed to have stashed a fair proportion of France's national gold reserves in here. The sight of it was breathtaking, even to Ben, who'd seen some treasures in his life.

Then there were the jewels. The back wall of the safe was reserved for glass-fronted cabinets filled with watches, tiaras, necklaces that sparkled under the lights like liquid rivers of diamonds. Loose gemstones of all shapes, sizes and colours. Little velvet cases with their lids open to display the priceless wares inside. The entire contents of Tiffany's in New York might have been loaded on trucks and shipped here to Le Mans. Quite what Auguste needed it all for was a mystery in itself.

But in any case, the old man's personal collection of booty wasn't what Ben's attention was fixed on, after he spotted the cigar box.

It sat alone on a shelf, quite incongruous among all the eye-boggling wealth on display. Just a plain, slim cardboard box with its lid closed and bearing the brand name MONTECRISTO.

Auguste wasn't a smoker, as far as Ben knew. And if he had been, in billionaire fashion he'd have some kind of super-expensive and elaborate humidor to store his Cuban cigars in. So what was in the box? Ben stepped over to it and lifted the lid.

And there was the answer. Nestling in a piece of jeweller's tissue was a single chess piece. A small chunk of rare white opal carved in the shape of a horse's head.

'What've you got there?' asked Valentina, coming over to see what he'd found.

Ben gently removed the white knight from the tissue and showed her. 'What we've been looking for,' he replied.

'But I thought all the chess pieces were stolen in the attack.'

'This one's a little different from the others,' Ben said.

He turned the knight over in his hands, knowing exactly what to look for. Fixed to the piece's circular base was the little round piece of green felt that would act to cushion it against the hard surface of the chessboard. Ben used his thumbnail to prise up a corner of the felt, then peeled it right off. Underneath was a hole drilled into the middle of the piece. And inserted into the hole was a shiny plug that Ben already knew was made of the rare metal osmium.

Which was all the proof Ben needed that this white knight wasn't one of the original pieces from Auguste's Napoleon set. It was the very same copy that he'd commissioned from his old pal and sometime partner in crime, Silvano Scarpa. And that whatever was inside it was obviously valuable and important enough to require that it should be stored here in this impregnable vault.

'Tuesday,' he said, beckoning his friend over from where he'd been transfixed by the stacks of cash and gold bars. 'You know a lot about hi-tech stuff and computers and things.'

'I'm no expert,' Tuesday replied with a modest shrug. 'But not too shabby.' The reality was that he had a talent for technology that left Ben and Jeff looking like a couple of clueless old fogeys.

'I think there's something sealed inside this chess piece,' Ben explained to him. 'A bug of some kind, with a miniature recordable drive. You think you could get it out?'

'I don't see why not,' Tuesday said, examining it. 'But this type of stone, or whatever it is, looks like pretty brittle material. I can't guarantee it wouldn't split when I try to get that plug out.'

'Smash it with a hammer for all I care,' Ben said. 'We need to get at whatever's inside.'

'No problemo, pal. Leave it with me.'

The white knight wasn't the only item that Auguste had been keeping in the cigar box. Next to it, not wrapped in tissue but sealed in a little polythene pouch, was a USB drive. Ben didn't need a computer expert to tell him how to access whatever information was stored in there.

'I think we have what we came for, folks,' he said. 'Now let's find a laptop and take a look.'

They were back in the corridor with the walk-in safe closed up behind them when the walkie-talkie radio clipped to Jeff's belt gave a chirrup and a fizz and the gruff Scots voice of their security team member Cormac Wallace came crackling over the speaker.

Jeff snatched up the radio. 'Dekker. What's up, Mac?'

'Uh, you'd better get over here, Jeff. We've a situation at the main gate.'

Chapter 39

Racing down the driveway through the rainy darkness to the main gate, Ben and the others quickly discovered what was up. The sudden appearance of an unidentified black sport minivan pulled up outside the entrance had the security team edgy and unclipping the retaining straps on their concealed holsters in readiness for trouble.

The minivan's headlight beams cut brightly through the slanting rain, shining on the security hut and barrier and the team of soggy men assembled there watching it intently and holding back from getting any closer. The gate flood-lamps reflected off the vehicle's slick black bodywork and showed the solitary shape of a man at the wheel. It felt like a standoff that could explode into violence at any moment.

'How long's he been there?' Jeff asked Wallace.

'Just a couple of minutes,' Wallace replied, rainwater pouring in rivulets from his beanie hat as he gazed fixedly at the mystery van. 'Looks like the driver's on his own, unless there's more of them in the back. Guy's just sat there, not moving, staring at us. We didn't know what to do.'

'Could be them again?' Tuesday wondered, narrowing his eyes against the van's lights.

'Yeah, but what's he doing sitting at the gate?' Jeff said.

'It's creepy,' Valentina said, hugging herself.

Ben peered at the van. Then he smiled and started walking over the rain-streaked concrete towards the gates.

'Ben?' Jeff called after him.

As Ben approached the gates in the glare of the van's headlights, its driver's door suddenly swung open and the figure of the driver stepped out.

'Hello, Jaden.'

Wolf's appearance had changed since he and Ben had last crossed paths, in Afghanistan a few months earlier. The beard that had helped to make him pass as a native fighter was shaven clean and his hair was buzzed ultra-short. But the golden smile was still there, gleaming in the dazzle of the floodlights the other side of the gate's iron bars. He was wearing a well-used old combat jacket, jeans and army boots.

'What a surprise, eh?' he said.

'Nothing much surprises me about you any more,' Ben replied.

'Likewise. I just passed by a smoking bomb crater a few miles down the road, with half the French police crawling over it like someone stepped on an ant nest. Thought it looked like your handiwork. Been busy, I see.'

'Right now I'm busy wondering what brings you to this neck of the woods.'

Wolf shrugged. 'Must admit I don't generally tend to keep up with current affairs, up in my little nook of the Spanish mountains. It's all bullshit anyway. But you'd mentioned you were helping out your rich pal Kaprisky, so I looked it up to see what'd been happening with him. Then I thought, wow, maybe you could do with a helping hand.' He nodded towards the back of the van. 'And turns out I was right, too. Got a little something for you I picked up along the way.'

Jeff and Tuesday were coming over. 'Hey, look what the cat dragged in,' Jeff chuckled, recognising Wolf. They'd only met Ben's old SAS comrade once before, but working together to bring down a cabal of child-sacrificing satanists had been a bonding experience.

Ben signalled back to the guard hut to open the gates and raise the security barrier. Wolf got back in his van and drove on through. 'Crappy weather you have in these parts,' he commented as he stepped out again and the small crowd gathered around him. 'Hasn't stopped pissing it down since I crossed the French border.'

'Valentina, this is Jaden,' Ben said. 'A very old friend of mine.'

'*Enchanté, Mademoiselle*,' Wolf said, flashing his most charming smile at her. For a former professional assassin and possibly the most dangerous man Ben had ever known, Wolf could be full of the social graces when he wanted to be. Valentina smiled uncertainly back and let Wolf shake her hand.

'Don't let his appearance alarm you,' Tuesday stage-whispered. 'He's really not a dangerous psychopath. Just likes people to think he is.'

'Although there are a few of the genuine articles around,' Wolf said. 'You can never be too careful. In fact I happened to stumble on a couple of them as I was checking around your perimeter a few minutes ago.'

Wolf blipped open the back doors of his van, and Ben realised with a start that this was the 'little something' he'd said he'd brought them. They all drew close to see as Wolf pulled open the doors.

'Caught these malingering in the bushes on the south side of the estate,' he said. 'There's a little gated entrance there. Seemed to me they were planning on getting in that way and paying you a social call. But I got to them first.'

Lying on the bare metal floor of the back of Wolf's van were a pair of men. One of them was securely trussed up with a plastic cable tie binding his wrists behind his back, two more around his ankles and knees, a large rectangle of duct tape over his mouth, and struggling violently to get free. The other wasn't bound up at all, and wasn't moving.

Valentina gasped and stepped away.

'Never mind him, Miss,' Wolf said. 'He won't hurt you. He's what we call in the trade "dead".'

'She can see that,' Ben replied.

'Apparently he preferred it that way to being captured alive,' Wolf said. 'Each to their own.' He reached inside the van, grabbed the other one and dragged him out. As Wolf's prisoner slumped to the wet ground, Ben realised that it was Messer. Which meant that the dead man was the driver of the truck, with whom Messer had escaped.

One of the nastiest, most unscrupulous and highly-paid hitmen on the planet. And Wolf had been able to sneak up and take him down, just like that. Then again, Ben had long ago stopped marvelling at Wolf's predatory skills.

'They were carrying knives, no guns,' Wolf said. 'Then again, our friend Messer here didn't earn his name by being a slouch with a blade. Did you, matey boy?' he added, nudging the wriggling captive with his foot. 'Don't ask me where his brother is, though. They're usually inseparable, as a rule.'

'I know where he is,' Ben said. 'Lying on a slab with a sheet over him.'

Wolf's expression didn't change. 'That figures. Anyway,' pointing down at Messer, 'this one put up a bit of a struggle, so I had to bang him around a little bit. But he can still talk, if you were interested in pressing some truth out of him. Such as who might have paid him and his brother to take you out.'

'And to try to murder my Tonton,' Valentina said, eyes fixed on the prisoner. The rain was dripping from her hair and soaking her clothes. She didn't give a damn.

'All right,' Ben said. 'Let's see if he feels like talking.' He crouched down next to Messer under the floodlights and ripped the duct tape away from his mouth. The killer's eyes blazed at him.

'Remember me?' Ben said to him. 'I'm the man who shot your brother. And the same will happen to you unless you tell me what I want to know.'

Messer's lips drew back from his teeth and he spat. For a moment he stayed silent. Then the veins bulged in his forehead and he screamed out a string of abuse in his own language.

'What'd he say?' Jeff asked.

'Remind me where he comes from again,' said Tuesday.

Wolf said, 'Lithuania.'

Tuesday nodded. 'Right. Then I'm guessing he said something like "I'm gonna ice your ass, you motherfucker" in Lithuanian.'

Jeff elbowed him. 'Hey. Who's the foulmouthed one now?'

Hovering close behind Ben and looking at the prisoner as if he was some kind of dangerous animal they'd trapped, Valentina asked, 'Do you think he was one of the men who attacked the house?'

'I'm sure he was,' Ben replied. 'It's the kind of job he and his brother would have been recruited for. One of their other cronies was the man who posed as Georges that day. But the real giveaway is that Messer and his dead pal here were sniffing around the south gate, from where the attack team made their exit. That's how they knew about it.'

Messer spat again, his spit tinged pink with blood under the bright lights. He wouldn't take his crazed, unblinking eyes off his brother's killer.

'He's not going to talk to us,' Valentina said. 'Look at him. You can see it.'

'Probably right about that,' Wolf agreed. 'I never really expected him to.'

'So what the hell are we going to do with him?' Tuesday asked.

Ben looked at Wolf, then at Valentina. Obvious enough what Wolf's answer would be, given his former profession. Valentina, he wasn't so sure. Even so, her reaction surprised him.

'Maybe you're thinking about shooting him,' she said. 'But I don't want you to.'

Wolf looked disappointed. 'No?'

'It's your call what happens to him, Valentina,' Ben said. 'What do you propose?'

Her gaze was still fixed on Messer as she replied, 'First I want you to cut him loose so he can stand up.'

'I'm not sure that's a good idea,' Wolf said.

'It's what I want,' Valentina replied, in the tone of someone who was used to getting it.

Jeff slipped a folding knife from his pocket, flicked out the blade and handed it to Ben, who bent over the prisoner and used the knife to slash the ties holding his knees and ankles.

'Now help him to his feet,' Valentina said. Ben stood, grabbed Messer under the arms and hauled him upright. A small, dry smile came over Messer's face.

'Now cut the ties off his wrists,' Valentina said.

Wolf looked at Ben. Ben hesitated.

'You said it's my call,' she said. 'So please.'

'You're the boss,' Ben said. He moved behind Messer, slid the blade between the man's tethered wrists and cut the cable tie away. Messer's arms swung free. He rubbed at his chafed wrists. Breathing hard, his eyes filled with glowering hatred.

Now Valentina took a step closer to the prisoner, brushed her wet hair away from her face and addressed him personally. 'I don't know if you understand me. But I need to tell you something.'

'He understands you,' Wolf said. 'He knows every European language. Talk to him in Norwegian or Serbo-Croatian if you want.'

'All right.' She was looking levelly at Messer. The school-girl facing the hardened killer. Ben was amazed by her strength.

She said, 'Do you understand why I don't want these men to shoot you?'

Messer said nothing. His eyes flicked from Valentina to the others, then back again.

Until that moment, nobody had known about the little subcompact 9mm automatic she had hidden in her pocket. She whipped it out and pointed it at Messer. 'It's because *I'm* going to shoot you, for what you did. You piece of filth!'

Messer froze. Only Ben moved, stepping towards her.

'Don't try to stop me, Ben,' she warned him, a tremulous edge of desperation in her voice. 'I'll shoot myself if you do. I swear!'

Ben stepped back. She could be bluffing, but he wouldn't want to put it to the test. 'Don't do this.'

'I told you right at the beginning, Ben,' she said, so constricted with emotion that her lips hardly moved. The gun was trained steadily right at Messer and her finger was on the trigger. 'I told you I wanted these men brought in front of me so I could see them die. Face to face. Then you get your billion euros. That was the arrangement.'

'This is a mistake,' Ben said. 'The police will be here soon. Better to turn him over to them.'

'Let her do it, Ben,' said Wolf in a quiet, hard voice. 'If it's what she needs.' As though shooting a man could be a form of therapy.

Another clap of thunder growled in the sky above them. The storm wasn't over yet. The security guys stood impassively by, watching. They were a crew of tough, experienced men, nearly all from military backgrounds, who'd all seen and done a lot in their lives and were deeply loyal to Ben, Jeff and the Le Val team who'd trained them for the job they were being paid to do now. None of them was about to shy away from the scene that was unfolding down here by the main gates, on this dark rainy night far away from the eyes and ears of the few staff still residing on the estate. The sound of a pistol shot wouldn't carry far enough beyond the house to be heard. There would be no witnesses to the demise of this scumbag who'd brought death and suffering to the Kaprisky household.

Ben knew there was nothing he could do to stop it happening, in any case. The die was cast now. All he could do was watch Valentina pull the trigger and doom herself to a lifetime of regret. He knew all about those.

Valentina adjusted her aim to point the little pistol straight at Messer's head. Striker fired. No safety. All it took was a simple squeeze of the trigger. Messer just stood there silently staring at her, barely breathing, his eyes like lasers boring intensely into hers. Whatever was about to happen next he must have known there was no escape for him, surrounded by all these men. But maybe escape wasn't his plan. A glimmer of madness came over his expression. Almost as if he relished this moment.

Valentina's face was taut and pale. Her grip on the gun began to falter, and its muzzle wavered. A tear rolled from one eye, then the other. Her breath caught with a sob, and then her resolve cracked completely and she lowered the gun. 'I . . . can't! Can't do it!'

Then Messer flew at her, so fast and suddenly that the quickest eye could barely have followed it. In a fraction of a second, her pistol was out of her hand and into his.

He might have shot her then, point-blank range right in the face. Or he might have chosen this moment to turn the gun on the man who had killed his brother. That option would have made more sense to someone in his position, but nobody would ever know. Because in the very next fraction of a second after that, the slug from Ben's .357 Magnum was drilling him through the side of the head and he fell limp to the ground.

'Off to join his dear departed Kugel,' Wolf said. His own Colt Commander was in his hand too, and if Ben hadn't moved as fast as he had, Wolf's bullet would have been next in line to the target.

Valentina staggered on her feet as her legs turned to jelly, her face completely white. Her breath came in a ragged gasp and she started shaking. Ben quickly put away his gun and wrapped his arm around her shoulders as the shock hit her and the tears came flooding out. She pressed herself tightly against him, weeping convulsively. 'You're okay,' he murmured in her ear, caressing her wet hair as tenderly as if she were his own daughter. There was a spot of Messer's blood on her cheek. He wiped it off before she could notice it there. 'You're okay.'

'I couldn't bring myself to kill him,' she sobbed.

'I'm glad you couldn't, Valentina,' he told her.

'I hate myself for being so weak. I broke my promise.'

'No, you were strong,' he said. 'Because you turned away from doing the wrong thing. Don't you forget that. I don't want you to ever learn what it feels like to take another person's life.'

It was Tuesday who broke the silence that had fallen over the rest of the group. 'So now we have two dead guys to dispose of, before the fuzz turn up and catch us with them.

309

Anyone got any suggestions?' In the world of regular soldiering he'd come from, back in the day, enemy corpses just got left on the battlefield and were someone else's job to clean up.

'Seems to me we're in farm country out here,' Wolf said. 'Which means there's bound to be a farmer with a slurry pit somewhere in the vicinity. Nothing like slurry for dissolving a body, short of feeding it to pigs. And it's good for the environment.'

'You really have an answer for everything, don't you?' Tuesday said. Wolf shrugged.

'We'll take care of it,' Wallace said grimly.

'And then what?' Jeff asked. 'Not much chance now of getting either of these bastards to talk to us.'

'Maybe we don't need them anyway,' Ben said, holding up the USB flash drive. 'Now let's go inside and find out what this is really all about.'

Chapter 40

Ben, Valentina, Jeff, Tuesday and Wolf all hurried inside the house and upstairs to Auguste's study. Everyone was still dripping wet, but they were too intent on their purpose to bother to dry themselves off. 'Cosy little pad you have here,' Wolf said airily, looking about him. Tuesday pulled a chair up to the desk and immediately got to work on the replica white knight, using Jeff's clasp knife in an attempt to prise the metal plug out of the base. Meanwhile Ben grabbed Auguste's laptop and plugged in the USB.

As the machine whirred into life the worrying thought came to him that the data storage chip could be encrypted with password protection. But as he'd hoped, Auguste had already provided it with all the security it needed by locking it in his secret vault. The screen flashed into life, showing a window marked FLASH DRIVE. With Valentina close at his shoulder he clicked on it and a menu came up. The drive contained only two files, both unnamed.

'One of them is a video file,' Valentina said, peering at the screen. 'The other's a pdf document.'

'Which do you want to open first?' he asked her.

'The video first,' she decided.

He clicked the file open, then angled the laptop around so that they could all see the screen. Jeff and Wolf pulled up a couple more chairs. Valentina kneeled at the edge of the desk, as close as she could get to the computer. Ben stood beside her. He was worried about what they might be about to learn, and wished that she didn't have to be here.

The video file spent a moment loading. As it opened, they saw that it had been recorded inside this very room. The camera had been set up at the end of the desk where Valentina was crouching. Sitting in the now empty leather swivel chair with his back to the window, curtains drawn, was Auguste Kaprisky. The time and date stamp in the corner of the screen showed that the video had been shot only days ago, on the day prior to Auguste's meeting with Fritz Kohler in Berlin. He was wearing a dark suit and tie and looked solemn and composed, like a president making a special address to his people on some important occasion.

'I'm amazed,' Valentina muttered. 'Tonton hates being filmed. He'll do anything to avoid even having his picture taken.' And it was true that the old man was notoriously camera-shy. Which could only mean that Auguste must have had a very significant reason for recording this video.

As they were about to find out.

A hush fell over the room. Then Auguste's monologue began. He spoke in a clear, sober and authoritative voice, looking directly into the camera with a strangely penetrating look that made the watchers feel as though he was addressing them personally.

'I have recorded this videotaped presentation with three principal aims. Firstly, it is intended to act as an indictment against a group of individuals whose identities and criminal activities I will be describing in some detail. Secondly, it will

312

also function as my witness statement with regard to these activities, of which I have first-hand knowledge. And thirdly, to my shame, it is intended to serve as my personal confession of my involvement in unspeakable crimes against humanity. I am deeply ashamed to admit that thanks in part to my collusion, deliberate or otherwise, these crimes are being perpetrated as I speak, or are in motion to be unleashed upon the world. It is my heartfelt desire to prevent them from ever reaching their fruition, for the salvation of mankind.'

Valentina was staring boggle-eyed at the screen. If there was any residual shock left in her system from what had happened earlier, it was all gone now, dwarfed in comparison to this. She burst out, 'WHAT?!'

'That's quite an opening statement,' Tuesday observed dryly. Ben held up a finger to shush him as Auguste went on:

'If you are watching this video, you will no doubt be aware that I am speaking to you from beyond the grave. It may be that my death will have occurred from natural causes, for although I am currently in excellent health it cannot be denied that I have reached a certain age and my remaining time in this life is necessarily limited. More likely, however, my death occurred not from natural causes but was precipitated more suddenly. For I believe it is entirely possible that my co-conspirators in these crimes may suspect me of treachery against them. In that case I will surely not survive, for my colleagues are ruthless men for whom the act of murder is insignificant. In anticipation of such an outcome I placed instructions with my attorney Gabriel Archambeau, in the form of a sealed letter to be opened only after my death, which would reveal the whereabouts of the computer flash drive on which this video, the only existing copy, is recorded. I now offer you my posthumous confession, in the hope that it can help to undo the evil that is being plotted against humanity.'

Valentina looked at Ben. 'So Gabriel knew about it all along!'

'But not what it was,' he replied.

Onscreen, Auguste paused to gather his thoughts and then continued. 'At this point I must go back in time to explain how I came to the situation in which I find myself now. Some years ago, in 1989, having achieved a certain level of status in the world of business and economics, I was cordially invited to join an organisation whose existence is known to very few people. I myself had only been vaguely aware of it before then. Its obscurity is no accident, but the result of careful dissimulation and secrecy on the part of its members. This I had always naively assumed to go hand in hand with the so-called elite status of the individuals within the group, whose meetings had to be held in the most stringently private settings for security reasons. More recently I have come to understand there were other, darker, reasons for keeping its identity unknown to the world. Reasons that have come to the fore by such stealthy incre-ments that by the time I learned the full implications of their plans and how far they had already advanced, it was too late.'

Ben realised he'd been holding his breath. He laid a gentle hand on Valentina's shoulder and felt it as rigid as stone.

'More on that subject in a moment,' Auguste said. 'First let me take a minute to focus on the organisation itself. Its membership is restricted to fifteen at any given time. No woman has ever been invited to join. Vacancies only arise upon the death of an existing member, and once inducted into this extremely exclusive club it is not otherwise possible to leave or retire. The group's meetings take place once every three months, each lasting two days and held at a variety of secret, isolated locations that I reveal in the accompanying notes. This has been going on for many years, since its founding not long after the turn of the last century. Throughout that time it has only ever been known as "The Forum". Past members include figures from the all-powerful top banking families, members of the nobility, and some of the richest and most influential magnates and leaders in the world. Today the Forum continues to draw its membership from a select number of extremely wealthy individuals, some of whom possess fortunes far in excess of my own.'

Jeff gave a low whistle. 'Talking *serious* money.'

'Shush,' Valentina snapped at him.

Ben's mind had flashed back to Auguste's appointments diary, with its cryptic reference to 'F' that had eluded him until now. F for Forum. The final puzzle solved.

'The Forum's current Chairman is the British billionaire investment banking tycoon Sir Simon Asquith. His vice chair is an Austrian called Klaus Speer. Further detailed information on these two men and its other members is included on the document that accompanies this video. They presently include four former heads of state, including a former British Prime Minister and a United States President, whose names are very well known to the world. Less well known publicly are those of Matthias Rothstein and Georg Eisenberg, the chief executives of two of the world's largest and most powerful pharmaceutical giants, who themselves represent two of the wealthiest families on the planet that have been manipulating global economics and politics for literally centuries. Also on the list is the American business mogul Julius Berkeley III, whose name will be well known to you and whose so-called philanthropic works across the world, through his Berkeley Foundation, have earned him the admiration of a completely unwitting public.'

'Berkeley? The computer games guy?' Tuesday said, surprised.

'I think he's a little more than that,' said Wolf.

'Always knew the little runt was a no-gooder,' Jeff growled.

Valentina threw them all a nasty look. 'Shhh! People!'

'Other longtime members include Jean-Claude Dorn, the Belgian owner and chief executive of the Dorn Group, the umbrella organisation under which the bulk of the world's food manufacturing companies operate – not, as most people believe, as rival competitors but in the form of a global monopoly. Closely allied to the food industry, as well as the pharmaceutical industry, is Arlin Hainsworth Baumbach, the director of the world's most important genetic research development firm, who is also named as one of the chief perpetrators of the crimes I am about to reveal. As is Noah Jaggard Petersen, a highly regarded scientific entrepreneur who, thanks to influential friends with extremely powerful resources, is the leading developer of future artificial intelligence and transhumanist robotics technologies.'

'What the hell is a transhuman robot when he's at home?' Jeff said in a low voice, so as not to incense Valentina a third time.

'Better hope we don't live long enough to find out,' Tuesday whispered back.

'The Forum's members also represent a range of other industries,' Auguste Kaprisky went on. 'The public are not widely familiar with the name Erich Stahl, but as the supreme head of the trillion-dollar conglomerate Midas International he is perhaps the most powerful media mogul alive. Midas has spent the last forty years consolidating its control over the world's multimedia companies. It owns most of the major news corporations and several of the biggest newspapers in Europe, Britain, Canada and the US, has invested heavily in social media and acquired controlling interests in the film, television and advertising industries worldwide. Then there is Paul Li Huang of the Huang Communications Group, China's leading internet and broadcast media agency, working closely with the Chinese government. Between them, these parent organisations and the vast web of subsidiaries under their control dominate a large proportion of the world's media. These are the men who, in effect, dictate the content of much of the information received by the global public.'

'Well, I guess they have that one pretty well wrapped up,' Tuesday said.

'You may ask why I became involved with the Forum,' Auguste continued, 'and that is a very important question. When I accepted the invitation to become a member, I considered it an honour and an opportunity to play a part in furthering what I then believed to be the organisation's key ambitions: to act as a think tank and political influencer helping to foster and support the noble causes of human wellbeing, health, prosperity, freedom and happiness. All my life I have been staunchly a humanist. I do not, *cannot* accept the concept that there is an "elite" of powerful people at the top of society, occupying a lordly position of authority and control over the common people. On the contrary, I have always held that it is we, the one per cent who, thanks to our wealth and privilege, are well placed to ensure the stability of the economic and political worlds, who are there to serve our fellow man and responsible for helping to create a better existence for all.'

Wolf shook his head and muttered something very softly under his breath that might have been 'What a naive twat'.

'It is hard to say exactly when my first misgivings began to materialise. From quite early on in my involvement with the Forum, I had been dimly aware of an ideological under-current permeating the group's philosophy and goals, one that sat uncomfortably with the values I believe in. At first these ugly ideas tended only very occasionally to surface in our discussions, and then only by way of the most oblique and passing references, so that they seemed of little overall importance. Little by little, however, steered with great guile and cunning by particular members who seemed to me to want to push their agenda subtly to the forefront, they gained increasing traction over the years. With growing discomfort it slowly began to dawn on me that this had been their aim all along. It was like watching the gradual corruption of a benign and just political system, from the first glimmers of infiltration by dark and sinister influences that grow imperceptibly more disturbing as it moves inexorably towards becoming an instrument of brutal tyranny and oppression. The rise of dictatorships has followed the same course, again and again all throughout history.'

'So what were these ideas?' Jeff said, sounding frustrated. Valentina didn't turn on him this time, because she must have been wondering the same thing.

Auguste paused to sip from a glass of water, then continued. 'So what were these new ideas?' he asked startlingly, as though he'd been able to hear Jeff. 'Let me explain. As I have said, all my life I have been a humanist, with all that that implies. Now I was beginning to sense the steady influx of a form of dogma into the Forum's agendas and policies that was not only deeply distasteful but increasingly more alarming. The catalyst for this change was the emergence, many years ago, of what was to develop into what we now call Green politics. What began as an earnest and well-intentioned ecologically minded philosophy aimed at reshaping the future of the world for the benefit of all mankind slowly morphed into something more akin to the anti-humanist doctrine of Thomas Malthus.'

'Who's that?' Valentina asked. Her turn to interrupt.

'An English political economist in the nineteenth century,' Ben explained, pausing the playback for a moment. 'He preached that there were too many people and we should encourage disease and death to keep the numbers down.'

'But that's horrible,' she said, wrinkling her nose.

'There are a lot of horrible people in the world, Valentina.' And Ben had a nasty feeling they were about to learn a lot more about them. Reluctantly, he let the video play on.

'A key concept at the heart of the Forum's new ideology came under the header of "Limits to Growth",' Auguste resumed. 'This set of ideas encourages us to believe that the greatest enemy of humanity, our environment and the planet is, in fact, humanity itself. Using their considerable high-level connections, this emerging element within the Forum initiated a set of data studies raising the alarm about the dangers of population growth. They purported to show, in the most unimpeachably scientific terms, that the era of plentiful natural resources – energy, food, even water – that mankind has enjoyed throughout modern history was set to come to an end within a few short years, and that certain adjustments had to be made in order to counter this trend before catastrophic results ensued. We ourselves are collectively responsible for this crisis, the science made clear.

'And of course this was nothing new. The studies drew comparisons with other species: when, for example, a herd of elephants has become so numerous as to reach the point of destroying its own environment, the long-established practice of animal husbandry teaches us that those excessive numbers must be thinned for the sake of the collective. The logic is simple enough. If this fails to happen, there would simply be too little to go round and the entire herd would perish. Based on this same premise, as stewards of the planet it was incumbent on us to devise ways and means of applying a similar system of control to our own species.

'In other words, we were being told that the only solution to avert global disaster from diminishing resources was to take active steps to reduce the human population itself.'

Chapter 41

None of the five in the room spoke as those words sank in, with all their terrible implications. And as Ben had feared, there was much worse to come.

On the screen, Auguste took another sip of water and pushed on with his narrative. 'Needless to say, this was all presented in the most reasonable language, in the guise of a benevolent strategy to protect humanity and save the planet. Everything they say and do appears to be in the best interests of the peoples of the world. But the truth is very different. The conclusion of the Forum's scientific study left us facing two key issues. First: just what do we mean by the term "overpopulation"? What proportion of the world's nearly eight billion human inhabitants is considered as excessive and therefore in need of elimination? On what basis are we to determine who should live, and who should die? And second: having established a target figure to which we wish to reduce this apparently overlarge population, what is the most practical, efficient and expedient way of achieving this goal?'

'As in, how do we go about killing everyone,' Tuesday muttered. 'Is this crap for real?'

From the solemn, grave expression on Auguste Kaprisky's face, this crap was very real indeed. He'd never been a man to joke around.

'As these discussions became more and more involved over the long succession of meetings that followed, many of my fellow Forum members came forward with their own suggested solutions, and I was quite horrified by the open enthusiasm with which they seemed to embrace the idea. The representatives of the food industry believed they held one possible key to solving the problem of excessive human population. If food supplies could be artificially limited, say by instigating a global supply chain crisis or significantly hampering production, things could simply follow their natural course. Instead of doing all we could to feed the world, we would quietly allow the hungry to die. There were, they proposed, various ways of achieving this without its appearing to be a deliberate act: the sabotaging of crops and food processing plants could easily enough be put down to energy and manpower shortages, extreme weather or even cyber attacks; while the mass destruction of cattle, poultry and swine could be attributed to disease, real or fabricated. The already highly politicised climate change agenda could be deployed in a new role, touted through our vast media connections as the trigger for a needed revolution in agriculture that would completely change the landscape of food production. This, by replacing traditional sources of nutrition with new "Green" alternatives such as the mass consumption of insects, would provide a convenient means of reducing excess population by means of malnutrition and starvation. While the finger of blame for all this, as far as the general public were concerned, would be pointed at the universal scapegoat, climate change. Hence emphasising still further the apparent need to reduce the number of humans on the planet, who, lest we should ever be allowed to forget, are the real culprits behind the whole thing and thus have brought their own destruction on themselves. The perfect deception, exonerating the architects of genocide from all moral responsibility. Not to mention, from any suggestion of blame.'

'Have to hand it to those clever bastards,' Jeff grunted. Tuesday was shaking his head in disbelief at the cynicism of it all. Valentina just looked stunned.

'Other members suggested other approaches for achieving the same goals. One of these came from our American philanthropist friend Julius Berkeley, who reminded us of the widespread vaccination programmes financed by his foundation in Third World countries like India and Africa that had, in the name of promoting health and wellbeing, led to the deaths of hundreds of thousands of children. Preliminary medical trials had provided ample evidence that certain vaccines were dangerously toxic. Yet despite this, or perhaps indeed because of it, the inoculation programmes had been aggressively promoted by healthcare institutions and government authorities, generously incentivised to do so, while any dissenting voices were actively silenced. Then there were the covert sterilisation initiatives that had been conducted in similar parts of the world, also to devastating effect.

'For these reasons Berkeley was a strong advocate of the idea that the most effective solution to our overpopulation problem was a medical one. It was also the most lucrative, he argued. While the deliberate disrupting of the global food supply was undoubtedly an efficient way of taking excess numbers "off the board", as he put it, such a strategy benefited

323

no one economically. Quite the opposite in fact, given the massive wastage and destruction involved. In stark contrast, a medical approach could potentially yield trillions of profit – that is to say, while the population was still large enough to generate such massive revenues. He made these points convincingly enough to get the representatives of the pharmaceutical industry on the Forum committee very enthusiastic. Needless to say, the Berkeley Foundation is a major stakeholder in their companies.'

Auguste's emotions showed only in the stony hardness of his expression as he went on in the same calm, solemn tone. 'As I sat listening to these intelligent, rational, successful men calmly discussing what could only be described as the deliberate genocide of their fellow human beings, I began to realise to my horror that these ideologies had been there all along, waiting for the opportunity to fully take root and flourish. It came to my notice that some of the members had been conducting their own private discussions, a Forum within a Forum if you will, slowly but steadily and with infinite patience hatching their plan. Now their agenda was coming out into the open, infecting the minds of my fellow Forum members like a cult belief system. Was such a thing really possible? I could scarcely believe what I was witnessing.

'You will ask, did I not make any attempt to counter this madness? Yes, I did. However, I had to be very careful how I couched my criticism. To attack their plans simply on a moral basis would carry no weight at all, for these godless and unscrupulous men. Returning instead to the scientific studies that formed the basis for their projections of population disaster, I pointed out that these were founded entirely on computer models. How were we to know that these were trustworthy? Was it not the case, I argued, that computer models were notoriously prone to error and subject to manipulation? Had experience not shown time and again that one can obtain precisely whatever results one wishes, depending on how the data are programmed? I spoke at length and made my reservations very clear – but my objections were ignored. All I managed to achieve was to bring disapproval and, I sensed, a degree of suspicion on myself.

'I now faced the terrible realisation that the apparently philanthropic, liberal and humanitarian organisation I had joined, or had thought I had joined, was slowly revealing itself to be anything but. Deeply disturbed, I began to look more closely into the history of the Forum, and discovered that one of its founders was a man called Dr Karl Ravensfeld. An epidemiologist by training, having gained his medical degree at the University of Jena in 1896, he published several books and many scientific papers in which he promoted his Malthusian view of human pregnancy as a form of disease, which needed to be eradicated in the same way that medicine sought to eradicate smallpox, yellow fever and other dangerous conditions. In his private practice Ravensfeld took to sterilising and aborting his female patients with tremendous zeal, and was proud of having personally prevented thousands of human lives from ever happening.'

'Ravensfeld? Ravin' mad, more like,' Jeff grumbled.

'My research then took me deeper, prompting me to investigate the family tree of the Berkeley dynasty. Our Forum colleague Julius Berkeley likes to style himself as a self-made billionaire, but as I discovered, he is only the inheritor of a long line of extremely wealthy and powerful Berkeleys – and in more ways than one. His grandfather, Julius Berkeley the First, was a prominent supporter of the American Eugenics movement, with links to the Nazi Party; while his father, Julius Berkeley II, financed illegal coerced sterilisation programmes in Peru, Mexico, Chile and Guatemala during the 1950s and '60s. As I learned, the activities of the present-day Berkeley Foundation, bolstered by the hundred-billion-dollar fortune of its chief executive, are only a continuation of that dynasty's ambition to reduce the human population to what they consider a sustainable number.

'And what might that number be? That was the question I asked myself over and over, while my Forum colleagues were strangely reticent to be too specific on the subject. But it so happens that in the course of my private investigations I was able to find out just exactly what these criminal lunatics have in store for the future of humanity.'

Chapter 42

At this point in his narrative, Auguste Kaprisky switched gears to tell them a story.

'In 1979,' he said, 'a man going by the name "Robert C. Christian" approached the Elberton Granite Finishing Company of Elberton, Georgia, USA, with an unusual proposal that he claimed he was making them on behalf of "a small group of loyal Americans". What he wanted to commission them to build was a twenty-foot granite monument, to be erected on a five-acre parcel of land purchased for the purpose, some miles outside the town of Elberton. It was an unusual location for such a monument, and the nature of the thing itself was even more unusual. On hearing his proposal the director of the company decided that "Christian" must be deranged, and tried to dissuade the man by quoting him an enormously inflated sum for the job, the equivalent of nearly four hundred thousand dollars today. To his surprise, however, the quotation was accepted without hesitation.'

'What's this shit got to do with anything?'

'Be quiet, Jeff.'

'The monument became famously known as the Georgia Guidestones. It consisted of six large granite slabs, arranged in a design reminiscent of a Neolithic stone circle like the

British Stonehenge. According to the exacting instructions provided to the builders, it was inscribed with what purported to be a message for humanity, a guide for a new "Age of Reason". This message took the form of a set of ten commandments, translated into a variety of modern languages as well as cuneiform Babylonian, ancient Greek, Sanskrit and Egyptian hieroglyphics. The commandments dictate a number of ideological principles for mankind: "To be not a cancer on the Earth, leave room for nature"; "To guide reproduction wisely, improving fitness and diversity"; "To balance personal rights with social duties"; "To establish a world government that would oversee the affairs of individual nations". If this sounds to you like a blend of totalitarian socialist ideology mingled with ecological extremism, you would not be far wrong. But the best is yet to come, with the commandment that proclaims the need "To maintain humanity under five hundred million in balance with nature".'

'Half a billion people,' Jeff said with a deep frown. 'That's, like—'

'About a sixteenth of today's world population,' Tuesday replied. 'Half of what it was in the year 1800.'

Jeff looked at him. 'Why'd you always cling to all this weird information?'

'Guys,' Ben said.

'It took me a year of digging,' Kaprisky went on, 'with the invaluable aid of several private investigators in Georgia and elsewhere, to discover the true identity of the man who commissioned the building of the Georgia Guidestones under the pseudonym "Robert C. Christian". His real name was Nestor Grindlay. Born in Maple Grove, Minnesota in 1923, he went on to become a key US associate of none other than Sir Simon Asquith, who in 1979 already played an important role within the Forum and would later rise to become its Chairman. Grindlay, too, was a senior member and economic adviser to the committee until his death twenty years later.'

'He was one of them!' exclaimed Valentina, as captivated as she was horrified by the story.

'And so here lay the answer that none of my fellow members would openly give,' August said, 'but which was literally carved in stone as part of their secret vision of the future of mankind. A vision that for anyone of sane mind can only be regarded as a nightmare. To reduce the current world population to half a billion would entail the systematic genocide of nearly *seven and a half billion innocent souls*. Consider that the total fatalities in all the wars of history combined are estimated at around one billion, a mere fraction of this number, and you will gain some perspective on the monstrous, evil, demonic nature of their plan.'

'No fucking way,' Jeff muttered. 'There'd be nobody left.'

'Fifteen out of every sixteen people we know would be dead,' replied Tuesday, the maths prodigy.

'Perhaps that is why, on July 6 2022, the Georgia Guidestones were blown up by a person or persons unknown, using high explosive charges,' Auguste said. 'Knowing who erected them, one can speculate that the time had now come to erase the too-obvious evidence of their stated intentions for the global population. Indeed, the monument had long attracted the suspicion of conspiracy theorists around the world, many of whom regarded it as a shrine to a sinister new world order, or even as the Ten Commandments of the Antichrist.

'I have never thought of myself as a conspiracy theorist,' he went on, allowing himself a small, dry smile. This was about as close as Auguste Kaprisky was capable of coming to humour. 'And I still do not. Because these are *not* theories. They are facts. Here are some more. Why did the world's mainstream media largely ignore the sinister message of the Guidestones for all these years? Simply, because the Forum exerts such influence over news outlets everywhere, writing the scripts and pulling the strings that make the puppets dance to their will. Likewise, why did the US Federal authorities so quickly intervene when the Guidestones were targeted in earlier minor acts of vandalism, such as being spray-painted with conspiracy slogans in 2008, yet barely lift a finger to find the perpetrators of the bombing? Surely, this was a far more serious crime? Yet the FBI have been conspicuous by their absence from the case, apparently content to leave it in the hands of the local sheriffs. Again, one may speculate that the authorities did nothing because they were told to do nothing. It is impossible for the general public to imagine the kind of power that the Forum wields.'

Auguste took a long pause, as though he was measuring his words for what was coming next. Ben sensed that the old man was building up to an even worse revelation. As though anything could be worse than what he'd told them already.

Yet, Ben was right.

'So by now we begin to understand the sheer unimaginable scale of the Forum's genocidal ambitions,' Auguste said. 'They have even stated them publicly. But how do they intend to carry them out? This is the last great question to be addressed, and I'm afraid that the answer is also painfully clear.'

'Let's have it, then,' Jeff said angrily. 'What have the fuckers got planned for us?'

And now here it came at last.

'In a vote from which I abstained,' Auguste said, 'the members more or less unanimously elected to execute their plans using a medical strategy as outlined by the monster Julius Berkeley. It now transpires that this course of action has been years in development, a secret project co-funded by his foundation and the pharmaceutical bosses to the tune of billions of dollars, with collusion from shadowy elements of government and the military defence-intelligence complex. Thanks to emerging biotechnology that has only recently taken the quantum leap from the realms of science fiction into reality, they now have the means to insert deadly gene-altering components, created in their bioweapons laboratories, into revolutionary new lipid nanoparticles. These are a minute, microscopic delivery system, carriers if you will, that when injected into the body are designed to be capable of penetrating the cell wall and entering the nucleus itself, where they can deploy their payload. By this means it is possible to effectively re-program the DNA of the recipient in order to create inside their own cells an entire armoury of toxic pathogens, chimeric semi-synthetic virus proteins and animal venoms that will spread around the body, infest the circulatory system and organs, eat away natural immunity to illness, affect brain function, cause fatal cardiac inflammation, disable the body's ability to detect and neutralise latent cancer cells, provoke an explosion of autoimmune

331

disorders, and a host of other pathologies specifically engineered to destroy and end lives. And to do all this in such a way that there would be no smoking gun, no possible trail of evidence leading back to the murderers. No evidence, indeed, that any crime had even been committed. No such act of mass murder has ever been conceived before now. If successfully implemented, the death toll would make even the Nazi Holocaust or Stalin's Reign of Terror pale into insignificance by comparison.'

Auguste pointed a bony finger at the camera. For the first time in his video presentation, he looked angry and emotional. 'Make no mistake, they have the resources and power to ensure that these almost completely untraceable biological nanoweapons will find their way into a wide range of medications and inoculations routinely used by billions of people across the world. For those who survive the acute physical damage, or in whom these effects may take some time to cause progressive organ failure and eventual death, the biotechnology is designed also to target the reproductive system, causing swathes of infertility, spontaneous abortion and severe birth defects on an unprecedented scale. This is no idle threat. It is real, and they have every intention of carrying it out in the near future. Indeed it may have begun even as I speak. Nobody would ever know. And it must be stopped before it is too late.'

Valentina looked aghast. 'I think I'm going to be sick.'

'Me too,' echoed Tuesday.

'They can't do this!' she burst out. 'I mean, how can they?'

'They can do whatever they want, kid,' Wolf said with a shrug. 'They have the power. Might is right, simple as that.'

'But what about rule of law? What about governments? Aren't they in charge? Wouldn't they stop something like this from happening, to protect us?'

'Valentina,' Ben said patiently, reaching out to pause the video again. 'You heard what your Tonton said. These people *own* governments. They hold the purse strings to all the big banks and control all the money. They can buy and sell nations, manipulate elections. They can instate the world leaders they've groomed to be their puppets and depose the ones who cause trouble for them. They can finance wars and decide which side they want to win, while selling arms to both sides. They tell the media what to say, so that everything Joe Public hears on the TV is all one huge lie to suit their purposes. They run the entire medical and pharma industry, technology, economics, education, all of it. Jaden's right. Men like these, with the kind of wealth they have at their disposal, they're above the law.'

He hated telling her these hard realities of life. It felt like drowning kittens in a sack.

She fell silent, breathing hard, struggling with her denial. Then nodded resignedly. 'Fine. What the hell do I know? I'm just a kid, I suppose. Like everyone keeps telling me.'

'They might be above the law,' Jeff said. 'But that doesn't mean someone can't do something about it.'

'No,' Ben said. He restarted the video and Auguste went on talking.

'The destruction of the Guidestones came as a signal to me that something was about to happen. And of course by now I knew exactly what that "something" was to be. The evil cabal at the heart of the Forum were about to implement their Final

Solution on the world, to make their long-held statement of intent a reality at last. Therefore, I decided that I, too, must act. The very survival of humanity depended on it.'

'Oh, Tonton,' Valentina sobbed. Tears welled in her eyes.

'But what to do?' Auguste asked. 'I had already voiced my dissent, to little avail. Meanwhile their plan is so grossly outrageous, so surreal in its enormity, that anyone attempting to denounce it to the outside world would be ridiculed as a babbling lunatic. Unless, of course, they could provide evidence so compelling and undeniable that the world would *have* to take the threat seriously. My first priority, therefore, was to gather such evidence. If you are watching this video, you will also have possession of the chess piece stored in the same hiding place as the flash drive. As you may be aware by now, this chess piece is no ordinary white knight. It is a special replica that I had made, containing an ultra-sensitive recording device, which I contrived to smuggle into the most recent of the Forum's meetings.' He added by way of a parenthesis, 'Details of the location of that meeting, and of the next, are included in the pdf document I have provided.'

'Awesome,' Tuesday said, holding up the white knight to gaze at it in wonder.

'It goes without saying that gatherings of the Forum are subject to the strictest of security measures,' Auguste went on. 'The extreme secrecy of matters discussed prohibits the carrying of mobile phones or any other type of electronic device inside the conference room, or anywhere close to it. Any member found breaching this hallowed rule would face the most ruthless punishment. Particularly a member like myself, who had already attracted a certain amount of ill feeling due to my vocal opposition and abstention from voting on the matter, which had not gone unnoticed. But I was undaunted by the great personal risk I was taking, as it was the only way that I could capture the proof I needed. And it was worth it. Contained inside the chess piece is irrefutable, high-quality audio evidence that can put an end to their schemes for ever. In it you will hear the voices of Sir Simon Asquith, his henchman Klaus Speer, Julius Berkeley III, Matthias Rothstein, Arlin Baumbach, Jean-Claude Dorn, Noah Jaggard Petersen and several others, openly finalising their plan to unleash the lethal bioweapon on an unsuspecting global public. You can hear them laughing at the stupidity and worthlessness of the "useless eaters" they so despise, and whose mass destruction they have longed for all these years. You can hear their sick fantasies of a depopulated world, cleansed of the filth of humankind, a terrestrial paradise or Garden of Eden where they believe they will stroll around as gods for the rest of eternity.'

'This is gonna blow the lid off big-time,' Tuesday murmured, staring at the white knight in his hand. 'The shitstorm to end all shitstorms.'

'You get that audio device out of there,' Ben told him.

'You damn well betcha I will.'

'What are we going to do with it?' Wolf asked.

'I don't know yet,' Ben said. 'But we'll figure it out.'

Auguste was looking tired by now, the long monologue of his testimony having taken a lot out of him. Before he started winding down to his conclusion there was one more item he needed to mention. 'Shortly after gathering my evidence I made contact with a Berlin-based investigative journalist called Fritz Kohler. Having examined the credentials of many of his peers I selected Herr Kohler as someone I could trust to bring this information to a wider public and give it the recognition it deserved. I was cautious, however. At our introductory meeting in Berlin I fed him only a bare minimum of detail, enough to persuade him of my legitimacy and seriousness, whilst enticing him to learn more. We have arranged a second meeting, to be held in the near future here at the estate where I can speak more freely and intend to bring him fully up to date with my knowledge.'

Valentina glanced at Ben. 'Berlin?' she said.

Ben nodded. 'Fritz was Mia's fiancé.' He hadn't told her a great deal of what had happened during his trip to Germany, but she was insightful enough to read between the lines and her look told him that she understood everything.

Auguste went on, 'However, I fear that my former colleagues have hardened their suspicions towards me. After that last meeting I sensed a sea-change in their attitude and am inclined to believe they now regard me as a potential threat. That being so, then my days are numbered as these men do not suffer their political opponents to live. By the time this video is seen, the viewer will know whether or not that second meeting with Herr Kohler did in fact take place. If not, then it is certainly because my enemies have got to me first. In such a case I can only trust that the information will safely reach his hands now. Herr Kohler, if you are watching this, I would like to express my gratitude once again for your willingness to expose these vile crimes. It was a pleasure meeting you, and I only wish we could have worked more closely together.

'And this brings me to the end of my testimony, as there really is nothing left for me to say. Perhaps I have reached the end in other ways too. I have lived a long and fulfilling life and accept that if it is now almost over, then so be it. I go to my grave in the hope that my efforts will have achieved their purpose in bringing my killers, and the would-be murderers of billions of others, to a swift and severe justice. My only regret is that my departure from this life will wrench me away from the one person in the world whom I truly adore. Valentina, you are the apple of my eye, the sunshine in my heart and the breath in my lungs. I love you far more than words can say, my dear sweet child. Please forgive me for my many faults and mistakes, and remember me for ever as your Tonton.'

Valentina was in floods of tears now. But they were tears mingled with joy, knowing that her hero of a granduncle was alive despite everything.

'In the meantime I leave it to you, dear viewer, to ensure that these dangerous lunatics will be utterly destroyed as they deserve, in the greatest scandal and political takedown of all time. Please consult the supplementary material I have provided, a wealth of additional detail that may be of use. Thank you, and goodbye.'

Chapter 43

For a long moment afterwards, it felt as if all the air had been sucked out of the room.

'Holy shitbags,' Jeff said.

'That certainly was something,' commented Tuesday.

The others said nothing. Valentina, because she was unable to speak for the tears. Wolf, because Wolf was generally economical with words at a time like this; and Ben, because he was already grabbing the laptop, closing down the video file and bringing up the supplementary document. Within an instant it was flashing up onscreen and they were all gathering closer around the desk to look.

As Auguste had indicated, the document consisted of a long and detailed set of notes on all of the other fourteen members of the Forum, himself excluded. At the head of the list were a number of names of the most key players, arranged in order of importance within its hierarchy. He'd written their profiles up as meticulously as a police report. Each one included a photo, along with name, date and place of birth and nationality. For the members whose identities were more prominently in the public eye, such as the former heads of state and the well-known American billionaire philanthropist, he'd been able to lift their falsely smiling faces from official websites and mainstream media. Others, more reclusive and perhaps less willing to be recognised in public, had clearly been photographed covertly from afar without their knowledge. Auguste must have been tracking them for months.

And he'd done his research, too. Each man had been allocated a potted history of his background, career and even interests. The information ran into several pages.

'He's even found out where they all live,' said Valentina. 'Look at this one. Sir Simon Asquith, owns this big country pile in Surrey, England, called Brasenose Hall. Doesn't look a patch on this place, I have to say.' Not at all competitive, was Valentina. 'Then there's his vice-chairman, Speer. Another billionaire science entrepreneur, PhD in bioelectrical engineering, owner of several patents in cybernetics and prosthetic medicine. Lives in Hungary.'

'Any relation to Albert Speer the Nazi?' Tuesday wondered aloud.

Valentina said, scanning down the list, 'And here's that horrid little American Julius Berkeley, with his spread in Bellevue, Washington.' She sniffed desultorily. 'It looks more like a mining camp than a mansion, if you ask me. Ben, what are you doing?'

Ben had stepped away from the desk to go over to the safe where Auguste's diary was kept. Quickly re-entering the now familiar access code he retrieved the book and leafed back through the pages to revisit the dates of those previously baffling entries that he now understood were the three-monthly meetings of the Forum. There they were: the most recent that Auguste had managed to secretly record, and the next which was due to take place just six days from now.

Interesting timing, in more ways than one. Ben reflected that if Auguste's illicit audio recording was about twelve weeks old, it suggested that his fellow members' growing suspicions hadn't reached a critical point until sometime later, when they must have had operatives covertly watching his rendezvous in Berlin with Fritz Kohler. That had been the clincher. The delay between that last Forum get-together and the combined moves against Auguste and Fritz meant that the time window before the next big meeting of the gods had been shortened. Maybe they'd been expecting to be able to invite a new member during that period to take the place of the freshly deceased. How disappointed they must be.

His mind turning over furiously, Ben replaced the book in the safe and went back over to join the others around the desk. 'Did Auguste say that he'd provided the locations of the Forum meetings in this document?' he asked.

'Hold on,' said Valentina. 'We'll have to scroll down past all this member information. There's so much of it.' She deftly worked the laptop's touchpad, clicked a few times and said, 'Okay, yes, here we are. The last meeting was held on Jumby Bay Island in Antigua, nearly three months ago. Some kind of fancy private resort, by the sound of it. Colonial villas, beaches and palm trees.'

'How jolly nice to be able to hide away in your tropical paradise retreat, sipping on a banana daiquiri while conspiring to murder most of the global population,' Tuesday said.

'And the next one?' Ben asked.

'Hold on,' she said again, moving down the page. 'Here it is. The next one is in Hungary. Lake Balaton.'

'Our boys certainly like to move around, don't they?' Jeff said. 'See the world and plot to destroy it, at the same time.'

'Hold on a minute,' said Wolf, who'd been silent for a while. 'Go back to the other page. The one with the info on the Forum vice-chairman, Speer.'

Valentina looked at him. 'Why?'

'Because he lives in Hungary. Be interesting to know where exactly. Could be somewhere near the location of the next meeting. Or the same, even.'

'You think these guys'd use their own homes for something like that?' Jeff asked doubtfully.

'Think about that stately home we knocked over, where all the devil- worshipping scumbags used to meet up to eat babies and stuff.'

Valentina was thankfully too absorbed in the laptop to pick up on the baby-eating reference.

Reaching the section on Klaus Speer Valentina said, 'Here he is. There's a ton of info about him, actually. A chess grandmaster, man of great learning and culture and longtime friend of Tonton's, before he saw him for who he really was. And here's the bit about where he lives. You're right,' she said to Wolf. 'Lake Balaton. Ever heard of it before?'

'Not me,' Tuesday said. Valentina whipped out a smartphone and got to work tapping and swiping at the screen with the second-nature dexterity of her tech-savvy generation. Maybe in a few thousand years' time, teenage kids would have developed spaghetti-like fingers to work these devices yet more efficiently. That was assuming the Forum's genocidal plans didn't prevent those future generations from ever being born. 'Here we go,' she said. 'Lake Balaton is the biggest freshwater lake in Central Europe, eight miles wide and nearly fifty miles long.'

Jeff asked, 'He lives *on* the lake, or *by* the lake?'

'Doesn't say,' Wolf replied, scanning the page.

'Maybe there's another island,' Tuesday suggested. 'They seem to like their islands. Makes sense, I suppose. Nice and private.'

'Eight miles by fifty is a lot of water,' Jeff said. 'Should offer all the privacy anyone needs.'

'A chess grandmaster,' Ben said thoughtfully. 'That's an interesting coincidence, don't you think?'

'And a man of great learning and culture, whatever that's worth,' Wolf said. 'Well, a murdering nutcase who can quote Shakespeare and knows about wine and opera is still a murdering nutcase, in my book.'

'Damn right about that,' Jeff said. 'But here's another thought, guys. I hate to say this, but if that last meeting was almost three months ago and they were already so close to putting this bloody plan of theirs into action, then how do we know they haven't already started rolling with it?'

'Then everybody will die,' Valentina said. 'The end of the human race as we know it.'

'Not necessarily,' said Ben. 'It doesn't have to happen that way.'

Jeff turned to look at him. They'd been friends for a long, long time and nobody knew Ben as well as he did. The look in Ben's eye was one he'd seen before. 'What's on your mind, mate?'

'Something you said earlier,' Ben replied. 'These people might be above the law, but that doesn't mean *someone* can't do something about them. Someone who doesn't always answer to the law, if they can help it.'

Wolf gave a predatory smile. 'Someone, as in . . . us?'

'Tell us what you're thinking, Ben,' Tuesday said.

'We have some options,' Ben replied. 'We can retrieve the audio device hidden inside that chess piece. And if we can figure out how to make it work, we can send the recording to someone in Fritz Kohler's line of business who'd know what to do with it. Then we can sit here on our arses for as long as it takes, waiting for the shit to hit the fan. But what if it doesn't? What if it just goes nowhere?'

'Which seems like a pretty likely outcome,' Wolf said. 'Along with another dead reporter, a ton of payoff money and a lot of covering up. Same old, same old. You still believe in the justice system, I have a bridge for sale. On Jupiter.'

Ben nodded. 'Alternatively, we take a more proactive approach. We know these men are due to gather together again in just a few days' time. And we know where. It's not that far away from here. Paris to Budapest is only about fifteen hours by road.'

'And a lot faster by private jet,' Valentina said.

'Proactive is good,' Jeff said. 'I like the sound of proactive. Find out where they're hiding and stamp the filthy bastards all out in one fell swoop. Like destroying a rats' nest.'

'Or hand them over to the cops,' Ben said. 'Then again, that's a waste of time if the lawmakers are too afraid to prosecute them. You have to consider who these people are, and the power they have.'

'Then they have to go down,' Wolf said. 'All the way down. In a way that makes sure they're never coming up again. That's the only way that makes sense.'

'Right,' Jeff said.

Ben looked at his friends. 'You know I can't ask any of you to come with me.'

'Since when did you even need to ask?' Tuesday said, putting on an offended expression.

Jeff's eyes glittered and a wicked grin spread over his face. 'As a matter of fact, mate, you just fucking try and stop us.'

Chapter 44

Lake Balaton, Hungary

Surrounded by miles of quietly rippling open water, the circular ramparts and gun emplacements of the great fortress commanded a dominating view of the lake on all sides. Its foundations were said to have originated from Roman times, though the massive stone walls and towers themselves had been built during the long, bloody Hungarian–Ottoman wars of the early sixteenth century, to help prevent the warships of the Turkish Sultan Selim 'the Terrible' from laying waste to Christian cities up and down the length of the strategically important waterway. Much later, the fortress had served as a munitions store and battery in the 1945 Plattensee Offensive conflict between German troops and the Red Army, the Wehrmacht's short-lived last hurrah on the Eastern Front.

The shores of Örvényes could be glimpsed from the top of the battlements on a clear day. But right now it was a murky, rainy night and the fortress stood shrouded in drifting mist, the wetness gleaming on its black stonework as the dark waters below lapped at the rocky base of the island on which it stood. From somewhere out there in the mist could be heard the two security patrol boats assigned by the fortress's present-day owner to maintain a constant watch over the surrounding lake.

On the outside the massive edifice looked almost unchanged from centuries ago, but internally it had undergone radical modernisation and restructuring, thanks mostly to that same owner, Klaus Speer. At this moment, in a brightly lit modern conference room deep inside the labyrinthine walls of the fortress, he was sitting alone at a long table surrounded by fourteen empty chairs. Though in fact Speer wasn't completely alone, as on the big screen opposite him was displayed the face of his boss Sir Simon Asquith. Blotchy and wrinkled, prolapsed and stained with liver spots, it wasn't a face that lent itself particularly well to being magnified to take up most of the wall at the top of the table. The Chairman's harsh, belligerent voice rasped from hidden speakers around the room as he talked, or barked, at his subordinate.

Their secure video conversation was a pre-meeting briefing ahead of the big event scheduled for five days from now, and once again its main focus was their organisation's current biggest headache: namely, the ongoing nuisance posed by the involvement of this associate of Auguste Kaprisky's, Benedict Hope. Word had reached them a few hours earlier of the failed attempt to eliminate him in France. That had been their last contact from their man Messer. Since then, absolute radio silence – and they could only assume that meant the worst.

'It's a disaster,' Asquith was saying angrily. 'Another total bloody cock-up. Everything we throw at this bastard Hope, he seems able to survive it.'

'It's no more than another minor setback,' Speer countered. 'We'll deal with him.'

'So you keep telling me,' said the huge irate face on the wall.

That wasn't the only bad news they'd received that day. Meanwhile, the latest report from their insider in the local Le Mans police informed them that Kaprisky had come out of his coma and appeared to be rallying. 'You assured me this wouldn't happen, Speer,' Asquith grated.

'With all respect, sir, I wouldn't have made that guarantee. I said there was a slim chance of his recovery. A *slim* chance, as opposed to none at all. I believe I was right about that.'

'So it seems, unfortunately. And now the question is what the hell we're supposed to do about it.'

Speer replied, 'Nothing. Nothing at all.'

Asquith's already hideous blown-up face twisted into a grimace. 'Oh, that's good,' barked the voice from the speakers. '*Nothing*. That all you can suggest?'

'That is to say,' Speer elaborated patiently, 'we do nothing for the moment. I suggest that instead we bide our time, quietly forging ahead with our plans. Let nature take its course, If indeed Kaprisky is set to make a full, if somewhat unexpected, recovery, we wait for him to be back on his feet. Then we strike again.'

Asquith snorted, 'Surely you don't propose mounting a second attack on the house? After what happened before? With this Hope lurking about to bugger things up for us even worse than the first time?'

'No, that would be foolish. This time we'll adopt a different approach. Rather than risk attacking his defences right in the middle, we focus our assault towards where he's weakest.' Speer could actually see his strategy in front of him like chess pieces positioned on an imaginary board, floating in mid-air. And like all winning chess strategies, it depended as much on the psychology of their opponent as it did on material strengths. 'Consider for a moment where that weakness lies. What's the one thing Kaprisky cares about most in all the world?'

'You mean, apart from trying to blow up everything we've been working towards, spent billions putting into action?'

Speer could see he was going to have to spell it out for him. 'More than that, even. The girl.'

'The girl,' Asquith echoed. That seemed to have got his interest. A lascivious little smile, or something like it, tugged at the wrinkles around his mouth.

'Sooner or later she'll have to leave that estate,' Speer said. 'She can't stay tucked away in there like a canary in a gilded cage for ever. And when she does come out, and travels back to that school of hers in Switzerland, that's when we'll strike.'

'And do what with her?'

'I haven't figured out the endgame yet,' Speer replied. 'A kidnapping, for sure. There'll be no shortage of local thugs available for that purpose. Once we have her, Kaprisky will agree to whatever we demand of him for her release. We can draw him to a ransom drop and then kill them both. It'll look like just another abduction gone ugly. He's a billionaire. It happens. The public won't think twice about it. People still remember the Getty case. The business with the severed ear.'

'You're forgetting that this Hope character is some kind of kidnap recovery specialist. Kaprisky has used him before in that capacity, according to my sources.'

'That's assuming Hope is still living and breathing by then,' Speer said. 'Even if he is, the old man will be too terrified and panic-stricken to waste time involving him, the police or anyone else. Especially after receiving a couple of fingers or an ear in the post.'

Asquith considered, and gave a cold nod. 'Very well. Sounds like an effective strategy. Make it so.'

'I'm pleased you approve.'

'Speaking of strategies, the last time we spoke, you told me in no uncertain terms that you would be disposing of that infernal board game. I'm assuming you've done so?'

Speer balked at its being called a 'board game', but showed no reaction. 'The chess set? Of course. And as I said, you can rest perfectly assured there will be no trace of it for anyone to lay eyes on, ever again.'

'That's something, at least. Right. Well. I think that's all, Speer. I have other important business to attend to. I'll see you in five days' time.'

'Thank you, sir,' Speer said graciously. 'I look forward to it, as ever.'

The screen went dark. Speer ended the call connection. '*Verdammte alte Fotze*,' he muttered to himself in his native German as he flicked off the conference room lights. From there he headed along the winding corridor to a special locked doorway, and beyond it to the stone spiral staircase that descended to a lower tier very few people ever were allowed to enter.

This was his sanctum sanctorum, his Holy of Holies, to which nobody had access but himself and a small handful of cleaning and serving staff. The huge open-plan space was all one circular room supported on columns, its almost perfect symmetry broken only by the stairway shafts that connected the floors below and above, bypassing this one entirely. Speer's private space was sandwiched between Levels 2 and 3, and so he liked to joke to himself that he lived on Level Two and a Half. This had been the main deck, so to speak, of the fortress's once formidable artillery battery. Where the massive circular array of forty-two-pounder cannons had once pointed out from their emplacements across the waters of the lake was now a grand curved expanse of windows that filled his rooms with light during the day and offered an almost all-around view that made him feel as invulnerable as Zeus looking down from Mount Olympus.

Speer had fallen in love with and purchased this property as a near-ruin many years ago, and been personally responsible for its total interior redesign. Architecture was just a hobby for him, of course, but one for which he had a tremendous talent that he believed he must have inherited from his grandfather Albert, a close associate of Adolf Hitler. Little Klaus had been just ten years old when his dear old granddad had been released from prison, after serving twenty years for his prominent part in Hitler's war machine as Minister of Armaments, among other functions. The young boy had been fascinated to learn about his grandfather's true calling as an architect, which had led him to design some of the most iconic constructions of the Third Reich including its Chancellery and the Party rally grounds at Nuremberg.

The older Klaus had tried to incorporate some of that architectural splendour into the refurbishment of his beloved fortress. It was the one place on earth where he felt completely satisfied and contented, and his personal living space down here was his most favourite of all. If Speer had been at all given to such vulgar, common expressions, he might have thought of it as his man cave or bachelor pad. Neither of which was really an appropriate term: firstly because the word 'cave' scarcely did justice to the exquisite perfection of good taste and finery with which he'd surrounded himself down here. And secondly because 'bachelor', with all its implications, would give rather the wrong impression of a man who, in all the years he'd lived alone in this place, had not once experienced – still less submitted to – the temptation to exploit his very private lifestyle to entertain intimate female company. Nor intimate male company, for that matter. Unlike the majority of his peers in high-level political affairs Speer considered himself quite above such gross matters of the flesh, to the point where he disregarded them with a pronounced sense of revulsion and loathing. Not for any sort of moralistic reason, but simply because he felt, and had always felt since his earliest childhood, a marked detachment from his fellow humans, the 'useless eaters' who comprised the vast majority of the population, in whom he could see no more value than in an insect. Sometimes he wondered musingly if he even belonged to the same species at all, beyond the superficial physical similarities.

No, Speer's true passion was for inanimate things, for beautiful objects, as well as for the acquisition of knowledge and for ideas in their purest form. Of all of those, none was purer than the game of chess that he utterly revered. And of all the treasures that he'd collected over a lifetime of great wealth, none gave him more cerebral pleasure, or indeed half as much, as the one he'd acquired by force from the collection of Auguste Kaprisky. There it sat on a table near the west window: the priceless Napoleon chess set, to be kept well out of sight of the Chairman when the rest of the Forum arrived on the island for their meeting, days from now.

Speer walked over to the table and stood admiring his prize. He had a game in progress, pitting his considerable ability against the fiendish mind of his Komodo chess computer's highest difficulty level, and at the moment he, playing white, had the advantage. The artificial brain had made its latest cunning, unexpected move while he'd been talking to Asquith. Speer shifted the black bishop accordingly, then pondered the new threat it posed for a long moment, scrutinising his position and thinking in multiple spatial and temporal dimensions about all the possible ways things might go from here, before he decided on his response by advancing his white queen three diagonal squares to put pressure on the covert, as yet innocuous but potentially deadly enemy stratagem he perceived quietly developing in the background.

Things were getting interesting. Speer relished the challenge of going up against a truly brilliant opponent. Allowing his thoughts to stray briefly from the intricacies of the game, he wondered whether this Benedict Hope, evidently a highly skilled warrior from what they'd been able to find out about him, might be seen as the martial equivalent of the Komodo chess machine. A very tough nut to crack, at all events. Speer respected that, but he was no less determined to see his real-life enemy defeated. And he believed it was just a matter of time.

Speer turned his attention back to the Napoleon set. It pained him bitterly that he had so far been unable to possess the original board. Perhaps one day, he told himself, he might have the opportunity to go back to the scene of the crime and take that too. But in the meantime, even though their acquisition had led him and his Forum associates nowhere in terms of knowledge, even though the attack had turned out to be a complete failure, even though he still couldn't understand how on earth Kaprisky had managed to deceive the Forum members so cleverly, just the sight of these magnificent chessmen made him forget all his concerns and filled his soul with light and beauty like the sun's rays streaming through cathedral windows. Now that they were his, nothing on earth could persuade him to dispose of them. Not even a direct order from his Chairman, a man who wouldn't hesitate to have him butchered for disobedience. What was he supposed to do, toss the chess pieces into the lake and watch them sink to the bottom, these priceless historic artefacts lost for ever? What kind of soulless, barbaric philistine could even contemplate such a thing?

To hell with Asquith, Speer thought. One day soon he'll die and I'll become Chairman in his place.

Or maybe I'll kill him myself.

Chapter 45

Deep into the night, Ben, Jeff, Tuesday, Wolf and Valentina sat in Auguste's study thrashing out their plan of action. Having long since unanimously agreed on the need to travel to the Lake Balaton region of Hungary as soon as possible, they still had a thousand details to wrangle over before they arrived at a coherent strategy.

It was Tuesday who'd come up with the thought. 'Just one small point, folks. Does any of us speak an actual word of Hungarian?'

Which made everyone go quiet for a moment until Jeff remembered their guy Baz Baczko. 'His mother's from Szentendre.'

'Now look who clings onto weird information,' Tuesday challenged him.

'Hey, beat me up for just happening to remember what the guy told me one time. Anyhow, he speaks a bit of it. Hungarian, I mean.'

'A bit of it?' Tuesday said, raising an eyebrow. 'Like "hello", "goodbye" and "please can you tell me the way to the airport"?'

'Even if he just knows a few basic words, that's better than the rest of us,' Ben said. 'Think he'd come along and help out?'

Jeff laughed. 'Do bears shit in the woods?'

'He went off with Liam to dump that little Peugeot,' Tuesday said, making Ben feel a twinge of guilt about the young couple deprived of their car. 'But he might be back by now.'

'Let's find out,' said Wolf.

As it happened, Baz and Liam had returned some thirty minutes ago, and had been drinking mugs of cocoa in the security guard quarters when Jeff radioed down to summon Baz to the study.

Baz was a large, imposing guy in his late thirties, lean, muscular, broad-shouldered and handsome in a craggy, flinty kind of way, a young Charles Bronson. His attitude was as tough as his appearance, and three minutes of listening to their proposition was all that was necessary before he grunted, 'I'm in.'

'How's your Hungarian?' Jeff asked.

'*Elég jól beszélek*,' Baz replied with a shrug. Showing off.

'That'll do,' Ben said. 'Welcome aboard.'

'I reckon some of the other blokes would be up for it, too,' Baz said. 'In fact they'd give an arm to come in.'

'What d'you think, Ben?' Jeff said, turning to him. 'Call it a six-man team? Us four, Baz and one extra?'

'And me,' Valentina piped up. 'Makes seven. Or six and a half, maybe.'

'Absolutely not you.'

'I can help. I've been helping already, haven't I?'

'You know you have,' he replied, 'and we couldn't have done any of it without you. But now you can help even more by staying here out of harm's way. Remember, you're on lockdown and you're not to venture outside of this estate

355

until further notice, okay? Why else do you think we brought in extra men to keep you safe?'

'Lockdown,' she muttered sourly. 'I hate that idea.'

She might have hated it, but after some gentle but firm persuasion she had little choice but to accept it. 'All right, you win. Now what about your base there? If there's a town nearby we could rent you an apartment or a house there. Or something in the countryside. Or there must be some hotels in the area.'

Ben shook his head. 'We can't fix a location until we know exactly where the target is. We'll want to be as close by as possible without attracting any notice. Forget hotels, they're too public and six foreigners will stick out like a sore thumb in a place like that.'

'Got to be some old shack we can use,' Wolf said. 'We can scout the place when we get there.'

Not to be outdone, Valentina replied, 'But we do know that Speer is either on the lake or close to it. So how about a boat? That would give you a mobile base where you'd be self-sufficient and able to stay out of sight while you hunt around for your target.'

'What kind of boat?' Jeff asked. As an SBS operative, he'd been around waterborne craft of all shapes and sizes for many years and knew every aspect of sailing inside out.

'What do I know about boats?' she said airily. 'One that's big enough for six people to live on. There must be thousands of them to choose from in the area that we can charter at a moment's notice. Or buy. Who cares about money?'

'I like the way this girl thinks,' Wolf said. 'A boat would be ideal. Something like a mid-sized motor cruiser with three cabins and space to store our kit. We could mooch up and down the lake all day long and nobody'd be any the wiser about what we were up to.'

Ben agreed. But immediately thinking of Lucas Dennim and his favourite boy's toy *Spirit Dancer*, he reminded them of the need for such a vessel to be as inconspicuous as possible. 'It can't be too large or ostentatious in any way. Especially as three of us have to keep a very low profile, since our faces will be known to the enemy.' They'd already spent some time discussing the problem of their compromised anonymity: Ben's most of all, but also Jeff's and Tuesday's, thanks to their association with Le Val. They had to assume that the enemy knew who they were by now. 'All we need is for word to get out that there's some stupid movie actor or celeb sailing around the lake incognito on his fancy yacht. Next thing you know, we're swarmed with people trying to spot him. So a boat, yes, but keep it basic and simple. Any old plain Jane fishing tub would do fine.'

'But I want you to be comfortable,' Valentina objected. 'Not crammed together like sardines in some leaky, stinky old rust bucket without decent facilities. You might be living there for days.'

'It's not a pleasure cruise,' Ben said. 'And we're all pretty used to roughing it, Valentina, trust me.'

'As long as I can bring my teddy bear,' Tuesday said with one of his most disarming grins, and Valentina laughed for the first time that day. It was good to bring some levity to the conversation.

Around three a.m., Valentina finally gave in to exhaustion and bade them good night, promising that she'd contact

Gabriel and start the ball rolling first thing in the morning. Soon after that, the rest of them called it a night too, and drifted off to their quarters for a few hours' rest before things started to become very active indeed. Wolf was happy to kip in the security guys' lodge house with the others.

Ben returned to the Swiss cottage, but even though his head was swimming with fatigue and he felt physically worn out from his exertions of that day, he was too full of thoughts and needed to spend some time winding down before he could get any sleep. He stood out on the dark balcony looking across at the moonlit woodland of the estate, smoking Gauloises and mulling over the complexities and dangers of what he and his friends were about to embark on. Their plan would be leading them straight into the heart of the enemy's lair, where you could forget about dealing with their goons in twos and threes like before. He had no doubt whatsoever that the Forum would surround themselves with a numerous and well-equipped security presence that even a team of skilled, experienced operators would have a tough time penetrating. There was a good chance that not all of them would be coming out alive. But he knew that reality wasn't lost on the others. They were walking into it with their eyes wide open, and taking deadly risks was nothing new to any of them.

Their mission to Lake Balaton wasn't the only thing on his mind that was keeping him from sleep. With every hour that passed since the attack earlier that day, it seemed to him more and more puzzling that the police still hadn't made their appearance. He couldn't understand it. What was holding them up? They had all the evidence they needed to bring them straight to the estate and take him away for questioning, pending all kinds of serious criminal charges they could throw at him. He couldn't allow that to stand in the way of the plan. If they turned up now, they'd have to catch him and that wouldn't be easy for them. But sooner or later, he knew he was going to have to face the consequences of what had happened.

Eventually he flicked away the stub of his last Gauloise and headed back inside the dark, silent cottage feeling strangely low and depressed. He had been into battle many times before now, faced all kinds of risks and dangers, found himself more than once staring almost certain death right in the eye and never flinched from any of it. But this gloomy feeling of deep unease that hung heavily over him now was something else, and it was new to him.

In the bathroom before going to bed, he gazed at himself in the mirror and saw a gaunt-faced stranger looking back. That was when he understood what he was feeling.

'Am I afraid?' he asked his reflection.

The look in his own eyes confirmed the answer. Yes, he was afraid. To have come this far through life, survived so many dangers, endured so many tough times, only to end up spending years locked behind bars simply for the crime of trying to protect his own skin while looking after the interests of his friends, was a prospect he wasn't at all sure he could bear. He had no concerns about his ability to withstand the physical environment of prison. But could he survive psychologically? If anything could break his spirit it was the helplessness and the frustration of being trapped like a tiger in a cage. That was what truly frightened him the most, more than pain or blood, more than mutilation or loss of limbs, more even than death.

If that sort of existence was the future that lay in store for him, he thought to himself as he stared in the mirror, then maybe it would be better if he didn't make it back from Hungary at all. Then if fate did spare him and he came home in one piece, he'd sooner go on the run and spend the rest of his life as a hunted fugitive than submit to captivity.

He smiled grimly at his reflection. *So be it,* he decided. *I don't care. To hell with them.*

With that thought he turned away from the mirror. The feeling of unease was gone again, and he felt strong and ready. In the morning they would put their plan into action.

And they did.

Chapter 46

The sixth man elected to the team was Cormac Wallace, after a bout of fierce competition from the others, who exactly as Baz had predicted were falling over one another to be picked. 'Guys, the rest of you have just as important a job to do,' Ben told them over an early breakfast, 'by staying here and making damn well sure the place is secure. Even behind the walls of this estate, we're outnumbered and outgunned. And trust me, I wouldn't trust anyone but the best to defend it.'

The next debate, unresolved from last night's long discussions, was over how best to get to their destination. Valentina had been pushing for them to make use of the Gulfstream again, and there was no arguing against its being the fastest means of landing the team into position. But now they had a clearer idea of the kind of reach and power the enemy had at their disposal, Ben was concerned that the team's arrival by air could be detected via the local airport authorities. An ostentatious private jet with the legend KAPRISKY CORP emblazoned in huge red letters on both flanks was like a giant flying billboard advertising their plan, hardly his idea of keeping a low profile. The days of zipping discreetly about the world were over.

The rest of the team agreed with Ben that the most anonymous means of travel was by road. Still slurping down the last of his morning coffee, Tuesday scoured the local listings of motors for sale and found a second-hand Renault cargo van being offered at a surplus fleet auction just a few kilometres the other side of Le Mans. Within fifteen minutes he and Jeff were off in Jeff's Ford Ranger with a bundle of cash from Auguste's secret walk-in safe to make the purchase. On their way back in tandem to the estate they stopped at a scrapyard, where in exchange for another wodge of Auguste's banknotes the manager of the *casse auto* agreed to let them have a set of plates from a crash-damaged wreck of the same make and model. Their new transport was worn and battered with nearly two hundred thousand on the clock but Clark Jenner, who had been a REME mechanic in his last life, checked it over and gave it a clean bill of health. The van had a three-seater bench up front and enough space in the back for the rest of them to stretch out in reasonable comfort – more than they'd have been able to expect from riding in an army truck, back in the day.

Yesterday's thunderous rainstorm had given way to a fine, bright morning. The hours were rolling slowly by with still no sign of the police showing up at the estate gates and Ben, feeling the pressure of their possible appearance at any time, wanted to get away without delay. They faced a road trip of over 1700 kilometres, but the best part of five days gave them a reasonable time margin to get to their destination and make their preparations before the Forum gathering got underway. Once all the necessary provisions for their journey had been raided from the kitchen stores and packed into the van, they said their quick goodbyes – Ben hated a fuss every bit as much as his friends did – and set off.

They'd be driving in shifts, stopping only for fuel, and Ben was taking the wheel for the first stint, with Wolf and Baz Baczko riding up front beside him. He left the estate satisfied that Valentina and Auguste would be well protected there. From Le Mans they headed north, adding a lengthy but unavoidable leg to their journey in order to stop by Le Val and loot all the kit they could carry from the armoury. As well as enough weaponry and munitions to start a small war their inventory of tactical training equipment contained sufficient quantities of items like bulletproof vests, night vision, communications and expedition gear to equip the six-man team several times over. Ben was zipping up one of the black NATO-issue holdalls they'd carry all the gear in when he spotted the mobile phone jammer on a shelf. It was the device he'd mentioned to Valentina before, something probably very similar to the one the raiders had used in their attack on the Kaprisky residence. And it occurred to him now that it could come in very handy, where they were going. He grabbed it off its shelf and stuffed that into the bag too.

With everything packed and the van ready to set off once more, Ben said another goodbye to his German shepherd dog Storm, who had thought his beloved master was home for good this time and was barking with frustration at being left behind again. From Le Val's quiet corner of rural Normandy their route took them back down south to Rennes, then revisiting Le Mans before veering northeast through Gabriel Archambeau's city of Chartres and then onwards to skirt Paris. Next on the itinerary was Reims in the heart of champagne country, then Metz, and a while after that they were coming up on the German border. It made Ben think of Mia, and wonder how she was faring in her new life.

They were approaching Saarbrücken when his phone interrupted the tedium of the journey. By then he had switched places with Wolf and was lounging in the passenger seat with a Gauloise. It was Valentina, calling with the excited announcement that she'd found them the perfect boat in Hungary, and in just the right location. 'It's only an eensy ordinary little tub of a thing, exactly like you said you wanted,' she assured him. 'Extremely cramped and uncomfortable, with hardly enough room inside for the six of you to breathe.'

'Sounds ideal,' Ben said. 'Nice work.'

'I was going to ask Gabriel to charter it for a week or two,' she explained. 'But it turned out there was no way of doing that without getting into all kinds of paperwork that could have connected it back to Kaprisky Corp too easily. I was pretty sure you'd want to avoid that. So I bought it.'

'You bought it.'

'Oh, it wasn't all that expensive. Gabriel can always write it off as a tax deduction, or whatever. Not that it matters. And it seems buying a boat is a lot less complicated than buying cars and things. Especially when you offer a few thousand over its market value.'

Ben rolled his eyes. 'Where is it?' he asked, and noted down her directions to the marina where it was moored, near Balatonfüzfó on the far northeastern corner of the lake.

'We have a boat?' Jeff asked as he ended the call.

'We have a boat.'

On they went, roads, roads and more roads, the boredom intercut only by food and fuel stops. Germany was blanketed by rain clouds that dulled the journey even more as Jeff and Tuesday took their turns at the wheel. By seven that evening, after nine hours on the road, they hit Heidelberg; a while later Regensburg. Conversation was minimal. After the first few hours the non-drivers had become too brain-numbed by the constant, steady drone and vibrations of the bare metal van cab even to play cards in the back. Beyond Regensburg the route curved southeast through Leggendorf and Passau, and as evening turned to night they were crossing into Austria. Somewhere near Vienna Ben took another turn at the wheel. Not long after that, the road signs in his headlights started showing names like Hegyeshalom and Mosonmagyaróvár. For a while their route through Hungary ran more or less parallel with the Danube River, not that they ever saw it in the darkness, before they reached the town of Gyór and turned southwards down Route 82 for the last ninety-minute leg to Balatonfüzfó.

By the time they reached the far eastern tip of Lake Balaton and followed Valentina's somewhat garbled directions to the marina where their boat was moored, it was three in the morning and they'd been on the road for seventeen straight hours. Which, by Ben's reckoning, wasn't bad progress. They climbed out of the van with a lot of yawning and stretching, grabbed the bulging, heavy holdalls from the back and checked in at the reception office. The marina was managed by a portly little guy called Jozsi, who had been bribed by Valentina to the tune of a couple of hundred thousand Hungarian forint, five hundred euros, to keep the place open late for them and show them to what would be their new floating base for the foreseeable future.

Jozsi was in a grumpy, taciturn mood at this time of night despite the extra cash, and he sullenly led them from the office and along a floodlit jetty with boats tethered up on both sides, gently bobbing on the dark, rippling lake. A chilly mist drifted over the surface of the water like smoke. Baz was doing all the talking for them, as the only team member who knew Hungarian.

'Which one is it?' Ben asked, looking around him at the moored vessels under the glow of the floodlights. There was a lot more variety among the boats than there'd been at Dinner Key Marina in Miami, everything from modern cabin cruisers to banged-up old fishermen's workhorses that looked pretty much like what he'd outlined to Valentina. One in particular caught his eye. It was small and squat and filthy and its hull was dented and patched, and if it had been a road vehicle it would probably have belonged on a scrap heap like the van that had donated their number plates. Perfect for their needs. 'That one?' he said, pointing.

Baz pointed the scabby old vessel out to Jozsi and said something in Hungarian. Jozsi frowned, shook his head and jerked his thumb further up the jetty. Ben looked, and saw what he was indicating at.

Cormac Wallace spotted it at the same instant. 'Ah, fer fuck's sake!' he burst out, eyes popping from his head.

'Whoops,' Tuesday said.

'Perhaps not quite what we had in mind,' muttered Jeff.

Ben's heart sank. The promised 'eensy ordinary little tub of a thing' was an apparently brand new Beneteau Oceanis Clipper, eleven metres of slick, gleaming white sailing yacht with easily enough space for ten people to travel in luxury.

It was as far a cry from an old fishing boat as he could have imagined, and looked exactly like it belonged to someone with serious cash to burn. Lucas Dennim, eat your heart out. It was a good thing Valentina wasn't a mere millionaire, the way she threw money about without a second thought.

'I told her we needed to keep a low profile,' he groaned. 'Didn't I make myself clear?'

'Your very words, mate,' Jeff said, shaking his head in dismay.

Wolf was the only one who could see the funny side of it. 'Leave the choice to a billion-euro heiress, and what did you think would happen?' he laughed. 'A rich kid like her doesn't see the world like we do, Ben. To her, anything smaller than a two-hundred-foot tri-decker with a helicopter pad, five-star restaurant facilities, full staff and staterooms like the *Titanic* really is just an ordinary little tub. Don't hold it against her. That's the life she was born to.'

Ben's first instinct had been to call her and start yelling. But he knew his friend was right, and in any case it was too late now to start complaining. 'I suppose we'll just have to slum it,' he said to a smiling Wolf.

Jozsi handed a slip of paperwork to Baz, which Baz passed on to Ben with a quizzical look, and which Ben returned to Jozsi with a fictitious signature that received only a glance and seemed to satisfy him. The marina manager stumped back to his office and the team got to work loading their kit aboard while Jeff took over as ship's captain, totally in his element despite his misgivings about the boat. They cast off from their moorings, the engines fired up with a roar and a churning of propellers, and they went burbling off across the misty water.

Chapter 47

They spent the remainder of that night moored in a sheltered nook on the northern banks of the lake. When everyone else had gone to bed, exhausted from the endless journey, Ben lingered alone for a while on the gently rocking foredeck, watching the stars through breaks in the mist. Then he flicked his cigarette into the water with a hiss and went back below to stretch out on his bunk in the V-berth and snatch some rest for himself, too.

Sleep was slow in coming and quickly over. As the first colours of dawn crept over the horizon, the boat's galley filled with the scents of fresh coffee and fried bacon and the six bleary-eyed team members gathered around the dinette table in the yacht's plush main saloon to replenish their systems with all the energy they were going to need for the coming day.

The mist had lifted and the rising sun was shimmering over the surface of Lake Balaton. The far shore lay far enough away to be completely out of sight, and they might have been at sea for all the vast expanse of water that stretched out to the south and west. With nearly six hundred square kilometres of lake area to cover, it was as well they got an early start. There was a fresh breeze gusting from the north and Baz and Cormac busied themselves raising the mainsail, rather than use motor power. Jeff took up his position at the wheel and Tuesday, the closet tech nerd, immersed himself in the onboard GPS and radio apparatus down below.

Meanwhile Ben and Wolf unpacked five pairs of high-powered binoculars from their kit and ran through a weapons check in the event they ran into any unexpected trouble during their reconnaissance of the area. The ordnance they'd brought from Le Val consisted mainly of the compact and quick-handling MP-5 submachine guns that all six team members, especially the two ex-Special Forces men among them, were so familiar with. In addition to the MP-5s Tuesday had packed his favourite Accuracy International L115A3 rifle, a long-range tool he could ply like a magic wand and which had once earned him the kudos of being one of the top snipers in the British army. The rifle could be broken down into its component parts and stowed in a zippered case that doubled as a backpack. For extra brute firepower they'd brought along a trio of Remington 870 'shorties', ultra-compact twelve-bore shotguns with pistol grips and barrels cut down to just eight and a half inches, useless at anything more than across-the-room range but highly effective in close-quarter combat. They'd no idea what kind of action they might encounter but it was good to consider all eventualities. Everybody had a knife, an identical professional killing tool with a rubberised handle and seven inches of wicked black double-edged blade. Silent, and deadly. And they all knew how to use them.

Lastly, Ben had supplemented his own personal armament with his faithful old Browning service pistol. It might lack the outright stopping power of Auguste Kaprisky's magnum

369

revolver but it carried a payload of more than twice as many rounds and fitted his hand like a well-worn glove. He'd carried the venerable Browning for so many years, on so many missions both in and out of the military, that he swore there was a hollow behind his right hip made by the gun nestling there, and felt strangely undressed without it.

With the northerly wind swelling their mainsail they glided quietly away from the shore and out into the open lake, dappled all around by the soft golden light of the sunrise. The only sounds were the ruffling of the canvas above them and the whoosh of the water running along their sides. There was an atmosphere of stillness, almost of serenity, but then Ben had always felt that way going into unknown danger. He moved all the way forward along the deck to take up his position at the bow railing, his binoculars hanging close to his chest and a radio handset in his pocket. Wolf crouched at the starboard rail a few feet away, eyes slitted against the sun, as calm and silent as a rock.

For the rest of that morning and into the afternoon they explored the waters of the long, wide lake, cruising as unobtrusively as possible and carefully scanning the water and the shoreline. Baz and Cormac occupied the port side rail, their binoculars glued to their eyes. Tuesday's observation post was the flying bridge, where he sat perched right up above the wheelhouse with the wind in his hair and a huge irrepressible grin on his face. There were a few other craft on the lake, mainly pleasure boats and smaller motor cruisers, none of them remotely as showy as theirs, and every time one passed by close enough for its occupants to come out and stare enviously at the stately sailing yacht Ben silently cursed Valentina for saddling them with this white elephant.

He told himself he was being overcautious. They'd covered their tracks well getting here and nobody could have any idea of their purpose. To the unknowing eye this serious-looking group of men with binoculars must have appeared to be a bunch of birdwatchers, or maybe a team of conservationists carrying out an ecological survey of the lake's natural habitats. The truth was, they themselves didn't yet know what they were searching for.

But early that afternoon, having covered some forty kilometres of water from the northeastern tip down towards the lake's widest point, they found it.

As the strange sight slowly appeared over the flat blue horizon, at first Ben thought he was looking at some kind of volcanic island, like the ones his unit had come across in the Pacific Ring of Fire many years ago on a military exercise. But then as Jeff steered a course closer towards it, he realised that the huge, dark, dome-shaped mass rising up from the middle of the lake was too even and symmetrically formed to be anything but a man-made structure.

'It's a fort,' Wolf said from behind Ben's shoulder, speaking for the first time in hours. And Ben could see that once again, his old SAS comrade was perfectly right.

Whoever had built it, it had been there for a long time. The ancient fortress stood on a small island of black rock that might once, millions of years ago, have been a natural promontory before the land bridge connecting it to the lake shoreline collapsed or was eroded away. Its massive circular stone walls formed a squat, wide circle about a hundred and fifty feet high, tiered like a cake with its batteries of old gun emplacements overlooking the lake and the distant shores to each side. It had clearly been designed to withstand attack from a large waterborne force, certainly larger than anything half a dozen men with a handful of weapons could muster. Even for a fleet of ships, back in its day it would have been almost impossible to take by storm.

A voice inside Ben's head told him, 'This is it. It has to be.'

As they came closer and the fortress loomed larger, they could see and hear that they weren't alone on this stretch of lake. From behind the island emerged a pair of identical fast-moving boats, curving in opposite directions in a wide loop of the fortress, cleaving the water with their sharp bows and leaving foamy white wakes behind them. 'Security patrol boats, looks like to me,' Wolf said, echoing Ben's thoughts.

Ben brought his binocs up to his eyes and steadied himself against the rail to get a better focus on one of the boats as it bounced over the water. He counted five men aboard, all wearing identical orange high-visibility jackets. One of them was sitting slouched at the rear of the stern cockpit with a black Heckler & Koch rifle hanging from its sling over his shoulder, in the casual manner of a person who carries a firearm all day, every day, as part of their professional duties.

'They're armed and they mean business,' Ben replied to Wolf, lowering his binocs. 'Only a pro close protection team gets a pass from the law to carry full-auto weapons in public, anywhere in Europe. Makes you wonder who and what they're protecting, doesn't it?'

Wolf nodded. 'Yup. Looks like we came to the right place, all right.'

Ben keyed his radio and told Jeff to steer wide of the island, in case they gave the impression of being too curious about it. The whole trick now was to appear as uninterested as possible, while observing their target very closely. Everyone except Jeff left their posts on deck and went below, so that each man could go on watching discreetly from a porthole. With his binoculars turned up to full magnification Ben studied the island now some three hundred yards off on their port side as Jeff heeled the yacht around in a long, wide anticlockwise turn. The base of the fortress, water-smoothed and streaked with moss and lichen, was solid dark stone wall all around except for a single opening, a south-facing archway at water level that was closed off with a huge iron grating like the portcullis of a medieval castle. From this distance it looked to Ben as though the lake waters flowed right into the archway, so that with the gate raised it would provide access to boats carrying people or supplies.

Interesting.

Angling his binoculars up the line of the walls, he scanned along the crenellated battlements at the top. Impossible to see over them, of course, but he guessed that the Forum members, when they started arriving, were probably more likely to be flown in by helicopter than to cross over the lake by boat. There would certainly be some kind of landing pad up there within the circle of the walls, possibly not big enough for a heavy cargo-carrying chopper but fine for lighter aircraft delivering individual delegates to their meeting.

As Ben lowered the binocs back down to look again at the portcullis before it disappeared out of sight around the curve of the fortress wall, he saw the patrol boats still speeding round and round the island in their loops and circles and figures of eight. Did whoever was in charge of the old fort generally keep up such active guard duty, twenty-four/three-six-five, he wondered, or was this a temporary stepping up of security ahead of the coming Forum conference? That would be more proof, in his mind, that they'd come to the right place.

Then, as he watched the patrol boats, Ben spotted another vessel, a medium-sized motor cruiser, coming from the direction of the shoreline, further away but closing the distance every second. His guess was they were maybe four kilometres from land at this widest part of the lake. The motor cruiser was clearly headed straight for the island, its course made obvious by its long, curving wake.

Keying his radio again, he said, 'Jeff, bring her back around but give it a nice wide berth.'

Instantly, he felt the yacht slope under him as Jeff heeled it tightly over to starboard, and their pace slowed as the wind dropped out of her sails. That was fine, because Ben wanted to buy time to watch the incoming boat from shore. He moved across to the opposite porthole to catch it as they came around. For a minute the approaching vessel was blocked from his sight by the fortress. When it re-emerged into view it was much closer and he was able to get a better look through his binocs.

It was no patrol boat, he was sure of that. Larger and slower and sitting more heavily in the water, it seemed more likely to be some kind of supply vessel. As he kept watching, it drew up to the arched entrance at the foot of the fortress, cut its engines and sat there bobbing for a moment as the iron portcullis drew up to let it pass under the arch. The engines restarted with a churn of white water from its propellers. In the last few moments before he lost sight of it, it disappeared inside the fortress and the iron portcullis came down to close it in.

Then the yacht had glided on too far and Ben could no longer make out the archway around the curve of the fortress's base – but it didn't matter. He'd seen all he needed to see already.

He got back on the radio and said, 'Jeff, get us out of here before someone starts to take notice of us.'

Chapter 48

All six men agreed that, beyond any shadow of a doubt, they'd found what they were looking for. The presence of armed security around the lake fortress alone proved that something big was about to take place there. Now it was time to work out the critical next phase of their plan. Under motor power now as they sailed into the wind, they returned in a hurry to their unofficial mooring point, the nook where they'd spent the night. Coffees were brewed and sandwiches unpacked, and the team convened around the cabin table for a council of war.

During their first planning discussion back in France, Ben had touched on the question of catering arrangements for the conference. Fifteen Forum members, most of them old and fat and too well used to luxury living, plus their various entourage – personal bodyguards, assistants and lackeys, plus the general protection personnel laid on for the event which could amount to dozens more – would all add up to an awful lot of food and drink being consumed during the two days of the meeting. Somebody would have to supply that large quantity of provisions, and someone else would also have to do all the cooking, preparation, serving and cleaning up. It had only been a passing thought at the time and they hadn't developed it in any detail. But now, based on what they'd seen, Ben realised that his idea might provide them with their best way of getting inside.

'We can't storm it,' he told them. 'On land, some isolated house or conference facility, we might have had a chance. But not this. It'd be crazy to even try.'

'Fucking bone, mate,' Jeff agreed, loudly slurping his coffee. 'Not unless we had a troop or two of SBS frogmen with a couple of armoured gunboats to back us up.'

'And air support,' Tuesday said glumly.

'But what if we could slip in there without anyone even noticing?' Ben said.

'That'd help,' Wolf replied.

'So here's what I'm thinking,' Ben said, and outlined the plan that had started taking shape in his mind from the moment they'd seen the supply vessel arriving at the fortress. The boat was almost certainly a frequent visitor, he explained. If Klaus Speer lived on his little private island for any length of time at a stretch, it was a sure bet that he had his personal groceries – fine food, wine, champagne, all the bare necessities for a Master of the Universe – brought to him on a regular basis, maybe once a week, maybe more often. This far ahead of the Forum meeting, Ben was willing to hazard a guess that today's delivery had been one of those.

'But come the big event, you can be sure there'll be a hell of a lot more to-ing and fro-ing back and forth,' he said. 'How many deliveries do you suppose it'll take to supply all the grub for his Forum pals and all their entourage?'

'A lot,' Wolf said. 'And it'll all be done in a last-minute rush, too. These guys don't eat frozen dinners or tinned corned beef, I'm thinking.'

'It's terrifying how fast some of those gourmet delicacies can lose their freshness,' Tuesday said, rolling his eyes. 'I mean, beef Wellington wrapped in mushrooms and savoury crêpes will hardly last half a day. To say nothing of your ballotine of salmon stuffed with hake mousse, in a champagne butter sauce and glazed vegetables on the side. Just shocking, darling.' The others laughed.

'Not to mention,' Ben added, 'as well as all the fresh foodstuffs and drink, they'll be ferrying across all the catering staff they're going to need to dish it all out to them. So we're talking about quite a few boat crossings, all happening very close to when the delegates start appearing, maybe even after they've arrived.'

'Sounds reasonable,' Jeff said. 'Go on.'

'Now, we saw that the supply boat seemed to have come directly across the lake from the far shore, instead of travelling along its length like we did,' Ben said. 'What that tells us is that there must be a pick-up point across there, a dock or jetty where the boat moors up to get the supplies loaded on board. Which also tells us that there must be a road down to the shore, where the trucks bring the goods from some local source, or maybe a variety of sources, not too far away. The trucks unload down by the shore, the stuff all gets transferred onto the boat, the boat carries it across, then has to come back to pick up the next delivery. All pretty labour-intensive and convoluted, with a lot of moving parts to the process.'

'That's what you get for living on an island,' Cormac said.

'And it works out well for us,' Ben replied.

'I can see where this is going,' Wolf said, smiling one of his nasty carnivore smiles. 'I like it.'

'First thing we'd need to do,' Ben said, 'is find out where the trucks are coming from. This is a fairly tourist-friendly area, so there are bound to be some five-star hotels and restaurants nearby able to provide fancy enough food and wine for our illustrious VIPs. If we knew which one had the contract to cater to the conference, that would give us the exact route the trucks would be taking to the pick-up point.'

'And if we had that?' Jeff said, with a knowing look.

'Then we'd be in a position to hit them the same way they hit the Kaprisky estate,' Ben replied, 'when they hijacked the cook's van to smuggle their team through the security gates, Trojan horse style. My idea is to return the favour in kind.'

'Why go to the trouble of finding out the truck route?' Baz asked. 'Why not just hit them at the pick-up?'

'Because more than likely the supply boat belongs to the fort,' Ben said. 'Which means they'll probably have at least a couple of their goons with guns and radios hanging about close by. To get on board the boat without causing a stir, we need to be in that truck when it turns up. That's where you come in, Baz, being the one who speaks Hungarian. You'll be doing all the talking to the boat crew while the rest of us are busy with the heavy lifting.'

'Gotcha,' Baz said, nodding.

'But what makes you so sure we can get on the boat at that point?' Tuesday asked. 'What if the boat crew just takes it from there, leaving us lot standing on the shore scratching our heads?'

'Because I'd be surprised if the job of bringing all that delicate food and wine over the lake would be entrusted to a bunch of guns for hire,' Ben said. 'I think the restaurant or hotel guys would be hired to make sure it arrived safely at the fort. I'm pretty certain our friend Speer would insist on everything being done right. That's how I'd do it.'

'Okay,' Tuesday said. 'So the stuff's aboard the boat, and so are we. Next thing the security guys radio the fort to say they're incoming.'

'Right,' Ben said. 'And we set off. Now, the fort is pretty much on the widest point of the lake. That's a lot of water to cross, and the trip probably takes twenty to thirty minutes.'

'During which time the security guys find themselves suddenly knocked on the head,' Jeff said.

Ben nodded. 'We neutralise the crew, take over the boat, grab their weapons and dress up in their gear.'

'Neutralise,' Cormac said, 'as in, kill 'em an' dump 'em overboard?'

'Why not?' Wolf replied with a cold glimmer in his eye. 'You think they wouldn't do the same to us?'

'It doesn't have to go that far,' Ben said. 'If there's a hold or a storage locker aboard, we might be able to stuff them in there out of sight. A bit of duct tape will do wonders to keep them from causing any trouble. Then as we draw up to the arched entrance they raise the gate and we sail right inside, and nobody's any the wiser. The moment we're in, we get off the boat as quickly as possible, split up into three two-man teams and set about taking down the rest of the security presence. Again, if possible, we can deal with the guards without causing any fatalities. It's the Forum we're there for.'

'How jolly civilised of us,' Wolf said.

'What happens to the food?' Tuesday asked, frowning.

'We gobble it up while we're on the water,' Jeff replied. 'Shame to let all that lovely nosh go to waste, don't you think?'

'I'm serious. What happens when they find an empty boat, nobody there to deliver the stuff and all their guys gone? What's to stop them raising the alarm?'

'Us,' Wolf told him.

'Too late by then anyway,' Jeff said. 'Once we're in, we're in.'

Tuesday didn't seem convinced. 'I can see other problems, too. For instance, what if there's another layer of security before we can get through the gate?'

'If we need to make further radio contact with the fort, Baz can talk to them,' Ben said.

'Okay, but what if they ask for something else, like a passcode?'

'Give us a break,' Jeff muttered.

'And that's not all,' Tuesday said, looking far from happy with the plan. 'What if the delegates haven't even arrived yet at this point? Seems to me this is all about timing and luck. There's so much to go wrong.'

'Those are chances we'll just have to take,' Ben said. 'All the more reason why we need to know exactly where the trucks are coming from, and exactly how many shipments of cargo are crossing over from the pickup point. That way we can make sure we get on the last boat, to maximise our chances of success.'

'Sounds all right to me,' Jeff said. 'You worry too much, Tues.'

'Devil's in the detail, people,' Tuesday said.

'I agree it's not perfect,' Ben admitted. 'But I think it's our best way in. Our only way in, for that matter. Unless you want to fly in posing as Forum members.'

'We're a bit too young and handsome for that,' Jeff chuckled. 'Besides, the bastards smelt a rat, they'd blow us out of the air faster than a fart in a fan factory.'

'I think we have a plan,' Wolf said. 'I'm in.'

Jeff nodded. 'Me too.'

'Whatever you say,' Tuesday chimed in, still a little sceptical.

Baz and Cormac added their agreement. Now Ben suggested a two-pronged approach to tracing where the food and wine supplies were coming from. 'Mobile reception here is too sketchy for much of an online search. I'll call Valentina and get her to text us a list of all the high-class catering firms in the area, as far afield as Budapest. Plus all the decent hotels and restaurants around the lake. One of us will go ashore and start going round making discreet enquiries to find out which one of them is supplying the conference. That's got to be you, Baz.'

'Fine by me,' Baz said.

'Meanwhile, two more of us will pick up the van from the marina and head along the opposite bank of the lake to search for the pickup point. We might get lucky and spot another truck turning up, which we can follow back to source. Doubling up on any intel we can learn from Baz's reconnaissance.'

'We'll need a second vehicle, for Baz to drive around in,' Tuesday said, still worried about the details.

'Forget it, I'll use taxis,' Baz said. 'Won't be a problem. And it's more anonymous that way.'

'So it's settled,' Ben said. 'We start in the morning.'

Chapter 49

In the event, they started sooner than that. Valentina's comprehensive list of all the local hotels and restaurants arrived within the hour, arranged in order of star rating with the fanciest ones at the top. It turned out that Lake Balaton was a gourmet's haven, with resorts like Balatonfüred, Keszthely and Siófok crammed chock full of high-end joints offering the classiest of Hungarian cuisine. Valentina excluded the run-of-the-mill establishments adapted to a more modest budget, not just because she personally regarded anything below a four-star rating as a greasy-spoon café, but because she rightly judged that Speer and his billionaire pals wouldn't touch them with a twenty-foot pole.

Before her text landed, Tuesday had been struggling with his phone's scrappy internet reception to find a good cover story for Baz. It was decided that he was to pose as the 'Galloping Globetrotter', a blogger who wrote pieces on his travels around Europe and conveniently gave no real name or displayed any images of himself online. Maybe he wasn't as good-looking as Baz. But it provided the perfect front for their teammate to go around asking about the mysterious fortress he just so happened to have spotted on the lake and was interested in writing about.

Baz wasn't particularly thrilled with the idea. 'It's a moronic name. Galloping Gobshite, more like. Besides, do I look like the writerly type to you?' he complained to Jeff. 'I can barely scribble a shopping list anyone could read.'

'It's only a blog, mate. Any half-brained ape could stump up one of those.'

'Oh, thanks.'

By mid-evening, Ben and Jeff had accompanied Baz back on shore to the marina. They soon found out that Lake Balaton's local taxi services were far above anything available in their own corner of rural Normandy. Within just a few minutes Baz was picked up by a friendly driver who jabbered happily in rapid-fire Hungarian as they set off towards the first port of call, a five-star hotel incorporating a famous fish restaurant just a few kilometres down the north shore of the lake.

As the taxi disappeared in one direction, Ben and Jeff clambered into their old van and headed off in the other, heading around the tip of the lake to follow the road that hugged the southern shoreline all the way along its length. Their target, if they were going to find anything at all, would be located approximately twenty-five to thirty kilometres along the south shore, where the lake was at its widest.

Ben sat at the wheel and let the smoke from his Gauloise drift out of the crack in his window. They drove mostly in a comfortable silence, two guys who'd known each other so long and been through so much together that they could intuit each other's train of thought with the barest minimum of conversation. They didn't need to talk about the progress of their plan, or the deadly danger the team would be going into when the operation started to roll. Or about the fact that either one of them, possibly even both of them, might not return home to Le Val alive. They'd been here before, many times. What most normal people would have experienced as unbearable stress and fear was just another part of life for men like them.

It was a long, winding drive down the lakeside road. The area was somewhat more densely populated than they'd expected, with a good number of tourist resorts, bars and small towns clustered along most of the shoreline. At the point closest to Ben's estimate of where the supply boat had come from, they came across another marina on a beach inlet, almost a small enclosed port with various jetties and numerous boats floating on the dark water. They parked the van nearby and got out. A night mist had fallen, hanging over the shore. There was a marina reception office, but it was closed up with no lights in the windows. They walked along each jetty, looking at the boats on the off chance that one of them might be the motor cruiser they'd seen delivering to the fortress. It wasn't there.

They returned to the van and sat for a few minutes considering. Training his binoculars far across the misty lake, Ben could dimly make out the distant movement of coloured navigation lights and spotlamps from the patrol boats continually circling the fortress. Only a few shards of light glimmered from the windows of the dark fortress itself, reflecting on the water. The place seemed very still and quiet, utterly remote and inaccessible even on this busy, popular and well-populated lake. It seemed the perfect location for a man like Speer, within convenient reach of all the luxuries and services that the rich thrived and depended upon, yet so insulated from the world in its own protected bubble. Try finding a wilderness hideaway where you could order in filet mignon and vintage Château Lafite Rothschild at the drop of a hat.

'What do you reckon?' Jeff asked, pointing at the marina. 'Seems to tick all the boxes. Right part of the lake, bang on its widest point. Easy enough to get a truck in there to unload stuff. I'd say this has to be it, no?'

Ben said nothing for a moment. Maybe Jeff was right. But something in Ben's instinct was telling him this wasn't the place. 'Let's keep looking.'

They headed a few kilometres further down the shore road, but no more suitable places appeared and soon afterwards, knowing from their GPS that they were now past the widest point of the lake, they gave up and reluctantly doubled back. A couple of hundred metres before they reached the marina they'd just come from, Jeff suddenly said, 'Hold on, what's that? Pull over.'

Ben hit the brakes, stopped and reversed back to the narrow side road entrance, now to their left, that they'd missed earlier and only spotted this time thanks to Jeff's eagle eyes. It had been easy to drive straight past in the darkness, because of all the bushes either side.

'Looks like this goes all the way down to the water,' Jeff observed.

'To me, too.'

'Fancy checking it out?'

'I certainly do,' Ben said, and turned down it. Forty metres on, they saw their guess had been right. The bushes either side of the narrow road gave way to tall chain-link fencing, with large forbidding signs marked MAGÁNTERÜLET! and a barred metal gate flanked by security cameras on masts. Ben rolled the van to a halt.

'Call me stupid,' Jeff said, 'but I have the feeling someone doesn't want us going down there.'

'Where on earth did you get that idea?' Ben replied, smiling. He pointed at the gateway and the line of the chain-link fence running off to its left. 'See the camera blind spot there?'

Jeff nodded, knowing exactly what was in his friend's mind. 'Go for it.'

Ben reversed away from the gate and back up to the top of the side road, where they left the van and tracked stealthily around in a wide circle on foot through the bushes. Approaching from the left, they carefully emerged into the camera blind spot, scrambled over the chain-link fence and dropped down the other side to continue along the private road. Sure enough, it led them all the way down to the lakeside, and a single broad boat jetty in its own little cove sheltered from view of the nearby marina. Several kilometres away across Lake Balaton, the dim lights of the fortress twinkled through the mist. No sign of its supply boat, but there was no doubt in Ben's or Jeff's mind that this was the private mooring that served as the pickup point for the supply deliveries across the water.

'What now?' Jeff asked. 'You want to hang around in case anything happens?'

'I doubt we're going to see anything this time of night,' Ben said. 'We might as well head back to base.'

'Not a bad night's work,' Jeff said as they returned along the shore road a few minutes later.

'Except we still have no idea what direction the delivery trucks might come from. There are so many restaurants around here, it could be any of them.'

'Maybe it doesn't matter,' Jeff said optimistically. 'We could still hit them on the private road.'

Ben shook his head. 'That'd be taking a risk. Too close to the boat.'

'The whole thing's a risk, mate.'

'I know.'

'Maybe Baz will get lucky.'

'Maybe.'

A lot of maybes. A lot of reasons to feel discouraged. But when Ben's phone went off a few kilometres out from base, their uncertainty vanished. And with that came some unexpected news.

The call was from Baz, sounding a little relaxed after a few drinks as well as very pleased with himself, because he'd scored a direct hit with his first shot, the upmarket hotel and fish restaurant at the top of Valentina's list.

And it seemed the whole Galloping Globetrotter thing hadn't been such a terrible idea after all, because it had enabled him to get talking to a pretty, loquacious and not altogether discreet waitress in the hotel bar. The young Charles Bronson charm probably hadn't done any harm either. Anyhow, expressing his writer's curiosity about the lake fortress and wowing her with his amazing blog and travel adventures around the world, Baz had come away with a lot of information.

Ben pulled the van over, killed the engine and put the call on speaker so that Jeff could listen in to what Baz had to report.

The waitress's name was Maris, and she loved to natter. In the unstoppable flow of words poor Baz had learned that she was twenty-eight, an Aries, and she had a bad-boy older brother called Andor who had been employed at the same hotel until two months ago, when he'd been fired – completely unjustly, in his opinion – after being caught splashing around nude with some equally drunken female companions in the hotel swimming pool.

More importantly, before that unfortunate incident, Andor had been closely involved with putting together the many food and drink orders that came from the fortress and organising their delivery, and so he knew a lot about what went on there. The local catering trade loved the place, Maris had said, because it was an industry in its own right. She'd never personally seen the rich guy who lived there, and he apparently kept himself to himself surrounded by a lot of security, but it was well known that he held large events on his private island at least once a year that were worth a lot of money to the region.

That's amazing, Baz had said, playing innocent. Who is this rich guy? Must be someone seriously important.

Nobody knows anything much about him, Maris had replied. Some kind of big shot, anyhow, with all these high-powered billionaire friends. Someone said they'd seen the German Chancellor and the Canadian Prime Minister there once, though that was just rumour and hearsay. Whatever the case, the events at the fortress were always a really big deal. Lots of money spent, champagne and brandy flowing through the place like a river and the hotel having to take on a ton of extra staff to do all the cooking, serving and cleaning up. They were ferried out there, literally, by the boatload.

And as a matter of fact, Maris had added, it so happened that another such shindig was scheduled to take place in the very near future. The hotel was already gearing up for the big event, what with the manager running around yelling at everyone like a crazy person and the head chef whipping all the sous-chefs into working overtime to put together all the fancy dishes and Andor's former colleagues busily loading crates of expensive booze onto their vans in preparation. Wouldn't that make a great scoop for the Galloping Globetrotter blog, when the helicopters carrying all the bigwigs started landing? Baz had agreed enthusiastically that it would. Talk about being in the right place at the right time. He might even be able to snatch a photo of someone famous!

'They're already preparing for it so soon?' Ben said, surprised and wondering what this might mean for their plans. 'The meeting's still three days away.'

'That's what I was about to tell you,' Baz replied. 'We don't have three days. She says it's happening tomorrow. They'll be arriving in the morning, first thing.'

Ben and Jeff looked at each other.

'Are you completely sure about that?' Ben asked Baz.

'Sure as sure. Made her repeat it.'

Jeff gave a low whistle. 'Well, I'll be damned. Those sneaky old dirtbags only went and changed the date on us.'

Chapter 50

First thing the next morning, Maris's prediction proved to have been right on the money. Out of the clear blue sky over Lake Balaton came the first chopper, a brilliant white Sikorsky S-76 that thudded in over the fortress battlements, hung there for a moment twinkling in the sunlight and then gently descended out of sight as it touched down on the landing pad within the walls. It remained there just long enough for its exalted passenger and his people to disembark, before the pilot flew off again to return to some unknown base and await further instructions.

'And so our first chicken has come home to roost, boys and girls,' Jeff said, shading his eyes with his hand as he watched the chopper disappear into the far distance. 'Only another thirteen to go.'

'Won't be long before the next one,' said Ben. 'By the time they're all in place and settled in, we'll be ready to give them a surprise.'

The two of them were back in the van, accompanied by Wolf and Tuesday, where they'd all been sitting impatiently for the last hour. From their elevated viewpoint, parked in a small grassy layby on a narrow, deserted stretch of road about quarter of a mile inland of the southern shore of the lake, they had a partial view of the water beyond the trees and could just about make out the tops of the fortress battlements far, far away. Across the road from where they were parked was a thicket of bushes, in which Baz and Cormac were hiding and poised for action at an instant's notice.

This quiet, lonely stretch had been carefully picked out of the route from the hotel to the private quay as the best spot to intercept the delivery truck that, thanks to Andor, they knew would be carrying several dozen crates of best vintage wines, champagne and cognac for the conference. The first two food trucks had already rolled at dawn, along with a minibus conveying the catering staff down to the boat. The Masters of the Universe would be receiving a five-star luxury breakfast on arrival, before the opening day's proceedings began.

Ben and the team had been very lucky, and they knew it. If it hadn't been for Tuesday's Galloping Globetrotter inspiration and Valentina's efficiency in sending the list of hotels and restaurants around Lake Balaton, they might well have missed the boat, both figuratively and literally. Ben wasn't happy that so much had depended on chance, but there wasn't time to dwell on that now. The tension was rising as they sat waiting for the truck to come around the corner. When it arrived, the sequence of moves they'd been verbally rehearsing over and over since last night would have to be carried out with lightning speed and precision.

'Another one,' Wolf muttered, pointing up at the second chopper flying over the lake. Like the first, it came in to land, then a few minutes later took off again. Soon afterwards it was followed by a third, then a fourth. The Forum gathering was slowly taking shape.

The fifth chopper was a growing bright yellow speck in the sky when the delivery truck suddenly appeared around the bend.

'Here they come,' Jeff said. 'Party time.'

Ben already had the engine running. At exactly the right moment he slammed the van into gear and lurched out from the verge into the road, cutting the truck off and forcing it to stop with a squeal of brakes. In the same instant Baz and Cormac erupted from the bushes on the other side and were pointing guns at the windscreen and driver window.

'Drop it,' Baz growled in Hungarian at the wide-eyed driver, who'd grabbed a phone. The guy did as he was told. While that was happening at the front of the truck, at its rear Tuesday was quickly planting a pair of emergency traffic cones to make it appear to any passing motorists that happened to come down the road that there had been a breakdown. They even had a set of jump leads out from the van to fake it convincingly.

The road was still empty. Ben and Jeff wrenched open the truck's doors and its three occupants were dragged out and bundled briskly across to the cover of the bushes on the other side, where they were subdued without using excessive force, professionally tethered up and left where they'd be out of sight and reasonably comfortable for the next few hours. The traffic cones were tossed into the bushes after them. Ben jumped into the van and the others into the truck, Wolf at the wheel, and they sped away from the scene with Ben following. From start to finish the hijack had taken fifty-one seconds.

Now they headed fast towards the pickup point that Ben and Jeff found last night. Ben left the van up on the main road and joined the others in the truck, and they drove down the private road. Everything seemed on course. As they approached the chain-link security fence and the blue vista of Lake Balaton opened up again in front of them, they saw another helicopter landing at the fortress. That made six.

The metal gate was unlocked. Beyond it, the same motor cruiser they'd seen yesterday was moored waiting for them at the jetty, with three armed guards standing by. Ben thought that one of them was the guy he'd seen at the back of the patrol boat, smoking a cigarette. He was smoking another one now as he opened the gate wide to let them come rolling down the track to the jetty.

As they passed through the gate, the cigarette guy approached the driver's window. His black H&K rifle was slung from his shoulder, the buttstock slapping his hip as he walked. Wolf rolled down the window and just stared at him. For a moment Ben thought the cigarette guy was going to request some ID or ask what happened to the regular delivery crew. But all he did was wave them on through.

'So far, so good,' Tuesday muttered.

'Lemon squeezy, mate,' Jeff said cheerfully.

'No English,' Ben warned them. 'Keep it buttoned and let Baz do the talking.'

They climbed out of the truck, opened up the back doors and started unloading the jinking crates of ten-thousand-euro-a-bottle Bordeaux and super-elite champagne and spirits. 'Six of you to transport a few boxes of booze?' the cigarette guy said to Baz, laughing.

Baz shrugged, unfazed, and replied in Hungarian, 'This is expensive shit. Your boss wouldn't be too pleased if we dropped one, would he?'

'Right about that.'

'Want to give us a hand?'

The cigarette guy blew smoke, grinned and shook his head. 'Not what I get paid for. You boys carry on.'

The guards stood around looking jaded as the crates were piled up on the jetty next to the boat. Jeff hopped aboard as though he'd been doing it all his life, which was almost true, and Ben passed him one box at a time, which he stowed in the cargo area behind the cabin. The two of them spoke only in grunts and gestures, not that any of the guards was paying the remotest attention to them. During the few minutes it took to transfer all the goods onto the boat, two more helicopters came thudding down over the lake and landed one after another at the faraway fortress, the second one hovering at a safe distance while the first delivered its VIP occupant and then took off again. That brought the number up to eight.

The very last box to be stowed aboard the boat contained not bottles, which had been removed and thrown in the bushes with the truck's original crew, but the six compact MP-5 submachine guns from Le Val and various other equipment including Tuesday's takedown rifle in its zippered carry case. When the box and its secret contents were in place, two of the guards jumped into the cabin while the cigarette guy slipped the boat from its mooring point. Ben and the team gathered at the stern end of the deck, each man remaining silent but acutely tuned into his comrades' thoughts. The diesels fired up with a roar and the propellers churned white water, and they moved off from the jetty. As Ben had anticipated, at this widest point of the lake it was going to take maybe twenty minutes to reach the fortress. The plan was unchanged from before: when they were about halfway across, they would make their move against the guards and capture the boat as quickly and efficiently as they'd done with the truck. These three bozos wouldn't know what had hit them.

Until then, all was peaceful as the boat chugged across the smooth blue expanse. It was a fine morning. Sunlight sparkled on the ripples and on the broad white wake curving behind them. The dark, vast hulk of the fortress crept gradually closer, like a strange volcano rising from the surface. The patrol boats were looping round and round the island, as always, throwing up white bow waves as they sped bouncing over the water. Closer by, a small flock of ducks had flown across from the shore and came down to bob along in single file, now and then upending to dabble underwater. Wolf stood at the stern rail, watching the birds with a kindly expression on his usually tough, battle-hardened face.

As the bobbing row of ducks drifted by, a sudden shotgun blast punched the still air and an explosion of water and feathers erupted from the surface where one of them had been quietly dabbling and minding its own business. The rest of the flock scattered in a panicked flapping of wings and a chorus of quacking. Ben turned, looked down the deck and saw one of the guards, the cigarette guy, rack his pump-action twelve gauge for another shot at the escaping birds. He was laughing, along with his two cronies, who seemed to find the sight of the poor broken creature floating on the water highly amusing. So this was what they did to liven up all these dull trips back and forth across the lake.

The cigarette guy shouldered his gun and swung the muzzle up and along to track the flight of the lead duck, ready to blast it out of the air. But he never got to pull the trigger, because in three long strides Jaden Wolf had crossed the deck, grabbed the barrel of the weapon, jerked it off target and then slammed the hard steel into the guy's face, splitting the skin of his forehead wide open and smashing him violently to the deck. Then the shotgun was swinging butt-first in a sweeping arc and catching the second guard in the chest as he jumped forward to defend his buddy.

It was happening a little sooner than planned – but what the hell, Ben thought as he and the others moved in to finish the job. The third guard had managed to make a grab for his automatic rifle when Ben twisted it out of his hands and snapped his neck. The other two, one of them streaming blood from his face and the other clutching at his broken ribs, attempted to put up a resistance but quickly met a similar end.

'Well, I suppose that solves the issue of keeping them out of trouble,' Jeff said laconically when the three lifeless bodies were stretched out on the deck at their feet.

'I didn't like them anyway,' Wolf replied. 'Bunch of arse-holes, hurting defenceless ducks just for fun.'

'They had it coming one way or another,' said Cormac. They stripped the dead guards of their jackets, radios and spare ammunition, dragged their bodies to the stern end of the boat and tipped them into the wake with three soft splashes. Then Wolf, Jeff and Baz donned their jackets to take their place. 'Brand spanking new and unfired,' Wolf said, inspecting his Heckler & Koch rifle. 'Just like I thought. They certainly provide their boys with a lot of nice kit, don't they?'

Jeff took over the controls of the boat. As they continued towards the fortress they saw two more helicopters arrive. That made ten. Ten had become twelve by the time the supply boat had reached the base of the fortress and gone chugging up to the stone arch entrance on its south side.

Up close, the building was simply enormous, its craggy curved walls looming high and intimidating over them. Baz was ready with his radio in case there was any need to communicate with the people inside. But instead the massive portcullis just cranked into action and rose up, steel cables winding on great pulley wheels to hoist several tons of iron grating.

Jeff grinned at Tuesday as though to say, 'See? Always worrying over nothing.' But his own expression was tense and hard as he feathered the throttle and steered the boat carefully, slowly, through the huge arch. The chug of its motors reverberated around the cavernous space. There were several stone docking bays inside, each with a boat moored up to it. Jeff steered the supply vessel into the one empty bay and the iron portcullis came grinding down to close off the arch.

And then they were in.

Chapter 51

It had only been two or three minutes since Klaus Speer last looked at his watch, but he glanced anxiously again at it now. A dozen of his guests had arrived and were settling into their private quarters, for a short break and a freshen-up before the morning session of their meeting formally got underway. The last two should be arriving any time. Ah yes – peering out of a gun emplacement window – here came the Dorn Group Sikorsky. That left just the VIP Airbus that Speer had chartered specially for the Chairman.

This was to be the fourth Forum meeting held at Lake Balaton over the years. Speer was a fretful host at such times, apt to fuss over the smallest thing like an old mother hen and snappishly delegating detailed tasks to his minions. His home might not be as spacious as the tropical paradise on Jumby Bay Island or some of the other venues that regularly hosted the Forum's gatherings, but it did offer seclusion, security and a degree of luxury second to none. And nothing, nothing but the best would do for his colleagues. Everything must be perfect.

Speer felt especially honoured that his peers should be gathering here for this particular occasion, on the eve of the rollout of the grand master plan that had been in development for so many years. Its goals had been a focus for decades – centuries, even, long before the Forum came into existence and took over the role as their principal driver. Again and again and again they had felt as though they were on the brink of making their mass depopulation agenda a reality, only to be frustrated by the limitations of the science. There was really no other way to do it. Contaminating public water supplies was crude, logistically too challenging and ultimately a waste of money and effort, since it just became too dilute to have enough effect. Likewise it was pointless trying to spray the toxins from the sky, because unless one were to bomb entire populations with super-concentrated clouds of the stuff it would only tend to dissipate in the air. The best way, decided after years of debate, was to find a means of delivering the harmful gene-altering substances directly into the body, the way that a snake or a wasp injects its venom straight into its victim's bloodstream.

But their work had been beset by all kinds of setbacks and difficulties. The mRNA material necessary for their scheme to work was so terribly fragile that the slightest environmental disturbance could render it useless. Any contact with air, with water, with even the tiniest fluctuation in temperature, and it just fell apart, unravelled – the science term was *denatured* – and became inert. Only by a state-of-the-art combination of the latest innovations in genetic engineering and the development of the microscopic lipid nanoparticles wrapped in polyethylene glycol, the carrier of the genetic weapon agent into the very nucleus of the human cell, had their plan become possible to put into effect.

Speer was no geneticist, and left such things to experts like fellow Forum member Arlin Baumbach and the many other specialists on their vast payroll. His own particular area of expertise as a bioengineer was the additional experimental feature built into their scientific marvel, the graphene-based self-assembling intra-body biotechnology that he was convinced would enable the surviving population, without their knowledge of course, to be physiologically hooked up to a global digital communications and information grid, a global hive brain that he had grandly dubbed the 'Internet of Minds'. His ingenious, revolutionary innovation was set to redefine the very essence of what it meant to be human. And to elevate its creator, the great Klaus Speer, to the immortal position of something very close to a god.

The main purpose of their meeting would be to decide on the exact date by which the first batches were to be distributed to the global public, via the Forum's vast pharmaceutical industry networks. The reason why the conference had been brought forward by two days was because their teams of lab scientists, working day and night for months on end, had managed to complete the first several million doses ahead of the original deadline. Billions in bonuses would be paid out as a result, on top of the enormous sums already tied up in the secret deal that involved all the major nations of the world. Even for someone with Speer's uncanny mental capacity for details, the logistics of such a large-scale rollout were mind-bogglingly complex.

As Speer stood there deep in thought about all this, he heard a door open behind him and turned to see his personal assistant, a much-harried and overworked little man called Huber, step furtively into the room.

'I apologise for disturbing you, sir,' Huber said in his obsequious way, 'but I thought you would want to be informed that Sir Simon Asquith's pilot has radioed to say they will be landing imminently.'

Speer nodded. 'Good, good. I'll be there in one moment.'

Huber cleared his throat and frowned nervously. 'There's something else, I'm afraid, sir. The supply boat has arrived with the wine and champagne. It came in ten minutes ago.'

'So what?' Speer snapped at him. 'Why come and tell me about it, man? See to it that the crates are brought up to the kitchens as usual. Do I have to oversee everything personally?'

Huber's look of anxiety became more pronounced, his protruding Adam's apple bobbing up and down as if he was trying to swallow a whole potato. 'Well, the thing is, sir,' he said stiffly, 'we may have a problem.'

That was a word Speer wouldn't tolerate being uttered in his presence, not now. 'Problem? What problem?'

'Well, sir, it seems that the boat delivered the beverages all right. The crates are there, as they should be. But apparently there was nobody aboard. It's down there in its docking bay, empty.'

Speer stared at Huber as though he'd lost his mind. 'What? How is that possible? Are you saying that the boat delivered the supplies all by itself?'

'No, sir. I shouldn't think that possible either.'

'Obviously it isn't,' Speer said abruptly. 'So where are the hotel employees whose job it was to bring them across? Where are the boat crew?'

'I don't know, sir. There seems to be no sign of any of them. I checked the security control room and the cameras aren't picking up any trace.'

'Who's down there now?' Speer demanded, and Huber gave him the names of the personnel who had gone down to meet the boat, only to find it empty. 'Tell them to bring the boxes up themselves,' Speer ordered him irritably.

'I'll do that, sir. But does this mean . . .?'

'Does it mean what?'

Huber swallowed again before daring to utter the unutterable. 'That we have a security breach? And if so, should we take the appropriate emergency precautions?'

The virtual chess pieces whizzed about the board of Speer's mind in a frenzy of logical calculation as he computed this awful idea. 'Appropriate emergency precautions' equated to one thing only, which was to whisk everyone who mattered down to the boat bays, get them aboard the fast cruiser and evacuate the fortress. It was an extreme solution to a problem he couldn't yet be sure existed. If the cameras were showing nothing, perhaps there was nothing to show. The last thing he needed was to sound a false alarm and make himself look a dithering weak-minded fool in front of his fellow Forum members, especially with the Chairman about to land any minute. He couldn't be seen to fly into a panic over nothing.

But at the same time, what if it wasn't nothing? What would it say about him, if he couldn't run his security systems properly? If he allowed the Forum to be exposed to even the smallest risk?

403

He needed to make a decision, and fast.

He told Huber, 'Alert the guards, but do it quietly. There's to be no commotion. None whatsoever, is that understood? Everything must seem perfectly under control, which I'm certain it is anyway. There's bound to be some simple explanation. The idiots on the boat must have got at the spirits aboard and are rolling about drunk somewhere. Find them, lock them up and I'll deal with them later. Keep me informed of exactly what's happening. In the meantime I have to go up and greet the Chairman.'

'Very good, sir.'

The black Airbus had just landed as Speer headed up towards the helipad on Level 5. Moments later the great Sir Simon Asquith appeared, wind-ruffled and in a predictably foul temper after his journey. 'I don't know why I ever consented to our meeting in this bloody place,' he grumbled as Speer met him and his two silent bodyguards, Hoare and Jupp. 'Being surrounded by all this water plays merry hell with my rheumatism.'

Speer was all apologies and assured him that the air-conditioning and moisture control systems of the fortress were absolutely top-notch. As ever, all efforts had been made to ensure his colleagues' comfort, etc., etc. While he fawned and grovelled and bowed and scraped to his chief he was thinking how happy it would make him if Asquith just dropped dead, right here, right now in front of him. When the Chairman had gone stalking discontentedly off to his luxury apartment on Level 4, Speer set off towards the main conference area. Beside the big boardroom where the Forum would be spending much of their time over the next two days was a lavish dining room. The long table at the top of the room was covered with all manner of breakfast dainties, bagels and croissants, toast and marmalade, rich-smelling coffee, four different varieties of herbal teas and jugs of freshly pressed fruit juice. Some serving staff were finishing laying down the breakfast covers on smaller tables, working quickly and efficiently as the first VIPs started filtering into the room. Three of Speer's colleagues had arrived ahead of the pack and were helping themselves to tea, coffee and orange juice. As usual, their conversation was about money, investments, big deals, bigger profits.

'Hey, man,' called out Julius Berkeley III in his loud, brash manner, interrupting their conversation as Speer walked in. He always greeted Speer that way, which Speer found vulgar and irritating. For such a pencil-necked little homunculus, Berkeley's big mouth could fill a room like a flock of honking geese. Noah Jaggard Petersen, tall and bald and gaunt at Berkeley's side sipping jasmine tea, was much less outgoing, even less so than usual, which Speer knew was because Petersen was only jealous of his brilliant nanotech invention and wished it had been his idea.

Julius Berkeley pointed at the buffet table. 'Say, dude, are those pastries gluten free? The cute little ones there with the icing on top.' Berkeley didn't have an intolerance, he just liked to be in control of everything and draw all the attention.

'Why of course,' Speer replied with a polite smile. He had no idea whether they were gluten free or not, and in any case he was too distracted to remember. Berkeley shot out a greedy little hand, grabbed a pastry from the top of the pile and sank his million-dollar capped teeth into the icing. 'Fuckin' A,' he said, chewing and grinning at the same time with his mouth open. 'So like I was sayin',' he resumed his conversation with Petersen, turning his back on Speer.

Speer left them to their big money talk, stepped away down the corridor and whipped out his phone to call Huber. 'Well?'

'There's no sign of them, sir,' Huber said. 'Security have done a thorough sweep of the lower floors and found nothing.'

'Double the detail and keep looking, damn it. They can't have just vanished into midair.'

It was all very unsettling. Speer's suspicious mind, more than his instinct, was nagging at him that something was wrong. He had no intention of letting his colleagues know about it just yet, but if there had indeed been some kind of security breach he was anxious to make sure he himself was protected in the event of any disturbance. His own personal bodyguard, newly promoted having amply demonstrated her talents in her former role within the Forum's wider organisation, had been allocated a small, simple suite of rooms down below, in a lower section of the fortress that had once been part of the gun battery's powder magazine.

'Will there be anything else, sir?' Huber asked anxiously, hanging on the line and waiting to be dismissed.

'Yes. Ask Miss Voss to report up here to me right away.'

Chapter 52

The arrival of the last helicopters could be heard from far below, in the dark bowels of the fortress where the six-man team were hiding. When Ben, Wolf and Jeff's Special Forces units had been deployed on assault raids back in the day, sometimes they'd had detailed intel on the internal layout of the target and sometimes they hadn't. Something this size, Ben wished they'd found a way to study architect plans before going in. But you couldn't always have what you wanted.

The upper levels of the fortress were sure to have been heavily refurbished and modernised, but down here everything was as it would have been centuries ago, with bare block stonework and ancient, heavy iron-barred door-ways. Hurrying away from the docking area after abandoning the supply boat they'd climbed a flight of stone steps worn smooth in the middle, leading to a vaulted stone passage with rooms either side. One of those was a gloomy, windowless bare-walled storeroom stacked with empty drinks crates and sundry supplies. That was where they'd taken refuge for a while, before moving on with the next phase of the mission. The plan now was to wait until the Forum members were settled into place, and then strike hard and fast in the hope of getting them all in one place.

To do that, it had been arranged that the team of six would divide themselves into two-man subunits. Jeff would pair up with Tuesday, Wolf with Baz, Ben with Cormac. That would enable them to spread through the fortress, dealing with whatever resistance they met along the way, and giving the impression of a much larger invasion force. Bluff could sometimes be as effective a strategy as speed and surprise.

While they waited they checked their weapons one last time. Tuesday was carrying his dismantled sniper rifle in its zippered backpack. Each pair of men was equipped with one of the three Remington 870 ultra-short shotguns, useful for breaching locked doors. Ben was happy to leave his co-partner Cormac in charge of that part, leaving him with the same familiar duo of MP-5 submachine gun and Browning pistol that he'd used on a thousand missions. Everybody had their knife and a walkie-talkie with a mic and earbud. The extra piece of kit they'd packed was the mobile phone jammer from the Le Val armoury, which Ben was carrying in a lightweight knapsack.

He took off the knapsack, unzipped it and took out the jammer. The thing was a black metal box with several stubby antennas bristling from its top. It bore no manufacturer's name, being a specialist military item not available to the general public. Anti-terrorist teams routinely used these to cut off the communications into and out of terror cells prior to a raid. The device was capable of selective frequency jamming so that anything outside of a predetermined range would be blocked. This meant the team could set their own radios to a certain channel and still be able to communicate with one another, while nobody else would be able to.

Likewise, the jammer would take out wi-fi signals, internet reception and disable any kind of wireless CCTV surveillance system within a five-hundred-metre radius. The jamming signal could have trouble penetrating thick stone walls, but that was just a chance they'd have to take.

Ben activated the device, felt it give a brief pulse as it powered up, and set it in a corner. The moment it was turned on, the enemy's communications would be scrambled. They'd know it, of course, and it might alert them that something was up. The mysterious disappearance of the supply boat's occupants would already have got them worried. Ben expected that they'd be sending down a security team to check things out any moment now.

He was right. Not many minutes had gone by when he tensed, hearing the sound of footsteps echoing in the passage outside the door, and signalled for the others to stay quiet. Moments later, the footsteps came right up to the door of the storeroom and someone tried the handle. When the door began to open, Ben and Wolf were pressed to the wall behind it, knives drawn, and the other four team members had retreated silently into the shadows.

Four armed security guards entered the room, the lead man shining a torch. The team waited for all four to be well inside before Ben kicked the door shut behind them. What happened next was very quick and silent. It wasn't a pleasant part of the job, and nobody in their right mind would ever be able to get used to carrying it out. But it was the kind of close, brutal warcraft, the art of sudden death, that they were trained for and were all highly proficient in. The four guards weren't. They wouldn't have stood a ghost of a chance, even if they hadn't been outnumbered by fifty per cent and taken completely by surprise. Not a shot was fired. Ugly, but supremely efficient.

Once the bodies had been piled up out of sight under some bits of old sacking, the team exited the storeroom and continued upward to the next tier, designated Level 1, where the modernised section of the fortress began. The stairs arrived at a landing that branched off into a long passage going left and right, with another stairway opposite bearing straight upward. No sign of life or movement, but there soon would be, once the dead guards were missed.

They split up into their prearranged pairs, with no more than a slight nod as they parted. Jeff and Tuesday headed left, Wolf and Baz headed right, and Ben and Cormac took the steps that carried them up to Level 2. The higher you went, the more luxurious the interior of the fortress became, with thick carpeting underfoot and tasteful art on the walls. Soft, soothing choral music, Palestrina or Byrd perhaps, was being piped in through invisible speakers. Ben palmed his radio and whispered. 'Checking in.'

'Rog,' said Jeff's voice in his ear.

'All groovy here,' came Wolf's. Groovy. He sounded as though he was enjoying himself.

Ben and Cormac moved on. No resistance met them yet. No teams of guards with machine guns and hand grenades appeared to blast the intruders back into the water. But when the action did kick off, things were set to get pretty noisy around here.

Chapter 53

Jeff and Tuesday had taken the left branch of the passage on Level 1. They padded quietly and stealthily along it, checking doors as they went, each man covering the other. It soon appeared that this floor of the fortress was more devoted to practical storage than accommodation. Nothing like a conference room full of greedy, evil billionaires was in evidence.

The fortress was a warren of passages, hallways and corridors. It felt like being on a large cruise ship, or inside the world's most luxurious lighthouse. Their path branched out twice, and then Jeff and Tuesday came to a spiral stair shaft with an arrow sign pointing upwards. Jeff motioned with his weapon and led the way.

'Is it just me, or is this a hell of a long gap between floors?' Tuesday asked in a whisper when they seemed to have been climbing for a long time. Jeff nodded, thinking the same thing. He was no architect, but it seemed to him as though there must be an extra level sandwiched between the main ones, a layer of the cake that could only be accessed some other way. Like Tuesday, he was wondering what that hidden layer might contain. Maybe that's where they would find the evil old men lurking, like woodlice under a rotting log.

They soon found something else.

The stairway shaft finally came out on what they guessed was Level 3. Jeff and Tuesday emerged cautiously, the tension rising with every passing minute. The place felt empty, but they knew it wasn't. Stalking onwards, the passage came to a T, with heavy fire doors to the left and right about fifteen metres apart. Tuesday signalled to say, 'Which way?'

Jeff shrugged and was about to say something like 'Your choice, mate.'

That was when the fire door to their left burst open and four armed men wearing security uniforms like the guards downstairs came flooding through it, more backing them up from behind. Almost in the same instant, the fire door on the right opened too, with more men emerging out of that one, weapons raised. Jeff was thinking that the security guards might have spotted them on a hidden camera system. Which suggested either the jammer signal couldn't penetrate the thick inner walls of the fortress, or else that the CCTV was hard wired. Or that, sometimes, shit just happened.

Too late to worry about it now. He and Tuesday were trapped in the middle, their only retreat the way they'd just come.

Jeff quickly counted ten guards. But ten against two seemed like a walk in the park to Jeff Dekker. Partly because he was very, very good at what he did. Partly because he had Tuesday Fletcher to back him up. And also because Jeff had never once in his life retreated in the face of an insane risk.

The guards were all raising their weapons, but Jeff and Tuesday, poised back to back in the open ground of the corridor, raised theirs faster. Jeff yelled at them, 'Drop your guns and give yourselves up or we shoot!'

Maybe these guys didn't speak English, because they didn't seem to heed the warning.

And that was when things got noisy.

To point a loaded weapon in the direction of a living human and pull the trigger was something almost anyone could do, physically speaking. Children could do it, and often did. But to hold your nerve, stand fast in the face of deadly return fire and still hit what you aimed at – that was the trick that few men in the rent-a-goon business ever mastered, because it took the kind of training, experience and mindset that only a real professional soldier could bring to the table. Jeff and Tuesday had it. The guards hadn't.

Jeff didn't flinch as bullets ripped up the corridor. He marked his target, fired, saw his man go down, fired again. Short bursts, fast and accurate, hitting centre of mass and instantly moving on. Another down. Another. The bulk of Tuesday's battle experience had been coolly nailing the enemy one bullet at a time from a thousand yards away rather than the hell-for leather mayhem of close-quarter combat that Special Forces excelled in. But he'd had the best teachers in his Le Val comrades. He rattled off one magazine, dumped it, clipped in another. Three, four, five guards on his side went down, and then there was nobody more coming through the fire doors either side, and the corridor was clear apart from dead bodies.

'You good?' Jeff said to Tuesday.

Tuesday replied, 'I'm good.'

Jeff got on the radio to Ben and Wolf. 'The show's officially begun, folks. No keeping our presence a secret any longer.'

Chapter 54

'Sir, sir, all phone and radio communications are down,' a pale-faced and terrified Huber reported to Speer outside the conference room doorway. He was badly out of breath from his mad dash up the stairs from the security control centre, where to his horror he'd realised that they had a far worse problem than his boss was willing to admit. The comms equipment was fine. Everything was working as it should, power lights blinking, controls fully functional. Except for the fact that the entire network had just been rendered totally, suddenly, unresponsive by some external force that Huber couldn't account for. Now nobody within the fortress could talk to anyone else or make contact with the outside. The patrol boats buzzing around the island were completely incommunicado.

Inside the conference room, amid a buzz of general chatter through which Julius Berkeley's voice could be heard the loudest as ever, the Forum were settling themselves around the long table. Everybody had enjoyed a satisfying if brief power breakfast and they were ready to launch straight into their morning agenda. There were a lot of smiles and amiable laughter. Dictating the fate of billions of global citizens was cheerful, heartwarming work. None of the delegates would have the slightest idea that the phone network was down, as they'd surrendered all their personal devices before entering the room, in keeping with the strict rules of the meeting.

'Calm yourself, Huber,' Speer hissed.

'You don't seem to understand,' Huber babbled, his deference to his superior temporarily forgotten. 'We're cut off. Everything's dead. It's terrible.'

'It's a technical fault,' Speer assured him, trying to sound assured himself. 'It must be. Have security found the missing boat crew yet?'

'How should I know? I can't get through to anyone,' Huber said helplessly. 'We're under attack. I'm certain of it.'

'Keep your damn voice down.' Speer didn't want the Chairman to hear. He didn't want to hear it either. 'Now listen, Huber. You've got this wrong. There's got to be some rational exp—'

But then the sudden staccato eruption of very loud noise from below them shattered Speer's train of thought, along with any hope that this was just some technical glitch. There was no mistaking the sound of automatic gunfire. And it was coming from directly beneath them on Level 3.

Sir Simon Asquith had been the last to arrive in the conference room, and he'd only just lowered himself into the comfortable leather wing chair at the head of the table. 'What the bloody hell is that?' he exploded, surging to his feet, looking about him with his jowls turning the colour of beetroots. Everyone knew what it was. The former heads of state stared at one another, aghast. The pharmaceutical chief execs looked as if they needed to swallow some of their own pills in a hurry. Only Noah Jaggard Petersen appeared relatively calm. 'What the fuck?' Julius Berkeley screeched in panic, nearly falling out of his chair. 'What's happening? Mitch! Tug! Help me!'

Mitch and Tug were Berkeley's personal bodyguards, a pair of thirty-something ex-US Secret Service agents who between them tipped the scales at over five hundred pounds and had seriously weighed down the helicopter on its way here. Against all Forum protocol they now lumbered inside the conference room to protect their master, tearing Micro-Uzis from their suit jackets. The shooting down below intensified, then faltered and died away. But the Forum were now in full-blown alert mode.

'Call the chopper!' Berkeley yowled. 'Get the me fuck outta here!'

'Can't do it, boss,' Mitch said, checking his phone. 'No signal.'

'This is intolerable!' shouted the Chairman, standing with his fists on the table.

'You got that fuckin' right, bud,' Berkeley yelled back at him. He turned to his men. 'Come on. We're leaving.'

'How, boss?' Tug asked, empty-faced.

'There's a speedboat down there in the boathouse, right?' Berkeley said. 'I know there is. I saw it last time I was here. Big ol' powerboat. Mitch, you can drive a boat, can't you?'

'Sure can, boss.'

'Then let's go,' Berkeley said. 'What the best way out of this shithole?'

'Stairs down are just down the corridor, boss.'

Berkeley strutted towards the doorway like a small angry rooster, the giants at his heel toting their machine guns.

'This is all that prick Speer's fault,' he snarled as he stepped out into the corridor. Speer wasn't there. 'I'm gonna kick his Austrian ass so hard he'll be wearin' it for a hat. Speer! Speer! Where the fuck are you?'

Speer was in fact rushing away from the conference room as fast as he could, accompanied by his own bodyguard who'd been lurking further down the corridor. As slender and lithe as Miss Voss might appear, with the spiked hair and angular beauty of a fashion model, she could have put either of Berkeley's heavyweight lunks on the floor and beaten his brains out before he knew what had hit him. The sound of gunfire had sprung her into action and she was ready for a war. Speer motioned for her to follow him as he ran. 'Down to my quarters. Now!' She obeyed without a word as he led her towards the private doorway that would take them to the shelter of Level Two and a Half, his private domain. He could hold out there until this attack was repelled.

They raced on. Speer was fit for his age, for any age. Unlike the majority of his Forum associates, who were wheezing heart attacks waiting to happen. As he sprinted down a long winding passage with Miss Voss right behind him, he heard the sound of more gunfire from a different part of the fortress and his mouth went dry. He croaked, '*Mein Gott.*'

Speer knew that he should have acted sooner. But it was too late to waste time on regrets. He had to focus instead on getting himself to safety. Who in heaven's name could be invading the fortress? Speer had no idea. Or maybe he did, he realised as he ran. There was only one man who would dare attempt it. Only one man who'd have been capable of locating them here. Which meant Hope must know everything.

Hope had to die. And Speer had to live. He didn't care about anything else at this moment.

Chapter 55

The small group of three security guards Wolf and Baz had encountered moments ago on their way up towards Level 3 had offered little resistance. A burst from Wolf's submachine gun and a blast from Baz's 870 shortie had taken them down in short order, and now the pair were approaching the stairway they'd been looking for. Level 2 was clear. The target would be somewhere on the upper floors. Wolf and Baz raced up the steps two at a time and found themselves in another long passage.

Wolf checked his radio. 'How are we doing, boys and girls?'

Jeff responded first: 'All clear this end of Level Three. Moving up to the next.'

Then Ben: 'Good to hear you're still with us, Jaden.'

'Only because I've nothing better to do,' Wolf replied with a grin. He keyed off his radio and they kept moving.

There was a bend ahead. Wolf cocked his head to one side and narrowed his eyes, hearing something. The approaching footsteps from around the bend sounded to him like three people moving at a run, two of them large and heavy, the third lighter and smaller.

Wolf signalled to Baz with a raised fist and they positioned themselves either side of the corridor, ready for them.

Wolf's ears were as sharp as his wild canid namesake's. Sure enough, around the corner came the three figures he'd expected. Except maybe not quite the same. The one in the middle was a short, angry-looking bespectacled middle-aged man in a pink crew-neck pullover and nicely creased chinos and very shiny shoes. To his left and right were a pair of huge meatheads wearing dark suits and carrying Uzi submachine guns, who dwarfed him as though he were an eight-year-old. Wolf recognised the smaller, older man as Julius Berkeley III, from his pictures. He looked even weedier in real life. So much for a Master of the Universe. The bodyguards looked pretty well-fed by contrast, but big guys always moved slowly.

As though to prove it, the two knuckleheads halted mid-step, crouched on bent knees and brought up their Uzis to fire. Wolf and Baz were far ahead of the curve. Before either of the bodyguards could get off a shot they were twitching and jerking in the full-automatic stream from the two MP-5s. They hit the floor like downed elephants.

Wolf had expected a man like Julius Berkeley to either scream and run for cover or drop to his knees and beg for mercy. He'd known a lot of filthy rich people in his time. Worked for several of them, and done jobs on a few others, back during his assassin days. In his experience, rich guys were so used to having their lackeys do everything for them that they couldn't so much as fart without someone there to catch it in a bag. But Julius Berkeley surprised him by reaching into the pocket of his chinos, pulling out a shiny little Ruger .380 auto and firing twice in rapid succession. He snatched his first shot in too much of a hurry and it went wide, but at the pop of the second Baz staggered and dropped his gun.

Wolf only saw it happen in his peripheral vision, because he was so focused on Berkeley. The assumption was that his partner was down. The follow-up assumption was that the next two rounds in Berkeley's little pistol were for him. Wolf enjoyed living and he had little desire to quit this world just yet. So without hesitation, he put three nine-mil rounds in Berkeley's chest and drilled a fourth straight between his eyes.

Berkeley's glasses flew off and he toppled over backwards as though he'd been chainsawed off at the ankles. Wolf stepped over to him and put a fifth round in his head. Superfluous. But then Wolf thought the guy deserved the extra finishing touch, all things considered.

Wolf hurried back to Baz.

Chapter 56

Ben and Cormac had cleared their end of Level 3 and were emerging from the stairwell to the next tier up when they came face to face with Klaus Speer hurrying in the opposite direction. Ben knew the Austrian instantly from the image in Auguste's dossier.

Speer wasn't alone. Running two strides behind him was a slim woman of about thirty. She had spiked black hair and wore black jeans and a black jacket, and there was something strangely familiar about her. As she caught sight of Ben her face hardened with recognition, too – and in the same instant he knew where he'd seen her before. Not just seen her, but spoken to her.

'*Miss, why don't you go and work on your tan or something?*'

That had been on the deck of Lucas Dennim's yacht, a million miles away in the Bahamas. On that occasion she'd been blond-haired Candi, the Miami Beach bikini bunny that Dennim had picked up on his travels. Today, it was clear she was anything but that. The way those implacable ice-blue eyes locked on Ben's was the way a hawk fixes on a mouse scampering through the long grass. All systems go, ready to swoop without the least hesitation. And in a split second's realisation, seeing her here, Ben knew that Lucas Dennim must have come to a bad end.

'Candi' stopped in her tracks and her hand whipped inside her jacket. Speer had too much momentum going to slow down in time, and he tried to duck past Ben and Cormac. 'Not so fast, pal,' the Scotsman said. He blocked Speer's way and stopped him cold with a punch that split his lips and knocked him off his feet. Before Speer hit the floor with a grunt of pain and surprise 'Candi' was tearing a Desert Eagle automatic from her jacket. The handgun was huge in her small, hard fist, and its report was even bigger in the confines of the passage. The high-energy slug caught Cormac in the side of the neck and blood flew up the wall. Cormac twisted and dropped, but Ben didn't have time to watch him fall as he brought the MP-5 to his shoulder and planted its foresight on 'Candi'.

Whatever her real name was, she was as fast on her feet as she was a deadly shot. She skipped sideways like a dancer into an alcove as Ben's three-shot burst chased her across the passage, firing as she went. The light fixture above Ben's head exploded and the passage went dark. He fell back to a doorway and let off another burst, but he was firing blind. He activated the tactical light on his weapon and in its thin white beam saw the woman dashing towards the fallen, gasping Speer, yanking him to his feet as though he weighed nothing, and the two of them racing for the stairwell. She bundled her principal roughly down the steps ahead of her and went bounding down them in his wake, angling her pistol one-handed back towards Ben as she ran.

Ben went to shoot, but as he was pressing the trigger another shot boomed from the Desert Eagle and he felt his weapon jolt violently as if it had been kicked by a horse.

The shockwave through his hands was as stunning as the knowledge that the gun had saved his life by a freak chance. He pressed the MP-5's trigger but it wouldn't work. That wasn't going to stop him from going after her.

He let the damaged weapon clatter to the floor and sprinted down the steps in pursuit, moving so fast there wasn't time to draw the Browning from his belt. Speer made it to the bottom of the stairs. 'Candi' didn't. Ben caught her three quarters of the way down, tripped her and sent her tumbling. The gun fell from her hand and bounced down the steps. She landed like a cat and kept running. Ben was two steps behind her. Ahead, Speer was staggering and weaving like a lunatic, spilling blood from his damaged lips and making a sound like '*Asshhk – urghgle*'. A doorway on the left: 'Candi' ripped through it and disappeared. Ben hesitated for a split second, wondering whether to go after her or stay on Speer. Speer was his primary target, but the woman was dangerous and needed to be eliminated first. There was blood on the floor, a trail of big round spots Speer was leaving behind him. Ben could use that to catch him later.

He ducked into the doorway and found himself in a large, brightly lit kitchen. Stainless steel sinks and food preparation and storage units, tall fridges, free-standing islands, an industrial cooking range the size of a small car. Three kitchen staff members were standing bunched in a corner, staring at him like terrified rabbits at the sight of a fox. Ben said to them, 'Go,' and whatever words of English they could speak, they seemed to understand him and bolted from the room.

Ben looked around him. And then she flew at him.

She'd yanked a chef's knife from the block, eight inches of broad triangular blade that came flashing towards him too viciously and too aggressively for him to do anything but jump back out of its way. She was cutting the air so hard and fast he could hear the hissing *whoosh* of the razor-edged steel. As he retreated past the cookery range he spotted a large frying pan on its surface and grabbed it. Heavy cast iron, eighteen inches in diameter, as thick and solid as a club in his hand. It wasn't much in the face of a concerted knife assault, but it was a hell of a lot better than nothing at all.

She came at him again, advancing relentlessly, her pale blue eyes fixed on his like a predator's. The most unnerving thing about her was the total silence of her attack. Her knuckles were white on the black knife handle as the blade came jabbing towards him from all angles, fast as the needle on an electric sewing machine, darting at him now this way, now that way, each stab aimed with surgical precision at a vital organ. One after another after another, Ben deflected them with the heavy skillet, like a medieval combatant using his shield to parry sword blows. Every time the blade was blocked by the pan it screeched metal against metal and flexed under the impact, leaving deep gouges. A strike like that into soft flesh would drive the knife eight inches deep, right in up to its hilt. Here she came again. Jab. *Screech.* Another vicious lunging jab. Another *screech*. The only sound in the large room, apart from the thud of his heart inside his head. She was doing all the advancing and he was doing all the retreating. He didn't know how much longer his reflexes were going to keep saving him. The look on her face was one of absolute, emotionless concentration, like something not human. No doubt. No fear.

Perhaps too little fear. Because fearlessness and overconfidence were close cousins, in battle. Now she stepped a touch too close on the offensive, and he saw an opening. He kicked out the sole of his boot in a straight jab that caught her just below the knee, not hard enough to break the joint but enough to knock her off balance as the knife thrust coming for his face went off its mark. Before the blade could come slicing back edgeways for his eyes he caught her a hard blow with the edge of the skillet. It smashed into the side of her face, shattering her nose and cheekbone, and suddenly she wasn't quite as pretty any more as the blood washed down in a red mask.

Not pretty, but still as deadly and even faster. Ben was forced back a couple of steps as the knife flashed at him again. He was too slow to parry one slash and felt the steel bite the edge of his wrist. But her vision was impeded by the blood, her depth of field perception not what it had been before the edge of the skillet had caved half her face in. She misjudged the next strike, leaving herself open for a critical instant in which Ben delivered a truly savage blow and felt the edge of the heavy instrument do some serious damage. She staggered and he hit her again, just as hard and more precisely, a downward blow that split her head open and sluiced red all down her front. She staggered again. Eyes burning at him through the blood, blinking fast and losing focus now. He kicked out again, driving her into retreat. She stumbled against the edge of a kitchen island, her fingers involuntarily loosened their grip on the knife handle and she wobbled and then fell. Ben moved in and killed her with a stamping kick to the throat.

Being forced to kill a woman was not a nice thing. But then, a woman slicing your guts out with a sharp knife wasn't any better than a man doing it.

Ben left her where she'd fallen and went after Klaus Speer.

Chapter 57

With Speer and Berkeley gone, just thirteen Forum members were left in the conference room. Twelve of them were all looking to their Chairman to do something. And a man as accustomed to high command as Sir Simon Asquith naturally assumed that leadership role.

Asquith knew that whoever was attacking them, it wasn't the police or anyone else in authority. No, it was that same damned man who'd taken it upon himself to thwart all their plans, almost certainly at the behest of Auguste Kaprisky. How else could they have known the location of the Forum meeting?

This was all Speer's fault. Thanks to his weak planning, Kaprisky had survived. And now because of Speer's incompetent security arrangements, the traitor was going to be allowed to take his revenge on the Forum.

Speer would pay dearly for this. The Chairman would see to that.

But first and foremost, he and the remaining Forum members had to get out of this mess. And there was no time to waste, because the unknown force of attackers could overwhelm the guards on the lower tiers and reach Level 4 at any moment. The members' only protection then would be the limited number of personal bodyguards they'd been able to bring along. Asquith had his two faithfuls, Hoare and Jupp. The ex-US President had managed to cram four onto his helicopter. Over thirty steely-eyed professionals in total, armed to the teeth. Surely that would be enough to save them?

But what if they weren't? Asquith hadn't survived this long by taking chances, or by placing trust in his fellow men. He wasn't inclined to start now.

'It's a fortress, for God's sake,' said Erich Stahl. 'There must be somewhere secure for us.'

'Not here, that's for sure,' raged the ex-President. 'Jesus Christ, Asquith, how could something like this happen?'

'We're getting out of here,' the Chairman said calmly.

Arlin Baumbach shook his shiny-domed head. 'What? By helicopter? How's that work, when we can't contact anyone on the outside?'

'Not by helicopter,' the Chairman replied. 'Berkeley was right. There's a fast speedboat down below. That's how.'

'All fifteen of us?' Jean-Claude Dorn shouted, staring wildly at him. '*Mais putain*, there would never be the room!'

'We'll make room,' the Chairman said. 'Bodyguards stay behind.'

'But Berkeley and his men are already on their way down there,' said the former British Prime Minister.

'I know they are,' replied the Chairman. 'That's why we have to get there before they do.'

A man like Sir Simon Asquith always did his homework. His private investigators had provided him with the architect's plans for the Lake Balaton fortress years ago, when Speer had first proposed holding meetings here. As a result, the Chairman knew far more about the layout of the place than the likes of Julius Berkeley, that crass little inchworm. For instance, he happened to know that there was a secret back stairway leading directly down from Level 4 all the way to the boathouse, designed as an emergency escape route. He also happened to know the location of the manual switch that independently operated the portcullis, in case of a major power failure.

The Chairman led the way out of the conference room, with the billionaire tycoons and former heads of state tailing after him like obedient children. Outside in the corridor, Asquith's men Hoare and Jupp along with the rest of the assembled bodyguards had their weapons drawn and were waiting anxiously for further instructions. The sporadic crackle of gunfire could still be heard coming from different parts of the fortress, creeping closer now.

'Your sidearm, Hoare,' the Chairman commanded, putting out his hand for it.

Hoare frowned. 'Sir?'

The Chairman snapped his fingers impatiently. 'You heard me, man. Hand it over.'

The former mercenary hesitated for just an instant, then did as he was told. The Chairman slipped the heavy Sig Sauer .45 into his pocket. 'I shall be taking charge of the evacuation,' he said crisply. 'Your men are all to remain here as a rearguard and repel the attack. I believe that the leader is a former British Special Forces officer named Hope, Benedict Hope. You are to take him alive if at all possible. Kill the rest. Then rejoin us on shore as soon as possible, bringing me the prisoner for interrogation. Afterwards you may deal with him. Understood?'

'Very good, sir.'

Then the Chairman turned to his twelve Forum members, the last of them filtering hurriedly from the conference room. 'Now, gentlemen, if you would like to follow me. There's not a moment to lose.'

Chapter 58

As he left the kitchen Ben could see no sign of Speer himself, but he quickly picked up the trail of blood spots the Austrian had left behind. Big, bright red splashes the size of pennies, scattered in an erratic line along the corridor. *You don't get away that easily, Speer.*

Before he could take up the chase, Ben had other business to attend to. He ran back up the stairs to where Cormac was lying inert on the floor, and his heart sank at what he saw there. The heavy-calibre gunshot to the side of the guy's neck had done terrible damage. Cormac wasn't breathing. Ben pressed his fingers to the man's bloody neck. No pulse.

'Sorry, Cormac,' Ben murmured. He snatched up the dead man's short-barrelled shotgun and hurried back down the stairs to retrace Speer's trail. As he ran he could hear more shooting from elsewhere on Level 3. He keyed his radio and tried to raise Jeff, Tuesday, Wolf and Baz, but got no response.

Speer first. Then he could start worrying about the rest of his friends.

The blood spots began to thin after a few dozen yards, but there were still enough for him to track the fugitive's escape route the length of a long passageway, down a short flight of steps and from there across a landing to a door where the scanty trail thinned out altogether and went no

432

further. It was a heavy door with no glass, security hinges and a strong combination keypad lock. There was a red smear on the handle and another on the keypad buttons.

Ben stood back from the door, worked the pump on the Remington 870 shortie, jammed its stump of a barrel hard against the lock and pulled the trigger. The deafening blast made the door judder violently on its hinges and tore a fist-sized hole right through, leaving a mangled mess where the lock had been. He smashed the door open with a kick and ran on through, finding himself at the head of a sealed, smooth stairway shaft curving downwards. There was another blood spot on the third step. He raced down the shaft, wondering where the hell it was leading and then realising that it was taking him down to the intermediate floor he'd guessed must lie between the second and third levels as he and Cormac had worked their way upwards earlier. At the bottom of the curving shaft was a second door. This one wasn't locked, but hanging slightly open. The handle was also smeared red.

Ben nudged the door the rest of the way open with the shotgun barrel. It swung wide on smooth hinges and he was met with bright sunlight from the all-around windows and a sweeping view of the sparkling lake.

So this must be Klaus Speer's private little pad, he thought as he stepped into the huge round room. And an impressive space, filled with the trappings of wealth and good taste. The furnishings and artwork might even have impressed Auguste Kaprisky. But what mattered to Ben right now were the whereabouts of its owner, because he was nowhere to be seen.

Ben gazed around him at the gleaming exotic hardwood floor and expanses of antique oriental rugs, looking for more blood spots. None. He looked over as a small movement caught his eye. Was it a soft gust of breeze from the open window that had made that floor-length satin fleur-de-lys curtain ripple, or was there someone hiding behind it? He walked across to the window, prodded the curtain with the gun barrel and felt only limp material. Then he peered out of the window itself, thinking that maybe there was some kind of fire escape ladder down which Speer might have clambered to safety. But there was just the craggy curve of the stone wall, barely a foothold or a handhold all the way down to the jagged rocks and the water's edge a hundred feet below. Ben was a proficient climber, but even he wouldn't have fancied his chances of making it down there without a rope.

Now something else caught Ben's attention. There was a small round table to the left of the window, positioned where it would get the late afternoon sun. The table's surface was inlaid with an eighteen-inch chequered square. A chessboard. And sitting on the chessboard were the elegant pieces that looked so familiar to him, because he'd not only seen them before, but played with them.

The Napoleon set.

Of course. It was no real surprise to him that a man of Speer's cultivated tastes wouldn't have disposed of an artefact of such historic value and importance. Not even if his Forum boss specifically told him to get rid of the evidence of their crime, which Ben was pretty sure they would have insisted on.

A game was in progress on the board. The contest looked fairly evenly matched, with both sides locked in some dense and thorny strategy and a few captured pieces from both black and white sitting on the sidelines.

'Been playing with yourself again, Speer,' Ben said out loud. He picked up a white knight, looked at its base, then did the same with the other. Both originals. He smiled to himself. Kaprisky had fooled them nicely, switching the fake piece with its recording device back for the real one on his return home. They must have been so sure they'd recaptured the incriminating proof, only to find themselves scratching their heads wondering what happened.

On a sideboard nearby was a beautiful wooden case lined with blue velvet, with thirty-two hollows cut out for the chess pieces. It wasn't the original box, which hadn't left the Kaprisky residence. But it would do nicely for carrying the Napoleon set home to where it belonged.

'What does it take?' said a strangled voice. Ben turned and saw Klaus Speer advancing towards him, limping badly on a sprained ankle. His mouth and chin were stained with drying blood and russety spots and spatters of it were all down the front of his shirt. His silver hair was all awry and his eyes looked dull and dead. He could have been two hundred years old.

'What does what take?' Ben asked him.

'To make you go away,' said Speer. 'What does it take?'

'You're talking about money,' Ben said.

A strange, wild kind of light came into those dead eyes and brightened the man's totally defeated expression. 'Oh yes. More money than you've ever imagined. I have it. I'll give it to you.'

'Funny,' Ben said. 'Someone already offered me a billion euros to kill you and your Forum friends.'

Speer shook his head and raised his hands, showing his bloody palms. 'I can double that. I can triple it!'

'No need to go that far,' Ben said. 'I work pretty cheap.'

Then he raised the shotgun and blew a great ragged hole in Klaus Speer's chest. Speer was thrown backwards against the window. Ben shot him again and the huge expanse of glass behind him came crashing down like the face of a calving glacier. Speer tumbled out of the shattered pane without a sound.

Ben stepped over to the window and reached it in time to see Speer's cartwheeling body hit the rocks below. He bounced once, then rolled into the lake and the water washed over him pinkish-red.

Ben's radio crackled. Relief flooded through him when he heard a familiar voice in his ear.

'Ben?'

'Jeff. Where are you?'

'Roof. Uh, best get up here pronto, mate. Looks like we're screwed.'

Chapter 59

By the time Ben had pounded back up the stairs and raced all the way to Level 5 it was already too late to do much. Jeff, Tuesday and Wolf were standing at the northern wall of the battlements, beyond the helipad.

'Look,' Jeff said, pointing out across the lake. Ben followed the line of his finger and saw what he was showing him. It was a boat, some kind of fast powerboat, though it was hard to tell from such a distance as it sped away from the fortress, bouncing on the water and tracing a long white wake.

'It's them,' Wolf said, handing him a pair of binoculars.

Ben went to the battlement and steadied himself against the rough stonework to watch the escaping boat. It was at least a thousand yards away and widening the distance with every passing second.

'The guards have all legged it and are hiding somewhere,' Jeff said. 'The ones who still could. Where's Cormac?'

Ben shook his head. 'Baz?'

'Caught one in the shoulder,' Wolf said. 'He'll live.'

Ben was pleased to hear that. But now the Forum were about to get away. If that happened, all this, Cormac's death, had been for nothing. He asked, 'Tuesday, can you make that shot?'

'Wish I could,' Tuesday said with a rueful look. He held up a dripping, clawed right hand to show Ben where a bullet had ripped up the tendons across the back of it.

Ben looked back at the boat. It had to be twelve hundred yards away by now, little more than a little black smudge at the end of the long, curving white wake. Two more boats were coming to meet it. The patrol boats, Ben guessed. In a few moments their courses would intersect, and then the security men aboard the patrol boats would escort the Forum members to shore, and that would be the end of it. No chance of ever getting to them again.

Unless.

'Let me try,' he said. He reached for the zipper on Tuesday's backpack.

'It's a long way, buddy,' Wolf replied. 'I'd have tried myself, if it wasn't so far.'

'Let me try anyway,' Ben said. The rifle came out of the backpack in four sections. Barrel, receiver, butt stock and scope. He slotted the pieces together, flipped out the legs of the folding bipod and rested the weapon on the edge of the battlement wall. Worked the bolt back and then forward, sliding a tapered, shiny cartridge into the chamber. He locked the bolt. Safety off. By now the boat was probably fifteen hundred yards away, a tiny receding dot even in the magnification of the powerful scope.

'What's she set to?' he asked Tuesday, meaning the zeroed range.

'One,' Tuesday replied, meaning one thousand.

Which meant Ben was going to have to aim high, so that the bullet's arced trajectory at this extreme range would bring it down like a rainbow onto the target.

'Here goes,' he said.

He sucked in a deep breath, let half of it out, and felt his body go very still. Nothing existed except him and the target. The vanishing powerboat was banking towards the shore. The two patrol boats were almost on it now.

The perfect trigger break is the one that comes virtually as a surprise, at the exact moment when all the stars are lined up for the optimum shot. No flinch, no deviation at the last instant, no interference from the shooter whatsoever. This was one of those. Ben felt the recoil of the weapon snap against his shoulder and then the projectile was gone, streaking through the wide open space between them at the target at over three thousand feet per second. At this range it was going to take about one and a half achingly long seconds to hit the target.

If it hit anything at all.

Ben held his breath.

And then it hit.

Far, far away, the speeding powerboat was tracing a smooth, steady curve over the lake. All of a sudden it seemed to veer wildly off course, its new direction taking it straight towards the two patrol vessels that had been coming up on its starboard side to escort it. The parallel wakes were suddenly about to criss-cross.

'No,' Jeff murmured. He snatched up the binocs.

'Yes,' Wolf said.

As they watched, the distant white lines came together and then touched, as the out of control powerboat impacted the side of the first patrol vessel, tore straight through it, slicing it in two, then smashed into the second while still travelling at maximum knots.

Through the rifle scope Ben saw the explosion as a small orange-yellow flash, turning into a great red flower that blossomed up before it was engulfed behind a tower of black smoke. The sound of the blast reached them moments later, like distant thunder.

The occupants of the first patrol boat might have survived. But there would be no such chance for the others.

Wolf was grinning the way a mako shark does after swallowing a tuna fish. 'Thousand quid says you can't do that again,' Jeff muttered, shaking his head in disbelief.

'Not sure he needs to,' Tuesday said. Fifteen hundred yards away, the remains of the burning boats slipped silently into the lake, leaving a scattering of smoking wreckage on the water.

Ben was about to speak when he saw the movement from the corner of his eye, and turned quickly to see the large group of men standing there behind them on the rooftop. A lot of men. More than thirty, pointing a semicircle of guns at them. Jeff, Tuesday and Wolf all turned as well.

'Time to give it up,' said the tall man in the middle of the semicircle. He spoke with a British accent and was smartly dressed in a dark suit with an old regimental tie. A former soldier, before he'd become a close protection agent for a VIP scumbag.

'You want a bet?' Wolf replied, with a dangerous flash in his eye. Jeff and Tuesday were silent and rock-still, cats watching a dog.

'Give it up,' the tall man in the regimental tie repeated. The spokesman of the group. 'Guns on the floor. Hands on your heads. You're done. You,' he said, waving his gun at

440

Ben, 'I have orders to take alive for interrogation. The rest of you, well, that's up to you.'

Ben lowered the rifle, but he didn't let go of it. The Browning pistol was still tucked into his belt behind his right hip, untouched. Wolf and the others still had their MP-5s and made no move to drop them either. Tuesday had no issues with working a submachine gun left-handed.

'Your principals are dead,' Ben told the tall man. 'That severs all ties. Your jobs are finished. It's not your fight any more.'

'My fight's with you,' the tall man said. 'It's what we were paid for.'

Ben gave a shrug. 'Be my guest. Who wants to go first?'

'He means die first,' Wolf explained, for those who hadn't got it.

'Thirty of us. Only four of you,' said the tall man. 'Some odds.'

'That's true,' Ben said. 'You might get us all. But how many of you will get to walk away? A dozen, maybe? Ten?'

'Try none,' Jeff said.

The tall man made no reply. 'You killed our employers,' said another guy. American.

'So go find yourselves some more,' Wolf told him. 'Plenty of worthless pieces of shit in the world needing protection. Unless you want to look after someone decent for a change. They don't pay as well, I know.'

'It's a time limited offer,' Ben said to the tall man. 'We don't like people pointing guns at us. In a couple more seconds we might be less inclined not to take it personally.'

The tall man still said nothing. One second of silence. Then he lowered his gun.

'That's what I call an intelligent play,' Wolf said.

'All right. So where do we go from here?' the tall man asked.

'That's easy,' Ben replied. 'We turn off the jammer device that's blocking your phones and radios. Then you can call whoever you need to come and get you. Then you get to go home.'

The tall guy nodded. 'Home. Yeah. Sounds good to me.'

Then slowly, all thirty of them put away their weapons, turned and walked away over the rooftop.

Tuesday let out a long breath. 'That was interesting.'

'Invigorating,' said Wolf.

Far away across Lake Balaton, the column of black smoke leaned high into the clear blue sky and slowly dissipated. Tiny figures could be seen swimming from the sinking wreck of the first patrol boat. None from the others.

'Well, folks, I'd say it's time for us to go home too,' Jeff said.

'Not quite,' Ben replied.

Chapter 60

In the coming weeks, months and even years, a host of inquiries and investigations would seek to unravel the mystery of what exactly had taken place at the fortress on Lake Balaton. Perhaps the real truth, even if it were discovered, would never be revealed to a shocked public. Perhaps it would; only time would tell.

But none of that was of concern to Ben and the others right now as they worked to clear up any trace of their having been here, and get away from this place as fast as they could. First and foremost, none of the team were going to be left behind, dead or alive. The body of Cormac Wallace was wrapped in thick black plastic bags from the fortress kitchen and carried down to the supply boat along with all their kit. Wolf and Jeff found a first-aid box in the same kitchen and raided it for bandages and painkillers to treat Tuesday's damaged hand and the wound in Baz's shoulder. The bullet from Julius Berkeley's .380 had gone right through, causing an impressive amount of bleeding but no permanently disabling damage. Wolf helped him down to the boat.

Meanwhile, Ben had other tasks to attend to. After returning to Speer's quarters to retrieve an item of importance he ran back below to the storeroom where they'd planted the mobile jammer. The moment the device was deactivated and the phones were suddenly live once again, he called Valentina to tell her it was over, and what to do next.

By the time the supply boat had reached the shore, the Kaprisky jet was already being prepped for takeoff from Le Mans Arnage Airport. The team's van was still where they'd left it, a short way from the private jetty. Ben at the wheel, Jeff and Wolf beside him and the walking wounded with poor Cormac in the back, they drove fast to Hévíz-Balaton Airport near the city of Keszthely at the western end of the lake. The hardworking Gabriel Archambeau had once again been pressed into working his influential magic, to ensure that there would be no red tape complications about bringing the team home.

Not many hours later, the bright red Kaprisky Corp helicopter was whisking the five and their fallen comrade back to base. A private ambulance was waiting for them when they landed, to take Baz, Tuesday and Cormac to the clinic. Also anxiously waiting for the chopper was Valentina, her hair waving loose in the windstorm from its rotors and the tears of joy streaming down her face. Ben was happy to see her, and he held her tight as she flew into his arms.

'It's really over?' she kept saying.

'It's really over.'

'I have more news.'

Sometime early that morning, Auguste Kaprisky had opened his eyes like a man awakening from a long, strange dream. Then he'd swung his legs out of his hospital bed, plucked the drip tube from his arm, stood up and walked out of his room to interrogate the incredulous clinic staff as to what the hell he was doing in this place. One of the nurses had been so shocked to see him that she'd spilled a tray of medications all over the floor.

Valentina and Ben rode over to the clinic in the golf buggy. They were met by Doctor Theroux, who led them to the lounge where Auguste was eating his first solid meal since the attack. 'He's been giving them a really hard time,' Valentina told Ben as they followed the doctor down the gleaming white corridor. 'I don't think he really understands how close he came to dying.'

'But he's okay?' Ben asked. Visions of brain damage, memory loss filled his mind.

She grinned. 'See for yourself.'

'Take this vile slop away at once and bring me something I can eat!' came the loud cry from inside as they approached the lounge. It was followed by a terrified nurse scampering from the room clutching a part-eaten plate of scrambled eggs and toast. Ben stepped into the room and the indignant expression on the old man's face changed to a beaming smile. 'Benedict!'

'Hello, Auguste.'

'I can't tell you how good it is to see you, my friend,' Auguste said, gripping Ben's hand with amazing strength for a man who'd just come out of a deep coma. 'Tell me, is it true?'

'The Forum is finished,' Ben told him, and the old man closed his eyes and nodded, a small tear of relief rolling down his cheek. Then his eyes snapped open, and he gripped the arms of his chair and went to get up. 'Then we must celebrate!'

Valentina gently pushed him back down. 'Shh, Tonton, you heard what the doctor said. You mustn't over-exert yourself.'

'Oh, what silly nonsense! We have to drink to this moment. Benedict, you would like champagne, wouldn't you? Nurse! Nurse! Bring us champagne! And three glasses!'

'I have something for you,' Ben said. He reached into the bag he was carrying and brought out the beautiful wooden box.

Stunned into silence, the old man slowly opened the box. His face lit up when he saw what was inside. 'My pieces! The Napoleon set!' He marvelled at them for a moment, then turned to his grandniece and grasped her arm. 'Quick, my angel, run back to the house and ask someone to bring me the board. It seems so long since I last played. Ben, a game with you?'

'No thanks, Auguste,' Ben replied with a smile. 'I've already had my chess apprenticeship.'

Ben stayed only a few minutes at the clinic, just long enough to have a glass of champagne – Auguste's wishes couldn't be denied by anybody – and then say goodbye.

'You cannot be leaving already?'

'Not just yet,' Ben said.

Back at the house, he met with Gabriel Archambeau and they spoke about arrangements for Cormac. His body would be flown to his native Scotland, where sadly he had no immediate family to grieve for him. The funeral would be held at a small church in a little village called Portknockie, on the Moray Firth, where he was born. Ben intended to be there, and would be one of the pallbearers taking Cormac on his final journey.

'You look tired,' the lawyer said. 'Come, let's sit in the yellow salon and have a glass of brandy.'

Ben hadn't eaten a scrap all day, and brandy on top of champagne was perhaps pushing things, but he was too exhausted to refuse. In the comfortable salon, Gabriel poured them each a generous measure of cognac. 'How much do you know?' Ben asked him.

'Oh, I have a reasonable grasp of the situation,' Gabriel replied. 'Valentina has filled me in on some of the details. I take it you're wondering about the next step, with regard to Auguste's, ah, shall we say, investigations?'

'The white knight,' Ben said. 'Or more specifically, what's inside it.'

Gabriel rolled his brandy pensively around the inside of the glass, pursing his lips. 'Hmm. From what I understand, Auguste's former colleagues are no longer in a position to move ahead with their plans. Correct?'

'Not personally,' Ben said. 'But what's to stop someone else from picking up where they left off?'

'Like cutting the head off the mythological hydra,' Gabriel mused. 'It simply grows two more in its place. But then, what if all the heads have been cut off at once? That seems to be the case here. In the present state of chaos, I'd say it will be a long time before they can reorganise themselves. And now that Auguste is back with us again, I'm sure he'll have his own ideas about how best to utilise the incriminating evidence.' He chuckled. 'And believe me, the effect

447

will be devastating. No, I don't think we have too much to fear from these people in future.'

As they talked, there was a knowing look in the lawyer's eye and a little smile that made Ben think he had something more up his sleeve. He was right.

'I suppose you're also wondering why we haven't heard from the authorities, regarding your little incident here in France?'

'It had crossed my mind,' Ben said. He was still bracing himself for their appearance and it baffled him that there'd been no mention of it since his return from Hungary.

'Then I think I can answer your question, and allay any concerns you might have. You see, about, oh, it must be twenty-five years ago now, our dear friend Auguste went through a brief period where he contemplated getting involved in motor sports. As unlikely as it might seem, for him. His intention then was to put together his own rally team for international competition. He was quite serious about it, going so far as to create a hand-built prototype, based on the classic old Lancia Stratos, which I'm sure you know was a highly successful rally car, in its time.'

It seemed a wild story. But at the mention of the Stratos, Ben began to understand that Gabriel had a particular purpose in telling it. 'I see.'

'Auguste's design was closely modelled on the original, but with a brand new proprietary engine and modified chassis. If it had ever gone into production it would have been called the Stratosky.' The lawyer made a sickly grin. 'His idea, not mine, I hasten to add. But it never did go into production. For which I was quite grateful, I must say.

448

Nothing will drain the coffers dry faster than venturing into motor racing. Look what happened to Lord Hesketh.'

'Are you saying that the car I drove was the only one ever made?' Ben asked.

Gabriel nodded. 'Even its engine block was bespoke. There was no legal requirement for either it or the chassis to be marked with any kind of identification numbers, and so they were left blank. The vehicle was never road registered, and only ever used on the estate. It wasn't even insured. Valentina shouldn't really have let you use it. But that's of little importance. The point is that, as you might imagine, such a vehicle wouldn't come up on the police computer. Technically speaking, it didn't exist.'

'So they weren't able to trace it to the estate?'

'How could they? Nor to you personally. The same applies to the revolver I understand you borrowed from Auguste's study. Unregistered, therefore untraceable.'

And the ejected .357 shell casings Ben had left all over the field hadn't shown any trace of fingerprints, because he'd fed them from a speedloader. It was all beginning to make sense to him now.

'Of course, the police had their suspicions,' Gabriel said. 'Mainly because the incident took place so close to the estate where all the trouble had happened recently. Perhaps too much of a coincidence. But they don't have a shred of proof. And you were never here. Not officially.'

'What about the couple whose car I took? They were witnesses. They saw me.'

'Christophe and Danielle Bobier. Yes. But in the event, the statements they gave to the police were so wildly

449

contradictory that the officers just gave up on them. She reported seeing a small man with a foreign accent, and he saw a tall man with a limp and black hair. Utterly useless. But the police are quite accustomed to these things.'

'So where does that leave me?' Ben asked.

'Well, speaking as a legal professional, I'd say that leaves you in the clear, my friend. Nothing to worry about, and free to go home. Before you do, however, there's just one other matter we should perhaps discuss.'

'What matter is that?'

'The matter of the reward that Valentina offered you in return for a successful outcome of your mission,' Gabriel said. 'If mission is the right word. I believe the agreed sum was one billion euros?'

'I don't know how I could square it with the taxman,' Ben said.

'I think you can leave that up to me,' Gabriel said slyly. 'We have our little ways and means around these things.'

Ben smiled and shook his head. 'I was only joking, Gabriel. I told Valentina I don't want her money. I meant it.'

'Her offer was in earnest. Not to state the obvious, but it's an awful lot to turn down. Are you sure?'

'Perfectly sure,' Ben said. 'For myself. But I'm sure the budget will stretch to a couple hundred thousand each for all the guys who came to help us out. They've earned it.'

'Consider it done.'

Gabriel put out his hand, and Ben shook it.

Maybe some lawyers weren't so bad, after all.

EPILOGUE

Ben stayed on the estate for a few days after that, living in the Swiss cottage. It was a beautiful, warm late September and the trees were just beginning to turn gold. Autumn was the loveliest time of year in France. The heat and humidity of summer were long gone and the air was crisp and clean. He spent some time with Auguste and Valentina over those days but mostly stayed on his own, relaxing, reflecting and thinking about getting back to his life. It would soon be time for him to head up to Scotland for Cormac's funeral. Maybe he'd take a tour of the Highlands while he was there. He had a friend who lived in those parts, Grace Kirk. Someone who had meant a very great deal to him, at one time. He hadn't seen her in quite a while.

Jeff and Tuesday had already headed back to Le Val. The Kaprisky clinic doctors had patched up Tuesday's hand and it would soon be good as new. Baz had needed only a minor operation on his shoulder and a few weeks of convalescence would see him back in the game, now a little richer for the experience.

As for Jaden Wolf, he'd slipped off sometime before dawn the morning after they'd got here. No goodbyes, not a word, just a note that Ben found under the door of the cottage. It said:

TILL NEXT TIME
J

Ben smiled to himself when he read the note. That was Wolf to a T, going his own way as always, searching for the life of peace that Ben had always wanted too. A dream that never quite seemed to come true for either of them. It had been that way all along. Trouble was their creed, their only talent, and no matter what men like them did, no matter how hard they tried to run from it, it always seemed to find them.

It wouldn't be long before trouble found them again. When it did, each man knew that the other would always be there for him.

Ben folded the note and put it in his pocket.

'Till next time,' he said.